"If I kissed you and meant it, you'd have cause to worry, Miss Simms."

"I would?"

He approached her slowly, making his voice low and cool. "You would. A true kiss would stir you in your deepest places. It would keep you lying awake in your bed all night long. Restless and beset by . . ." He paused. "Flutterings."

Her brow lifted in amusement and a sly dimple formed in her cheek. "Flutterings?"

"Yes," he pronounced in a definitive tone. "Flutterings."

She smothered a laugh.

Good Lord. This wasn't happening. He could not be having this conversation. *Flutterings?* Stupid, asinine word, but he was committed now. He couldn't back down. He was the duke in this room, he reminded himself. And she was just a serving girl. It was time they both remembered it.

Except she wasn't *just* a serving girl. She was a serving girl with aspirations, keen business sense, shockingly good taste in poetry . . . and slight, enticing curves his hands ached to explore.

By Tessa Dare

Coming Soon

Tessa Dare

Any Duchess Will Do

AVON

An Imprint of HarperCollinsPublishers

This is a work of fiction. Names, characters, places, and incidents are products of the author's imagination or are used fictitiously and are not to be construed as real. Any resemblance to actual events, locales, organizations, or persons, living or dead, is entirely coincidental.

AVON BOOKS
An Imprint of HarperCollins*Publishers*
10 East 53rd Street
New York, New York 10022-5299

Copyright © 2013 by Eve Ortega
ISBN 978-0-06-224012-5
www.avonromance.com

First Avon Books mass market printing: June 2013

Avon Trademark Reg. U.S. Pat. Off. and in Other Countries, Marca Registrada, Hecho en U.S.A.
HarperCollins® is a registered trademark of HarperCollins Publishers.

Printed in the U.S.A.

12

For librarians and booksellers everywhere,
who gather books and build shelters for tender souls.

Acknowledgments

As always, I am deeply thankful to Tessa Woodward, Helen Breitwieser, Jessie Edwards, Pam Spengler-Jaffee, and everyone at Avon Books/HarperCollins.

To Courtney, Carey, Leigh, Bren, Laura, Kara, Susan, and The Unnameable Loop—all my love and gratitude. I could not write a book without your friendship and support. I would be foolish to even try.

And lastly, endless appreciation to my loving husband, children, parents, and family, who make it so blessedly difficult for me to crawl inside characters less fortunate.

Chapter One

Griff cracked open a single eyelid. A bright stab of pain told him he'd made a grave mistake. He quickly shut his eye again and put a hand over it, groaning.

Something had gone horribly wrong.

He needed a shave. He needed a bath. He might need to be sick. Attempts to summon any recollection of the previous evening resulted in another sharp slice of agony.

He tried to ignore the throb in his temples and focused on the tufted, plush surface under his back. It wasn't his bed. Perhaps not even a bed at all. Was it just a trick of his nausea, or was the damned thing moving?

"Griff." The voice came to him through a thick, murky haze. It was muffled, but unmistakably female.

God's knees, Halford. The next time you decide to bed a woman after a months-long drought, at least stay sober enough to remember it afterward.

He cursed his stupidity. The epic duration of his celibacy was no doubt the reason he'd been tempted by . . . whoever she was. He had no idea of her name or her face. Just a vague impression of a feminine presence nearby. He inhaled and smelled perfume of an indeterminate, expensive sort.

Damn. He'd need jewels to get out of this, no doubt.

Something dull and pointed jabbed his side. "Wake up."

Did he know that voice? Keeping one hand clapped over his eyes, he fumbled about with the other hand. He caught a handful of heavy silk skirt and skimmed his touch downward until his fingers closed around a stocking-clad ankle. Sighing a little in apology, he rubbed his thumb up and down.

A squawk of feminine outrage assailed his ears. An unyielding object cracked him over the head, but hard. Now to the pounding and throbbing in his skull, he could add ringing.

"Griffin Eliot York. Really."

Bloody hell.

Forget the headache and piercing sunlight, he bolted upright—bashing his head again, this time on the low ceiling. Blinking, he confirmed the unthinkable truth. He wasn't in his bedchamber—or any bedchamber—but in the coach. And the woman seated across from him was all too familiar, with the double strand of rubies at her throat and her elegant sweep of silver hair.

They stared at one another in mutual horror.

"Mother?"

She smacked him again with her collapsed parasol. "Wake *up*."

"I'm awake, I'm awake." When she readied another blow, he held up his hands in surrender. "Good God. I may never sleep again."

Though the air in the coach was oven-warm, he shuddered. Now he most definitely needed a bath.

He peered out the window and saw nothing but vast expanses of rolling green, dappled with cloud-shaped shadows. The coach's truncated shadow indicated midday.

"Where the devil are we? And why?"

He tried to piece together memories of the previous evening. This was hardly the first time he'd woken in unfamiliar surroundings, head ringing and stomach achurn . . . but it was the first time in a good long while. He thought he'd put this sort of debauchery behind him. So what had happened?

He hadn't imbibed more than his usual amount of wine at dinner. By the fish course, however, he seemed to recall the china's acanthus pattern undulating. Swimming before his eyes.

After that, he recalled . . . nothing.

Damn. He'd been drugged.

Kidnapped.

He snapped to alert, bracing his boots on the carriage floorboards.

Whoever his captors were, he must assume they were armed. He was without a blade, without a gun—but he had eager fists, honed reflexes, and a rapidly clearing head. On his own, he would have given himself even chances. But the bastards had taken his mother, too.

"Do not be alarmed," he told her.

"Oh, I wouldn't dream of it. Bad for the complexion." She touched the double strand of rubies at her throat.

Those rubies. They gave him pause.

What shoddy excuse for a kidnapper used the family coach and left the captive wearing several thousand pounds' worth of jewels?

Devil take it.

"You."

"Hm?" His mother raised her eyebrows, all innocence.

"You did this. You put something in my wine at dinner and stuffed me in the carriage." He pushed a hand through his hair. "My God. I can't believe you."

She looked out the window and shrugged. Or rather, she gave the duchess version of a shrug—a motion that didn't involve anything so common or gauche as the flexing of shoulder muscles, but merely a subtle tilt of the head. "You'd never have come if I *asked*."

Incredible.

Griff closed his eyes. Times like these, he supposed he ought to remind himself that a man only had one mother, and his mother only had one son, and she'd carried him in her womb and toiled in labor and so on and so forth. But he did not wish to think about her womb right now—not when he was still trying, desperately, to forget that she possessed ankles.

"Where are we?" he asked.

"Sussex."

Sussex. One of the few counties in England

where he didn't claim any property. "And what is the purpose of this urgent errand?"

A faint smile curved her lips. "We're going to meet your future bride."

He stared at his mother. Many moments passed before he could manage coherent speech.

"You are a scheming, fiendish woman with entirely too much time at leisure."

"And you are the eighth Duke of Halford," she returned. "I know that doesn't mean much to you. The disgraces at Oxford, the gambling, the years of aimless debauchery . . . You seem determined to be nothing more than an unfortunate blot on the distinguished Halford legacy. At the very least, start on the next generation while I still have time to mold it. You have a responsibility to—"

"To continue the line." He closed his eyes and pinched the bridge of his nose. "So I've been told. Again and again."

"You'll be five-and-thirty this year, Griffy."

"Yes. Which makes me much too old to be called 'Griffy.'"

"More to the point, I am fifty-eight. I need grandchildren before my decline. It's not right for two generations of the family to be drooling at the same time."

"Your decline?" He laughed. "Tell me, Mother, how can I hasten that happy process? Other than offering a firm push."

Her eyebrow arched in amusement. "Just try it."

Griff sighed. His mother was . . . his mother. There was no other woman in England like her, and the rest of the world had better pray God had broken the mold. Like the jewels she delighted in wearing, Judith York was a formidable blend of exterior polish and inner fire.

For most of the year, they led entirely separate lives. They only resided in the same house for these few months of the London season. Apparently, even that was too much.

"I've been patient," she said. "Now I'm desperate. You must marry, and it must be soon. I've tried to find the most accomplished young beauties in England to tempt you. And I did, but you ignored them. I finally realized the answer is not quality. It's quantity."

"*Quantity?* Are you taking me to some free-love utopian commune where men are permitted as many wives as they please?"

"Don't be ridiculous."

"I was being hopeful."

Her lip curled in a delicate scowl. "You're terrible."

"Thank you. I work hard at it."

"So I've often lamented. If only you applied the same effort toward . . . anything else."

Griff closed his eyes. If there was any conversation more tired and repetitive than the "When will you ever marry?" debate, it was the "You're a grave disappointment" harangue. Only in *this* family would it be considered "disappointing" to successfully oversee a vast fortune, six estates, several hundred employees, and thousands of tenants. Impressive, by most standards. But in the Halford line? Not quite enough. Unless a man was reforming Parliament or discovering a new trade route to Patagonia, he just didn't measure up.

He glanced out the window again. They seemed to be entering a sort of village. He slid open the glass pane and discovered he could smell the sea. A salted-blue freshness mingled with the greener scents of countryside.

"It is a prettyish sort of place," his mother said. "Very tidy and quiet. I can understand why it's so popular with the young ladies."

The coach rolled to a halt in the center of the village, near a wide, pleasant green that ringed a grand medieval church. He peered out the window, gazing in all directions. The place was far too small to be Brighton or . . .

"Wait a minute." A vile suspicion formed in his mind.

Surely she hadn't . . .

She *wouldn't*.

The liveried footman opened the coach door. "Good day, your graces. We've reached Spindle Cove."

"Oh, *bollocks*."

When the fancy coach came trundling down the lane, Pauline scarcely gave it a glance. Many a fine carriage had come down that same road, bringing one visitor or another to the village. A holiday in Spindle Cove was said to cure any gently bred lady's crisis of confidence.

But Pauline wasn't a gently bred lady, and her trials were more practical in nature. Such as the fact that she'd just stumbled into a murky puddle, splashing her hem with mud.

And that her sister was near tears for the second time that morning.

"The list," Daniela said. "It's not here."

Drat. Pauline knew they didn't have time to go back to the farm. She was due at the tavern in minutes. This was Saturday—the day of the Spindle Cove ladies' weekly salon, and the Bull and Blossom's busiest day of the week. Mr. Fosbury was a fair-minded employer, but he docked wages for tardiness. And Father noticed.

Frantic, Daniela fished in her pocket. Her eyes welled with tears. "It's not here. It's not here."

"Never mind. I remember it." Shaking the muddy droplets from her skirts, Pauline ticked the items off in her memory. "Dried currants, worsted thread, a bit of sponge. Oh, and powdered alum. Mother needs it for pickling."

When they entered the Brights' All Things shop, they found it packed to bursting. While the visiting ladies met for their weekly salon, the villagers purchased their dry goods. Villagers like Mrs. Whittlecombe, a cobwebby old widow who only left her decrepit farmhouse once a week to stock up on comfits and "medicinal" wine. The woman gave them a disdainful sniff as Pauline and Daniela wedged their way into the shop.

Pauline could just make out two flashes of white-blond hair on the other side of the counter. Sally Bright was busy with customers three deep, and her younger brother Rufus ran back and forth from the storeroom.

Fortunately, the Simms sisters had been friends with the Bright family since as far back as any of them could remember. They needn't wait to be helped.

"Put the eggs away," Pauline told her sister. "I'll fetch the sponge and thread from the storeroom. You get the currants and alum. Two measures of currants, one of alum."

Daniela carefully set the basket of brown speckled eggs on the counter and went to a row of bins. Her lips moved as she scanned for the one labeled CURRANTS. Then she frowned with concentration as she sifted the contents into a rolled cone of brown paper.

Once she'd seen her sister settle to the task, Pauline gathered the needed items from the back. When she returned, Daniela was waiting with goods in hand.

"Too much alum," Pauline said, inspecting. "It was meant to be just one measure."

"Oh. Oh, no."

"It's all right," she said in a calm voice. "Easily mended. Just put the extra back."

She hoped her sister didn't notice the sneering expression on old Mrs. Whittlecombe's face.

"I don't know that I can continue to give this shop my custom," the old woman said. "Allowing half-wits behind the counter."

Sally Bright gave the woman a flippant smile. "Just tell me when we can stop stocking your laudanum, Mrs. Whittlecombe."

"That's a health tonic."

"Of course it is," Sally said dryly.

Pauline went to the ledger to record their purchases. She secretly loved this part. She flipped through the pages slowly, taking her time to peruse Sally's notes and tabulations.

Someday she'd have her own shop, keep her own ledgers. It was a dream she hadn't shared with anyone—not even her closest friend. Just a promise she recited to herself, when the hours of farm and serving work lay heavy on her shoulders.

Someday.

She found the correct page. After the credit they earned from bringing in eggs, they only owed sixpence for the rest of their shopping. Good.

Bang.

She whipped her head up, startled.

"Good gracious, child! What on earth are you doing?" Mrs. Whittlecombe slapped the counter again.

"I . . . I'm p-puttin' back the alum," Daniela stammered.

"That's not 'da aw-wum,'" the old woman repeated, mocking Daniela's thick speech. "That's the sugar."

Oh, bollocks. Pauline winced. She knew she should have done it herself. But she'd wanted so fiercely for Daniela to show that wretched old bat she could do it.

Now the wretched old bat cackled in triumph.

Confused, Daniela smiled and tried to laugh along.

Pauline's heart broke for her sister. They were only a year apart in age, but so many more in understanding. Of all the things that came a bit more difficult for Daniela than other people—pronouncing words that ended in consonants, subtracting from numbers greater than ten—cruelty seemed the hardest concept for her to grasp. A mercy, in Amos Simms's family.

"Not the clayed sugar," Rufus Bright moaned.

Sally boxed him across the ear.

"I just scraped it from the cone," he apologized, rubbing the side of his head. "Bin was almost full."

"Well, it's entirely useless now," said Mrs. Whittlecombe smugly.

"I'll pay for the sugar," Pauline said. She felt instantly nauseous, as if she'd swallowed five pounds of the stuff raw. Fine white sugar came dear.

"You don't have to do that," Sally said in a low voice. "We're practically sisters. We should be *real* sisters, if my brother Errol had any sense in his head."

Pauline shook her head. She'd ceased pining for Errol Bright when they parted ways years ago. She certainly didn't want to be indebted to him now.

"I'll pay for it," she insisted. "It was my mistake. I should have done it myself, but I was in a hurry."

And now she would certainly be late for her post at the Bull and Blossom. This day only grew worse and worse.

Sally looked pained, caught between the need to turn a profit and the desire to help a friend.

In the corner, Daniela had finally realized the consequences of her error. "I can put it back," she said, scooping from the sugar barrel and dumping it into the alum, muddling both quantities with her flowing tears. "I can put it right."

"It's all right, dear." Pauline went to her side and gently removed the tin scoop from her sister's hand. "Go on," she told Sally firmly. "I think I have some credit in the ledger."

She didn't just *think* she had credit. She *knew* she did. Several pages beyond the Simms family account, there was a page labeled simply PAULINE— and it showed precisely two pounds, four shillings, and eight pence of credit accrued. For the past few years, she'd saved and scrimped every penny she could, trusting Sally's ledger with the safekeeping. It was the closest thing to a bank account a serving girl like her could have.

Almost a year, she'd been saving. Saving for something better, for her and Daniela both. Saving for *someday*.

"Do it," she said.

With a few strokes of Sally's quill, the money was almost entirely gone. Eleven shillings, eight pence left.

"I didn't charge for the alum," Sally murmured.

"Thank you." Small comfort, but it was something. "Rufus, would you kindly walk my sister home? I'm due at the tavern, and she's upset."

Rufus, apparently ashamed of his earlier behavior, offered his arm. " 'Course I will. Come along, Danny. I'll drive you in the cart."

When Daniela resisted, Pauline hugged her and whispered, "You go home, and tonight I'll bring your penny."

The promise brightened Daniela's face. It was her daily task to gather the eggs, count and candle them, and prepare them to sell. In return, Pauline gave her a penny a week.

Every Saturday evening she watched Daniela carefully add the coin to an old, battered tea tin.

She would shake the tin and grin, satisfied with the rattling sound. It was a ritual that pleased them both. The next morning the same treasured penny went into the church offering—every Sunday, without fail.

"Go on, then." She sent her sister off with a smile she didn't quite feel.

Once Rufus and Daniela had left, Mrs. Whittlecombe crowed with satisfaction. "That'll be a lesson for you, bringing a simpleton around the village."

"Go easy, Mrs. Whittlecombe," a bystander said. "You know they mean well."

Pauline flinched inwardly. Not that phrase. She'd heard it countless times over the course of her life. Always in that same pitying tone, usually accompanied by a clucking tongue: *Can't be hard on those Simms girls . . . you know they mean well.*

In other words, no one expected them to *do* a cursed thing right. How could they? Two unwanted daughters in a family with no sons. One simple-minded, the other lacking in every feminine grace.

Just once, Pauline wanted to be known not for *meaning* well, but for *doing* well.

That day wouldn't be today. Not only had everything gone wrong, but as she regarded Mrs. Whittlecombe, Pauline couldn't muster any good intentions. Anger bloomed in her chest like a predatory vine, all sharp needles and grasping tendrils.

The old woman placed two bottles of tonic in her netted bag. They clinked together in a way that only increased Pauline's anger. "Next time, keep the fool thing at home."

Her hands balled into tight fists at her side. Of course she wouldn't lash out at an old woman the way she'd once fought the teasing boys at school, but the motion was instinctive. "Daniela is not a thing. She is a person."

"She's a half-wit. She doesn't belong out of the house."

"She made a mistake. Just like all people make mistakes." Pauline reached for the bin of ruined white sugar. It was hers now, wasn't it? She'd paid for the contents. "For example, everyone knows I'm incurably clumsy."

"Pauline," Sally warned. "Please don't."

Too late. With an angry heave, she launched the bin's contents into the air.

The room exploded in a blizzard of white, and Mrs. Whittlecombe was at the storm's dead center, sputtering and cursing through a cloud of powder. When the flurries cleared, she looked like Lot's wife, only turned to a pillar of sugar rather than salt.

The sense of divine retribution that settled on Pauline . . . it was almost worth all that hard-earned money.

Almost.

She tossed the empty bin to the floor. "Oh, dear. How stupid of me."

Griff regarded his mother and that smug smile curving her lips. This time she'd gone too far. This wasn't mere meddling. It was diabolical.

Not *Spinster* Cove.

He'd never visited the place, but he knew it well by reputation. This seaside hamlet was where old maids went to embroider and consumptives went to dry.

Accepting the footman's hand, the duchess alighted from the coach. "I understand this place is just bursting with well-bred, unmarried young ladies."

She motioned toward a lodging house. A sign dangling above the entrance announced it as THE QUEEN'S RUBY.

Griff blinked at the green shutters and cheery window boxes stuffed with geraniums. He'd rather bathe in water teeming with sharks.

He turned and walked in the opposite direction.

"Where are you going?" she asked, following.

"There." He nodded at a tavern across the square. By squinting at the sign hung over the red-painted door, he discerned it was called the Bull and Blossom. "I'm going to have a pint of ale and something to eat."

"What about me?"

He gestured expansively. "Make yourself comfortable. Take a suite at the rooming house. Enjoy the healthful sea breezes. I'll send the coach for you in a few weeks." He added under his breath, "Or years."

The footman followed a respectful pace behind, holding the open parasol to shade the duchess.

"Absolutely not," she said. "You're going to select a bride, and you're going to do it today."

"Don't you understand what sort of young ladies are sent to this village? The unmarriageable ones."

"Exactly. It's perfect. None of them will turn you down."

Her words drew Griff to a sharp halt. He swiveled to face her. "Turn *me* down?"

For the obvious reasons, he avoided discussing his *affaires* with her. But the reason he'd been celibate lo these many months had nothing to do with women turning him down. There were many women—beautiful, sophisticated, sensual women—who'd gladly welcome him to their beds this very evening. He was tempted to tell her so, but a man couldn't say such things to his own mother.

She seemed to interpret his silence easily enough.

"I'm not speaking of carnality. I'm speaking of your desirability as a husband. Your reputation leaves a great deal to be desired." She brushed some dust from his sleeve. "Then there's the aging problem."

"The 'aging' problem?" He was thirty-four. By his estimation, his cock had a good three decades of working order ahead, at least.

"To be sure, you're good-looking enough. But there are handsomer."

"Are you sure you're my mother?"

She turned and walked on. "The fact is, most ladies of the *ton* have given you up as a marriage prospect. A village of desperate spinsters is precisely what we need. You must admit, this worked nicely for that scampish friend of yours, Lord Payne."

God's knees. So *that's* what was behind this. Curse that rogue Colin Sandhurst and his bespectacled, bookish bride. Last year, his old gambling friend had been sequestered in this seaside village without funds, and he'd broken free by eloping with a bluestocking. The pair had even stopped at Winterset Grange, Griff's country retreat, on their way to Scotland.

But their situations were completely different. Griff wasn't desperate for funds in any way. Neither was he desperate for companionship.

Marriage simply wasn't in the cards for him.

His mother fixed him with a look. "Were you waiting to fall in love?"

"What?"

"It's a simple question. Have you delayed marriage all these years because you're waiting to fall in love?"

A simple question, she called it. The answers were anything but.

He could have taken her into the tavern, ordered a few large glasses of wine, and taken an hour or two to explain everything. That he wouldn't be marrying this season, or any season. Her only son would not be merely a blot on the distinguished Halford line, but the very end of it, forever, and the family legacy she held so dear was destined for obscurity. Her hopes of grandchildren would come to naught.

But he couldn't bring himself to do it. Not even today, when she was at her most infuriating. Better to remain a dissolute-yet-redeemable rascal in her eyes than be the son who calmly, irrevocably, broke his mother's heart.

"No," he told her honestly. "I'm not waiting to fall in love."

"Well, that's convenient. We can settle this in one morning. Never mind finding the most polished young beauty in England. You choose a girl—any girl—and I'll polish her myself. Who could better prepare the future Duchess of Halford than the current Duchess of Halford?"

They'd reached the tavern entrance. His mother stared pointedly at the door latch. The footman jumped to open it.

"Oh, look," she said upon entering. "What luck. Here they are."

Griff looked. The scene was even ghastlier than he could have imagined.

This tavern didn't seem to be a "tavern" at all, but more of a tea shop. Young ladies crowded the establishment, all of them hunched over tables and frowning in concentration. They appeared to be engaged in one of those absurd handicrafts that passed for female "accomplishment" these days. Quilling paper, it looked like. They weren't even using fresh parchment—just ripping pages straight from books to fashion their queer little trivets and tea trays.

He peered at the nearest stack of volumes. *Mrs. Worthington's Wisdom for Young Ladies*, each one read. Appalling.

This was everything he'd been avoiding for years. A roomful of unmarried, uninspiring young women, from which the common wisdom would argue he should find a suitable bride.

At the nudging of a friend, one young woman rose from her chair and curtsied. "May we help you, ma'am?"

"Your grace."

The young woman's brow creased. "Ma'am?"

"I am the Duchess of Halford. You would properly address me as 'your grace.'"

"Ah. I see." As her nudging friend smothered a nervous giggle, the fair-haired young woman began again. "May we help you, your grace?"

"Just stand tall, girl. So my son can see you." She turned her head, surveying the rest of the room. "All of you, on your feet. Best posture."

Pain forked through Griff's skull as chair legs screeched against floorboards. One by one the young ladies obediently rose to their feet.

He noted a few pockmarks. One case of crooked teeth. They were none of them hideous, just—fragile in some cases. Others were unfashionably browned from the sun.

"Well," the duchess said, striding into the center of the room. "Jewels in the rough. In some cases, very rough. But they are all from good family, so with a bit of polish . . ." She turned to him. "Take your choice, Halford. Select any girl who strikes your fancy. I will make her into a duchess."

Every jaw in the room dropped.

Every jaw, that was, except Griff's.

He massaged his throbbing temples and began preparing a little speech in his mind. *Ladies, I beg you. Pay this raving madwoman no attention. She's entered her decline.*

But then, he thought—a quick exit was too kind to her. Surely the only proper punishment was the opposite: to do precisely as his mother asked.

He said, "You claim you can make any one of these girls into a suitable duchess."

"Of course I can."

"And who will be the judge of your success?"

She lifted a brow. "Society, of course. Choose your young lady, and she'll be the toast of London by season's end."

"The toast of London, you say?" He gave a doubtful laugh.

He scanned the tavern for a second time, planning to declare mad, instantaneous love for the most shrinking, awkward, homely chit available—and then watch his mother sputter and flail in response.

However, from the amused glances the young ladies exchanged, Griff could sense that there was more courage and wit in the room than his first impression might have indicated. These young women were no fools. And though they each had their flaws and imperfections—who didn't?—none were unsuitable to a shocking, insurmountable degree.

Damn. He'd looked forward to teaching his overstepping mother a lesson. As matters stood, he supposed he'd be better served to just mutter a few apologies, drag the duchess back to the carriage, and drop her at Bedlam on the way home.

And then, with a creak of hinges and a slam of the rear door—

His salvation arrived.

She came stumbling through the back entrance of the tavern, red-faced and breathless. Her boots and hem were spattered with alarming amounts of mud, and a strange white powder clung to her everywhere else.

A serving girl's apron hung loose around her neck. As she gathered the tapes and knotted them behind her back, the cinch of laces revealed a slender, almost boyish figure. Less of a shapely hourglass, more of a sturdy hitching post.

"It's ten past, Pauline." The male voice boomed from the kitchen.

She called back, "Beggin' pardon, Mr. Fosbury. I'll not be tardy again."

Her diction and accent were not merely uneducated and rural—they were odd. When she turned, Griff could make out the reason why. She had a hairpin clenched in her teeth like a cheroot, and she mumbled her words around it.

The tardy serving girl clutched another hairpin in her hand, and when her eyes—leaf-green, bright with intelligence—met Griff's, she froze in the act of jamming that pin through the tangle of hair piled atop her head.

God, that hair. He'd heard ladies describe their coiffures as "knots" or "buns." This could only be called a "nest." He was certain he glimpsed a few blades of straw and grass in there.

Clearly, she'd been hoping to enter unnoticed. Instead, she was suddenly the center of attention. That mysterious white powder that clung to her . . . it caught the light, shooting off tiny sparks.

He couldn't look away.

As the breathless young woman alternated glances between Griff, his mother, and the amused ladies filling the rest of the room, her unfinished coiffure disintegrated. Locks of unpinned hair tumbled to her shoulders, surrendering to gravity or indignity, or both.

This would be where the average serving girl would duck her head, flee the room, and await her employer's wrath. No doubt there'd be sniffling or sobbing involved.

But not this serving girl, apparently. This one had just enough pride to trump etiquette *and* good sense.

With a defiant toss of her head to distribute her brandy-colored locks, she turned and spat the last hairpin aside.

"Bollocks," he heard her mutter.

Suddenly, Griff found himself battling a grin. She was perfect. Coarse, uneducated, utterly graceless. A touch too pretty. A plainer girl would have better suited his purpose. But fair looks notwithstanding, she'd do.

"Her," he said. "I'll take her."

Chapter Two

Another girl's prince has arrived.

That was Pauline's first thought, when she stumbled in and spied the finely dressed man silhouetted in the door.

She watched it happen every few months in this village. These young ladies sought refuge in Spindle Cove for the oddest of reasons. Their harp-playing lacked grace, perhaps, or the color of their eyes was unfashionable at Court this season. And then—to the utter astonishment of everyone except Pauline—some handsome earl or viscount or officer came along and married them.

None of them spared so much as a glance for the serving girl.

So which lady was this one after? Whoever she was, she'd be set for life. Everything about the man's appearance—from ivory buttons to fitted leather gloves—blared his wealth in trumpet notes. And if his garments screamed "riches," everything beneath them spoke of power. It would be easy for a gentleman to go soft and paunchy, but he hadn't. The close cut of his dark green topcoat revealed broad shoulders and defined muscles in his upper arms.

His face was strong, too. Boldly sloped nose, squared jaw, and a wide, confident mouth. There was nothing pretty about his features, but when taken together, they had an undeniable masculine appeal.

In short, he was no trial to look at. But even if he weren't—Pauline couldn't take her eyes off the man.

Because he wasn't taking his eyes off her.

And the way he looked at her—like she was the answer to every question he'd never thought to ask—had her heart beating faster than a trapped hare's.

"Her," he said. "I'll take her."

"You can't choose her," an older woman replied, clearly testy. "That's the serving girl."

Pauline spared the lady a brief glance, sizing her up as a silver-haired woman who was small of stature and long on self-importance. She had a rail-straight spine. She'd need it, to hold up that unholy ransom in jewels.

"She's a girl," the man replied evenly, still looking at Pauline. "She's a girl, and she's in the room. You said I might choose any girl in the room."

"She wasn't in the room when I said that."

"She's in the room now. And once I saw her, I had eyes for no one else. She's perfect."

Perfect?

Pauline looked to the window, expecting a pig

to fly through it. A pig strumming a lyre and speaking Welsh, perhaps.

The gentleman moved toward her, navigating the room with ease. As he approached, each heavy, rhythmic footfall made her acutely aware of her wild, sugar-dusted hair and mud-spattered hem. She took comfort from the signs of his own flawed humanity. On closer view, he was unshaven, and his eyes were rimmed with red—from lack of sleep or too much drink, or both.

Pauline inhaled slowly. His clothing carried the fading whiff of some masculine, musky cologne. The scent curled inside her, warming her in low, secret places.

"Tell me your name," he said.

He spoke in a voice that was low and rich and . . . magnetic, apparently. She could feel every person in the room sway in his direction, to better make out his words.

"I'm Pauline, sir. Pauline Simms."

"Your age."

"Twenty-three."

"And are you married or betrothed?"

She bit back a startled laugh. "No, sir. I'm not."

"Excellent." He inclined his head. "I am Griffin Eliot York, the eighth Duke of Halford."

A duke?

"Oh, Lord," she muttered.

"Actually, Simms, what you're meant to say is, 'your grace.'"

She dropped her gaze to the floorboards and made an off-balance curtsy. "Your grace."

Waving off her belated attempts at deference, he went on. "My mother has grown impatient with my unmarried state. She enjoined me to take my choice of any woman in this room, with the promise that she could make that woman into a duchess. I've chosen you."

"Me?"

"You. You're perfect."

Perfect. Again, that word. Pauline's mind couldn't handle all this at once. She had to break the information into small morsels.

This robustly handsome, self-possessed, wonderful-smelling man was the eighth Duke of Halford.

Out of all the ladies in this room, he was choosing her, the serving girl.

To be his future duchess.

You're perfect.

Chills raced from the nape of her neck to the soles of her feet, leaving her breathless. Either the whole world had turned on its ear, or after twenty-three years of never being good enough . . . in the eyes of one man—in the eyes of this *duke*—she was perfect.

The duchess cast a cool gaze on her son. "Unnatural child. You live to thwart me."

"I don't know what you mean," he replied calmly. "I'm doing precisely as you asked."

"Be serious."

"I am serious. I've chosen a girl. Here she is." The duke made a sweeping gesture from Pauline's tangled hair to her muddy shoes, painting her with humiliation. "Go on, then. Make her a duchess."

Ah. She understood everything now. She *was* perfect in his eyes. Perfectly dreadful. Perfectly graceless. Perfectly wrong to be a duchess, and by making her an example, the duke meant to teach his interfering mother a lesson.

How clever of him. How obnoxious and insufferable, to boot.

It's your own fault, Pauline. For that one, mad instant, you were a fool.

She didn't find him so handsome anymore. But he still smelled wonderful, drat him.

There was a pause, which no one in the room dared interrupt. It was as though they were spectators to a championship match of some sort, and the duke had just scored a critical point.

Every head swiveled to face the duchess, waiting for her move.

She had no intention of forfeiting. "Well, then. We'll go to the girl's parents."

Brazen strategy, thought Pauline. Two points to you.

"I'd love nothing more." Halford pulled his coat straight. "But I must be returning to Town at once, and I'm certain Simms can't leave her post."

"Certainly I can," Pauline said.

Both the duke and his mother turned to her, clearly irritated that she'd dared interrupt. Never mind that she was subject of their argument.

"I can leave my post anytime." She crossed her arms. "I don't need a post at all, do I? Not if I'm to be a duchess."

The duke gave her a blank look. Obviously, he hadn't expected this reaction. She was probably supposed to stammer and protest and run blushing into the kitchen.

Unlucky for him. He'd picked the wrong girl.

Of course, she knew he'd meant to pick the "wrong girl," but he'd picked the *wrong* "wrong girl." Pauline enjoyed a good laugh as much as the next person, but already she'd lost too much today. She couldn't part with her last tattered remnant of pride.

"Mr. Fosbury," she called in the direction of the kitchen, untying her apron strings. "I'll be leaving now. I don't expect I'll be coming back today. I'm taking this duke 'round to the cottage so he can ask for my hand in marriage."

That brought Fosbury out from the kitchens, looking perplexed as he wiped his floury hands on an apron.

Pauline gave him a reassuring wink. Then she turned to the duchess, smiling wide. "Shall we, your grace?" She made a show of giggling. "Oh, pardon. Did you want I should call you 'Mother'?"

Ripples of hushed laughter moved through the room. The look of aristocratic discomfort on the duchess's face was immensely satisfying.

Whatever stubborn, unfeeling game this duke and his mother were playing, they were gaining a third player in Pauline.

What's more, Pauline was going to win.

Turning her gaze to the duke, she gave him a bold, unashamed inspection. No chore there. The man truly was a fine specimen of masculinity, from broad shoulders to sculpted thighs. If he could ogle her, why couldn't she look right back?

"Cor." She unleashed her broadest country accent as she tipped her head to admire the lower curve of his tight, aristocratic arse. "I'll have great fun with you on the wedding night."

His eyes flared, swift enough to make her insides wince. Could teasing a duke amount to a hanging offense? He certainly possessed the power and means to make her regret it.

But when all the Spindle Cove ladies broke into open, boisterous laughter, Pauline knew it would be fine. She wasn't one of the Spindle Cove set. She was a servant, not a well-bred lady on holiday. But they would stand by her, just the same.

Miss Charlotte Highwood rose and spoke in her defense. "Your graces, we are honored by your visit, but I don't think we could part with Pauline today."

"Then we find ourselves in conflict," the duke said. "Because I don't intend to part with her at all."

The dark resolve in his words sent odd sensations shooting through Pauline. He meant to continue this farce? Stubbornness must run in this duke's family the way green eyes ran in hers.

The duchess tilted her head toward the door. "Well, then. The coach is waiting."

And that was how Pauline Simms, tavern serving girl and farmer's daughter, found herself bringing a duke and his mother home for tea.

Well, and why the deuce not?

If these Quality meant to embarrass her in front of all Spindle Cove, it was only fitting they should sacrifice some pride of their own. She couldn't wait to see the duchess's face when they pulled up before her family's humble cottage. It might do them good to see how common folk lived—to sit on rough-hewn wooden stools and drink from chipped crockery. She and Sally Bright would be laughing over this story for the rest of their lives.

After giving directions to the driver, Pauline joined them inside the coach. She slid a hand over the calfskin seat, marveling. She'd never touched an actual calf this soft.

She was certain no one of her station had ever been a passenger inside this conveyance, and judging by the grim sets of their jaws, she would guess neither the duke nor the duchess were pleased to have a sugar-dusted serving girl and her muddy shoes joining them now.

Which only made Pauline more resolved—she was going to wring this experience for every last drop of amusement.

For the entirety of the ten-minute drive to her farm cottage, she reveled in inappropriate behavior. She bounced on the seat, testing the springs. She played with the window latch, sliding the glass pane up and down a dozen times.

"What does your father do, Miss Simms?" the duchess asked.

Other than shout, curse, rage, threaten? "He farms, your grace."

"A tenant farmer?"

"No, he owns our land. Some thirty acres."

Of course, thirty acres would be nothing to a true landed gentleman, much less a duke. Halford probably owned a thousand times it.

As the carriage left town, they passed by the Willetts' fields. Mr. Willett's oldest boy was out working in the hops. Pauline put down the window for the thirteenth time, stuck her arm out and waved gaily.

She put her thumb and forefinger in her mouth and whistled loud. "Gerry!" she called. "Gerald

Willett, look! It's me, Pauline! I'm going to be a duchess, Ger!"

When she settled back inside the carriage, she caught the duke and his mother exchanging a look. She propped one elbow on the windowsill, covered her mouth with her palm and laughed.

As they neared the cottage, Pauline rapped on the carriage roof to signal the driver. When the coach had rolled to a stop, she reached for the door latch.

"No." With the crook of her parasol handle, the duchess snagged her by the wrist. "We have people for that."

Pauline froze, taken aback. She *was* one of the people for that. Or had the old lady forgotten?

The duke knocked the parasol aside. "For God's sake, Mother. She's not a wayward lamb."

"You chose her. You told me to make her a duchess. Her lessons start now."

Pauline shrugged. If the woman insisted, she would wait and allow the liveried footman to open the door, lower the step, and assist her down with white-gloved hands.

As the duchess alighted, followed by her son, Pauline dipped in a deep, exaggerated curtsy. "Welcome to our humble home, your graces."

She opened the gate and led them through the fenced poultry yard. The gander was after them immediately, honking and ruffling his wings. No one could tell Major he didn't outclass a duke. The duchess tried a freezing look, but quickly resorted to wielding her parasol in defense.

"That'll do, Major." Pauline clapped her hands. Then she ushered her guests inside. "This way, your graces. Don't be bashful. Our home is yours. We're all family now."

The door lintel was low and the duke was tall. He would have to duck to avoid bashing his head. He paused at the threshold. For a moment Pauline thought he'd simply turn around, return to the carriage, and drive off to London.

But he didn't. He bent at the waist and passed through the doorway in a single, fluid motion.

She had to smile at that. The arrogant duke, literally stooping to enter her family's cottage.

Once inside, the two visitors swept a look around the small, sparsely furnished abode. It wasn't difficult to take in the whole dwelling at a glance. The house was only some dozen paces wide. A stone hearth, a few cupboards, table and chairs. Faded print curtains fluttered in the two front windows. To the side, an open doorway led to the only bedroom. A ladder climbed to the sleeping loft she and Daniela shared.

The rear doorway led to the exterior area where they did all the washing. Soft splashes indicated someone was washing up after the noon meal.

"Mother," she sang out, "look who I brought home from the Bull and Blossom. The ninth Duke of Halstone and his mum."

"Halford," the duchess corrected. "My son is the eighth Duke of Halford. He's also the Marquess of Westmore, the Earl of Ridingham, Viscount New-thorpe, and Lord Hartford-on-Trent."

"Oh. Right. Suppose I should learn it all proper, shouldn't I? I mean, seeing as how it'll be my name, too." She grinned broadly at the duke. "Fancy that."

His lips quirked a fraction. Whether in irritation or amusement, she didn't dare to guess.

"Will you sit?" she asked the duchess.

"I will not."

"If you need the privy," she informed them in a confidential tone, "you go through that door, back around the woodpile, and left at the pigs."

"Pauline?" Mother came through the back door, wiping her hands on a towel.

"Mother, there you are. Has Father gone back to the fields?"

"No," said Amos Simms, darkening the same doorway her mother had just traversed. "No, he 'asn't. Not yet."

She found herself holding her breath as her father peered at the duke, then the duchess.

Lastly, he turned a menacing glare on Pauline.

A sharp tingle of warning volleyed between her shoulder blades. She would pay for this later, no doubt.

"What's all this, then?" her father demanded.

Pauline swept an arm toward her guests. "Father, may I present His Grace, the eighth Duke of Halford, and his mother. As for what they're doing here . . ." She turned to the duke. "I should let his grace explain it."

Oh, excellent. The girl wanted him to explain it.

Griff exhaled, running a hand through his hair. There was no satisfactory explanation he could offer. He had no bloody idea what he was doing in this hovel.

Something sharp jabbed him in the kidney,

nudging him forward. That damned parasol again.

Oh, yes. He recalled it now. There was a reason he was here, and the Reason Herself needed a sharp lesson in minding her own affairs.

He snatched the parasol from his mother's grip and presented it to the farmwife. "Please accept this gift as thanks for your hospitality."

Mrs. Simms was a small woman with stooped shoulders. She looked as faded and wrung out as the dish towel in her red-knuckled hands. The woman stared at the furled parasol, seemingly dumbfounded by its tooled ivory handle.

"I insist." He pressed it toward her.

She took it, reluctantly. "That's v-very kind, your grace."

"Never enter a house empty-handed. My mother taught me that." He shot the duchess a look. "Mother, sit down."

She sniffed. "I don't believe I—"

"Here." With his boot, he hooked a rough wooden bench and pulled it out from the table. Its legs scratched across the straw-strewn dirt floor. "Sit here. You are a guest in this house."

She sat, arranging her voluminous skirts about her. But she didn't try to look pleased about it.

For the next minute or so, Griff learned how it felt to be a menagerie exhibit, as the collected Simms family stood about, gawking at them in silence.

"Mrs. Simms," he finally said, "perhaps you'd be so kind as to offer us some refreshment. I would have a word with your husband."

With evident relief at her dismissal, Mrs. Simms drew her daughter into the kitchen. Griff pulled a cane-backed chair away from the table and sat.

As Simms settled on the other chair, the burly farmer narrowed his eyes. "What can I do for you, yer grace?"

"It's about your daughter."

Simms grunted. "I knew it. What's the girl done now?"

"It's not something she's done. It's what my mother would like her to do."

Simms cut a shrewd glance toward the duchess. "Is her grace needing a scullery maid, then?"

"No. My mother would like a daughter-in-law. She thinks I need a wife. And she claims she can make your girl"—he waved in the direction of the kitchen—"into a duchess."

For a moment the farmer was silent. Then his face split in a gap-toothed grin. He chuckled, in a low, greasy way.

"Pauline," he said. "A duchess."

"I hope you won't be offended, Mr. Simms, if I admit doubts as to the likelihood of her success."

"A duchess." The farmer shook his head and continued chuckling.

The boorish, sinister tone of his laughter had Griff shifting his weight on the chair. To be sure, it was an absurd idea. But even so, shouldn't a man defend his own daughter?

He cleared his throat. "Here's my offer. A man only has one mother, and I've decided to indulge mine. What say I take your daughter to London? There, my mother might have her best crack at transforming her from a serving girl into a lady sufficiently polished and cultured to be a duke's bride."

Simms laughed again.

"Of course, in the much more likely event that this enterprise fails, we will return your daughter to you. At the least, she'll come home with a few new gowns and some exposure to the finer things in life."

"My girl don't need new gowns. Nor any of your finer things."

Just then the girl in question returned to set the table. The dish she placed before Griff was possibly the ugliest teacup he'd ever seen—a cheaply painted bit of china no doubt birthed in some cutrate factory and passed down through several owners. But before releasing the saucer, she gave it a brisk quarter turn, so that the pathetic, limp flower on the cup would face him and the saucer's chip was on the hidden side.

The meaning in the gesture wasn't lost on Griff. She was a proud one, no question. Also smartmouthed and bold enough to bait a duke and his dragon of a mother. None of those traits were desirable qualities in a serving girl, much less in a bride.

But they were qualities Griff appreciated in general, and he was beginning to admire this Pauline Simms. Just a bit, and just for herself. During her few minutes in the kitchen, she'd tied back her hair. Her figure remained unremarkable, but now he could see she was more than a little pretty. High cheekbones, gentle nose, eyes tipped at the corners like a cat's. Quite fetching, really, in a rustic, country way. All the farmhands must be mad for her.

You've sworn off women, a voice inside him nagged.

Well, that oath needed some amendment. He'd

sworn off *involvement* with women, perhaps. That didn't mean he was going to poke out his eyes. A bit of casual appreciation never hurt anyone—and he suspected it might do this particular woman some good.

"If you're set on her, we can talk." Simms scratched his jaw. "But I can't let her go easy."

Good, Griff thought. No right-thinking father should let a bright, pretty daughter go easily.

The farmer lifted his voice. "Come 'ere, Paul."

She obeyed. As she moved toward them, her mouth was a tight line.

"Look at these 'ands of hers," Simms said, taking his daughter by the wrist and extending her hand and forearm for Griff's inspection.

Her fingers were slender and graceful, but her palm showed the calluses and scars of menial labor—labor more strenuous than serving pots of tea to spinsters. No doubt she helped with the farm work, too.

Simms shook his daughter's wrist, and her hand flopped up and down. "No one else has hands this small. Nor an arm this thin." He made a circle of his thumb and forefinger, easily ringing Pauline's slender wrist. "I've a mare about to foal. Ain't no one else on this farm what can reach up inside and grab the foreleg, if need be."

The farmer slid the ring of his thumb and forefinger from Pauline's wrist all the way to her elbow, visually demonstrating just what equine depths his slender-armed daughter would be called to explore.

Griff's missed breakfast now seemed like a blessing.

"Jes' look at that," Simms said. "She can reach all the way to the womb."

"*Father.*" Pauline snatched her arm away.

"That's worth something, right there," her father said. "Can't let her go without compensation. In advance."

Unbelievable.

Mr. Simms was a farmer. A poor farmer, yes— but not a destitute one. He owned thirty acres. His cottage was humble, but sound. No one was starving under this roof. A strange nobleman entered his home, and he offered, for all intents and purposes, to sell his daughter?

What of the girl's safety? What of her reputation? Griff wasn't the sort of nobleman to buy himself a virgin for despoiling, but Mr. Simms couldn't know that. This was the point where any decent father—hell, any sort of real man—would at least demand assurances. If not tell Griff to take his feudal offer and go straight to the devil.

But Mr. Simms didn't. Which told Griff he was a shoddy excuse for a father and no kind of man at all. The farmer wasn't the least bit concerned about his daughter's health or reputation. No, he just wanted to be compensated in advance. For his extra trouble when the mare foaled.

"This is truly your only objection?" he asked pointedly, giving the farmer a chance to redeem himself.

Mr. Simms frowned. "Not the only objection."

Well, thank God.

"There's the wages she brings home," he continued. "I'll need those in advance, too."

"Her *wages.*"

Griff had the sudden urge to hit something. Something wearing a coarse homespun shirt, dirt-caked boots, and a greedy sneer. That was it. His mother would need to learn her lesson in some other way, at some other time. He needed to leave. This interview either ended now or it ended badly.

Drawing on some generations-old reserve of ducal composure, he rose to his feet. "Perhaps this was an ill-considered plan. The chances of your daughter succeeding in London society are minuscule, and the risks to her are too great." He made his way toward the cottage door, pausing only to catch his mother by the elbow and pull her to her feet. "If you'll excuse me, my mother and I will be on our—"

"Five," the farmer called.

"Excuse me?"

"I'll let her go for five pounds."

Griff could only stare at him. "Good God, man. Are you serious?"

He cracked his neck. "All right, then. You can have her for four pounds, eight. But not a penny less."

Bloody hell. Griff passed a hand over his face. Now he looked as though he was haggling for the girl, determined to ruin her life for the lowest possible price.

"What an excellent bargain." Irony dripped from his mother's words. "I don't think you could find a more economical choice."

"I hope you're happy with yourself," Griff said.

The duchess arched a brow, deflecting all censure back at him. "Are you?"

No. He wasn't. He felt like a first-rate ass. He'd thought himself so damned clever, picking the serving girl out of the spinster crowd. And now he'd invaded her home and forced her to watch while her own father placed a price of four pounds, eight shillings on her health and happiness.

Even for him, this was low.

Miss Simms emerged again, moving toward the table with teapot in hand. Their gazes locked, and her eyes taught him some bold, nameless shade of green. Deep in some unexplored virgin forest, there was a vine of that color, just waiting to be discovered. And there was something essential in this girl's nature that was far, far better than this place.

Just then, Griff observed a telling sequence of events.

A clatter rose from the rear of the house.

With a quiet curse, Pauline Simms stumbled. Hot tea sloshed on the cottage's dirt floor.

"Paul, I told you—" The farmer's hand went up in threat.

And standing four full paces away, Pauline— the girl who would hold her own against a duke— flinched.

He'd seen enough.

"Mother, go ahead to the coach." He quelled her objection with a small gesture, then turned to the girl. "Miss Simms, a word outside. Alone."

Chapter Three

Pauline followed him out the front door and around to the side of the house. The south side, where there were no windows for the family to peer at them. Neither could the duchess view this corner from the carriage. It was just the two of them, alone with a late-blossoming apple tree and the ridiculousness of it all.

She hoped they might have a good laugh and part ways. There would be evening chores to be done before long, and she'd had enough of dukes for one day.

Apparently, he'd reached a breaking point, too. He stalked the yard in long strides. Back, then forth.

"I've reached a decision." He plucked a dead, dangling branch from the apple tree and tapped it on the fence rail. "Simms, you're coming with me to London. This very afternoon."

Her breath left her. "But . . . but why? For what purpose?"

"Duchess training, naturally."

"But you can't truly mean to marry me."

He came to a decisive halt. "Of course I don't mean to marry you."

Well. She was glad they had that settled.

"Let's set a few things straight at the outset," he said. "I might wear fine clothes and possess a splendid carriage, and I've rolled into your life on something that might resemble a whirlwind. Perhaps even a romantic one, to the untutored eye. But this isn't a fairy tale, and anyone who knows me could tell you . . . I am no prince."

She laughed a little. "With all due apologies, your grace, I hadn't formed any opinions to the contrary. I stopped believing in fairy tales long ago."

"Too practical for such things, I suspect."

She nodded. "I'm prepared to work hard for the things I want in life." Sadly, she was still wearing a full year's hard work spattered in her hair and frock.

"Excellent. Because what I'm offering you is employment. I mean to hire you as a sort of companion to my mother. Come to London, submit to her 'duchess training,' and prove a comprehensive catastrophe. Should require little effort on your part."

Pauline's jaw worked but no words came out.

"In exchange for your labors, I will give you one thousand pounds." He leveled his apple-branch switch at the cottage. "And you will never depend on that man again."

One thousand pounds.

"Your grace, I . . ." She didn't even know what to say—whether to call his proposal insufferable, or nonsensical, or a dream come true.

Impossible. That was the best word.

"But I can't. I just can't."

He moved closer. The sun caught amber flecks in his dark brown eyes. "You can. And you will. I will make it so."

She turned her gaze to the cottage, frustrated with his commanding demeanor and his stubbornly enticing scent. He smelled so wretchedly trustworthy.

"Don't worry about your clothes and your things," he said. "Leave it all. You'll have new."

"Your grace . . ."

He tapped the branch against his booted calf. "Don't play at reluctance. What can possibly be keeping you here? A post serving tea to spinsters? Farm labor, and sleeping space in a drafty loft? A brutish father who would eagerly sell you for five pounds?"

She set her teeth. "Five pounds is no paltry sum to folk like us."

And even if it weren't a vast amount, it was five pounds more than "completely worthless," which was how her father set a woman's value most days.

"Be that as it may," he said, "five pounds is considerably less than a thousand. Even a farm girl with no schooling can do that arithmetic."

She shook her head. Amazing. Just when she thought he'd exhausted the ways to insult or demean her, he proved her wrong.

He said, "My mother has too much time at leisure. She needs a protégé to take shopping and drill in diction. I need her diverted from matchmaking. It's a simple solution."

"Simple? You mean to bring me to your home . . .

buy me all new things . . . pay me a thousand pounds. All that, just to cure your mother of meddling?"

He shrugged in confirmation.

"I wouldn't call that simple, your grace. Much easier to just tell her you don't wish to marry. Don't you think?"

His eyes narrowed. "I think you enjoy being difficult. Which makes you the ideal candidate for this post."

Pauline was divided on how to receive that statement. For once, she was someone's ideal. Unfortunately, she was his ideal thorn in the side.

Nevertheless, his offer tempted in a perverse way. For once in her life she wouldn't be failing at success. She'd be succeeding at failure. No more would she hear, "But she *means* well"—the duke didn't want her to mean well at all.

"None of this matters," she said at last. "I can't leave Spindle Cove."

"I'm offering you a lifetime of financial security. All I'm asking in return is a few weeks of impertinence. Think of it as your chance to write the practical girl's fairy tale. Come away to London in my fancy carriage. Have some fine new gowns. Don't change a whit. Don't fall in love with me. At the end of it, we part ways. And you live wealthily ever after." He looked to the carriage. "Just say yes, Simms. We need to be going."

What would it take to convince him? She raised her voice, enunciating each word as best an uneducated farm girl could. "I . Can't. Go."

He matched her volume. "Well, I can't leave you."

The world was suddenly very quiet. The duke

went absolutely still. She could have thought him a statue if not for the stray apple blossom decorating his shoulder and the breeze stirring his dark, wavy hair. Somewhere above them a songbird chirped and whistled for a mate.

She swallowed hard. "Why not?"

"I don't know."

He tilted his head and stared at her with fresh concentration. She tried not to blush or fidget as his slow, measured paces brought them toe-to-toe. So close, she could see the individual grains of whiskers dotting his jaw. They were lighter than his hair—almost ginger, in this light.

"There's something about you." His ungloved hand went to her hair, teasing it gently. A little shower of crystals fell to the ground. "Something . . . all over you."

Good heavens. He was touching her—without leave, or any logical reason. And it should have been shocking—but the most surprising part was how natural it felt. So simple and unforced, as though he did this every day.

She wouldn't mind it, Pauline thought. Being touched like this, every day. As though there were something precious and fragile beneath the grit of her life, just waiting to be uncovered.

He dusted more fine white powder from her shoulder. "What *is* this? You're just coated with it."

Her answer came out as a whisper. "It's sugar."

He lifted his thumb to his mouth, absently tasting. His lips twisted in unpleasant surprise.

"Sugar mixed with alum," she amended.

"Oddly fitting." He reached for her again, this time leading with the backs of his fingers.

She felt herself leaning forward, seeking his touch.

"Pauline?" a familiar voice interrupted. "Pauline, who's that man?"

She jumped back and turned to spy Daniela peeking out from the west side of the cottage. After a moment of internal debate, Pauline waved her sister forward. There was no easier way to explain her refusal than to let him see for himself.

"Your grace, may I present my sister, Daniela. Daniela, our guest is a duke. That means you must curtsy and call him 'your grace.'"

Daniela curtsied. "Good day, your grace."

The words came out thick and nearly unintelligible, the way they always did when Daniela was nervous. Her tongue wasn't so nimble with strangers.

"The duke was just leaving."

Daniela curtsied again. "Goodbye, your grace."

Pauline watched him with keen eyes, waiting. People of his rank sent their simple folk to asylums or paid someone to tend them in the attic—anything to hide them from view. Still, he would be able to tell. Everyone could always tell within a minute of meeting Daniela.

The familiar anger welled within her, fast and defensive—a response learned from years of deflecting insults and slights. Her hand reflexively made a fist.

He probably wouldn't resort to name-calling. Idiot, numskull, half-wit, dummy, simpleton. Those words would be beneath a duke, wouldn't they?

But he would have some reaction. They always did. Even well-meaning people found some way to give offense, treating Daniela like a puppy or an infant, instead of like a full-grown woman.

Most likely the duke would curl his lip in disgust. Or turn his gaze and pretend she didn't exist. Perhaps he would sneer or shudder, and that would give Pauline just the surge of anger she needed to send him away.

But he didn't do any of those things.

He spoke in a completely unaffected, matter-of-fact tone. "Miss Daniela. A pleasure."

And as Pauline watched, the duke—God above, a bloody *duke*—lifted her sister's hand to his lips. And kissed it.

Lord help her, for the briefest of instants, Pauline tumbled headlong in love with the man. Never mind his promise of a thousand pounds. He could have had her soul for a shilling.

She briefly closed her eyes, rooting deep in her heart for all those reasons to dislike him. The most petty, stupid one came to her lips. "You didn't kiss *my* hand."

"Of course not." He glanced at the appendage in question. "I know where it's been."

Her cheeks flushed as she recalled her father's "demonstration" in the cottage.

"She is the source of your reluctance, I take it?" he asked.

Pauline nodded. "I can't leave her. And she can't leave home."

After a moment's quiet consideration, he addressed her sister. "Miss Daniela, I want to take your sister to London."

Daniela paled. Her chin began to quiver. The tears were already starting.

"I will bring her back," he said. "You have my word. And a duke never breaks his word."

Pauline raised a brow, skeptical.

He shrugged, conceding the improbable truth of the statement. "Well, this particular duke won't break this particular word."

"No." Her sister hugged her so tightly, Pauline reeled on her feet. "Don't go. I don't want you to go."

Her heartstrings stretched until they ached. They'd never been apart. Not for even one night. What the duke might describe to her as temporary, Daniela would experience as endless. She'd spend every moment of their separation feeling miserable, abandoned. But at the end of it . . .

One thousand pounds.

They could do anything with a thousand pounds. Escaping their father would only be the beginning. She and Daniela might have a cottage of their own. They could raise chickens and geese, hire a man now and then for the heavy labor. With prudence, the interest alone would be enough to keep them fed and safe.

And she could open her shop.

Her shop. So silly, how she'd come to think of it that way. She might as well have named it Pauline's Unicorn Emporium, as likely as it was to come to pass. It had always been just a dream for someday. But with one thousand pounds, that someday could be quite soon.

"God's knees." The duke's voice intruded on her thoughts. "Not you again."

Major, the old cantankerous gander, had found them once more, and he wasted no time in making the duke feel unwelcome. The bird stretched his neck to its greatest length, puffing his breast in a warlike pose. Then he lowered his beak and made a strike at the duke's boot.

With a crisp thwack, Halford deflected the goose with a flick of the apple bough. He jabbed the blunt end into the goose's breast, holding the enraged bird at branch's distance. "This bird is possessed by the spirit of a dyspeptic Cossack."

"He doesn't like you," Pauline said. "He's very intelligent."

With a short flight, Major managed to squawk free, and then they were starting all over again. Dueling, duke versus gander.

Halford stood light on his feet, one leg forward and one back, wielding the switch like a foil. "Winged menace. I'll have your liver."

Major cast some aspersions of his own. They were unintelligible to human ears, but no less vehement.

At her side, Daniela ceased to cry and began to giggle.

The tightness in Pauline's chest eased. "Daniela," she said. "Take Major to the poultry yard for me. Then come back."

Her sister spread her arms and shooed the gander toward the rear of the house. Once she was safely out of earshot, Pauline crossed her arms and faced the duke.

"If I agree to this . . ." She willed her voice not to shake. "If I go with you, will you return me home in one week?"

"A *week*?" He tossed the stick aside. "That's unacceptable."

"It's the only way I'll agree. It must be a week. We have a ritual of sorts on Saturdays, Daniela and I. She can understand this. If I promise to be back by next Saturday, she'll know I'm not leaving forever." When he hesitated, she went on, "I assure you, I can prove catastrophic within one week."

"Oh, I don't doubt that." He paused in thought. "A week, then. But we leave at once."

"As soon as I bid my sister farewell."

She turned and looked over her shoulder. Daniela was already on her way back from the henhouse.

"I need a penny," Pauline said. "Quickly, give me a penny."

He fished in his pocket and produced a coin, then dropped it in her outstretched hand.

She peered at it. "This isn't a penny. It's a sovereign."

"I don't have anything smaller."

She rolled her eyes. "Dukes and their problems. I'll be along in a moment."

Pauline drew her sister aside. She pulled her spine straight. The only way to keep Daniela from dissolving was to hold herself together. There could be no cracks in her resolve. She must be strong enough for them both, as always.

"Here's your egg money for this week." She opened Daniela's hand and put the coin in it, closing her fingers over the sovereign before she could notice the color wasn't right. "I want you to go upstairs and put it in the tea tin straightaway. Tomorrow, it goes in the collection at church."

Daniela nodded.

"I'm going with the duke now," Pauline told her. "To London."

"No."

"Yes. But only for a week."

"Don't go. Don't go." The tears streamed down Daniela's reddened cheeks.

Don't cry so, I beg you. I can't bear it.

Pauline very nearly gave in. To distract herself, she thought of the golden coin squeezed in her sister's hand. She imagined a thousand of them, stacked in neat rows. Ten by ten by ten by ten . . .

If only she could explain to Daniela what this would mean for them, and how it would better their lives in all the years to come. But her sister wouldn't want to hear more talk of change. She needed routine, comfort. Familiar tasks to see her through the week.

"I'll be back next Saturday to give you your egg money. I swear it. But you must earn that penny. While I'm gone, you must work hard. You cannot laze abed crying, do you hear? Collect the eggs every day. Help mother with the cooking and the house. When the week's gone, I'll be home. I'll be sitting with you in church next Sunday." She framed Daniela's round face in her hands. "And I will never leave you again."

She hugged her sobbing sister tight and kissed her cheek. "Go inside now."

"No. No, don't go."

There was no good to come of prolonging it. Parting wouldn't get any easier. Pauline released her sister, turned, and walked away. Daniela's sobs followed her as she went through the gate and entered the lane, where the duke's fine carriage waited.

"Pauline?" Her mother's voice, calling from the front step.

"I'll be home in a week, Mum." She didn't dare look back.

When she moved to enter the coach, her step faltered. The duke extended a hand. His hand was ungloved, and when his strong fingers closed over hers, a tremor passed through her.

"Are you well?" he asked. His other hand went to the small of her back, steadying her.

Pauline drew a deep breath. His strong touch made her want to melt against him, seeking comfort. She pushed the temptation away.

"I'm well," she said.

"If you need more time to—"

"I don't."

"Should you go to her?" he asked.

No. No, that would make everything worse.

It was useless to explain. What did it matter if he thought her unfeeling and callous, anyhow? She wasn't after his approval. She was doing this for his money.

"My sister always cries, but she's stronger than you'd think." She released his hand and mounted the stairs on her own power. "So am I."

It took a great deal to impress Griff. Many an afternoon in Court, he'd looked on as officers and dignitaries were awarded ribbons, crosses, knighthoods, and more for service to the Crown.

Some likely deserved their honors; many didn't. The pomp and ceremony had him jaded by this point, and God knew he wasn't prone to heroics himself. But he liked to think he could still recognize bravery when he saw it.

He had the feeling he'd witnessed a true act of courage just now. The girl had steel in her. He'd felt it, beneath his palm.

A good thing, too. Because if she was going to spend the next several days with the Duchess of Halford, Pauline Simms was going to need it.

"You have a week," he told his mother, settling into the coach.

"A *week*?" Twin spots of color rose on her cheeks, matching the rubies at her throat.

"A week. Simms's family can't spare her any longer than that."

"I can't possibly accomplish this in a week."

"If our Divine Creator could make the heavens, earth, and all its creatures in six days, I should think you can manage one duchess."

She huffed with indignation. "You know very well I'm not—"

"Wait. Hold that thought." Griff sent a hand into his breast pocket, searching. When he came up empty, he muttered a mild curse and fumbled in his waistcoat pockets, too.

"What on earth are you looking for?" his mother asked.

"A pencil and a scrap of paper. You were about to say you're not God, or something to that effect. I mean to have the exact quote, date, and time recorded. An engraved commemorative plaque will hang in every room of Halford House."

Her lips thinned to a tight line.

"You claimed you could make any woman the toast of London. If you can manage that with Simms in one week, I'll marry her." He leveled a single finger at her. "But if this enterprise of yours fails, you will never harangue me on the subject of marriage again. Not this season. Not this decade. Not this lifetime."

She glowered at him in silence.

Griff smiled, knowing he had her right where he wanted her.

He leaned back, propped one boot on his knee, and stretched his arm across the back of the seat. "If the conditions are unacceptable to you, I can turn this coach around right now."

She didn't object. He didn't turn the coach around.

They forged straight on, and Griff pretended to doze through a lengthy lecture on the vaunted family history. It was a litany of heroes, lawmakers, explorers, scholars . . . All the way from his far-flung ancestors in the Crusades to his father, the great, late diplomat.

Just as the duchess's tale was winding toward the debauched disappointment that was Griff, they paused to change horses and take dinner near Tonbridge.

Thank God.

"This," his mother informed her new charge as they alighted from the carriage, "is one of the finest coaching inns in England. Their private dining rooms are peerless."

Miss Simms made comical shapes with her lips as they entered the establishment. "I should think the Bull and Blossom is the superior place, for my money. More welcoming, and that's certain."

"A duchess does not look for an inn that is welcoming," his mother opined. "A duchess is welcome anywhere, anytime. She relies on the establishment to keep everyone else out."

"Really?" As they were shown into the dining room, Miss Simms turned to the stony footman. "Is that so?"

The footman pulled out a chair, staring forward at the wall.

She gave the blank-faced servant an amused look and waved her hand before his eyes. "Hullo. Anyone home?"

The footman remained still as a wooden nutcracker, until she gave up and sat down.

Griff took his own seat and summoned the waiter with a look, ordering an assortment of dishes. He was famished.

"Cor," Miss Simms sighed, putting her elbows on the table and propping her chin on one hand. "I'm famished."

The duchess rapped the tabletop.

"What now?" the young woman asked.

"First, remove your elbows from the table."

Miss Simms obeyed, lifting her elbows exactly one inch above the surface of the table.

"Second, mind your tongue. A lady never refers to the state of her internal organs in mixed company. And you will strike *that* word from your vocabulary at once."

"What word?"

"You know the word to which I refer."

"Hm." Dramatically thoughtful, Miss Simms put a fingertip to her lips and cast a glance at the ceiling. "Was it 'famished'? Or 'I'm'?"

"Neither of those."

"Well, I'm confused," she said. "I can't recall saying anything else. I'm just a simple country girl. Overwhelmed by the splendor of this inhospitable establishment. How am I to know what word it is I shouldn't say if your grace will not enlighten me?"

A pause stretched, as they all waited to see whether his mother could be provoked into repeating such a common slang as "cor."

Griff reclined in his chair, happy to wait her out. This was the most enjoyment he could recall at a family dinner.

His mother had been needing someone to manage. She certainly couldn't browbeat *him*—no matter what measures she'd resorted to yesternight—and the servants at Halford House were too well-trained and stoic. He'd been flirting with the idea of getting her a mischievous terrier, but this was better by far. Miss Simms wouldn't leave any puddles on the carpet.

Perhaps after this week was over, he'd hire his mother another impertinent companion.

But next time he'd find one who wasn't so pretty.

The girl sparkled. *Sparkled*, deuce her. Griff couldn't help staring. Hours of coach travel hadn't dislodged those sugar crystals dusting her form, and his eye couldn't stop searching them out. They were like grains of brilliant sand strewn in her hair, clinging to her skin. Even tangled in her eyelashes.

Worst of all, one tiny crystal had lodged itself just at the corner of her mouth. His awareness of it had long passed distracting and verged on maddening. Surely, he thought, at some point during dinner she would catch it with her tongue and sweep it away.

If not, he'd be tempted to lean forward and tend to the cursed thing himself.

"Miss Simms," his mother said, "if you think you can trick me into repeating your vulgarities, you will be disappointed. Suffice it to say, slang, blasphemy, and cursing have no place in a lady's vocabulary. Much less a duchess's."

"Oh. I see. So your grace never curses."

"I do not."

"Words like cor . . . bollocks . . . damn . . . devil . . . blast . . . bloody hell . . ." She pronounced the words with relish, warming to her task. "They don't cross a duchess's lips?"

"No."

"Never?"

"Never."

Miss Simms's fair brow creased in thought. "What if a duchess steps on a tack? What if a gust of wind steals a duchess's best powdered wig? Not even then?"

"Not even when an impertinent farm girl provokes a duchess to a simmering rage," she replied evenly. "A duchess might contemplate all manner of cutting remarks and frustrated oaths. But even in the face of extreme annoyance, she stifles any such ejaculations."

"My," Miss Simms said, wide-eyed. "I do hope dukes aren't held to the same standard. Can't be healthy for a man, always stifling his ejaculations."

Griff promptly broke the prohibition against elbows on the table, smothering a burst of laughter with his palm and disguising it as a coughing fit. The violence of it caught him by surprise. He couldn't recall the last time he'd laughed from so deep in his chest that his ribs ached. For that matter, he couldn't recall the last time he'd been tempted to lean across the table and catch a lush, clever mouth in a kiss.

For several months he'd been stifling . . . everything.

"Let it out, your grace. You'll feel better." She looked to him with false concern and a coy, conspiratorial smile.

Oh, he liked this girl. He liked her a great deal.

And that worried him intensely.

Chapter Four

Drat. So close. She'd almost had him laughing just then.

The duke had hired Pauline to provoke his mother, but somewhere in the past few minutes, Pauline had grown far more interested in provoking the duke.

For all his devil-may-care posturing, it would seem the devil did care about *something*. In the hours since they'd left Spindle Cove, a strange cloud of melancholy had gathered about him. She wanted to dispel it. Not out of charity, precisely— but because his brooding made her so acutely aware of her own sadness.

She was already sick with missing home.

She wondered if Daniela had stopped crying yet. Would she be able to sleep alone in the loft? Perhaps their mother would climb up to soothe her after Father had fallen asleep, bringing a dish of blancmange.

Pauline would tell herself that was the case. More

comforting that way. When she returned home independently wealthy, her sister would have a great bowlful of blancmange, every single night.

Speaking of food . . . On the table before her, the inn's servers spread a veritable banquet. Her stomach rumbled. She'd scarcely eaten all day, and she'd never been served a meal like this.

"Miss Simms," the duchess said. "Tell me what dishes you see on the table."

Pauline eyed her suspiciously, wondering what sort of test the older lady had in mind. The meal set before them was composed of a great many dishes, but none were exotic. She could name them all, easily.

"Ham," she answered. "Beef and Yorkshire pudding. Roasted chicken. Peas, boiled potatoes, and some sort of soup—"

The duchess rapped the table. "Wrong. All of it, wrong."

"All of it?" Pauline blinked at the unquestionably ham-shaped object on the platter before her. If it wasn't a ham, what on earth could it be?

"It's *h*am, Miss Simms." The duchess weighed heavily on the *H*. "Ham, not 'am. Yorkshire pudding, not 'puddin'.' Boiled potatoes, not 'biled.' And we eat roasted fowl, not vulgar chicken. After dinner, I'll give you some elocution exercises. Very useful in limbering the lips and tongue."

Well, that sounded . . . perfectly dreadful. For now, Pauline was far more interested in using her lips and tongue to eat. She reached for the carving knife embedded in the *h*am and used it to draw the platter toward her plate.

Rap, rap.

The duchess again.

"What is it I've done now?" Pauline asked. "I didn't say a word."

"It was your actions," the duchess replied, sending a glance toward the ham. "A duchess does not serve herself, Miss Simms."

"Very well." Pauline turned to the server. "You, there. Would you mind—"

Rap, rap.

The older woman cut her a look. "A duchess does not ask to be served, either."

Pauline regarded her empty plate with despair. "Then how, pray tell, does a duchess eat?"

"Observe me."

Pauline raised her head and watched.

"Are you regarding me very closely?" the duchess said.

"Yes, your grace."

"I shall only do this the once. A duchess need never repeat herself, you understand."

By this point Pauline was sure there was more steam between her ears than beneath the domed cover of the soup tureen. The duchess was like a walking, talking copy of *Mrs. Worthington's Wisdom for Young Ladies*. Pauline began to understand just what the Spindle Cove ladies were escaping when they came for holidays by the sea.

"I'm watching," she said tightly.

The duchess slid one eye—or at least, it seemed that way—to the waiting footman. Then she tilted her head by a nearly imperceptible degree, nodding once in the direction of the food.

The servants leapt forward and began serving food onto their plates.

"Praise be," Pauline muttered.

"Thank you, Simms," the duke replied, reaching for the carving knife. "I believe we will let that sentiment serve as table grace."

"The servants bring the vegetables, soup, fish, and all other dishes," the duchess explained. "The gentlemen at the table carve the meats."

As if in demonstration, the duke placed a thick, rosy slice of ham on Pauline's plate.

"Given your former employment," the duchess said, "I should think you would know all this."

"Etiquette is never strictly enforced in Spindle Cove," Pauline said. "And it's only ladies at the tables, anyhow. If they waited on a gentleman to serve them, they'd starve away."

"I can see we have a great deal of work ahead. What about your accomplishments? Do you sing, Miss Simms?"

"No."

"Play any instrument?"

"None."

"Have you any languages? Can you draw, sketch, paint, embroider, or produce any evidence of a ladylike finishing whatsoever?"

"I'm afraid not, your grace. I'm perfectly wrong for the position of duchess." She threw Halford a cheeky half smile.

But instead of smiling back, he gave her a look of cool displeasure. She didn't understand that look. It rattled her.

"Miss Simms," the duchess went on, "there is no magical combination of qualities that will make for a successful duchess. Beauty is useful, but not essential. Wit is desirable as well. Mind that I said wit, not cleverness. Cleverness is like rouge—liberal application makes a woman look common and desperate. Wit is knowing how to apply it."

The duke reclined in his chair. He seemed to have abandoned his own meal in favor of fixing Pauline with that intense stare.

She gathered an obscenely large forkful of potatoes and stuffed it into her mouth. She couldn't fathom the reason for his sudden broodiness. Wasn't this precisely what he'd hired her to do? He wanted her to be ill-mannered, didn't he?

"Lastly," the duchess continued, "the most important quality any Duchess of Halford needs is this: phlegm."

"Phlegm?" Pauline echoed, choking down her food. "It's forbidden to speak of hunger at the dinner table, but it's fine to talk about phlegm?" She poked at a bit of ham. "If it's phlegm you want, I can give you that. I learned how to spit with the farm boys. The trick is to start far back in your throat and—"

The duchess halted, just as she was about to spoon some asparagus soup into her mouth. She looked at the rich green broth, then set down her spoon.

"Not that kind of phlegm, Miss Simms. I refer to self-assurance. Unflappability. Aplomb. The ability to remain calm, no matter what occurs. Never underestimate the power of phlegm."

Ah, so she meant the way she and the duke had stared one another down that afternoon in the Bull and Blossom—neither of them willing to show a hint of weakness. The way they inspected the entirety of the farm cottage in a glance, sweeping a gaze around the rooms without even turning their heads.

The duchess cut her beef with delicate sawing motions. "Phlegm will be our greatest challenge, I suspect."

"I'm sure you're right on that score."

Whenever someone hurt Daniela—or anyone she loved—that thorny vine of rage blossomed in her chest. She didn't suppose she'd ever be able to suppress the response, nor did she wish to try.

"What good is rank and wealth," she asked, "if you can't even own your emotions? Aren't the Quality permitted to feel anything?"

The duchess replied, "Oh, we are permitted to *feel*. But we must never appear to be *ruled* by our feelings."

"I see. It would be unbearably common to sit at this table and just openly discuss our emotions about, say, love and marriage."

"Of course."

"So much more refined to kidnap one's son, then instigate a week-long farce with a serving girl. Is that it?"

She thought surely the duke would smile at that, but no. His gaze was now burning into her skin, like sunlight concentrated through a lens.

"I'm not sure I care for any phlegm." She took another bite and purposely spoke around it. "In fact, I'm sure I don't want it."

"For the last time, Miss Simms, this isn't a dish on the table to be taken or refused. If you're going to learn to be a duchess, phlegm is a requirement."

"Then I suppose we'll see who buckles first."

"I never buckle. A duchess has people to do the buckling for her."

Pauline shook her head. This week would be a challenge—but an amusing one, at least. The duchess did possess a sense of humor. However, the older woman underestimated Pauline, if she thought she could cow her.

Oh, she knew the Halford pride was strong. In the carriage, she'd listened to the family provenance. At *length*. No doubt a duchess born to generations of wealth, married into an even longer line of nobility, would believe herself to be indomitable. But Pauline had earned her stubbornness, fighting hard for it at every turn. On the other side of this week lay the prospect of a new, independent life. She wouldn't be swayed from that goal. Not even by a duchess.

Come *h*ell or *h*igh society, she would earn that one thousand pounds.

Eventually they all settled down to the business of eating. The servants removed the savory dishes from the table and replaced them with a variety of fruits and cheeses. Grapes, plums, nectarines. Pauline spied a dish of sherry trifle that had her mouth watering—layers of raspberries, sponge, whipped cream, all visible through the glass dish.

And then, to this overwhelming abundance of sweets, the footman set before her one more: a molded sculpture of blancmange.

The breath left her body, leaving only a keen, sharp ache.

Oh, Danny.

The wave of homesickness swamped her with

such violent force, she couldn't bear it. Not a moment longer. She pushed back from the table and fled the room, dashing into the stairwell.

This was a mistake. She had to leave. She had to go home. How many miles had they traveled? Fifteen? Twenty? She had a full belly, and the weather was fine. If she started now, she could walk home by dawn.

"Simms?" The duke's voice echoed down the narrow stairwell, arresting her on the landing. "Are you ill?"

"No," she said, hastily dabbing at her eyes before she turned to him. "No, I'm well. I'm sorry for leaving the table so abruptly."

Slow footfalls carried him down the stairs. "Don't be. It was the cap on a sterling display of poor etiquette. Well done, you. But my mother was concerned for your health."

"I'm fine, truly. It was just the blancmange."

"The blancmange?" He frowned. "I find it revolting myself, but the stuff almost never drives me to tears."

She shook her head. "It's my sister's favorite. I've been missing her all day, of course. But when that blancmange appeared before me, it all just . . ."

"Hit you," he finished for her, coming to join her on the landing. "All at once. Like a landslide."

She nodded. "Exactly so. For a moment, it was like the air went to mud. I couldn't even—"

"Breathe," he said. "I know the sensation."

"Do you?"

Perhaps he did, she thought, surveying the fine lines at the corners of his eyes, and the weariness that pooled like shadows beneath. She could believe he was intimately acquainted with this lonely, desolate feeling—perhaps even more so than she.

"Give a moment," he said. "It will pass."

The stairwell was suddenly very warm, and very small. The walls seemed to push them closer together. She was aware of his looming size, his male heat. His powerful good looks. And that rich, lingering hint of his musky cologne.

"Perhaps we should go back," she said.

"Wait. You have something"—he touched a fingertip to the corner of his own mouth—"just here. A stray bit of sugar, I think."

She cringed. How embarrassing.

She extended her tongue and ran it slowly from one corner of her mouth to the other, then back again. "Better?"

He blinked. "No."

She raised her hand to dab at her cheek.

"Stop. Just let me." He reached one hand forward, bracing the side of his palm against her cheek and brushing the corner of her mouth with his thumb.

Mercy. She was the farthest from home she'd ever been in her life, adrift in a vast, lonely sea of emotion. And his touch against her bare skin, so warm and assured . . . It was like someone throwing her a rope.

A connection.

He skimmed a light touch under her bottom lip. "You," he said softly, "have quite the mouth on you."

"So I've been told. It's my worst fault, I think."

"I'm not sure I'd agree."

She forced a cheerful tone. "I do have many faults to choose from. Impertinence, stubbornness, pride. I curse too much, and I'm terribly clumsy."

"Well." His touch stilled, and he tilted her face to his. "This week, all those faults make you perfect."

He *would* go and say something wonderful.

She tried to smile. It didn't quite work. Her emotions were chaotic, swinging back and forth between caution and thrill, and a mad voice inside her kept foolishly insisting that she needed to keep her lips very, very still . . .

Because this man was about to kiss them.

Pauline had been kissed a time or two. She knew how a man's face changed as he was preparing to do it. The small lines around his mouth disappeared, and his head made a subtle tip to one side. His eyelids grew heavy, lowering just enough to reveal a dark fringe of lashes.

His gaze focused intently on her mouth.

He leaned close.

Her insides trembled. This was the moment where she needed to . . . do something. Close her eyes, if she wished to be kissed. Take a swift step back, if she didn't.

She *shouldn't* want it. She hated to think what impropriety rakish dukes might expect of serving girls, and she didn't want to give the wrong impression. But it had been a very long time since she'd been kissed. And even longer since she'd heard any words so kind as the ones he'd just spoken.

In the end, she compromised by remaining perfectly, breathlessly still.

And he didn't kiss her.

He withdrew his touch and brushed past her, continuing down the stairs with a clatter of footfalls. "Simms, give my mother my regards."

"But where are you going?"

"I'm riding ahead to London," he called up to her. "Tonight."

Griff managed to procure a young gelding from the inn's stables. The horse was nothing to pace his favored bay warmbloods at home, but the beast looked strong and impatient—ready for some hard riding over open country. He'd do.

The moon was rising bright and round in the sky, ready to light his journey. Griff swung into the saddle, ignoring the thinness of the borrowed tack and the inconvenient tightness of his topcoat across his shoulders. These wouldn't be the most pleasant miles he'd ever covered on horseback, but comfort wasn't his priority tonight.

He had to get away.

That had been a very close thing, just now in the stairwell. A very close, warm, sweet, enticing, vulnerable thing.

Her lips had been so soft. A ripe berry-pink. Still glistening, where she'd searched them with her tongue. Quivering with emotion. He could have kissed them.

He'd wanted to, more than he'd wanted his next breath.

Sweet heaven.

Bloody hell.

He'd thought he was done with this. For months

now he'd ignored invitations and innuendos from women all over Town. A mud-spattered, sugar-dusted, smart-mouthed serving girl in drab linsey-woolsey could not prove his complete undoing.

As he nudged the horse into a canter, he realized he hadn't laid out a very good strategy for living the rest of his life as the New, Not-Truly-Improved, Just-Vastly-Less-Interesting Griffin Eliot York. For the past several months he'd been too absorbed by other emotions to feel any sensual deprivation. Any mild stirrings of unrest were quelled by routine physical exercise or the occasional halfhearted frig.

In retrospect, it seemed ridiculous to believe he—he!—could remain celibate for the remainder of his years. He should have known it would be coming: that day when his neglected cock *did* perk with interest, rise up and wave in a jaunty, "Ho, there—remember me?"

As his luck would have it, that day was today.

There was something about Pauline Simms that had him fascinated. She was so defiantly proud of her common origins, yet so hungry for approval.

This was a business arrangement, he reminded himself. He'd hired the girl to bedevil his mother, not to bewitch him. Her cleverness and lively, cat-tipped eyes should not be temptations. They were a desirable set of skills she brought to her post. Similar to the way one sought out a stonemason with brawn and foresight and steady hands.

The thought of employees helped him turn his mind toward mundane tasks. He'd need to warn the house staff that the duchess would be bringing a guest. Fortunately, his housekeeper, Mrs.

Thomas, was scarily efficient. A few words, and everything would be readied in advance of Miss Simms's arrival: room, maid, meals, bath.

God, yes. The girl needed a bath.

A proper bath. Not just a quick dousing to rinse away that glittering sweetness. A bath hot enough to soak those calluses from her hands and curl the short hairs at her temples. With a fresh cake of scented soap for scrubbing, and thick, downy towels to wrap her sleek, glistening limbs.

The image that came to his mind was so vivid, so lushly detailed in every texture of skin and soap and slickness . . . He had to pull the horse to a halt in the center of the road and recover himself.

The hard drumming of hoofbeats had ceased, but his ribs pounded with the furious thunder of his pulse.

Why her? Why now?

But as was the case with all the whys and wherefores he'd addressed to the darkness in recent months, no answers came back. Only one thing was clear. This just wouldn't do. Perhaps he could outride temptation tonight, but by the morrow, temptation would be living under his roof.

There was only one thing for it. He must pay a visit on his way back to Town.

He adjusted his position in the saddle, leaning over the gelding's neck to urge the beast faster. Midway on his journey through Kent, he turned his horse off the main road and instead took a winding, familiar spur.

He approached the village in the first gray whisper of morning—a tight cluster of cottages, wreathed in fog. A dew-glittered meadow offered some bluebells and primrose for the picking. Griff turned the horse out to graze and stretched his legs, gathering what twiggy wildflowers he could find. They weren't much, but it seemed poor form to show up empty-handed.

As dawn broke over the green horizon, he realized he was stalling. Stupid, to be anxious.

He walked past the white-steepled church, to the walled area behind it. The rusted churchyard gate swung inward with a whine of hinges, and he walked to the third row of monuments. He found the simply marked grave.

He remained there several minutes, silent and unmoving, before crouching to place his meager bouquet before the limestone cross.

When he tried to stand, he couldn't. Grief seized him with a savage, crippling pain. Like an auger drilling straight on his heart. It hollowed him out, left a round, aching hole—one he knew would never be filled.

This is what comes of indulging your desires.

After long minutes he could breathe again. Before he rose to leave, he kissed his fingertips, then laid them to the cool, grainy stone.

There. Temptation conquered.

Chapter Five

"Miss Simms," the duchess said. "Your nose will wear a hole in that windowpane. Duchesses do not gawk."

Pauline sat back on the carriage seat, chastened.

After traveling all night, they'd reached the bustling environs of London by early afternoon. It then took them three more hours to navigate the busy bridges and streets, making their way to Halford House. Her nose had been glued to the coach window for all of it, as she stared wide-eyed at the urban scenery. So much glass. So much brick. So much soot.

And so very many people.

Eventually the coach turned into an area of finer homes, many of them fronting wide green squares with immaculately trimmed hedges. They must be nearing the duke's house.

Pauline had been in fine houses before. Well, one fine house at least—Summerfield, the home of Sir

Lewis Finch. Sir Lewis's housekeeper sometimes hired extra help to clean house at Christmas or Easter. Summerfield was a grand manor, sprawling over several wings and filled with curiosities of every stripe. Every dusty old bit of bric-a-brac was priceless—at least, hired girls were expected to handle them like treasures.

By the time the coach rolled to a halt before Halford House, Pauline had convinced herself it would be well within the range of her experience.

She was wrong.

Nothing in life, dreams, or fairy tales had prepared her for this. And how she would keep from gawking, she had no idea.

To begin with, the house was massive. Four stories high, and wide enough that one would have to stand all the way at the opposite end of the square to regard it in its entirety. Close as she was when she alighted from the coach, Pauline had to tip her head nearly all the way back. She felt her jaw hanging agape.

And then, as the sun was just sliding beneath the city's uneven horizon, it lingered one last moment to splash brilliance across the square. The amber rays landed directly on Halford House, like a coronation. Every glass pane flashed like a diamond facet, and the white granite façade looked dipped in gold.

She was stunned.

Then the door opened. And she was stunned some more.

She followed the duchess through a gauntlet of eight liveried footmen. Once they crossed the threshold, there were more servants lined up in the entrance hall. Cook, housekeeper, house-maids, scullery maids, lady's maid.

The interior was accordingly impressive. Paint-ings on every available swatch of wall, ornate clocks chiming in welcome. Sumptuous uphol-stery in any place a person could possibly think to sit. It was really too much to take in with her eyes, but she didn't need to. She could feel this house's elegance in the soles of her feet. The wooden floors were expertly sanded and polished, and the carpets . . . oh, the carpets had pile so thick and plush, they made her insteps sigh with gratitude.

Pauline was introduced to the housekeeper, Mrs. Thomas—a woman who, in any other circum-stance, would have been handing her a bucket and brush, sending her to scrub a floor somewhere.

Today, she welcomed Pauline as a guest. She even curtsied. "Let me show you to your room, Miss Simms."

As she followed the housekeeper, Pauline wished she could leave a trail of bread crumbs. She'd never find her way back on her own.

Straight from the entrance, up the steps. Right at the top, and round the bend to the second, nar-rower flight of stairs. Then left down the wain-scoted corridor—the one with walls papered with a green toile pattern—or was it blue? This would have been easier in full daylight.

She counted the doors as they passed. One, two, three . . .

By the time the housekeeper stopped before the fourth door, it was all a blur.

The room was dark, and she was happy for it to remain that way.

Pauline numbly accepted assistance in stripping down to her shift, bathing the travel dust from her body, and climbing into the softest, warmest bed she'd ever laid upon. As her eyes closed and her legs stretched to the toasty depths of the bedsheets, she had the vague thought that someone had been here with coals in a bed warmer only moments before she'd entered the room.

Such excellent service. And for the first time in her life she was on the receiving end of it. It would have been folly to try to make it seem real, so she gratefully fell into dreams.

For several hours she knew nothing more.

She woke to darkness. And found she could not return to sleep.

She ought to have still been exhausted. She was exhausted, in truth. Her joints ached from the long hours in the coach, well-sprung as it was. Her mind was taxed to its limits from stretching to grasp so many unbelievable notions.

But she just couldn't sleep.

She was in a duke's house. Surely a duke didn't even call it a house, did he? House was too humble, too common a word. He called it a "residence." In the country, an "estate." Whatsit Manor, or Summat Castle.

She drew aside a corner of the heavy tapestry bed hangings and peered into the darkened room. Fortunately, it was nearing full moon, and the milky glow seeping in from the glazed windows (three of them! in one room!) gave her enough light to see the room she'd been too fatigued to explore earlier.

She could make out so far as the foot of the bed, to the upholstered bench at the foot of the bed, to the plush embroidered carpet, its oriental reds and brassy golds now soothed by night. The lotus pattern stretched for miles, it seemed. If she strained and blinked, she could see the edge of the dressing table and catch the glint of a full-length, gilt-framed mirror hanging on the wall. The looking glass was supported by sculpted marble cherubs. Mischievous cherubs. Evidently, they never slept.

Pauline gave a short, muted chirp of a whistle. It echoed back to her from the coffered ceiling. Goodness, the room was a cavern.

This one bedchamber could swallow her family's cottage whole.

And this was a guest room. Not even their best, she'd imagine. What must the other chambers be like?

On a side table, she spied a tea service, left over from when she'd arrived. Pauline supposed she should have rung to have it removed, but now she was glad she hadn't. A sip of cold tea with lemon might soothe her nerves.

She tugged the counterpane free and wrapped it about her shoulders before sliding from the bed. *"Oof!"*

It was a long way down. She landed with a thud, tangling in the counterpane and tumbling to the floor.

She wasn't hurt. Even this carpet was softer than her mattress at home.

Ruefully, she blinked at the little staircase toward the foot of the bed. She'd forgotten climbing the thing earlier that evening. Imagine, a staircase just for getting into bed. The duke's own bed must be so piled with feather beds, he probably needed six or eight steps. He probably lay drowning in satin bedsheets and downy pillows, cloaked in a nightshirt of regal purple velvet. The idea made her laugh.

A picture bloomed in her mind, crisp as daylight and all too real. The Duke of Halford, masculine limbs ranging across a wide bed. No toffish velvet. No flight of stairs. No swallowing maw of feather beds. Just rumpled dark hair, biceps flexed around a pillow, and soft white linen, luminous in the moonlight, tangled about his hips. Or maybe lower, just hugging the curve of a tight, muscled arse.

She tried to shove the image away. No luck.

That sealed it. Cold tea or no, now she'd never be able to sleep.

She picked herself up off the floor, gathered the counterpane tight about her shoulders as a wrap, and ventured out into the corridor.

It was darker here. Pauline stood still for a moment, trying to recall the housekeeper's sequence of turns. She'd tried to pay attention, but she'd been so overwhelmed and tired. Not to mention awed by the rows of ancient portraits, in some places stacked three high. All those scores of illustrious ancestors.

The girls back home would say this place was surely crawling with ghosts.

Somewhere above her, timber creaked. A cool draft swirled over her neck. Pauline swallowed hard.

Left. She was sure they'd come from the left.

She made her way slowly in that direction, keeping one hand out to trail her fingers along the wall. Every dozen steps, her fingertips skipped from wallpaper to the beveled wooden surface of a door. One, two, three . . . She counted six before pausing. She ought to have reached the stairway by now.

A sudden flare of light stopped her in her paces. Stopped her heart as well. Which ghostly Duke of Halford Past was that? Ducking, she raised her hand against the blinding flame and squinted through splayed fingers.

"Simms?"

She found the eighth—and only living—Duke of Halford, haunting his own house.

He held a lamp in one hand. With the other he yanked a door closed. She heard the scrape of a key in the lock.

"What are you doing?" he demanded, pocketing the key.

His angry tone surprised her. "Good evening to you, too, your grace. My journey to London was fine, thank you."

He was having none of it. "Why are you snooping around my private rooms?"

"I didn't realize they were your private rooms. I wasn't snooping. I took a wrong turning, that's all. I'll go back the other way." She turned to leave.

He caught her by the arm, swiveling her back to face him.

"Did my mother put you up to this?"

Pauline didn't even know how to answer. Put her up to what? Sleeplessness? Wrong turnings in a vast, darkened house?

"Are you looking to pilfer something? Answer me with one word."

"No." She drew up her spine.

"Then explain yourself. You're out of bed when you should be sleeping, in a corridor you have no reason to visit." He held the lamp high and examined her. "And you have a guilty look on your face."

"Well, you have an arrogant, wrong-headed look on yours."

That was a bit of a lie. The lamplight bleached the stark planes of his face and splashed weary shadows under his eyes. The rich brown of his irises was overwhelmed by cold, empty black. He didn't look especially arrogant, not right now.

Whatever he'd been doing in that locked room, it was private. She'd interrupted him in an unguarded moment. And because a big, strong man like him couldn't possibly admit to having an unguarded moment, he was going to make her twist and squirm.

She sighed. "Dukes and their problems."

"I don't appreciate your impertinence, Simms."

"Well, that's bollocks."

He drew her closer, and her heart began to race. Her bare foot grazed his. The shock of it traveled all through her.

"My impertinence is the reason I'm here, remember? It's why you chose me from a room of well-bred ladies. Because I'm perfectly wrong. Everything you'd never want in a woman."

He raked a gaze down her body. "I wouldn't say that."

The hard bob of his Adam's apple caught her gaze, dragged it downward. Her attention settled in the dark, chiseled notch at the base of his throat.

Her lungs chose that moment to go out on labor strike. She held her breath so long, she went a bit dizzy.

"Send me home tomorrow, if you like. But you'll find nothing's vanished with me. I wasn't stealing. Even if I were considering it—and I'm not—I'd know better than to try it my first night here. I've met your housekeeper. I've no doubt she keeps a list of every last drawer pull in every last closet and takes inventory on the regular. If I meant to steal, I'd wait for the last moment. So if you won't give me credit for honesty, at least give me credit for cleverness."

"I'll give you credit for nothing until I hear the truth."

"I've told you the truth." She pulled the counterpane tight about her shoulders. "I couldn't sleep. I thought I'd go down to the libr—"

"To the library," he finished for her. Sarcasm dried his words to brittle husks. "Really, that's what you mean to tell me. You were looking for the library."

Why did he sound so incredulous?

"Yes," she answered. But at this point all she wanted was to return to her bedchamber without further interrogation. Her sleeplessness would surely be cured. This man was exhausting.

"Very well." His grip tightened on her arm as he led her down the corridor. "If it's the library you're searching out, I'll take you there myself."

* * *

This wasn't working how Griff had planned. He thought he'd girded himself against temptation.

He hadn't counted on temptation herself materializing in a darkened corridor just outside his rooms, well after the hour of midnight. Her hair unbound yet again. Cloaked in her bedclothes, like a woman freshly tumbled. Skulking around his private chambers and looking even more fetching by lamplight than she had in afternoon sun.

Surely it was a trick of the shadows. Her eyelashes could not measure the length of his thumbnail. It was an impossibility.

Perhaps they grew longer with every lie she told. Really. The *library*.

Of all the trite, clichéd excuses to pull out of her ear.

He marched her counterpane-swaddled self down the corridor, then down the staircase and around a bend. When they reached the correct set of doors, he flung them both open wide for effect.

"There you are. The library." He handed her the lamp.

Blinking, she moved forward into the room, using the light to lead the way.

"Have your choice of books," he said. "I'll wait."

She stood in the center of the room, turning slowly. Awestruck, no doubt. Even he would admit it was an impressive collection. As it ought to be, having been amassed over a dozen generations. The room was two stories high and hexagonal in shape, due to some fit of whimsy on the fifth duke's part. He'd been an amateur architect, in addition to a naturalist and several other lofty things. One side of the hexagon served as the entryway, but bookshelves covered each of the other five, from floor to soaring ceiling.

"Go on, then," he prodded.

"Am I truly allowed to touch them?" she whispered.

"But of course. Someone ought to."

Still, she stood huddled in that twisted counterpane, face tilted to the rafters. "I don't even know where to start."

"What sort of books are your preference?" he asked, not bothering to hide the smugness in his tone. "Are you a great reader of philosophy? History? The sciences?"

"I like verses mostly. But I make no claims of being a great reader at all, your grace."

So. She admitted it that easily.

He crossed his arms. "Yet you claimed to be looking for the library."

"Yes. I wanted to see the books, not read them. I hoped to have a look through the collection. Perhaps make a list."

At last she ventured forward and ran her finger down the spine of a slender leather volume. She didn't even take it from the shelf, just touched it— gingerly, as though it might disappear into mist.

"How are they organized, do you know?"

"Not really. I suspect it's loosely by subject. My grandfather invented some system of classification and made a catalogue, but I've never troubled to understand it. I don't use the library often."

She raised the lamp and turned to him, blinking in disbelief. "You mean you live in this house, with all these books"—she waved the lamp in an arc—"and you never read them?"

He shrugged with nonchalance, belying the sore spot she'd poked. "I am an embarrassment to my forebears. I know this well."

"How much do books cost, anyhow?"

He gave up on drawing connections between these questions of hers. The hour was too damned late. "That would depend on many factors, I suppose. The nature of the book, the quality of the binding. Novels might be had for a crown or two, whereas a nine-volume set on the history of Rome . . ."

She waved off his answer. "I don't believe I want histories of Rome."

"The Romans weren't as boring as you'd think." History lectures were one of the few parts of his schooling he'd enjoyed.

"If you say so. But I doubt even the most bookish of Spindle Cove ladies will want to read nine volumes about it on holiday."

Griff watched as she nimbly climbed the rolling book stair, lamp in hand. She hung the lamp on a hook created for just that purpose and tilted her head to peruse the titles of the shelved books. Her hair fell to one side in a shimmering cascade, like poured brandy. She had a lovely neck—a smooth, graceful ivory slope.

"You mean to take books back to Spindle Cove?" he asked.

"As many as I can. You see, that's how I mean

to spend my thousand pounds—or part of it, anyway. I'm going to . . . Well, never mind."

"What do you mean, never mind? You're going to spend your money on books and then . . . ?"

She sighed. "If I tell you, you'll laugh. And if you laugh, I'll hate you forever."

"I won't laugh."

She gave him a dubious look.

"Very well, I might laugh. But you'll only hate me for a day or two."

"I plan to take books home and open a circulating library."

"A circulating library," he repeated—without laughing . . . noticeably.

"Yes. I'll rent out books to ladies visiting on holiday. And since I've little experience with libraries myself, I hoped to glean some ideas from yours. Do you believe me now, that I was out of bed with honest purpose—not with snooping or thievery in mind?"

He did believe her. A lending library for spinsters? Not even a champion liar could weave such a preposterous tale from nothing.

"Very well. I apologize," he said. "I misjudged you."

"You apologize?" She looked at him, shocked. "Those aren't words I expected to hear from your lips."

"Then you've misjudged me." His faults might be legion, but no one could say he didn't admit them openly.

"Maybe." She folded her bottom lip and sipped on it. "Well, then. While we're talking . . . perhaps you could suggest a book. What do you read, your grace?"

"I don't read much of anything besides estate correspondence. Never seem to find the time."

In demonstration, he lifted a newspaper from a side table and cast it aside. He felt a small twinge of guilt. Each morning, Higgs went to the trouble of ironing the thing, page by page. Griff seldom gave it a glance.

Instead, he moved to the room's large desk and lit a pair of candles. There was a broken clock there he'd been meaning to tinker with—one of the Viennese curiosities his father had collected. Really, he should have been a tradesman's son. He always felt more comfortable, more capable, when his hands were occupied.

Her questions followed him. "But if you did have time to read, what would you choose?"

"Plays," he answered. For no particular reason, other than to have the question gone.

"Oh, plays. Those would be good for the library. The Spindle Cove ladies are fond of staging theatricals." Clutching the counterpane about her shoulders with one hand, she used the other to pull the rolling ladder toward another bank of shelves. "Do you go often to the theater?"

"Not lately."

"But you did in the past, then." Genuine interest warmed her voice. "Why did you stop? How long has it been?"

His grip tightened on a screw he'd been loosening. No one questioned him about this. Not even his mother. He felt the unexpectedness of it first, like a cold splash of water to the face. But once the initial affront wore off, he was left feeling oddly relieved. Almost grateful.

Griff's peers, associates, friends from the club . . . they must have noticed his retreat from society this past year. But if they wondered at the reasons and speculated amongst themselves, not a one of them had directly asked him why. Whether they lacked the courage or the interest, he didn't know.

Pauline Simms had the courage. And the interest, it seemed. Her innocent question warmed a place inside him that had long gone cold.

For a moment he was tempted to answer.

But then he dismissed the idea. There was no way for a man of his wealth and rank to relate his personal trials to a serving girl without sounding completely insufferable. Miss Simms had been raised in poverty, with a simple-minded sister to protect and a violent father she couldn't escape. Despite it all, she retained her pride and a sharp sense of humor. Was this girl supposed to pity him for missing the Theatre Royal's spring season, when she'd never attended the theater for even one night?

She would chide him for his whinging, and justly so. He could hear it now: *Dukes and their problems.*

He worked another tiny screw free of the clock's back facing. "I don't see that it should be any of your—"

"Any of my concern," she finished for him. "I know. You're right. It's not my business, but I couldn't help asking. It's the oddest thing, your grace. Even amid all the ancient, moldering volumes in this library . . . I find you the most unreadable book in the room. Just when I think I understand you, you confound me again."

"Simms, I'm a man. I'm not that complex."

He set aside the clockwork, intending to call an end to this literary interlude and send her upstairs to her chamber. But when he looked up, he saw her.

All of her.

And his voice ceased to function.

She stood perched on the second highest rung of the ladder. The counterpane had slipped to a downy cloud on the floor, and she floated above it—just a wisp of woman, wreathed in the thinnest, most fragile linen shift he'd ever seen. The thing had been worn and washed and mended so many times, it was like a lace of cobwebs rather than proper fabric. And when she swung her body in front of the shining oil lamp?

The shift was utterly transparent.

He could see everything. She didn't have a boyish figure at all. No, she was all woman. Her small, apple-round breasts were capped with dark nipples. Her belly was sleek. When she perched on the ladder, stretching on tiptoe for another book, the curve of her silhouette called to him like a familiar melody. Arched foot, slender calf, sweetly flared thigh . . . and a rounded, graspable bottom.

True, hers wasn't a Rubenesque, buxom figure. No artists would paint her lolling about in white sheets. There was something wild and elemental about her. They'd be inspired to depict a dancing nymph or chasing dryad. Hers was a body that would always show to its best advantage in motion.

And bare.

Brilliant. Now his imagination rioted with thoughts of her naked *and* moving.

She turned on the ladder, facing him.

Eyes, he told himself. *Stay focused on the eyes.* She had lovely eyes, with that startling leaf-green hue and her impossibly long eyelashes. He needn't let his gaze wander anywhere else.

Not to her spritely breasts.

Nor the enticing, dark triangle nestled between her thighs.

Damn.

He was a man, as he'd told her. Not that complex. The reaction in his groin was pure, simple, and about four extra inches of straightforward. Surely she didn't realize how she appeared. She *couldn't* realize, or she'd jump down from that ladder at once and cover herself.

"Where are the novels?" she asked, matter-of-factly propping her elbow on the ladder's nearest rung.

An insidious thought occurred to him. If she didn't realize why he was staring, he could safely stare as long as he liked. He could drink in every bit of her, store up enough glimpses to fuel his fantasies for months.

"I think the novels are there," he answered brusquely.

He motioned to the wall in question. Then he positioned the dismantled clock like a shield, blocking her from his view. Behind it, he briefly rolled his eyes heavenward. Someone up there had better be adding a hash mark to his "Good Deeds" tally. Perhaps now his lifetime total came to five or six.

"Do you have any favorites to recommend?" she asked.

"No." He sighed with gruff impatience. He wished she would cease being so blasted friendly when he was striving to stop mentally undressing her. In his mind's eye she was two buttons from complete ruination.

"I don't read many novels, either," she said. "The few I've tried were like forests to me—I got lost. I prefer verses, when I can find them. Little posies of pretty words, easy to grasp and keep with you. There was a woman in Spindle Cove one summer who fancied herself a poetess. Her own poems were horrid, but I liked the books she left lying about. I committed my favorites to memory, so I could share them with my sister."

"And which ones were your favorites?" he asked, happy to let her speak so she'd cease asking questions.

She was silent for a moment. "I like this one. 'The maiden caught me in the wild, where I was dancing merrily. She put me into her cabinet and locked me up with a golden key.'"

Griff had the panel almost freed now, but his fingers slowed.

She went on, her voice gaining a dreamy, velvet texture. "'The cabinet was formed of gold, and pearl and crystal shining bright. And within, it opens into a world, and a little lovely moony night. Another England there I saw. Another London with its Tower. Another Thames and other hills. And another pleasant Surrey bower.'"

He stared at the gutted clock before him. It didn't seem to be a clock anymore, but a cabinet. One with a secret window onto a little lovely moony night. A different London, a different England. An entirely different world.

He was enchanted, just a little.

"The story goes all wrong from there," she said regretfully, "but I loved that bit. A cabinet of gold and pearl and crystal, with a little secret world inside. It's something beautiful to picture when I'm washing up glassware at the tavern. Or, you know, when I'm elbow-deep in a mare."

He looked up from the clock a fraction. Just enough to receive the mischievous, fetching smile she cast his way.

"What do you think?" she asked. "Could it ever work?"

No.

No, you bewitching creature. It could never, ever work.

"You mean the circulating library, I assume."

She nodded. "I have it all planned out, you see. There's an empty shop front on the village square where the old apothecary used to be. It's all shelves already, with a sturdy counter. Only needs a bit of sunlight and wood polish. Lace curtains maybe, and a chair or two for those who'd like to sit." Her mouth pulled to the side. "But the prettiness is all for naught, if it isn't a sound business idea."

"And you want *my* opinion?"

"If you're paying me a thousand pounds, I'd think you wouldn't want to see it squandered."

He chuckled. "You can't know how many thousands I've squandered on my own."

"Just give me your honest judgment. Please."

He squinted, easing a bit of clockwork loose.

"Honestly, I'm the wrong person to ask. No doubt the spinsters will queue up for your verses and novels. The only books I ever went looking for were the naughty ones."

She clutched the ladder rung. "Oh, your grace. You're brilliant."

Griff sat back in his chair, amazed. Never in his life had anyone said *that* to him. Not outside of a bed, anyway. "What's so brilliant about me, precisely?"

"A lending library full of naughty books. That's exactly what I need. I mean, not every book would necessarily be scandalous. But a good many of them should be. At home, the ladies can acquire all the boring, proper books they like, can't they? They come to Spindle Cove to break the rules."

Griff had a memory of the young ladies in that tavern, merrily ripping pages from an etiquette book to make tea trays. Yes, he could imagine torrid novels and radical pamphlets would do a brisk business in such a place.

And in making the inadvertent suggestion, he'd now be responsible for debauching-by-proxy an entire village of spinsters. This surely represented some sort of zenith or nadir of his life. He wasn't sure which.

"Where *are* the naughty ones?" She tilted her head back, peering into the farthest upper recesses of the room. "I suppose they'd be on a high shelf. Or did you have a locked cabinet somewhere?"

He laughed. "If I did possess a secret section of my library that consists entirely of books inappropriate for young ladies, you could hardly expect me to direct you to it."

"Why not? I'm no lady. Not that innocent, either."

Don't say that.

"It's very late, Simms."

"Very early, more like."

"Suffice it to say, it's very dark. And you're very unclothed, and we're much too alone." For the two of them to begin a perusal of erotic literature atop it . . . ? That fragile shift of hers wouldn't survive the hour. "I've no noble impulses, remember?"

Her cheeks flushed. "At least help me make a list?"

He drummed his fingers on the desk. "*Moll Flanders, Fanny Hill, The Monk*, a good translation of *L'École des Filles*. Those are a start."

She closed her eyes. "Done."

"You don't want to write them down?"

"I don't need to. I have a good memory."

She leaned heavily to one side as she scanned the shelf, seeming to float above him. Griff was nearly reduced to panting by the nubile shadow of her silhouette and the swirled-brandy fall of her hair. Yes, he'd perused his share of naughty books. None of them had affected him like this. He was hard as the mahogany desktop.

"Aha. Here's one I'll take to bed with me." She plucked a book from the shelf. "*Methods of Accounting and Bookkeeping.*"

"Now that should put you right to sleep." He chuckled. "But it's a good idea. Keep excellent written records, even if you do have a good memory. Don't accept credit. If you lend, always require a deposit. Few can match the aristocracy when it comes to shirking financial obligations."

She sent him a wary glance. "You don't shirk *your* debts, do you?"

"Last I heard, I'm the fourth-richest man in England. I never have a need to."

"Oh. Good." She clutched the bookkeeping tutorial to her chest and bent her head, inhaling deep. When she noticed his stare, she looked sheepish. "I like the way books smell. Is that odd?"

"Yes. A little."

But he found it oddly endearing, too. This had gone beyond a midnight chat in the library and progressed to something bordering on flirtation. Perhaps even a strange sort of friendship—on his side, edged with fierce, carnal attraction.

Whatever it was between them . . . it ended here, and it ended now.

He set aside the dismantled clockwork and rose from his chair, trusting the shadows to hide his arousal. "Upstairs with you, Simms. It's late, and I'm sure my mother has a full schedule of exercises in futile ambition planned for the morrow."

"Don't worry. I'm prepared to be a catastrophe."

"Very good."

She extinguished the lamp and descended two risers of the ladder. "Just to prove it, I shan't even curtsy when I leave this room."

"An excellent start. If you wanted to be truly shocking, you could start calling me Griff."

She looked to him. "Truly?"

He winced. A miscalculation on his part. He'd suggested it as a stroke of impropriety, but her flattered expression reminded him—familiarity of that sort could prove dangerous.

Speaking of danger . . .

"Take care," he warned. "The last rung is rather—"

She gasped and faltered. "Oh, bollocks."

Chapter Six

Time slowed. A fraction of a second showed Griff just how the accident would occur. Her toes would miss the last rung. She'd drop the book. She would make a desperate swipe with her hand, perhaps graze the ladder rail with her fingertips—but it wouldn't be a proper grasp. Her momentum would carry her forward.

And then she would fall to the ground, face first.

Granted, the fall was a matter of only a few feet, and she'd no doubt survive it whole and unharmed. But by the time his mind had reached the end of the scenario, his body was already in motion.

Putting one hand to the sofa back, he vaulted the thing in one swift motion. That obstacle cleared, he hurdled a leather ottoman in a single leap. Flinging his arms wide, he came to a skidding halt directly in front of the ladder.

Just in time to break her fall.

She fell heavy against his chest. He caught her in his arms.

And then—even when all was safe—he couldn't seem to put her down.

"Oh my," she breathed, looking at the room he'd just traversed. "That was quite an athletic feat."

"It was nothing."

The only manly reply, naturally. In truth, he suspected he'd pulled a muscle somewhere between vaulting the sofa and playing Jack Be Nimble with the ottoman . . . but he'd worry about the pain later. Other sensations demanded his attention now.

Good God. Just seeing her form had been a delight, but it was a pale shadow compared to the thrill of feeling her. Her nipples were every bit as assertive as her personality, jabbing at him through the frail, tissue-thin fabric of her night rail. They demanded his notice. More than mere notice—they wanted respect.

Hell, he would have offered them worship.

"It didn't seem like nothing." Her arms laced about his neck. "You're breathless."

"So are you," he noted.

"Fair enough." She gave him a smile so shyly sweet, it seemed to belong to some other girl. "Your reflexes are most impressive."

What a gift of a remark. Here was where he would normally reply with a suggestive, *You have no idea*, or *Years of practice, sweeting*. But he couldn't quite muster the tired rakish innuendo. An absurd idea visited him—that his entire misspent life of sport and leisure, whiling away the days fencing or boxing when he might have been building a legacy, had prepared him for this one moment.

For this one girl, who needed him to break her fall.

"I just couldn't watch you get hurt," he said, not understanding it.

"I thought you didn't have noble impulses."

"Believe me." He stared into her eyes and spoke the words without lewdness or irony. "I don't."

If he possessed a single grain of decency, he would have set her down long moments ago. Wicked as it made him, he loved the way she was clinging to his neck. As though the world around them were a vast, frozen waste and sharing the heat of his body was her only chance to survive. It was so easy to believe, for this moment, that she needed him. Needed his touch, his mouth, his heated breath. His bared, feverish skin all over hers.

Amazing, what acrobatic contortions the lusting male mind could achieve. He'd almost convinced himself that kissing her lush, sweet lips *was* the noble thing to do.

Almost. But not quite.

"I'll put you down now," he said.

She nodded.

And then she pressed her lips to his.

Praise and curses be heaped. The girl kissed *him.*

The kiss crashed over him in a turbulent wave. His senses opened like floodgates. Her lips were so soft. They tasted ripe as berries. She smelled of linen dried in the sun. Her skin was a lush blur of creamy pink in his stunned, still-wide-open eyes.

Even when the kiss ended, the sweet shock of it resounded in his every nerve. Primal urges echoed back.

More. Again. Now.

Lust was his old, familiar acquaintance. The rapid beat of his pulse, the taste of her on his tongue, the sudden tightening in his groin . . . he knew all these sensations quite well.

But there was something else in this storm of feeling. A deep, steady thrum in the region of his heart.

Her, it whispered. *I'll take her.*

That part was new. And terrifying.

He abruptly set her on her feet. Then he turned away, rubbing his mouth. "What the devil was that?"

"I would expect your grace to have more experience on the subject . . . but I thought it was a kiss."

He scrubbed a hand through his hair. "That shouldn't have happened."

"No, no. It was . . . it was good."

He swung to face her. "You call that good?"

"No. Not good. Fortunate, more like." She swallowed. "You can't deny there's been a certain tension building between us. I thought the kiss might help."

He stared at her in disbelief. "Help."

"Well, now it's done, you see." She turned away with a self-conscious shrug. "It's over. And obviously it wasn't anything special. We won't have to worry about an attraction."

It wasn't anything special? Not worry about an attraction?

Remarkable, how this girl could slash at his pride. Perhaps he should hand her a letter opener and invite her to complete the evisceration.

She reached to retrieve the book she'd dropped

and gathered it close to her chest, preparing to leave. "Good night, your grace."

Let it go, he told himself. *Let her go.*

"You can't judge on that kiss." He took a step forward—blustering on past logic and common sense, tripping straight into pigheaded foolishness.

"I can't?" she asked.

"No. That wasn't a proper kiss. It was a mere collision of lips. If I kissed you and meant it, you'd have cause to worry, Simms."

"I would?"

He approached her slowly, made his voice low and cool. "You would. A true kiss would stir you in your deepest places. It would keep you lying awake in your bed all night long. Restless, and beset by . . ." He paused, grasping for the female equivalent of an aching cockstand. " . . . flutterings."

Her brow lifted in amusement, and a sly dimple formed in her cheek. "Flutterings?"

"Yes," he pronounced in a definitive tone. "Flutterings."

She smothered a laugh.

Good Lord. This wasn't happening. He could not be having this conversation. *Flutterings?* Stupid, asinine word, but he was committed now. He couldn't back down. He was the duke in this room, he reminded himself. And she was just a serving girl. It was time they both remembered it.

Except she wasn't just a serving girl. She was a serving girl with aspirations, keen business sense, shockingly good taste in poetry . . . and slight, enticing curves his hands ached to explore.

She was delectable. Ripe as berries.

Her, the whisper came again.

Leave off, he told it.

"Flutterings," she mused aloud.

He nodded. He didn't even mind that she was mocking him. He wanted her to say that word again and again, because each repetition came with an erotic flash of her tongue. It stoked a wildness in him.

She pushed her bottom lip forward, considering. "I don't know that I've ever suffered flutterings, your grace. Perhaps they're unique to ladies of the higher classes. I don't possess that sort of delicate feminine nature."

He slid his hand to the back of her head, plunging his fingers through the raw silk of her hair. "Now that's bollocks."

And then he pulled her into a kiss.

Ah. So *these* were flutterings.

And this, Pauline gathered, was his idea of a proper kiss. An embrace with heat and purpose, and one that remained entirely in his command. He controlled the angle of her neck and the closeness of their bodies—and the slow, maddening rhythm of his tongue, sweeping between her lips again and again.

He kissed her forcefully, relentlessly, as though he were meting out some punishment she deserved. Twenty lashings with a strong, wicked tongue. Little could he suppose it was exactly what she wanted. What she craved, with every bone and sinew in her small, slender frame.

Yes. Thank you. May I have another.

Those few moments after she'd kissed him had been among the most miserable of her life. He'd acted so horrified and disturbed. She didn't know what she'd been thinking to try it. Only that she was so grateful to him for opening this vast, invaluable library to her, a common serving girl. For listening to her most secret dreams without mocking them—and what's more, perfecting them by giving her that brilliant, naughty idea.

He couldn't know. He couldn't know how much it meant.

And *then* he'd performed that dashing, heroic maneuver to break her fall.

When she saw him up close, a flash in his eyes gave her the strangest notion. That this was scarcely the first night he'd spent haunting the corridors, staying up much too late and far too alone. That he wasn't nearly so put out by the interruption as he would have her believe.

That he might need a kiss—and a little rescuing, too.

Of course he'd walk a bed of nails barefoot rather than admit such a thing. She ought to have guessed how he'd react. All men had their pride, and dukes worst of all. "Admitting weaknesses" must rank with "tickle fights" and "slug hunting" in his list of least-favored activities.

So he'd struck back at her with this. A kiss that was controlled, masterful, possessive. And Pauline couldn't say she minded in the least.

He held her to him so tightly, twisting one hand in the linen of her shift and making a snarl of her hair with the other. Later, she'd be brushing it until her arm ached, but it would be worth every last stroke. The sensations racing over her scalp danced on that delicious edge between pleasure and pain.

His chest was a solid wall of heat, inflaming her and bringing her nipples to tight, needy peaks. Nothing separated their bodies but a few tissue-thin layers of linen, but still she couldn't get close enough. She rubbed against him, hoping to soothe the ache. Pleasure arced straight to her core.

When she stretched her arms around his back, he growled in encouragement. The deep, vibrating sound traveled through her body and settled as a seductive hum between her thighs. She nestled closer still.

"That's it," he murmured against her lips. "That's right."

It was. The way they fit together felt so, so right.

He wasn't kissing her any longer. They were kissing each other. Taking pleasure. Giving comfort. Learning one another's taste.

His mouth gentled over hers, and his movements grew languid, playful. Their tongues partnered in a slow, sensual dance. She gripped the skin-warmed linen of his shirt, letting it glide between her fingertips. So supple, with so much strength beneath. A wild, feral curiosity seized her. She wanted to know everything about him. Was his body bronzed to match his face, or pale like carved marble? Did he have hair on his chest, or was it smooth?

What powered that fierce, drumming beat of his heart?

She told herself to stop the inquiries there, struggling to tether her imagination before it ventured further downward.

Apparently, he had no such concern.

He swept a bold, exploratory touch down her spine. A pleasant shiver chased his caress, skipping over her vertebrae. When he reached her bottom, his hand found a curve she didn't know she had, and he claimed it with a possessive squeeze. She savored his moan of satisfaction.

How wonderful. She was used to thinking of her body as all points and angles, but he made her feel soft.

She'd never felt like this, not in all her life. So wanted, so desired. So needed, and by a man who shouldn't need anything.

When he finally broke the kiss, he left her lips swollen and aching. The corner of her mouth was rasped raw by his whiskers, and she touched her tongue to it, coaxing the hurt. She'd be feeling this kiss for hours.

Possibly years.

He released a ragged sigh. "Simms. That was badly done of me."

Pauline laughed a little. "If *that* was badly done, I'm not sure I'd survive your best effort."

"No, no. It was badly done of me as your employer. I shouldn't like you to think I make a habit of chasing the help." He turned aside, scrubbing a hand through his dark hair. "When I want companionship, I have no difficulty finding it. I never need to s—"

"Sink to this?" Stung, she reached for the discarded counterpane. "If your aim is to let me down gently, you're failing."

Why did men have to ruin everything? The answer was simple, she supposed—because foolish women gave them the chance.

"Listen. I'm just trying to say it won't happen again. And I'm sorry."

"Sorry for kissing me? Or sorry it won't happen again?"

He approached and tucked the counterpane tight about her shoulders. "Both."

In the flickering candlelight, his face took on that same haunted, lonely look. If he truly had no difficulty finding companionship—and after that kiss, she could believe he didn't—why wasn't he off pleasuring his mistress, or entertaining a widow, or debauching a virgin tonight?

For a man with no desire to marry, he wasn't exactly reveling in his freedom.

"It was just a kiss." She gathered a lit candle from the desk. "What's a little kiss or two? Nothing."

He stopped and looked at her. "Did you hear yourself?"

"What?"

"You just said nothi*ng*. Not nothin'."

"No, I didn't. I said nothing. Nothing." She gasped. "Cor. I *did* say it. Nothing." She tested more words. "Kissing. Embracing. Fluttering."

"Let's just"—the duke held up a hand—"stop the exercise there."

Pauline clapped a hand over her mouth and laughed into it. "Oh, no. This can only be your fault. Your mother did say it was all in limbering the tongue."

He gave her a dark look.

"Don't worry, your grace. No matter how you pronounce it, it truly was nothing. Just a kiss."

Liar, her heartbeat pounded. *It was so much more.*

"I've been kissed before," she continued.

Liar, liar. You've never been kissed like that.

"I know not to make too much of it. This is hardly cause for alarm," she finished.

Liar, liar, hair afire.

"You're right," he agreed. "We both have our goals. You have your naughty bookshop to open, and I have my ribald life story to continue, unfettered by matchmaking. The only way this week can go wrong is if it ends with us engaged to marry, and God knows that's not going to happen."

He drew the doors shut, then turned to her. Their gazes caught in the warm, golden space above the candle flame.

Pauline forced a laugh. It came out high and wild and ridiculous, and she wished she could blame it on someone else. "Oh, heavens. Don't flatter yourself, Griff. The kiss wasn't *that* good."

And then she hurried up the stairs, trying to outrun that pounding accusation in her chest.

Liar, liar, liar, liar, liar.

Chapter Seven

By mid-morning the next day, Pauline was amassing quite the mental list of things duchesses didn't do.

Duchesses didn't curse, spit, serve themselves at the table, buckle in any sense of the word, or speak of their internal organs in mixed company.

But on a happy note, duchesses did not have chores. They didn't draw water, or feed the hens, or turn out the cow, or chase a loose piglet all through the yard. Duchesses didn't make their own breakfast, or anyone else's. That part was lovely.

And when the Duchess of Halford swept into her bedchamber, Pauline added one more item to her list:

Duchesses did not knock.

She startled and thrust the bookkeeping manual under the pillow before rising from the bed. She didn't want to explain how that book had come to be in her possession. Even if she'd spent the past hour or two reliving the scene in her memory.

Oh, that kiss.

Her lips still tingled.

"I'm glad to see you're awake," the duchess said, "even at this early hour."

This *early* hour?

"It's nearly eleven o'clock in the morning. I've been awake for ages." Never in her life had Pauline slept later than six. She turned her head and gazed out the window. "Half the day's gone."

"You're used to country hours. We operate on a different schedule in Town. The time for morning calls begins at noon. Luncheon might be taken at three. The evening is just getting under way at nine o'clock, and midnight suppers are *de rigueur.*"

"If you say so." Pauline woke with the dawn every day, without fail. Mornings would be her time for reading. Perhaps she could steal a visit or two to the library, once she finished the book-keeping text.

"My son seldom rises before noon," the duchess sighed. "But that's why we're getting an early start. We've a great deal of work before us."

Pauline scanned the room. "I would have dressed, but I didn't see my frock."

"Oh, that." The duchess waved a hand. "We burned that."

"You *burned* it? That was my best for everyday." As opposed to the two other frocks she owned, one of which was strictly for church.

"It's not going to be your best ever again. From now on, you wear better. Later we'll visit the shops, but I've had my modiste send over some samples for today. I'll ring for Fleur, and we'll have you dressed."

"Jolly good, your grace."

Pauline's spirits sank straight to the carpet. Two minutes into her undressing last night she'd realized she didn't get along with Fleur. Or more to the point, Fleur didn't get along with Pauline.

The lady's maid had golden hair and cornflower-blue eyes, and she floated into the room like a snowflake. Perfect, pale, and cold.

"Hmph," Fleur said. It was a very French sound, and it didn't sound complimentary to Pauline's hair, face, attire, or character.

The Halford driver and footmen had been present in Spindle Cove for everything, and Pauline knew how quickly gossip passed from one servant to the next. By now they all must know she was a mere country farm girl, not worthy of a lady's maid's attention. Surely the servants would resent her and the extra work she was causing them.

Fleur unpacked a set of tissue-lined boxes, drawing out a series of undergarments and three nearly identical frocks.

"They're all white," Pauline said.

"Of course they're white," the duchess replied.

Never in her life had Pauline worn a white frock. Perhaps not even at her own christening. White was the color for ladies, because only ladies could keep a white gown clean. If she had ever been so foolish as to make herself a light-colored frock at home, it would have been gray within three washings. Excepting aprons and stockings, everything she owned was either brown or dark blue.

Not any longer.

First she was cloaked in a snow-white chemise, then corseted within an inch of her life. The duchess selected the simplest of the frocks—a high-waisted morning dress in layers of sheer muslin—and Fleur lifted it over Pauline's head. The pale fabric descended like a cloud, wreathing her in airy prettiness. She stared down at her arms, so tanned and freckled when placed against the pristine muslin.

The duchess scrubbed her with an appraising look. "At least it fits in the shoulders. It's fortunate you're willowy."

Willowy? That struck Pauline as a generous way of describing her figure. Even willows had curves.

After fussing with the frock's loose waistline for a few moments, Fleur took a length of jade-green satin and slid it about Pauline's middle, cinching it tight and tying a bow in back.

"Hmph." This time, Fleur sounded satisfied.

"Yes, much better," the duchess agreed. "Now what can be done with her hair?"

Not much, appeared to be Fleur's opinion.

Once Pauline's hair was coiffed and pinned in a simple, upswept knot, she was left staring at a most unfamiliar reflection in the vanity mirror. Not a hair out of place, not a speck on her frock's scalloped lace overlay.

The duchess dismissed Fleur with a few words in French, then addressed Pauline's reflection in the mirror. "I am going to do something I never do. I am going to talk to you about my son."

Pauline's mouth opened. But even if she'd decided what to say, the duchess's look forbade her to say anything.

"I know. I know. But I can't speak to my peers about such things, and I'd never confide in the servants. I'm at my wit's end with Griffy, and I've no one else to tell."

Griffy?

"He's changed since last autumn. I noticed it the day I arrived in Town. My son was always a rascal as a young boy. Then he grew into a dissolute young man, always playing cards with his friends or hosting bacchanalian parties at that Winterset Grange. And there've been so many women."

No doubt, Pauline thought. Did last night make her one of them?

"But this past year, everything changed. He didn't even open the Grange last winter. He stayed in Town. For what purpose, I can't imagine. He never goes out to the clubs, shows no interest in friends or society. And then there's the locked room."

"A locked room, you say?"

She tried not to betray her heightened interest. With all that had happened in the library afterward, she'd almost forgotten surprising him in the corridor last night. He'd certainly behaved like a man with something to hide.

He also kissed like a man who craved warmth and comfort. But she wasn't about to tell the duchess *that*.

"A locked room," the duchess repeated. "He keeps one chamber of his suite locked day and night. Only he has the key. He doesn't even allow the maids to dust it. It's . . . it's perverse. Who knows what he's keeping in there?"

"I do hope it's not a collection of severed heads. Perhaps he's been trawling the countryside for impertinent serving girls, and I'll be number eleven."

The duchess harrumphed. "You're not number eleven. You're going to be his first—and only—bride."

"But I'm a commoner."

"The Halford legacy is sufficiently robust to withstand my son's debauchery. It can even survive a commoner as duchess. But it will end—forever—if there is no male heir."

"Surely the duke has decades yet to produce a son. You can't honestly believe he'll marry me."

"He *must*. I can't wait decades. You don't understand." The duchess halted. "I'd hoped it wouldn't come to this. Now I see I have no choice."

The older woman thrust one hand into her pocket and drew it back out, clutching something small and fuzzy.

"There," she declared. "Just look at it."

Pauline looked at it. A knitted object, of indeterminate purpose, made from light yellow wool. Part of it looked like a cap, and part of it looked like a glove, and none if it looked well made.

"What is it?" she asked.

"It's appalling! That's what it is. I don't even know how it happens. I haven't done needlework since I was a girl of fourteen. Even then it was crewel work and embroidery. Never knitting. But every night, for the past several months, I sit down for the evening, intending to read or write letters, and three hours later there's a lumpy, misshapen *thing* in my lap."

Pauline stifled a giggle.

"Go ahead, laugh. It's ridiculous." The duchess picked up the knitted mess and turned it over in her hands. "Is it a cap for a two-headed snake? A mitten for a three-fingered arthritic? Even I don't know, and I made the thing. The shame. I can't let the servants see them, of course. I have to stash them in a hatbox and smuggle them out to the Foundling Hospital on Tuesdays."

Pauline laughed aloud at that.

"A lifetime of elegance, poise, and jewels, and now I've come to this." She lifted the distorted mitten and shook it at Pauline. "This! It's absurd."

"Perhaps you should consult a doctor."

"I don't need a powder or a tonic, Miss Simms." The duchess sank into a chair and pressed the snarl of yarn to her chest. Her voice softened. "I need grandchildren. Little pudgy, wriggling babies to absorb all this affection unraveling inside me. I'm desperate for them, and I don't know what will become of me otherwise. Some morning, Fleur will come in to wake me and find I've been asphyxiated by a yards-long muffler. How gauche."

Pauline took the knitting from the duchess's hands and examined it. "This isn't half bad, in places. I could teach you to make a proper cuff, if you like."

The duchess grabbed it from her and stuffed it back in her pocket. "I'll take knitting lessons from you later. This week, you're taking duchess lessons from me."

"But, your grace, you don't understand. I don't even—"

Pauline shut her mouth. It had been on the tip of her tongue to say, *I don't even want to marry him.*

But something stopped her from saying it aloud. An impulse to spare the duchess's feelings, she decided. No mother would like to hear her son disparaged, and it would be impossible to explain why a serving girl would turn down the chance to marry a duke.

Explanations weren't necessary, anyhow. The duke in question was never going to propose.

"He's paying me," she blurted out. She just couldn't let the poor woman get her hopes up. Halford hadn't sworn her to secrecy, after all. "He's paying me to be a catastrophe. To thwart your every attempt at polish."

The duchess gave a delicate harrumph. "That's what he told you because that's what he's telling himself. He can't bring himself to admit that he's fascinated with you. You're a proud one as well. If I accused you of being infatuated with him already, you'd deny it."

"I . . . I do deny it. Because it isn't true."

As she spoke the words, Pauline's heart pounded in her chest.

Liar, liar, liar.

She *was* infatuated. Stupidly, impossibly infatuated with every little thing about the duke. No, not the duke—the man. The way he'd listened to her with true interest. The way he'd broken her fall, kissed her with such passion. The delicious, addictive way he smelled. Just that morning she'd harbored fantasies of stealing his discarded shirt from the laundry so she could stash it under her pillow.

Oh, ye gods! This was terrible. She even had flutterings.

Fleur reentered the room bearing a velvet-lined tray, which she placed on the vanity table.

Pauline gasped. The tray was covered in jewels of every type and color, sparkling in every conceivable setting—necklaces, bracelets, earrings, rings. But they did not come in every size. No, each gemstone was uniformly, alarmingly huge.

"That will be all," the duchess said, dismissing Fleur once again.

She turned her attention to the tray of jewels. "Not pearls, not today," she muttered, pushing aside a strand of perfectly matched iridescent orbs. "Topaz would be all wrong. It will be a few years yet before you can carry off diamonds or rubies."

Diamonds and rubies? The deluded woman kept speaking as if all these jewels would one day be hers. Pauline didn't know how to convince the duchess of the truth.

"Didn't you hear me, your grace?" she asked in a loud whisper. "Gri—I mean, the duke—is paying me to fail. He just wants to teach you a lesson, so he'll never be subject to your matchmaking again."

The older woman's hands settled on Pauline's shoulders. Their gazes met in the mirror. "How much did he promise you?"

"A thousand pounds."

The duchess seemed unimpressed. She placed her hands on either side of Pauline's face and pulled upward, elongating her spine until she sat ramrod straight.

"There. When your posture is correct, you have a marvelous neck for jewels." She tilted Pauline's head this way and that. "Never let anyone tell you to wear emeralds, simply because your eyes are green. It's what people with no imagination say.

On color alone, your eyes are a closer match to peridot. But peridot always strikes me as lamentably bourgeois."

"I don't often have people advising me on jewels, your grace," Pauline said, her voice muffled by the duchess's hands bracketing her cheeks. "This would be the very first time."

The duchess released her, turned, and lifted a necklace of light purple stones and gold filigree from the velvet-lined tray. As she draped the jewels about Pauline's neck, she said, "This is your stone. Amethyst. Rare, regal, yet sweet enough for a younger woman."

As the jewels found the dips and hollows of her collarbone, Pauline stared into the looking glass, amazed. The duchess was right—the amethysts' color did look well on her. The violet shade set off the golden tones in her hair and put a wash of pink on her cheeks.

Then again, perhaps the flush was born of excitement. She could scarcely believe such a thing was touching her bare skin.

"So my son has offered you a thousand pounds," the duchess said. "This necklace alone is worth ten times that."

Holy . . . Ten. Thousand. Pounds. Ten times a thousand pounds. A numeral one with four aughts after it. Hanging around *her* neck.

Fear gripped her with sudden, irrational force. She was terrified to move or breathe. If she even dared tilt her head to one side, perhaps the chain would break and the entire priceless business would slide into a floorboard crack—never to be seen again.

The duchess said, "Keep your eyes on the greater prize, my girl."

Pauline could do nothing but stare at the silver-haired woman in the looking glass. Odd. She hadn't pegged the duchess for a madwoman.

"Your grace, it simply won't work." She waved at her own reflection. "I'm not what he'd want. Much less what he'd need. He's the eighth Duke of Halford, and I'm a serving girl. Perfectly wrong. Just listen to me. Look at me."

"It's not I who needs a look at you." The duchess removed the amethyst necklace and replaced it in the tray, then motioned for Pauline to stand. "Come along. We're going to have an experiment."

Bemused, Pauline rose from the chair and followed. They went downstairs to the main floor, and the duchess guided her into a large, open salon. As they entered the room, she looked to Pauline and put a finger to her lips for quiet.

The carpets had been rolled back to the edges of the room, and Pauline quickly learned why. The room wasn't a salon right now, but some sort of gymnasium.

In the center of the floor, the duke and a masked opponent squared off against one another. Each man was clad in thigh-hugging buff breeches, a quilted waistcoat, and an open white shirt. Each man held a slender, shining sword.

Neither noticed them enter the room.

"*En garde,*" the masked man said.

Steel clanged in response.

Pauline looked on as the two swordsmen traded feints and thrusts. She was speechless in admiration.

While his opponent wore a mesh helmet to protect his face, the duke's features were fully visible. She could make out every furrow of concentration and drop of sweat on his brow. The exertion had matted his hair to his skull in dark, curling locks, and his open shirt clung to his torso. His musculature was revealed by the damp white linen, giving him the look of a marble carving come to life. Arms, shoulders, calves, arse—he was beautifully formed, everywhere.

The masked opponent sent a quick thrust toward the duke's torso, but the duke deflected it with a sharp flick of his own blade before going on attack. His lunges and thrusts had the grace of a dance, coupled with deadly force.

As the two battled on, the walls echoed with the exciting sounds of steel whooshing through the air and blades clanging against each other—and most thrilling of all, two athletic men grunting with the force of their exertion. The whole space hummed with virile energy.

If Pauline had been suffering flutterings since their kiss, this scene ratcheted those sensations to something even more profound. Stirrings? Quakings? She didn't want to name them.

In the center of the room, the men locked swords. The shining edge was just inches from Halford's face, and unlike his opponent, he wore no contraption of metal floss to guard it. A flick of the blade and he could be scarred or blinded.

Take care, she wanted to shout.

The duchess put a hand on Pauline's arm, restraining her.

Finally, with a primal growl, the two broke

apart—each man recoiling several paces backward.

As he swiped at the perspiration on his brow, the duke turned his head in the ladies' direction, briefly.

Briefly was all it took.

He saw her.

Even from across the room, Pauline felt it the moment his gaze locked with hers. The heated intensity made her skin tingle.

Halford must have felt more than a tingle. While he stood frozen in place, his opponent's blade nicked his upper arm. A line of red blood quickly soaked through his shirt.

"Oh!" Pauline clapped both hands over her mouth, horrified.

For her part, the duchess made a satisfied noise. "I call that a success."

Chapter Eight

Griff growled in pain, dropping his sword and pressing his free hand over the wound. "Damn it, Del."

"Not my fault. Why'd you stop defending?" His friend pushed back his protective mask and looked about the room. When his gaze found Miss Simms, he smiled broadly. "Hullo. I see for myself now."

Hullo, indeed.

Pauline curtsied, and Griff gave her a brisk nod.

He shouldn't have been so surprised. It was just that he hadn't seen her since the library last night, where they'd spent that time talking. Then embracing. Then kissing like lovers who'd been imprisoned in separate cells for ten years and were headed for the gallows at dawn.

Good God. Good God.

Today, he'd resolved to find her and have a brief, businesslike chat to set matters straight, assure them both it wouldn't happen again—but the talk wasn't supposed to happen like this. They were meant to be alone, but only to a safe degree. When he was too exhausted from hours of vigorous fencing to even contemplate lust, and when she was . . . not looking like that.

Are you all right? she mouthed.

No. No, he wasn't all right. He was devastated.

Yesterday she'd turned his head with impropriety and all those sparkling sugar crystals. Now she didn't sparkle any longer. She wore a frock of white so sheer and pure, the sun-burnished warmth of her skin shone through.

She *glowed*.

He'd always loved this: a woman's elemental effect on him, as a man. He used to live for these moments of raw, instinctual attraction. When a source of celestial-grade femininity wandered into the room, and his internal compass recalibrated. It was a sublime shift from internal chaos to single-minded determination. The difference between *Ye gods, what next?* and . . .

Her. I'll take her.

Damn. He wanted her. He had from the first. He understood it now, that some deadened part of him was kindling back to life.

But this was the worst possible time, and she was the least possible woman, and whatever effect she had on him, Griff knew he must make absolutely sure that no one in the room—not his mother, not his friend, not Pauline Simms—had any clue.

Well, aside from the bleeding.

Turning away, he used the edge of his sword to

shear a strip of linen from his shirt and used it to bind his wound.

"Your grace." Del stretched one leg forward and made a deep, courtly bow to the duchess.

"Lord Delacre." His mother inclined her head.

"Will you do me the honor of introducing your lovely friend?"

Don't start, Griff silently warned. *Not with her.*

He and Del had a long history of locking horns over conquests. In their most callow, youthful years they'd even made a sport of it, with wagers and a complex system of points. Griff had long outgrown such things, but there was no telling, where Delacre was concerned. He might still be keeping a tally somewhere.

"This is my guest," the duchess said. "Miss Simms, of Sussex."

"Well, Miss Simms of Sussex. It's a true pleasure to make your acquaintance. I am Lord Delacre, of wherever I'm least wanted." He lifted Pauline's hand and kissed it.

She lifted an eyebrow at Griff, and it was as though he could hear her teasing, *You didn't kiss my hand.*

But I saved you from falling on your face, he retorted with a quirked brow of his own.

For a moment they began to share a smile. And then it was though they both remembered the kisses that had followed said rescue—not to mention the implied intimacy of conversing in eyebrow quirks while other people looked on.

Her throat flushed. Griff looked away.

"Don't be worried about him, Miss Simms,"

said Delacre. "We're expert swordsmen, the two of us. Best in London. We have to be."

"And why's that?" she asked.

"Because we're the two greatest rakes." Del winked at her. "A reputation for expert swordsmanship is the best defense against being called out in a duel. No man, no matter how enraged, would put the choice of weapon in our hands." He set his practice blade aside. "Have you been long in London, Miss Simms?"

"Only since yesterday, my lord."

The duchess put in, "Miss Simms's parents have been unable to expose her to society, so I've offered to give the girl some polish here in Town."

"Judging by the slice in Halford's arm, I'd say you're off to a promising start," Delacre said. In a lowered voice, he told the duchess, "I know what you're up to. And as one blood-sworn to defend him against all marriage traps, I ought to object. But for once, your grace, I think we may be allies. There's no denying he's been a monk all season. Only less amusing."

"I heard that," Griff said curtly.

Del ignored him, still addressing the duchess in confidential tones. "Of course, we're not entirely aligned. You're his mother. You want to see him married. As his friend, my goal is different. I'd settle for getting him—"

"*Del.*"

"—out," Delacre finished, clapping a hand to his breast in innocence. "Getting him out. Of the house. What did you think I meant to say? You have a filthy mind, Halford. Positively diseased."

Annoyed, Griff swung his sword in idle threat, testing his wounded arm. With friends like these . . .

"This is excellent." Delacre clapped his hands. "Miss Simms needs an introduction to Town. Halford's been needing to use his—"

"*Del.*"

"—legs." Delacre raised his hands in innocence. "Obviously, we all need to attend the Beaufetheringstone crush this evening."

His mother sighed. "I will speak these words just once in my lifetime, I'm sure. Delacre, you make an excellent suggestion."

"It's a terrible suggestion," Griff muttered.

"Until this evening, then." Delacre gathered his things and sketched a quick bow. "I must be going. I like to wear out at least three welcomes before teatime. Otherwise, the day feels wasted." From the doorway, he leveled a finger at Griff. "You can thank me for this later."

Oh, I will gut you for this later.

"But I just arrived in Town," Pauline said. "I don't have anything to wear."

The duchess raised a brow. "Girl, you have so little faith in me."

Griff knew better. He put nothing past his mother when she had a goal in mind. But even if she managed to make Miss Simms look the part of a young lady, she couldn't remedy the girl's accent, education, woeful etiquette, and utter lack of genteel accomplishment. Not in a single day's time.

He wasn't worried.

Much.

* * *

A few hours later Pauline understood why the duke might price a week's maternal diversion at one thousand pounds and still think it a good value. The duchess could spend that sum in one afternoon, twice.

They visited the modiste first—an aging, turbaned woman who appeared better suited to fortune-telling than mantua-making. She surveyed Pauline with dramatic, kohl-rimmed eyes.

"Oh, your grace," the woman said, in a tone of despair. "What is this you've brought me?"

"She needs a week's full wardrobe," the duchess said. "Altered samples will do for today, but we need better for tomorrow. Morning, walking, and evening dress. A ball gown by Friday night. And she must look ravishing beyond compare."

"Ravishing? This?" The modiste clucked her tongue. "You ask too much."

The duchess lifted a brow and fixed the woman with a severe look. "I'm not *asking*."

The room froze over with an icy, tense silence.

Finally, the modiste clapped her hands, and a bevy of assistants rushed forward.

Pauline played scarecrow for hours, standing with her arms spread to either side while flitting seamstresses circled her. They measured every bit of her with tapes, from wrists to ankles, and draped her with lengths of shimmering fabric.

Once the seamstresses were finished pricking her with pins, it was on to the linen draper's, where Pauline learned just how many shades pink came in: scores. The duchess pored over bolt after bolt of satin in shades of blush, rose, berry, and one unpleasant, flaming shade she could only describe as "rash." The duchess had several fabrics cut and sent to the modiste.

Then it was on to the haberdasher's. And the milliner's. Then the glover's. By the time she'd tried on a dozen pairs of toe-pinching slippers, Pauline came to a realization.

Achieving the look of pampered elegance required a ridiculous amount of work.

While the duchess was directing the footmen in their efforts to secure fourteen parcels and hatboxes atop the coach, Pauline's attention strayed to a shop next door.

A happy flutter rose in her chest.

It was a bookshop.

She peered through the lattice of diamond-shaped windowpanes, greedily drinking in every detail and committing it to memory. In the window, someone had made a display of geographical titles—the travel memoirs of wealthy gentlemen, mostly. In the center lay an atlas, open to a tinted map of the Mediterranean Sea.

She noted the careful manner in which the unbound volumes were arranged on shelves. The titles were impossible to make out from this distance. Were they sorted alphabetically by title or by author? Or grouped by subject, perhaps? Maybe they were organized by some other method entirely.

Pauline cast a glance at the duchess. She was still wholly occupied with the parcels.

"No, no," she told the footman. "That one must go on top. I don't care that it's the largest. It mustn't be crushed."

A pair of ladies emerged from the bookshop,

turning to walk down the street in the other direction. Pauline peered through the window again. She saw no other customers within. After scribbling a few lines in a ledger, the shopkeeper disappeared into a back storeroom.

Her curiosity got the better of her common sense. While the duchess saw to the parcels, Pauline opened the door of the bookshop and ducked inside. She would only be a moment.

Oh, but she could have lingered for weeks.

The most glorious smell met her as she entered the establishment. Ink and paste and leather and crisp new parchment—all tinged with just the right amount of mustiness. It was the perfect blend of familiar and new, like the spice-laced comfort of walking into Mr. Fosbury's kitchen at Christmastime.

Beyond the display she could spy the shopkeeper's counter, with a slate of titles neatly labeled NEW PRINTINGS. Samples of various leather bindings were laid out for customers making a purchase—black, green, red, dark blue, and a scrap of light fawn-hued calfskin as impractical as it was lovely.

She walked to a shelf and let her touch linger on the spine of a book. A poetry volume.

Pauline didn't have much in common with the ladies who visited Spindle Cove. But she shared their love of the printed word. It seemed any young woman at odds with her place in life—be she a genteel lady or a serving girl—might find a happier home within the pages of a book.

"Who's that?"

The shopkeeper came out from the storeroom.

When his sharp gaze fell on Pauline, she snatched her hand away from the poetry volume, cradling her fingers in her other hand as if they'd been burnt.

The man eyed her with suspicion. "What do you want, girl? If you're selling pies or oranges, come 'round the back way."

"No, I . . . I'm not sellin' anythin'." The broadness of her accent pained her own ears. Never mind the new frock—she was instantly given away. "Anything," she repeated, making certain to attach the G sound this time. "I only wanted a look at the books."

The shopkeeper snorted. "If you're wanting horrid novels, you can find them down in Leadenhall. I don't permit girls to stand about gawping."

"I'm companion to the Duchess of Halford. She's waiting for me just outside."

"Oh, truly." The man laughed. "I suppose the Queen of Sheba had other plans today. Now out, before I chase you off with the broom. This isn't the place for you."

She couldn't move. His words threw her back to an old, hurtful memory. A book ripped from her white-knuckled hands. Pain splitting her head, from one ear to the other. Harsh words adding insult to the ringing in her ears.

That's not for you, girl.

She wanted to retaliate, stand up to the shopkeeper—but how? She had nothing. No coin to spend. No cultured accent or knowledge to prove his assumptions wrong.

She was visited by a powerful, childish temptation to throw a book at the man, but that would be less dramatic than sugar—not to mention, unkind to the book.

So she simply turned and left, cheeks hot and fingers shaking.

Someday, she promised herself, *I will own my own shop filled with lovely books. And it will be a home to me, and to Daniela, and to anyone else who needs it. No one will ever be turned away.*

Outside, the Halford coach now resembled a four-layer cake, with boxes and parcels tied to every available surface.

The duchess waved at her from inside the carriage. "Come along, then."

Pauline obeyed. She'd learned one thing from her quick survey inside the bookshop. She'd seen prices scribbled on the slates, and now she knew for certain . . .

One thousand pounds could purchase a great many books.

It was time to set aside all thoughts of kisses, flutterings, and haunted dukes. She'd been hired for one purpose—to be a disaster—and she simply couldn't fail.

Chapter Nine

Four petticoats.

Pauline had never dreamed that one woman could wear four petticoats. All at once, no less.

As she stared at her reflection in the mirror, she decided it would be more truthful to say the petticoats were wearing *her*. Her ivory silk skirts flared so dramatically, she didn't know how she'd fit through the doorway. She'd consider herself lucky if she survived the evening without plowing down any dogs or small children.

God help her if she needed to relieve herself.

As Fleur placed the final touches on her hair, Pauline stared wistfully at a cup of tea. It was going to be a long, thirsty evening.

"Listen to me closely," the duchess said. "There's a great deal at stake tonight."

Pauline nodded.

"If you want to win society's admiration, everyone must see you. No hiding in the corners or ducking behind the potted palms."

Note: Make bosom friends with potted palms.

"But though it's imperative to be seen, it's less important to be heard. Talk with the ladies, but not too much. That goes double for the gentlemen."

Which part? The talking, or the not too much?

"Tonight, you'll appear before the cream of London society. Let them see you as a lovely young lady with a certain freshness about her. A translucent petal, veiled in mystery. Someone they're dying to claim they've met, but don't truly know at all. Do you understand?"

Oh, yes. Clear as pitch.

In the corridor, her progress was slow. She wasn't accustomed to walking in such heavy skirts, nor in heeled slippers. Her gait resembled that of a wobbly foal. Perhaps a wobbly foal drunk on cider mash.

As they approached the staircase, her slipper heel snagged on the fringe of the carpet, nearly sending her sprawling. Pauline caught herself on a side table and endured several seconds of sheer agony as a porcelain shepherdess wavered back and forth on her base, deciding whether or not to fall.

"Miss Simms." Several paces ahead, the duchess whirled about to face her. "Have you forgotten how to walk?"

"I do know how to walk." She growled at the smiling shepherdess. "Just not dressed in all this."

"First, stand tall."

Pauline obeyed, even though she felt like kicking off the nefarious shoes and shrinking back to her bedchamber.

"Stop thinking about your feet. Imagine there's a string attached to your navel," the duchess advised. "Now let it pull you forward."

Amazing.

Simple as it sounded, the duchess's suggestion worked. When Pauline concentrated on her center, all the other parts fell into place. Her feet moved one in front of the other, and her shoulders just naturally pulled back. She felt taller, more assured. Floating.

As they neared the grand staircase, she felt an anxious twist in her belly. Her mind's eye supplied a vision—the silliest of fancies, no doubt—that the duke would be standing at the bottom of the stairs, waiting for them.

Waiting for her.

Oh, she hoped he would be there. She hoped he'd look up and see her—and then watch, enraptured, as she smoothly descended every last one of the two dozen steps like a silken mist. When she reached the bottom of the stairs, he'd take her hand and kiss it with those strong, passionate lips.

And he'd whisper just one hushed, reverent word:

Perfect.

It was a ridiculous fantasy. Completely absurd. And she wanted it to happen so desperately, she could scarcely breathe. After that encounter with the shopkeeper earlier, she could have used a fresh supply of confidence.

She reached the top of the staircase.

The duke wasn't there at all. So he didn't watch her stumbling down the two dozen stairs, and when she finally made her unceremonious landing, there were no kisses or compliments to be had.

They'd been waiting, stuffed into the coach—giant skirts and all—for a solid ten minutes before he finally joined them.

"Really, Griff," the duchess said.

He didn't apologize. "I had a letter to finish."

He cast a quick glance at Pauline, then looked away.

So much for her fantasies of enrapturing him with her radiant beauty. In the darkness of the carriage, with her hair pulled back so severely and all these petticoats wadded about her, she probably looked like a barn mouse who'd drowned in a dish of meringue.

Two minutes after departing from Halford House, the carriage rolled to a halt again.

"Here we are," the duchess said.

"Truly?" Pauline asked. "We might have walked."

The duchess only gave her a look, but Pauline didn't need it translated. *Duchesses do not walk.*

When they alighted from the carriage, they joined a small crowd of fashionable people spilling out the front door of the grand house.

"What's happening?" she whispered to the duke, trying to see around the horde of well-dressed people. "Why are we standing here?"

"It's a crush. We're all waiting to enter the ballroom and be introduced by the majordomo."

"He's going to announce me by name?"

"Of course," the duke replied.

"But . . . I've been serving ladies in Spindle Cove for the past several years. They all know my name. What if any of them are here tonight?"

"Simms is a common name. Sussex is a large place."

"They have eyes as well as ears. What if someone recognizes me?"

"Then the truth would be out, the game would be up, and we'd all have a jolly laugh at my mother's expense." He straightened his coat. "But truly, as you are tonight? No one will recognize you."

He sized her up with a leisurely, possessive sweep of dark eyes. And for the first time all evening, Pauline had an unhurried, well-lit look at him.

Good heavens.

They were well into the third day of their acquaintance. Could this truly be the first time she'd seen him freshly bathed, shaven, and properly dressed?

Apparently so. And one wouldn't think basic grooming could add so much to his masculine allure, but it did. It *did*. His black tailcoat and bone-colored breeches fit him like skin, hugging every contour of his broad shoulders and muscled thighs. The little touches of elegance— his smooth-shaven jaw, tamed hair, and exquisite sculpture of a cravat—only served as contrast to the raw strength ranging beneath the refinement.

He looked better than ever. And he smelled . . . oh, he smelled like an arousing, fevered dream. As he drew closer, she breathed him in. That intoxicating musky cologne—his valet must use it when pressing his shirts—mingled with the scents of soap and clean male skin.

Most affecting of all was the glint of hunger in

his gaze as he looked her over. As though he were a beast sizing up his prey. Judging the softest joint into which to sink his teeth.

Had he eaten anything today? she suddenly—absurdly—wondered. But she stopped herself from asking aloud. It seemed a very caretaking thing to inquire, and she wasn't here to care for him. No matter how tempting it was.

Remember that, Pauline.

"How is your arm?" she took the chance to whisper. She couldn't help caring that little bit.

"It's fine. It was nothing."

"But you were bleeding. I saw it."

He dismissed her words with a brisk wave of his hand. "Never mind my arm, Simms. We need to talk about your breasts."

Her cheeks went hot as coals. She looked around to make sure no one had overheard.

"They seem to have swollen to twice their proper size." He appraised them frankly. "I should call for a doctor. That can't be healthy."

Pauline's face suffused with heat. "You know very well it's only a corset. I'm in perfect health."

Except for these pesky flutterings all through her chest. And the sudden trouble breathing in his presence.

He clucked his tongue. "Your conduct had better be deplorable."

No difficulty there.

When they at last entered the fine house, a waiting footman offered glasses of ratafia from a tray. Pauline revised her resolution not to imbibe any liquids this evening. She accepted one and downed a hasty swallow.

That hasty swallow kicked her in the ribs. Someone had liberally seasoned the punch with brandy.

"Cor," she sputtered, choking on the strong aftertaste.

The room hushed. All through the entrance hall fashionably dressed people turned to stare.

"Corinthian," the duchess filled in, craning her neck to stare at the ceiling above. "I do believe you're right, Miss Simms. These columns *are* Corinthian."

Conversation slowly returned to normal, but Pauline didn't think anyone was fooled.

A well-dressed lady in middle years approached, flanked by two younger copies of herself. Daughters, obviously. All three women eyed the duke with rapacious interest before settling their keen gazes on Pauline.

"Your graces," the matron said. "Such a delight to see you this evening. Pray tell, who is your charming new friend?"

The duchess answered. "Miss Simms, this is Lady Eugenia Haughfell and her daughters."

Pauline curtsied. "Delighted, Lady Haughfell. Misses Haughfell."

Just those few words, and she was given away. The two fashionable daughters tittered with laughter behind their fans. If they would laugh to her face, she could only imagine what they'd say when her back was turned.

"Wherever did you come from, Miss Simms?" their mother asked.

"Sussex, my lady."

"And who are your people?"

"Her father owns land," the duchess cut in. "Her

parents have been unable to send her to Town, so I've invited her for a visit."

"Oh, your grace." Lady Haughfell twisted her lips at Pauline. "You do have such a heart for charity."

She and her daughters drifted away on a wave of giggles, leaving Pauline to feel awash in their scorn.

"*Haughfell*, girl," the duchess chided, pulling her aside. "Their family name is *Haughfell*."

Pauline wrinkled her nose. "What did I say?"

"Lady Awful."

"Oh." Cringing, she searched the woman out in the crowd. Judging by her ladyship's curled lip and the haughty stare she sent in her direction, Pauline wasn't sure she'd misspoken.

"No, no," the duke said. "To my ear it sounded more like Lady Offal. Either way, it was apt. The whole family is vile, and it's high time someone said it to their faces." He took the ratafia from Pauline's hand and downed it in a single swallow. "Do you know, I just might enjoy this evening."

His evident pleasure at her missteps didn't sit as well with her as it should. Pauline tried to ignore the stab to her pride. Satisfying her employer was a good thing. This was what she'd signed on for—a practical girl's fairy tale. No magical transformation. No sweeping romance. Just hard work, a job well done, and the shop of her dreams in reward.

So why did she keep hoping for something more?

Perhaps the ratafia was already muddling her brain.

Her discomfort only increased as they moved forward and she caught a glimpse of the elegant ballroom. The ceiling was supported by a great many columns—vast pillars of white, soaring high overhead. She'd never seen so many candles burning in one place.

"I'm not ready for this," she whimpered.

"Of course you're not," he said. "That's why you're here."

He offered his arm, and she threaded her gloved hand through the crook of his elbow.

The majordomo announced their party from the head of the stair. "His Grace, the Duke of Halford. Her Grace, the Duchess of Halford. Miss Simms, of Sussex."

Everyone in the crowded ballroom turned their way. Pauline felt countless curious eyes on her as they descended the short flight of stairs.

"What happens now?" she murmured through a tight smile.

"We make a casual circuit of the room," he said. "Then we part ways for the rest of the evening. You'll stay with my mother."

"Where will you be?"

"Elsewhere."

As they completed their circle of the ballroom, she briefly closed her eyes and thought of lining those apothecary shelves with lovely new books. Sharing dishes of blancmange with Daniela. Counting the duke's one thousand pounds.

In her distraction, she failed to note a streak of melted wax on the floor. Her foot slid straight out from under her.

Bollocks, bollocks, bollocks.

The duke's arm snapped tight, drawing her close and steadying her on her feet. She could tell he'd made the motion without even thinking. Those quick reflexes again.

She recovered herself and they drew to a stop near the punch bowl. The duchess drifted away, striking up a conversation with a woman wearing a turban festooned with ostrich plumes. She motioned for Pauline to follow her.

"Your grace," she whispered to Griff. "You really must release my arm now."

"I can't."

"Don't be noble *now*, of all times. Yes, it's terrifying to face all these strangers. I'm sure the rest of the evening will be a study in humiliation. But it's what I signed on for this week. Let me to it."

"I . . . *can't.*" He demonstrated, pulling away from her just a few inches until a taut cord of tension drew him back. "My button is caught."

Pauline tried moving away from him but encountered the same resistance. Keeping one eye on the curious crowd, she slanted a look at the place where his sleeve met her side.

"Oh, no."

The gown had been altered so hastily, the seamstresses must have missed a gap in the seam. When he'd steadied her just now, his cuff button snagged a loose thread. It was thoroughly tangled. No telling how many times it had twisted around.

"I'll get loose," he said smoothly, putting a punch cup in her free hand and filling it, just to give them both something to do. "Never fear. I've made a career of avoiding entanglements with women."

He tried again, grasping his sleeve with his free hand and giving it a firm yank. He didn't manage to free himself, but Pauline sensed the treacher-

ous pop of a stitch giving way. Her punch sloshed
from the silver cup back into the bowl.

"Don't." She clutched his arm, holding it still.
"You'll rip the whole seam. My gown will fall
apart."

He turned to her then, and gave her an intense,
thoughtful look.

No. He wouldn't actually do it.

Pauline glanced around the ballroom. She and
the duke had been standing here in quiet, linked-
arm conversation for a solid minute now, and
people were noticing. Everyone was watching
them—especially the ladies. Some looked envi-
ous, as though they wished to be the woman on
Griff's arm. Yet more of them wore possessive
expressions—as though they'd once been the
woman in his bed.

No matter which group they belonged to, she
was certain of one thing. They'd love nothing
more than to see her brought low.

She knew humiliation was the aim of the evening, but that would be . . .

"You *wouldn't,*" she said.

"I wouldn't," he said. "When I rip a woman's
clothes off, I almost always prefer to do it in private." He tilted his head toward a set of doors
across the ballroom. "We'll make for the gardens
and sort this out."

Arm linked tight with Pauline's, he began leading her back across the room they'd just traversed.
However, this time they couldn't make their way
unimpeded. Other guests kept slowing their
progress, drawing the duke aside for a word of
greeting or two.

Or three or four or five.

Pauline limited herself to monosyllabic answers and polite, shy smiles, not wanting to prolong conversation. What was most maddening, the less she spoke or interacted, the more favorably the ladies and gentlemen seemed to respond.

"You really must cease that," Griff said, drawing her away from a nattering pair of sisters.

"Cease what?"

"Being demure."

"I'm just trying to be brief," she replied.

"Yes, but that's where you've gone wrong. There's nothing like silence to ingratiate yourself with self-important people. It leaves them so much space to discuss themselves."

"Halford!" A ruddy-faced gentleman appeared out of nowhere, stopping them in their tracks.

Good heavens. How was it possible they'd made so little progress? Those doors to the garden were still some twenty yards away.

The man pumped Griff's free arm vigorously. "Haven't seen you for ages, old devil. Rumor had it you'd finally succumbed to the pox." He shot a toothy smile in Pauline's direction. "Who's this?"

"Miss Simms, of Sussex. She's in Town as my mother's guest. Miss Simms, this is Mr. Frederick Martin."

The gentleman bowed and gave Griff a conspiratorial wink. "Rather possessive of her, aren't you?"

"She's new in London. Just getting her feet."

In the corner, the small orchestra struck up the first strains of a waltz.

"Surely you'll allow me to steal her for one dance." Martin extended a white-gloved hand

and bowed over it. "Miss Simms, may I have the pleasure?"

Panic jumped in Pauline's chest. "Oh, I couldn't."

"Halford won't mind. When it comes to the ladies, he's always generous."

Pauline wasn't sure what the man meant by that remark, but she was certain she didn't like it.

"She's not dancing with you." The duke gave a heavy sigh. He sounded as though even he couldn't believe the words he was about to speak. "She's promised this dance to me."

With that, he pulled her away from Mr. Frederick Martin and led her onto the dance floor.

Pauline tried not to let fear show on her face. "What? Wait. I don't even know how to—"

"Just follow my lead. It's the only way to make a quick escape."

They waltzed their way around the ballroom. Because of the way his sleeve was caught on her gown, Griff had to hold his arm jutting out like a chicken wing. Without his hand on her back, he couldn't lead her properly. Pauline was left to chase him across the dance floor in tiny, tiptoeing steps.

At last they reached the doors to the garden.

"I've never seen that waltz before," an elderly matron remarked.

"A Hungarian variation, madam." He held open the door for Pauline. "All the rage in Vienna."

She couldn't stop giggling as they stumbled into the garden. "That was resourceful. I'll give you that."

"Now give me my freedom," he said. "Get me loose."

"You act as though this is my fault. It's your button. And it only snagged because you were too protective. If you'd allowed me to stumble a bit, we could have been on our way home by now."

She reached between them with her free arm, but quickly realized the situation could only be adequately inspected if her fingers were bare.

She thrust her hand out to him. "My glove. Help me off with it."

He loosed the ribbon garter at her elbow first, then set to work on the dozen tiny buttons stretching from her elbow to her wrist. It had taken ten minutes of struggling with fingers and teeth to close them earlier that evening.

He had them undone in ten seconds.

She lifted a brow. "Something tells me you've done this before."

"A time or two."

Or a thousand, she supposed.

He took her wrist, lifted her hand to his mouth, and caught the middle finger of her glove with his teeth. Then he slowly pulled.

The motion was wickedly sensual. Entrancing, even. When her hand slid free, she had no idea what to do with it.

"Oh. Yes." She felt between them, exploring the place where his button met her bodice seam. It seemed hopelessly twisted, by touch. Her attempts to make a visual inspection were thwarted—her artificially inflated bosom kept getting in the way.

"I could see it better if not for this ridiculous corset," she said.

"I'm good at removing those, too."

Pauline threw him a chastening look but he

didn't catch it. He was too busy glazing her breasts with his heated stare.

"Ahem."

"Sorry. I'm a man. We get distracted."

She flushed, pleased despite all her attempts not to be. Men might be distractible by nature, but they were hardly ever distracted by her.

"Fortunately," she said, "I still have a few powers of concentration left. You should remove your coat. Then you'd have both hands free. And if we still can't work the button loose, I can wait here while you go in search of scissors or a blade."

"I knew you were clever."

He tried shrugging his free arm out of his coat but made little progress. It was so tightly fitted, and his arms weren't lean.

"I need my valet for this."

"Let me play valet. I am a servant, after all."

He extended his wrist to her. "Hold the cuff."

She obeyed, and they began their second absurd dance of the evening: The duke flailing his arm while she attempted to hold the sleeve steady—and make sure that his other cuff didn't rip free and destroy her bodice. Every time he tugged on his sleeve, he just pulled Pauline forward. They ended up pivoting in a tight, useless circle. If their first waltz was a Hungarian variation, this one must hail from the moon.

He growled. "I should see about switching to a substandard tailor."

"Perhaps if I tried to work it loose this way."

Turning to face him as best she could, she slid her hand under his lapel, skimming over the silk front of his waistcoat and the firm wall of muscle beneath. Her heart stuttered when she brushed something that felt distressingly nipplelike—but she proceeded undaunted, working her hand up to his shoulder in an attempt to cleave the garment from his body.

"Lift your arm a bit."

He flinched, as if ticklish.

"Be still. I'm good at this, remember?" By twisting her arm and wriggling her fingers, she managed to ease her fingers higher. "No one can reach as high as I can."

"Good God, Simms. My arm is not a foal to be birthed."

"Almost there." She slid her fingers over the crest of his shoulder and partway along his sleeve.

"Simms."

She looked up. They were standing mere inches apart. His lips were very, very close to hers.

Her fingers involuntarily flexed, digging into his biceps. He winced.

"Oh." She sucked in her breath, apologetic. "I'm so sorry. I'd forgotten your wound."

"It's not my arm, Simms. It's everything. We're alone in the garden while a ball goes on. I can't stop staring at your breasts, and your hand is . . . violating my topcoat. It is time to face hard truths. As attempts at avoiding entanglement go, this one isn't working. At all."

"But . . . but it could be worse."

"It's hard to see how."

She didn't know what made her say it. The words just came from her lips. "You could be kissing me."

Chapter Ten

"*Kissing* you," Griff echoed. He tried to make it sound as though the words were some outlandish sentiment spoken in a foreign, unfamiliar tongue—and not the exact same thought he'd been harboring.

She was so close and so warm. They were entangled, and her deft, impertinent hands were all over him—reminding him just how long it had been since he'd been touched, stroked, fussed over. Given a damn about.

The hell of it was, none of her attentions were soothing in the least. Only provoking, arousing. Inflaming the hurt not only in his slashed arm, but in those raw, hollowed-out chambers of his heart.

"You're right," he told her. "Kissing is the one thing that would undoubtedly make this moment worse."

"Oh, Lord." She leaned forward until her brow met his chest. Then she lifted her head slightly.

Then let it fall forward again. After a few more repetitions, he understood the meaning behind this strange gesture.

His chest was the brick wall, and she was bashing her head against it.

Thunk. Thunk. Thunk.

"This is terrible," she moaned. "I can't fail at this, too. I just can't. My life before this was bad enough. What kind of hapless, hopeless person fails at failing?"

"I'm not following you."

She snuffled a little, using his pocket square to wipe her nose—without actually easing it from his pocket.

"At home," she said, "my sister and I, we're always those Simms girls who *mean* well. They say that because we can't *do* anything right."

Her breasts were now pressed against his chest, soft and springy. He shifted his weight from one foot to the other. Didn't help.

"I'm no stranger to humiliation," she went on. "The day you came into the Bull and Blossom, I'd been having the worst morning of my life. Everything went wrong. And I agreed to come to London with you because this was my chance. Surely, I thought, social disaster is the *one* thing I can do right. I'm expert at it." Her voice tweaked. "But just look at this. I can't even succeed at failure."

She wriggled the hand trapped deep in his sleeve. Those breasts trapped against his chest now shimmied in a little dance.

He took a deep breath. He had to take control of this situation, fast—or he would lose his grip entirely. "Listen, Simms. Let's just remain calm."

He sent a mental message downward: *That goes for you, too.*

"First, extricate your hand from my sleeve."

She obeyed, and he suffered all the same torture in reverse as her fingers dragged and wrestled over his shoulder, then his chest. But once it was done, he could step back, put some distance between them. They were only tangled in one place.

He nodded toward a nearby bench. "Now sit. Give me a moment, and I'll have this sorted."

He worked his own gloves free, then set about exploring the connection between his sleeve and her side. He found the place where his button had snagged. By now the cursed thing had twisted several times. He turned it this way and that, looking for the slack, resisting the urge to rush. Haste would only make it worse. This was a task that required patience.

Patience, and extreme fortitude.

God, what she did to him. Her brandy-colored hair made him yearn for a drink. He breathed deeply instead. A mistake. She smelled of French-milled soap and dusting powder and crisp, new linen. Now he wanted, quite desperately, to taste her bare skin. To run his tongue down that delicate slope of her neck, all the way to the graceful curve of her shoulder.

Then lower . . .

Lower, lower, lower.

"I had a dozen ways to be a disaster this evening," she said softly. "I'd thought them all out."

"Such as . . . ?"

"Eating far more than is ladylike, to start. Gentlemen despise indulgence in a lady."

This was news to Griff. "We do?"

"Of course you do." She gave him an incredulous look. "Secondly, I was going to express far too many opinions. A lady never airs her opinions."

"That can't be one of my mother's lessons. That woman never formed an opinion she didn't share."

"I didn't learn it from your mother. I read it in a book." Her voice took on an affected tone. " 'Save for unsightly mustaches, there are few things gentlemen find less appealing in a lady than a political opinion.' Well, I couldn't grow any whiskers. But I'm prepared to make six outrageous statements about the Corn Laws."

"The Corn Laws?" He couldn't help but laugh.

"You don't think it improper?"

"I think you're greatly overestimating a man's ability to heed conversation about the Corn Laws while confronted with a sight like this."

He let his gaze dip to her bosom, where it had been wanting to stray all night. Two soft, pale mounds pressed to the border of her neckline. Like twin pillows. His attention bounced back and forth between them.

"It's all right," she said in a playful whisper. "I can't stop looking at them either. This corset is a feat of engineering."

"I think it's sorcery."

"You're right about the illusion part. Here." She took his hand and brought it to her breast.

Griff froze, lust rocketing through him.

"There's cotton batting in the corset," she said. "Can't you feel it?"

She kept her hand over his, molding his fingers around the ample swell of fabric and the soft flesh beneath.

He swallowed hard. "Yes. I can feel it."

He could also feel *her*. Warm and supple and enticing.

"See? It's not real. So there's another strike against me." She adopted that strange tone of voice again. "A young lady who employs artifice to catch a gentleman's eye will *never* secure his admiration."

With profound reluctance, he let his hand slip from her breast. "Believe me. Right now, I only wish you could decrease my admiration. My admiration is currently rather . . . large."

She looked him in the eye and blurted out, "I'm not a virgin."

Damn. Just like that, he went fully erect, with a swiftness that rivaled swordplay. Upon reflection, he wasn't sure he could have drawn an actual blade that quickly. Were he wearing a metal codpiece, his cock would have met it with an audible clang.

"That won't help," he told her. "What makes you think that will help? I'm not a virgin, either."

"I didn't think you were, but—"

"But nothing. I was hoping to hear something like, 'I have a creeping skin disease.' Or, 'I hoot like a barn owl when I reach orgasm.' Those would be deterrents. I'm not sure the second is strong enough, actually. Curiosity might win out over trepidation."

"But noblemen don't want a woman who's lost her virtue. Mrs. Worthington was very clear."

"Who is this rabidly ill-informed person you keep quoting? Mrs. Who-ington?"

"She wrote an etiquette book. Haven't you heard of it? *Mrs. Worthington's Wisdom for Young Ladies.* That book is how I know exactly what a proper young lady should—and shouldn't—do."

"Did my mother give you that?" The title sounded vaguely familiar, but he didn't think such a book could be from his library.

"No, no. I've been reading it for years. There are copies of it all over Spindle Cove. Miss Finch—she's Lady Rycliff now—wanted to remove every copy from circulation. There are hundreds of them in the village, just heaped everywhere."

Griff frowned, remembering that first afternoon in the village. "Right. I remember it now. They had stacks of them. And they were ripping them apart to make tea trays."

She nodded. "They try to find uses for them. It used to be powder cartridges for the militia, but since the war's over, they've moved on to tea trays."

The logic in this eluded Griff, but he didn't want to interrupt.

"Anyhow," she went on, "a few years ago I took a copy home from the tavern. I knew they wouldn't miss it, and I'd never had a proper book of my own before. I wanted to see what it was that had the ladies so angry. A good half of the book *is* twaddle, I'll grant them. But the rest is just practical advice. Recipes for orange flower water. How to write invitations to parties and sew your own silk gloves. Suggestions for polite dinner conversation. Reading that book was like peering through a window onto a different world, until . . ." She dropped her gaze. " . . . until my father slammed it shut."

"Your father?"

"He found the book. I caught him staring at it. He can't read much, you know. But still, he stared at that title for the longest time. He didn't have to read the words to understand what it meant. It meant I wanted something more."

Reaching up, she plucked a low-hanging leaf and twirled it between her fingertips. "All my life, he'd made it no secret that he was disappointed in me. He'd wanted a boy to help with the farm, and he never hid the fact that he viewed me as useless. But when he found that book . . . For the first time, he was seeing it went both ways. That I might not be happy with the life he'd given me. Oh, it made him so angry."

Griff was becoming rather furious himself. Not with her. Never her.

"What did he do to you?" he asked.

She hesitated.

"Tell me."

"He picked up that book in one hand." She held the leaf in her fingertips and regarded it. "Said, 'That's not for you, girl.' And then he struck me with it, right across the face."

I'll kill him.

The intent roared to life in Griff's chest before his mind could even conceive the words. He was harboring elaborate fantasies of finding a horse and a blade, then haring down to Sussex to have a very short exchange with Amos Simms. One that began with "You rat-faced bastard" and ended with blood.

He was calculating just how long it would take, and how much daylight he'd have when he arrived. Whether he'd permit the man to beg for mercy, or skip straight to—

"I was nineteen years old," she said.

He closed his eyes and breathed deep, forcing himself to abandon his thoughts of the far-off villain who deserved to be run through. He should concentrate on the woman who needed him, here and now.

"Nineteen," she repeated. "Already a woman grown. I helped with the farm and earned wages for the family. And he struck me across the face like a child, just for wanting to improve myself. To learn." She let the leaf twirl to the ground. "Then he threw the book in the fire."

Griff cursed, sliding closer on the bench. He'd given up on disentangling his button for the moment. He didn't give a damn about the people inside, what they might think or conclude. For now, his only goal in this garden—in this life, perhaps—was to guard her. And to make her *feel* safe, which he suspected would be the more difficult task. Too many people had failed her that way.

"It didn't matter." Her chin lifted bravely. "I got another copy. And that time, I hid it somewhere else. When that book disappeared, I got another. Over and over again, until I found the way to outsmart him for good."

"What was that?"

A little smile curved her lips. "I learnt it by heart. Page by page, cover to cover. I committed the entire thing to memory. He couldn't beat that out of me, now could he?"

With a single fingertip, he tilted her face to his. Her eyes sparkled with the reflected torchlight. Brave and beautiful.

He marveled at the wild kaleidoscope of emotions she inspired in him. Violence, admiration, skin-scorching desire. The tenderness welling in his heart was almost too much to bear. No woman made him feel these things. Not all of them at once.

He cupped her chin in his hand and stroked the lovely cheek that had received such vile treatment. "You are never going back to that man again."

"No, I'm not," she said. "I'm going to have my very own circulating library, stocked with every book a proper young lady should never read." She sent a look toward the house. "Just as soon as I can get back into that ballroom and earn it."

He studied her delicate profile, amazed by the strength and determination writ there. She couldn't know how remarkable she was.

Perhaps . . .

Oh, damn. Perhaps he ought to tell her. Gather her close, turn her face to his. Give her the truth.

You're lovely. You're clever. You're turning me inside out, and I don't like it. I don't want to care for you. I've suffered enough over females who crawled inside my heart and deserted it after one week. But if I don't say these words right now, I'm the lowest of the low. So here it is. You're remarkable.

"Your stickpin," she said.

"What?" His mind reeled. It was as if wild horses had been dragging his thoughts to Blitherington, Clodpateshire—and they'd stopped just shy of a dizzying cliff.

"Your stickpin." She stared hopefully at the

diamond stud embedded in his cravat. "It's the answer. We can use it to cut the threads."

Right. She was too clever by half.

Her fingers flew to his neck cloth and she started tugging at the diamond stud. "How does it come apart?"

"There's a clasp." He dug under the folds of his cravat to find it. "Here. I'll hold the bottom and you take the top."

She gripped the stickpin in her fingertips and began to twist it loose.

"Careful there," he said. "Go slowly."

The way this week was going, it would be just his luck that she'd rip the pin free, pitch forward on the bench, and bury the sharp end in one of his vital arteries.

"Almost have it," she said.

He adored the way her delicate eyebrows knit in concentration, the way her bottom lip folded under her teeth. Oh, this was bad.

At last the golden pin popped free.

"Aha." She held it up between them, eyes shining with triumph—as though it were the sword in the stone she'd loosed, or the key to Aladdin's cave. Her smile could have lit the night sky. "We did it."

Wasn't that just his luck. She'd missed his vital arteries—and plunged the cursed thing straight into his heart.

"There," she said, teasing his button loose. "Our bargain is rescued. We're free of each other."

"I don't know about that."

He drew her close and took her mouth in a kiss. He sank into her, reassuring himself that the taste of her remained the same despite this new, el-

egant attire. That though the curves of her body
might be squeezed and shaped for public display,
he knew how they *felt*. Supple, warm, strong and
alive. He kissed her hungrily, relentlessly, savoring
her natural ripe-berry taste and the intoxicating
whisper of brandy on her lips. Pressing her further
and faster than any decent man would—because
he expected at any moment she'd push him away.

But she didn't. She just kissed him back, drawing him closer with a tilt of her head and a soft,
dreamy sigh. So generous, so achingly tender.

As he bent to kiss her neck, her fingers sifted
through his hair, sending jolts of pleasure down
his spine. Encouraged, he slid one hand to claim
her breast. He needed to feel her, fill his grasp
with her soft heat.

Instead, he got a handful of cotton batting.

"Deuced corset," he growled.

"I thought you liked the corset."

"I like this." He slid his thumb under her neckline. "I like you."

She sighed as he skimmed his touch lower, dipping to trace the curve of her slight, round breast.
He found the tight knot of her nipple and rolled it
back and forth.

When he claimed her mouth again, the shy sweep
of her tongue . . . it rocked him in his boots. Again
and again she caressed him. As though she were
painting him with sweetness in languid strokes.

A low, feral growl of yearning rose in his chest.
He wanted to thrust his hands under all this
bothersome fabric, explore the precious silk of
her skin. Feel her bared body pressed to his. Coax
sounds of pleasure she'd never made.

He wanted . . . *more*. Hours and days and nights of this, and not a moment of feeling alone.

But he knew that didn't work. Some of the loneliest moments in his life had been spent bodily tangled with somebody else. Perhaps she wasn't entirely innocent, but that didn't matter. He refused to drag this sweet, determined soul into depravity.

He pulled away from the kiss.

"Griff . . ."

"I shouldn't have done this." He withdrew his touch from her bodice and skimmed his lips over hers in a fleeting kiss. "I know we agreed that this . . ." He tilted his head and kissed her again, lingering. " . . . shouldn't happen again. Because it's a very bad idea, this."

He gave her one last, firm peck.

She kept her eyes resolutely closed. Those long eyelashes lay like fans on her cheeks. "What was it again, this thing we're not doing? Perhaps you could demonstrate *one* more time."

Sweet heaven. He wanted to demonstrate for hours, all over her body. That was the problem.

He kissed the tip of her nose, once. "There."

She opened her eyes, and their brilliant green savaged him. "You are a ruthless tease."

"You are an impertinent minx."

"Well." She smiled and shrugged, unrepentant. "That *is* what you wanted."

Yes. Damn it, it was. Apparently, after years of seducing every worldly, sophisticated woman in London, an impertinent minx of a serving girl was exactly what he wanted.

But Griff vowed to himself then and there . . .

This was one woman he would never have.

Chapter Eleven

"Last night was perfection."

The duchess drizzled a precise spiral of honey atop her buttered toast. Pauline briefly wondered if the older woman had chosen the citrine pendant at her throat to match her breakfast.

But she pushed the query aside, thinking it best to work one puzzle at a time.

"Perfection?" she echoed. "Last night? But it was terrible. *I* was terrible."

"My girl, we cannot argue with results." She waved a hand over a gilt-edged salver heaped with sealed envelopes. "So many invitations already."

"That doesn't make any sense."

"It makes perfect sense. Think of gemstones. Some jewels are prized for their exquisite cut and polish. Others are coveted by collectors, even when riddled with flaws, simply because they are so very rare."

"But I'm not rare in any way," Pauline objected. "I'm exactly the opposite. I'm *common*."

The duchess made a contrary snort over her bite of toast. "He *danced* with you."

"For all of ten seconds. Perhaps fifteen."

"That was more than enough. You don't understand. My son never dances. It's been years since he's danced with any unmarried lady, for the exact purpose of avoiding this speculation."

Pauline sighed. "But . . . but he only danced with me to escape his bothersome friend."

"The two of you disappeared into the gardens, and when you returned his cravat was mussed."

"We *had* to remove his stickpin. The duke's button was caught on my seam, and he couldn't get loose."

"Oh, I know he couldn't get loose." The duchess teased a folded newspaper out from beneath the heap of envelopes. "Precisely as it's printed in the *Prattler*. 'The Duke of Halford, Snared at Last.' "

Oh, no.

Pauline cringed as she scanned the newspaper gossip column. Just as the duchess had said, it was filled with speculation about the duke and "the mysterious Miss Simms."

Any thrill of overnight fame was lost on her. She was consumed by the common girl's worst daily fear: that of losing her post.

If the duchess was this happy with the results of last night, Pauline knew one thing.

The duke would not be.

He couldn't blame her for this scandal sheet, could he? If the evening had ended in anything other than humiliation, it was all his fault. *He* was the one who'd caught her when she slipped, tangling their clothing. *He* was the one who'd danced her out into the garden.

He was the one who'd kissed her. Touched her, so sweetly.

The duchess whisked the newspaper aside. "We've made excellent progress, but there remains a fair bit of road ahead. And you have your elbows on the table."

Pauline removed them grudgingly.

"This morning, our task is accomplishment."

"Accomplishment?"

"The next time you attend a social event, you'll stay longer than an hour. As is the case with all young gentlewomen in attendance, you may be called on to exhibit."

"Exhibit?" Pauline laughed.

Oh, this would be a joke. Her worries about accidentally succeeding in this duchess-training endeavor all melted that instant—like so much butter scraped across her warm, evenly browned point of toast. No scorched bread in this house.

"You mean to make me an accomplished lady in one morning? That's impossible."

"I mean to find the natural talent you already possess. There must be *one*."

Pauline paused, toast halfway to her mouth. "Your grace . . ."

She set the toast aside, suddenly uneasy. The duchess thought she had a hidden talent. Her, Pauline Simms. It was so strange—and rather wonderful—to have someone who believed in her, even this small bit.

Though Spindle Cove was stocked with unconventional ladies, none of them had ever taken much time to know Pauline. Her own mother was a sad, defeated shadow of a woman. She'd never had anyone like the duchess in her life—a guiding feminine presence who not only *believed* she could be something better than a farm wife or serving girl, but demanded she *try*.

But the more she came to treasure the duchess's confidence in her, the more Pauline worried about how this week would end. She hated the idea of watching the older woman's dreams unravel.

She said, "Please believe me when I tell you, nothing remotely matrimonial is ever going to transpire between me and the duke. It just . . . won't happen. Nevertheless, your grace, I'm starting to like *you*. You've been kind to me in moments, and I know you have a good heart under all that phlegm. I don't want you to form lofty expectations, only to have your plans spoiled."

In response, the duchess only gave a slight smile. She lifted a spoon and tapped at her egg sitting in its enameled cup. A delicate lattice of cracks bloomed over the egg's smooth shell.

Tap, tap, tap.

Pauline reached out with her own spoon and gave the egg a good, hard *crack*. She didn't know how else to make the older woman listen.

"Your grace, you must take me seriously. I'm trying to tell you to give up your hopes of grandchildren—at least, any mothered by me—and you're calmly eating a boiled egg. Are you losing your hearing?"

"Not at all. I heard you perfectly."

"You're smiling."

"I'm smiling because you said 'spoiled plans' and 'boiled egg.' Not 'spiled' or 'biled.'"

Pauline clapped her hand over her mouth,

aghast. Drat. The duchess was right. She *had* said the words correctly. What was happening to her?

She knew the answer to that question.

Griff was happening to her. When the duke kissed her, her head spun, her knees melted . . . and her elocution improved. Limber tongues and all that.

"Bloody hell," she mumbled into her palm.

The duchess gave a weak sigh and motioned to the servant for more tea. "Your H's still need work."

Griff woke up at the crack of . . . half-nine. Hours earlier than usual.

He'd always been the sort of person who felt most himself at night, and in this last year he'd become a veritable vampire. More often than not he went to bed as the sun came up and remained there until well past noon. But yesterday's debacle had made it clear to him he couldn't afford to doze though another day of his mother's scheming.

How had yesterday gone so wrong?

It had started with the frock. That damnable sweet, sheer, innocent white frock. She'd turned his head, and the rest of the day had been one mistake piling atop the next.

If he hadn't lost his concentration with Del, he wouldn't have been wounded. If he hadn't been wounded, he would have never agreed to attend that ball. If they hadn't attended the ball, he wouldn't have ended with her in that dark, fragrant garden, sliding his fingers over her tempting curves and contemplating acts of romantic lunacy.

The answer to this situation was plain.

No new frocks.

No attractive ones, anyhow.

No more kisses, either. That was obvious.

And most important of all, no more surprises.

As he walked through the house in search of them, Griff passed an unusual amount of clutter. Strange debris littered every room—all sorts of activities hastily abandoned. As though the house's occupants had recently fled an erupting volcano.

In the salon, he found various instruments of needlework strewn on the settee and table. In the morning room, an abandoned easel displayed a drippy mess of a watercolor. Nearby a few drawing pencils lay cruelly snapped in half.

He heard a faint melody, so he walked toward the music room. When he arrived, he found it empty of people—but every instrument in the place, from harp to harpsichord, had been stripped of its Holland cloth, dusted, and attempted.

Where were the servants? Why weren't they putting these rooms back to rights?

And he still heard that strange, slow melody. Like a drunken music box winding into a death spiral.

The tune ended. It was followed by an enthusiastic smattering of applause.

"Brava, Miss Simms," he heard.

And then, from someone else, "Give us another?"

The melody began again.

With slow, quiet footfalls, Griff traced the sounds to the dining room. He eased open the door a fraction.

At the far end of the room, he spied Pauline Simms. She stood before about fifteen water goblets lined up on the table, each one filled with a different amount of water, and she was pinging them with two forks.

He couldn't tell if they were pickle forks or oyster forks. And then he decided this absurd preoccupation with forks was why he didn't do mornings.

Anyhow, she was doling out a cheerful melody with these forks, as if each note were a bite of music.

No wonder the house was a shambles. All around her the assembled servants of Halford House stood looking on, rapt. Anticipating each musical morsel that fell from those precious little tines. None of them noticed Griff standing in the door.

The music was only part of the entertainment. As she worked, she pulled the most amusing faces. Delicate frowns of concentration, punctuated by disarming cringes when she struck a wrong note. When a lock of hair worked loose to dangle over her brow, she huffed a breath, blowing it away without skipping a beat.

She was working so very, very hard—so very, very earnestly—to create this display. It was absurd. Ridiculous. And utterly adorable.

Everyone in the room was enchanted, and Griff couldn't claim he was immune to her spell. She was enchanting.

When the last note faded, all the servants clapped.

"That was Handel, my girl," his mother said, beaming with pleasure. "How did you learn that piece?"

Pauline shrugged. "Just by listening to the village music tutor. She taught piano lessons in the Bull and Blossom."

"That's natural musicality," the duchess said. "You could translate that ability to any of several proper instruments, with practice."

"Truly? But, your grace, there's no time for

prac . . ." Her voice trailed off as she looked up—and saw Griff, standing in the doorway.

Their gazes tangled.

Without breaking eye contact, he could feel all the others in the room turning his way.

Griff knew he had a split-second decision to make. He was either going to be caught staring at Miss Simms, exposed for the enraptured, lusting fool he was, in front of his mother *and* all his servants—or he could do what he did best: hide his every emotion behind the mask of an indifferent, entitled jackass.

Really, there was no choice.

Jackass it would be.

He began to applaud in slow, smug claps—and continued long after the room had gone silent.

Long after the shy, endearing smile had fled her face.

He let one last, ringing clap echo through the sobered room. He brought out his most bored, condescending tone. "That . . . was . . . capital, Simms. You will certainly stand out from the debutante crowd."

She ducked her head, looking flustered. "Just an old trick I learnt at the tavern. Some nights are slow. The duchess asked after my musical talent, and this is the sum of it."

"Do you juggle tankards, too? Fold table napkins into jousting cranes?"

"I . . . No." She set aside the forks.

"Pity."

"Excuse me," she muttered, rushing out the dining room's other door.

Griff stared at the empty space she'd left. He hadn't expected her to take it quite that hard. She wanted to be a successful failure, didn't she?

Once she was gone, every footman and house-maid in the room turned in his direction. Their eyes shot beams of pure resentment.

"What?" he asked.

Higgs cleared his throat in subtle rebuke.

Good God. He'd lost them, their loyalty. Just like that.

"Really," Griff said. He ceased leaning on the doorjamb and drew to full ducal height. "*Really.* I've been your employer for years. In some cases, decades. Annual rises in pay, Christmas boxes, days off. Simms pings a fork on some goblets, and now you all side with her?"

Silence.

"You're servants. Stop standing about, and go . . . serve."

A dour parade of footmen and maids filed past him on their way out of the room, leaving Griff alone with his mother.

She opened her mouth to speak, but he held up a palm.

"I will do the talking," he said. He was the duke. He was solely responsible for six estates, a vast family fortune, and this very house—and he meant to assert that authority.

"I don't know what else you have planned for Simms this morning, but I intend to be a part of it. No more of this scheming and shopping in secret, only to ambush me with new frocks and water goblet sonatas. Am I understood?"

She lifted her chin. "Yes."

"Good." He clapped his hands together. "So what's on today's agenda, now that music is fin-ished? Whatever it is, I'm joining you. More shopping? Etiquette lessons? Some stab at exposing the girl to art or culture?"

"Charity," she said.

"Charity?"

"It's Tuesday. We're going to the Foundling Hospital. I visit every Tuesday."

The Foundling Hospital. The floor dropped out of Griff's stomach. Of all the places. He had no desire to spend his day at an orphanage.

"You only have a week with Simms. Why not skip this particular Tuesday?"

"Because it's an essential part of any duchess's duty—charity toward the less fortunate." Her brow quirked. "It's an essential part of a duke's duty, too."

Now he saw where she was going with this. And he didn't like it.

"On second thought," he said, "I can't go."

"Oh? Why not?"

"I have an urgent appointment. I've just remembered it."

Her eyes narrowed. "An urgent appointment with whom?"

"With . . ." He churned air with one hand. "Someone who needs to see me. Urgently. The land steward."

"He's in Cumberland."

"I meant the family solicitor." He looked down his nose at her. "I've decided to decrease your quarterly allowance."

She hmphed. "Well, then. You can discuss the matter with him today. His office is in Bloomsbury, directly across from the Foundling Hospital."

Griff sighed. Damn.

Chapter Twelve

Pauline was amazed. In London, it seemed even the orphans lived in palatial splendor.

The Foundling Hospital was a grand, stately edifice in Bloomsbury, surrounded by green courtyards and fronted by a formidable gate. Inside the building, the halls and corridors were lavishly decorated with paintings and sculpted trim.

As they walked down the center of the main hall, Pauline felt a cramp forming in her neck from staring upward at the artwork. But any pain in the neck was preferable to feeling the sting of Griff's indifference.

She couldn't even look at him. Not after that humiliation in the dining room.

It wasn't as though she took great personal pride in pinging tunes on crystal, but there'd been such malice in those slow, smug claps. She expected him to be displeased after last night, but she hadn't been braced for cruelty.

Men. Such capricious creatures.

She ought to have learned this lesson from Errol Bright. Whenever they'd stolen an hour or two alone together, he'd been all eager hands and fervent promises. But if they crossed paths in the village, he treated her as just the same old Pauline. At first she'd told herself it was romantic that way—they had a secret passion, and no one could guess. Eventually she'd realized the painful truth. All Errol's tender words in the moment were just that—in the moment. He'd never truly wanted more.

Now she'd made the same error with Griff.

Last night he'd made her feel beautiful and desired. This morning he'd made her feel small and stupid. No doubt she'd do well to take the duchess's advice: find some phlegm, and refuse to feel anything.

But that just wasn't her. And if she lost herself this week, she'd have nothing left.

As they moved through the Foundling Hospital, the duchess kept up a steady monologue. "This establishment was founded last century by Sir Thomas Coram and several of London's leading men—noblemen, tradesmen, the artists whose work you see displayed. The fifth Duke of Halford was among the original governors, and each of his successors has continued the tradition."

Pauline didn't think the *current* Duke of Halford cared a whit. He was so eager to be done with this place, both she and the duchess were trotting to keep pace with his long strides. If he didn't wish to be here, she couldn't understand why he'd come.

Once they passed out of the public rooms and into the actual home, the building's decor became markedly more austere. Evidently the palatial splendor was for show, not for the foundlings' benefit.

They passed a wide green courtyard filled with hundreds of children. All boys, clad in identical brown uniforms and arranged in orderly files.

"There are so many," Pauline murmured.

The duchess nodded. "And those are only the boys of school age. There are just as many girls in the other wing. And hundreds of younger children are spread throughout the surrounding counties. They're accepted as infants when their mothers surrender them, but then sent to foster families until school age."

"And then they're removed from those families again? That must be doubly cruel, to lose not only the mothers who birthed them, but then the only mother they've known."

"Still, they're better off than many," the duchess said. "They have their basic needs met, their education provided. When they're old enough, they have help finding posts in trade or in service. Our own Margaret in the scullery at Halford House was raised here, as were several grooms and gardeners at the Cumberland estate."

"It's very good of you to think of them."

"We have a duty, Miss Simms. For those of our rank and privilege, it is not enough to mean well. One must do some good."

The words prodded a tender place inside her. All her life she'd dreamed of doing better—for herself, and for her sister. So far she hadn't achieved even that. But the Duchess of Halford possessed the power, confidence, and funds to do good for whole swaths of people in need. It was a grand step up from dropping pennies in the church box.

Suddenly, the duke halted mid-step. "What *is* that miserable urchin wearing?"

He nodded toward a bench in the corridor. On it sat a child—a boy of perhaps eight or nine years. He was wearing the same brown uniform all the foundlings wore, but it was capped by a malformed knitted object, fashioned from yarn in an unfortunate shade of green.

To Pauline's eye, the mess of yarn appeared to be an abandoned sleeve, but the boy had the thing pulled over his head. It seized his crown in a lopsided, putrid-green hug, covering one eyebrow and ear entirely and riding high above his temple on the other side.

She fought a smile. It could only be the duchess's handiwork.

"What is that?" the duke repeated.

"I believe it's a cap," Pauline offered.

"It's a travesty." The duke approached the youth. "You there, lad. Let me have that cap."

The boy shrank from him, clutching one hand to his head and shielding his face with the other. He probably assumed that defensive posture often. He was a smallish child, Pauline noted. Pale and thin, with a fading bruise on his left jaw. Bullied by the larger boys, no doubt.

"You don't want to give it up? Fine." Halford removed his own brimmed felt beaver and held it out. "Here."

"Wh-What?" the boy stammered.

"I'm offering you an even trade. My fine, tall new hat for your . . . thing."

The perplexed boy removed his knitted head-gear, and the two of them made the exchange.

"Go on, then," the duke said, once the boy had the beaver in hand. "Put it on."

The boy obeyed, placing the duke's hat on his head. The thing came down to his ears, but by tipping the brim back and peering in the glass of a nearby window, he was able to survey his reflection.

It was probably because he was craning on tiptoe, but . . . Pauline could have sworn the boy looked three inches taller. A dangerous pang snatched at her heart.

"What's your name?" the duke asked.

"Hubert. Hubert Terrapin."

"Did they give you that name here, too?"

The boy nodded glumly.

"Well, at least the hat suits you," said the duke. He balled the tangle of green yarn in his hand. "Chin up, then. I know you're a foundling, but surely things aren't as bad as *this*."

The duchess cleared her throat with impatience, and their group continued down the corridor.

As they walked, Pauline couldn't help but steal glances at the duke. It was such a slippery thing, her disgust with him. At the slightest sign of decency on his part, the anger began to wriggle out of her grasp.

She tightened her hand in a fist. So he'd given a foundling his hat. What of it? He had dozens of hats, and could buy dozens more. Throwing money around didn't make him a good man. It just made him a wealthy man.

A wealthy man with a strong, handsome profile. And no more hat to shield his dark, touchable hair from her view.

He cut her a sudden, sideways glance.

"Aren't you going to put it on?" she asked, nodding at the green "cap" in his hands. "It *was* a trade."

He scowled at it. "Probably writhing with fleas."

"Impossible," the duchess insisted. "This institution has strict standards of cleanliness."

"Their standards are lacking," he muttered. "This is unacceptable. I know they're penniless, cast-off scamps without a possession in the world, but they must be permitted some pride."

Pauline's stomach twisted as she looked to the duchess, knowing the parcel the older lady carried beneath her arm was probably crammed with similar travesties of yarn—all misshapen, all rather useless. But every one of them the products of hope and motherly love.

Griff's insults might be unintentional, but surely they had to wound her. That hurt must go deep.

Twin smudges of color appeared on the duchess's high, aristocratic cheekbones, but that was the only reaction she showed.

She said, "We are not here to quibble with the fashion sense of foundlings. Today, we are here to tour the nursery. Come along."

The nursery?

At that, Griff balked. "No."

His mother turned. "What?"

"I said, no. A man must draw a line somewhere, and my line is definitely between this particular bit of flooring"—he gestured at the tile directly beneath his boots—"and the nursery door."

"Don't you like infants, your grace?" Miss Simms asked.

"Not especially. Noisy and noisome things, in my limited experience. I believe I've had enough touring the facility for one day."

"We've nearly walked the perimeter of this wing," the duchess said. "If your goal is to leave, it's faster if we go through the nursery."

He leveled a hard stare at his mother. "I know exactly what you're doing. You plan to take me in that room and pop a squalling, sticky creature in my arms. Because you think that experience will leave me vibrating with desire to make a squalling, sticky creature of my own. Perhaps there are men that ploy would work on. But I tell you, it won't work on me." He began a backward stroll. "I'll be in the carriage."

"Wait." With a quick curtsy in the duchess's direction, Pauline joined him. "I'll go, too. I've had a sneeze or two this morning, and I don't want any babies catching cold."

"Simms, you should stay with my mother."

"So should you." She paced him down the corridor, taking three steps for his every two. "You truly don't like being here, do you?"

"No. I truly don't."

"You could be a little more agreeable." She shook her head. "I'm starting to understand the duchess's frustration with you. And sympathize."

"My family has supported this establishment since its inception. I have no intent to discontinue that tradition."

"But you could be giving more."

"Very well. I'll donate an extra sum toward proper autumn apparel." He shook the green cap in his hand. "We can't have this sort of thing occurring."

"You needn't be so snide, you know." She took the cap from him. "It's ugly, yes. But clearly it was made with love."

"Made with love? *That?* That was made with incompetence, if not outright malice."

She sighed. "You don't understand. You're missing my point, and your mother's. When I say you could be donating more, I mean more than money. You could give your time and attention."

He shook his head. "The doctors and matrons who run this establishment want nothing from me but a timely bank draft."

"They seem happy to have your mother's involvement. She makes regular visits and brings . . . things."

As they moved back toward the main hall, they passed an empty room. Pauline noticed a familiar-looking face cowering in the corner.

"Hubert," the duke said. "That's you again?"

The boy approached them, mournful and hatless.

"What happened to your fine new hat?" Pauline asked. But the fresh split in the boy's lip told the story well enough. "An older boy took it from you, did he?"

The lad nodded.

She pulled Griff aside and whispered to him. "Griff, this is exactly what I mean. You can do something for him."

He showed his empty hands. "I don't have another hat."

"No, no. You made an impression on that boy earlier, and it had nothing to do with the hat. You spoke with him, treated him like a person *worth* something. Talk with him now. Give him some manly advice, or teach him to fight. It might be beneficial for you, too. It's good to feel useful now and then."

He cast a wistful glance toward the exit. "Simms, you seem to have forgotten that you are my employee. I hired you to distract my mother, not to give me advice."

"Well, then. Consider it a bonus."

Good God. Did her impertinence know no bounds?

"You're a powerful man," she went on. "And it's not only to do with your money or your title. You have the ability to make people feel valued, when you're not making them feel like rubbish."

She didn't understand. He wanted to help the lad. He truly did. But he wasn't in any condition to offer benign encouragement right now. This place had his viscera in turmoil. All the little footsteps pattering right over his heart . . .

"Sorry," he said curtly. "I just don't have the time."

Oof.

The punch seemed to come out of nowhere, though rationally he knew it must have originated at the end of her right arm. There was no doubt about where it landed—square in his gut.

He fell back a step, reeling.

"Hubert," she said, her eyes never leaving

Griff's, "since his grace can't spare the time, you're getting your fighting lessons from me."

"Simms, you can't be serious."

"Oh, I'm serious." She tugged off her gloves with her teeth and cast them aside. She circled him with raised fists, taunting. "What? You're not going to fight back?"

"You know very well I can't hurt a woman."

"Oh, please. You are entirely capable of hurting a woman. Expert at it, I'd guess." She feinted a jab to his ribs, then darted away.

Clearly she was angry with him, for reasons that had little to do with hats and foundlings. Griff would gladly let her take swings at him later, but he couldn't have this discussion right now.

He held up his hands. "I'm done here."

"Oh no, you're not." She dodged in front of him, blocking his only route of escape. "If you're not brave enough to throw a punch, I'm sure you can find other ways. Call me names, perhaps. Insult my origins. Or I know. Perhaps you could bring out that slow, obnoxious applause."

"Is that what this is about?" He narrowed his eyes at her. "You're vexed with me for not cheering your little water-goblet concert?"

"No," she shot back, defensive. Then she revised, "In part. You were purposely hurtful this morning."

"We made an arrangement, Simms. You agreed to be a failure. I'm paying you handsomely for the trouble. I thought that's what you wanted."

"Yes, but—"

"If the terms of our bargain are no longer satisfactory, I can send you back to Sussex."

"I signed on for a week of society's disdain. Not yours."

"Well, then. Consider it a bonus."

"Oh, you—" With a growl, she swung at him again.

This time he was ready. He caught her fist in his hand, enveloping the tight, small knot of knuckles and holding it fast.

"I told you everything last night." Her whispered words were barbed. "My dreams, my secrets. Everything. And this morning you treated me like nothing."

He made his voice low. "What is it you want, Simms? What is it you're wanting to hear? Am I supposed to say you're the equal of any well-bred lady?"

"Of course not. No. I don't want to be like those Awful Haughfells or any of their sort."

"Ah." He nodded slowly. "Now I see. You don't want to hear that you're their equal. You want to hear that you're their *better*."

She didn't reply.

"I'm supposed to deem your little water-goblet tune more enchanting than any Italian aria. Proclaim your wholesome country manners a breath of fresh air in my sin-clouded life." He laughed. "What else? Perhaps you're hoping to hear that your purity is the most intoxicating and rare of perfumes. Your hair smells like hedgerows and your eyes are like chips of wide-open sky, and God above, you make me *feel* things. Things I haven't felt in years. Or ever." With his free hand, he clutched his chest dramatically. "What is this strange stirring in my breast? Could it possibly be . . . love?"

She stared at his waistcoat button, refusing to look at him.

Somewhere in his brain a fragment of reason shouted that he was being a bastard and cocking everything up. But he wasn't acting on logic right now. He was torn between two impulses: the need to push her away from that raw, aching wound she kept poking, and the impossible desire to draw her close, possess her completely.

Most of all, he needed to leave this place before he went blind and mad with grief.

"I employed you for a reason, Simms. I'm not looking for a fresh-faced girl to teach me the meaning of love and give me purpose in life. And if you're looking for a well-heeled gentleman to make a fetish of your feisty spirit . . . perhaps you could find one here in London, but it won't be me."

"What a speech," she whispered, drawing close. "I'd be inclined to believe it, if it weren't for the way you kissed me last night."

Her angry warmth was palpable. Arousing.

"Oh, Simms. What kind of shoddy libertine do you take me for? I've kissed a great many women without caring for them in the least."

Hm. I don't believe I've ever seen that shade of green.

That was his last coherent thought, staring into her eyes. Then her left fist crashed into his face, and his world exploded with fireworks of bright red pain. He staggered a few steps backward. His skull rang like a bell.

Well. He deserved that.

When his vision focused again, he saw her talking to the boy.

"That's your first lesson, Hubert." She crouched before the wide-eyed lad, speaking to him on his level. "Don't fight fair. Life isn't fair, especially not life in a place like this. If you have a shot, take it. There's no call to be sporting about it, not with bullies."

She went on, "I grew up on a farm, see. A small one. A poor one. It was always one of my chores to mind the chickens. Now, newly hatched chicks are the sweetest, downiest, most innocent look-ing creatures on earth—but they're savage little beasts. They'll peck their own brothers and sisters to death if they sense a weakness."

As he listened to her, Griff felt his own defenses softening.

"It's the same with places like this," she went on. "There's always a pecking order. The big will torment the small, and the small will torment the smaller, and on down the line. It's the nature of chicks, and it's the nature of children, too. Don't dream it will change. You'll never be able to pummel every bully, and no amount of prayer or patience will convince them to change their ways. Just keep your head up and get what's yours. Your food, your schooling. Whatever they give you, don't squander it. All bread goes straight in your belly, and all the learning you can gather goes here." She tapped a fingertip against her temple. "Stash it away. Because once it's in you, it's yours. No one can take it from you. No schoolyard bully, no mean-tempered lessons master . . ."

Nor an abusive father, Griff silently added. He pictured her, a lock of hair dangling over her smudged cheek as she furtively memorized bits of etiquette and poetry between farm chores. Reading the same words again and again, until they were stashed away. Safe inside, where no one could rob her of them.

"Not even a duke," she finished.

Hubert eyed her silk day dress, with its flounce of lace. "You, my lady? You raised chickens on a farm?"

"I did. And as a child, I took more than my share of licks. But I got mine, just like I told you. It's how I've come this far. And if you find me impressive now . . . ?" She rose to her feet and patted the boy on the shoulder. "Come visit me next week. I'll be living wealthily ever after."

With a fiery glance at Griff, she left the room.

He started off in pursuit, somewhat hobbled by his aching . . . everything. God's teeth, what this woman was doing to him. He trailed her clipped footsteps down the corridor, catching up to her at the building's main entrance.

"Listen," he said, snaring her arm at the top of the steps. "About this morning. I wasn't trying to be the savage chick, or the pecking bully, or whatever it is you've likened me to."

"Don't apologize, please. Then I might feel compelled to apologize for hitting you, and I don't want to be sorry in the least."

"I'm not apologizing. Just explaining. I didn't mean to hurt your feelings, Simms. But if the damned things are really so fragile, you shouldn't let me anywhere near them. I told you, I'm no prince."

She squared her shoulders, apparently reaching

some decision. "You're right. You did warn me. And I shouldn't care what you think."

No, wait, he stupidly felt like contradicting. *I take it back. You should care. Please care.*

Because he could see it on her face—just like that, she'd decided she didn't need him. She would take her own advice to Hubert: complete her week's employment, take his thousand pounds, and never think of him again.

He *wanted* her to think of him. Not just this week, but always.

What an ass he'd been, baiting her with all those compliments she might hope to hear. Griff saw himself clearly now. He was the one yearning for approval. Long after this week was over, he wanted her to remember him as the beneficent, handsome duke who'd whisked her away to London and changed her life. No matter what other disappointments he added to his family legacy, he could console himself with the knowledge that there was a shopkeeper at the arse-end of Sussex who worshipped him. Who believed he had a heart of pure, chivalric-grade gold—or at least sterling—hidden beneath the arrogance and vice.

She was meant to be the one good thing he'd done.

And now she looked at him like something that slithered.

"You're right," she said. They exited through the front gates, where she drew to a halt in the drive. "Of course you're right. I've been a fool, wanting you to like me, approve of me. If you found anything in me to approve, you wouldn't have hired me in the first place."

"That's not true."

Now that they were out of the orphanage, he could breathe again. There were too many people about to do what he truly wished—which was to pull her into his arms for an embrace that might comfort them both. He settled for righting her sleeve.

"You don't understand, Simms."

She looked at his touch on her sleeve. "Oh, I understand you perfectly. You have good, generous instincts, but they're all smothered under that aristocratic phlegm. You're so choked with it, you're afraid to care about anything. Or at least, you're afraid to show that you do."

It started to rain then. Cold, fat drops struck the pavement with audible force. In moments the damp had flattened her clothing to her back and plastered locks of hair to her face, making her look small and alone.

"Simms."

She flinched from his touch. "What, Griff? What? Did you have something to say to me here? In the midst of a busy street, with people nearby—not in a darkened garden or locked room?"

"I . . ." He set his teeth. "Very well. I like you."

"You 'like' me."

"I do. In fact, I like you a great deal more than I should. And it's precisely because you *are* all wrong."

She stared at him, pursing those delectable, berry-pink lips. Far too many hours had passed since he'd kissed her.

He cursed. "I'm not explaining it right. I'm not

used to making these sorts of speeches. But can't we call a truce? Find somewhere to have a spot of—"

Before he could finish the thought, a woman in dark, shapeless wool rushed up to him. Like a raven, winging out of nowhere.

"Please, sir. I c-can't . . ." She sobbed from deep in her chest. "Please."

She darted away just as quickly, and it took Griff several instants to register that she'd left something behind.

A babe. Wedged into his arms.

Oh, Jesus.

Gray-blue eyes, scratchy little fingers. No nose or neck to speak of. All wrinkles, from head to tiny toes. Christ, why did they all have to look so much the same?

"Oh, goodness," Pauline said. "That poor woman."

"Wh—" He held the child slightly out from his body. His arms were frozen with shock. "Where is she? Where did she go?"

"I don't know. She must have meant to surrender the child. Perhaps she was afraid to come inside."

Griff scanned the busy environs, hoping stupidly for one flash of dark wool to stand out from the dark, woolen crowd. She'd probably stayed nearby. She was likely watching him now—this stiff, useless nobleman she'd trusted to do right by her child—and feeling keen regret.

The infant knew she'd been done wrong. She wailed up at Griff, puckered and red-faced, waving little fists clenched in anger. Drops of rain spattered her face and blanket. She opened her mouth so wide, her lips seemed to thin and disappear. Her toothless gums and little tongue were bright vermilion with rage.

You're a bloody duke, the babe seemed to shout at him. *Near six foot tall, thirteen stone. Do something, you worthless lump. Make it all come out right!*

"What should we do?" Pauline asked.

"I . . ."

Griff didn't know. With everything in his hollowed-out shell of a heart, he wanted to soothe the child's cries. But he couldn't. He just couldn't.

He passed the baby into Pauline's arms, muttered a few words of excuse that he'd never remember later. Then he turned and strode away, into the rain.

"Your grace! Griff, wait!"

He could shake off her calls, but the wailing carried high above the din of the streets, above the dark clatter of rain. Those wordless cries of accusation followed him all the way to the street.

Haunted him for miles.

Chapter Thirteen

Very early the next morning, Pauline woke in the darkness. She wrapped her body in a dressing gown, lit a taper, and made her way downstairs to the library.

She didn't find the man she'd spent a fitful night alternately worrying over and dreaming about. But she found something almost as intriguing.

The naughty books.

She plucked a volume from the shelf, built a fire in the grate, and settled in.

An hour or so later she was immersed in a scandalous encounter—a dairymaid's lover had his hands under her skirts and was questing determinedly higher—when the library door swung open with a whoosh of freezing air.

She startled, whipping her head up. Her attention was ripped from the story roughly, unevenly—like a sheet of pasted paper torn loose. Little scraps of lewdness clung to her. She was blushing so fiercely she worried her cheeks would glow in the dark.

Thank goodness the intruder wasn't the duchess or a servant.

Only Griff.

But she couldn't call him "only Griff." He could never be "only" anything. The intruder was life-altering, heart-muddling, oft-maddening Griff.

And she didn't know what they'd make of each other, after all that happened yesterday.

He tossed her a brief, dark look. She couldn't tell whether he was glad to see her or the reverse. "You're awake at this hour?" he said.

She closed her finger in her book, holding the page. "I wake early every morning. I'm a farm girl at heart. Can't sleep past five, it seems."

As he shrugged out of his coat and draped it over the back of a chair, she recognized it as the same one he'd been wearing when she'd seen him last. His jaw was unshaven. He was still hatless as well. And he looked every bit as miserable as when he'd left her at the front gates of the foundling home, squalling babe in arms.

However he'd spent his night, the activity hadn't succeeded in cheering him.

"Are you just coming in?" she asked, hoping she didn't sound too managing or . . . well, *wifely*.

He nodded.

What a stark illustration of the differences between them. This hour meant early rising for her, but late homecoming for him. The two of them were literally night and day.

But even night and day had to cross paths sometime.

"Where have you been?" she asked.

His answering sigh was a slow, weary rasp. "Simms, I honestly don't even know."

"Oh." She swallowed. "Well, I'm glad you're here now."

Wordlessly, he crossed to his desk and rolled up his uncuffed shirtsleeves. He lit two candles, sat down and regarded the broken clockwork he'd left waiting the other night.

"I hope your evening was more exciting than mine," she said lightly. "After dinner, your mother set me reading aloud from Scripture to improve my diction. I was told to read only the *H* words. *H*ath, *h*oly, *h*eresy. Rather a bore." She lifted the book in her hand and reopened to her current page. "Now that I've found the naughty books, the exercise seems much more interesting. *H*ard as *h*ornbeam. *H*eaving *h*illocks of bounteous flesh."

When that failed to coax a smile from him, she set the book aside and curled up in the chair. Propping her chin on her knees, she regarded him through the veil of lingering dark.

Something was very, very wrong. In a word (in an *H* word, no less—they seemed all the words she could think of now) he looked *h*orrible. *H*aunted, too—even more so than he had the first night.

And part of her suspected he needed to be *h*eld.

She wasn't sure how to initiate anything of that sort. To make the attempt seemed unwise, for many reasons. But there was one thing she could do for him—a skill learned through years of practice.

She rose from her chair, crossed to the bar in the corner and poured him a drink.

"When I started working at the tavern years ago, Mr. Fosbury told me I prattled on too much." She watched the amber liquid swirl into a glass. As she recapped the decanter, she made her voice gruff in imitation. " 'Pauline,' he said to me, 'you have to learn to tell the difference between men who come in wanting a chat, and men who just want to be let alone.' "

After crossing the carpet in slow, careful steps, she set the drink on the desktop just inches from Griff's elbow. He didn't look at it, nor at her. He rubbed the fatigue from his face and peered at the broken clock. As if he could stare at the thing hard enough that the gears would leap into motion of their own accord. Perhaps begin churning time in reverse.

"I took his advice," she went on, "learned to mind my conversations. But I also learned Mr. Fosbury had something wrong. There were men who wanted a chat and those who didn't." Gathering her courage, she laid a hand to Griff's shoulder. "But none of them wanted to be alone."

He drew a deep breath. His strong, linen-clad shoulder rose and fell beneath her palm.

She silently counted to five, as slowly as her skittering nerves would allow.

Nothing.

Well, then. She'd given him a chance. Nodding to herself, she lifted her hand and turned away. "I'll leave you to it, then."

"Don't."

The hoarse command froze her in place.

He swiveled his chair so that they faced one another, reached to take her by the waist, and drew her close between his sprawled legs.

Then he leaned forward—slowly, inexorably— until his forehead met her belly.

"Don't," he told her navel. "Don't leave."

Overwhelmed with some unnamable emotion, she stroked her fingers through his thick, dark hair. "I won't."

"I'm sorry."

"I . . . I know."

They remained that way for several moments. Touching. Breathing. Warming each other in the dark. Gratitude swelled in her heart. She hadn't let herself realize how worried she'd been for him. Not until this moment, when he was home safe. With her.

"How is she?" he murmured.

Something told her he didn't mean the duchess. "The babe?"

She felt his nod of confirmation chafe against her belly.

"The babe was a he, actually. And he's fine. I took him in to the matrons. They dressed him in clean swaddling, filled his belly with milk. He'll have been named and christened by now, I expect."

"I hope he fared better than Hubert with that naming part."

She smiled and stroked his hair again.

"I shouldn't have left you. I just . . ." He huffed out a breath.

"Don't be too hard on yourself. It was obvious the whole place set you on edge. Many a big, strong man has been sent into a panic by a wailing infant."

He lifted his head and gave her a searching look.

And her silly, girlish brain picked that moment

to decide he was the handsomest man she'd ever seen. Probably because he was the only man to ever look at her this way. Holding her together with his strong, sculpted arms while his heated gaze turned her to slag.

"Can we return to the conversation we were having just before all that?" she whispered. "We were standing at the gate. You were saying how much you liked me, asking for a truce. And I . . ." She grazed a light touch over his cheek. "I was about to apologize for this."

"Don't. I deserved the punches and then some. For most of my life I've been a first-rate jackass. For the past year I've been trying to be less of one. But I don't think I'm succeeding. I've merely graduated from first-rate jackass to flagship bastard."

"I don't know about that." She tamed a lock of his hair. "You've had your moments this week. Saved me from falling not once, but twice. You were perfect with my sister. And I suspect that when you offered me this post, you *thought* you were doing it to rescue me."

Now she wasn't sure.

Now she wondered if she was here to rescue him.

He said, "At any rate, I owe you an apology for everything today. Including the water goblets."

She laughed a little. "It truly was nothing. Just a silly tavern trick."

"I have embarrassing party tricks, too."

"Do you?"

"Oh, yes." He released her, reclining in his chair. "I can pleasure two women with both hands tied behind my back. Blindfolded."

"How boastful you are."

"Boasting would imply I'm proud of it. I'm not boasting."

Oh God. The look on his face told her he wasn't. The images now filling Pauline's mind made her a little bit queasy.

And very, very curious.

"I found the naughty books," she said. "I have questions."

"Oh, Lord." He rubbed both hands over his face. "No, Simms. No."

"But you're the only person I can ask. And you owe me for the water goblets."

He dropped his hands. "Very well. You have questions? Here are some answers. 'Yes,' 'No,' and 'Only with ample lubrication.' Apply them to your questions as you like."

She reached out and gave him a playful smack on the shoulder. "It's just that the books make it sound so ridiculous. All this pulsing and divine throbbing and unparalleled ecstasy and cataclysmic smelting of two souls into one."

"Cataclysmic 'smelting'? What book said that?"

"Never mind the smelting," she said. "But the rest of it. The unparalleled ecstasy part. Is it . . . is it really supposed to be that way?"

He sighed. "That particular question is best answered by experience."

"But that's just it, you see. I've had experience." She cringed. "A little bit of it. And it was nothing like that. No ecstasy whatsoever. Nor even any flutterings. That's why I was wondering if the books tell lies, or . . . or if it was just me."

"Simms." He rose from his chair and looked her in the eye.

It was killing her not to look away, but his expression made it clear he wouldn't answer otherwise. So she slid from the edge of the desk, met him toe-to-toe, and held his gaze directly.

Then waited, miserable.

"It wasn't you," he said.

In Griff's head alarm bells were sounding by the hundreds. He shouldn't have this conversation. Hell, he shouldn't even be here with her alone. But he needed to be with someone right now. And by God, she needed to hear this.

"It wasn't you," he said again.

"So the books *do* exaggerate," she said.

"I'm not saying that, either."

Her nose crinkled. "I'm so confused."

"That's because there are no simple answers. Can it be divine bliss? Yes. Can it be a dismal trial? Yes. It's like conversation. With the wrong person, it *can* feel forced, perfunctory. Boring as hell. But sometimes you find someone with whom the discussion just flows. You never run out of ideas. There's no awkwardness in honesty. You surprise each other and yourselves."

"But how do you find that person without . . . conversing all over town?"

Griff gave a dry laugh. "What a question. Find the answer and bottle it, and you'll have the most successful shop in England. I might even queue up myself."

He had "conversed" with many women in his life, and he wasn't proud of it. Oh, he had *been* proud of it once, and the women themselves had few complaints. But he'd come to realize it was a cold thing, when the best you could say of a bed partner wasn't "I love you" or even "I'm fond of you," but merely "I despise you a bit less than I despise myself."

But he meant what he'd said at the foundling home gates. He *liked* this woman. He could talk with her, as he hadn't talked with anyone in ages. And any man who'd let her go was a goddamned fool.

He reached for her, framing her sweet face. He traced her bottom lip with the pad of his thumb. "I don't have many answers, but I can tell you this much. It wasn't you."

He approached her, feeling the darkness compress and heat up between them.

"Griff." Her hand went to his wrist. "I wasn't asking for this."

"I know." He leaned in, tilting his head for the kiss. The anticipation of her taste set his pulse racing.

"But—"

"Simms. You asked the question. Don't interrupt when I'm making a point."

He hovered an inch above her lips . . . then reconsidered. A kiss wasn't what she needed. A kiss gave her too much room to hide. She needed to see him, see herself and how beautiful, how sensual, she was.

He ran his hands over the curves of her body, tracing them through her dressing gown. Her little gasp of pleasure thrilled him.

"I think I had a dream that went like this," she whispered. "Just last night."

"Don't tell me that." The vision of her dreaming fitfully beneath white sheets . . .

"What should I tell you, then? That you're the most attractive man I've ever known, and the mere scent of your cologne sets fire to my petticoats?"

"You should tell me to go to the devil." His hands went to the ties of her dressing gown. He paused, one finger looped in the corded sash. "But would you tell me so, if that's what you felt?"

She gave him a smile. "Don't you know me at all?"

He yanked on the knotted sash, drawing her to him. "I just know I'm desperate to touch you, everywhere."

Just this, he told himself. *Just touching.*

He would allow himself this much, and no more.

He worked the knot of the sash free and divided the edges of her robe, exposing the crisp white shift beneath it. This one was new—not nearly so frail and translucent as the one she'd worn the first night. But he found it arousing as hell anyway.

He slid his hands up and down her body, cupping her breasts through the chemise, then stroking downward to her hips and thighs. The linen softened and heated under the friction, molding to her form. He found her nipples and claimed them with his thumbs, teasing and rolling them to tight peaks. He slipped a button free, then another. Just enough so he could push the fabric aside, bend his knees, and finally—*finally*—suckle her the way he'd yearned to in that darkened garden.

As he kissed his way back up her neck, he sent one hand downward, arrowing straight for her sex.

He worked his fingers between her thighs, massaging the linen until he could cradle her sex in his palm. Even through the fabric, she was warm for him. Wet for him.

Dear God, he could have her so easily. Undo a few trouser buttons, push up her shift, and glide straight home. He could be in her in seconds.

"Nothing but your pleasure," he vowed to them both, stroking her with the heel of his hand and pressing his fingertips through the linen, dampening the fabric with her body's moisture. "You have my word. I don't mean to take from you. Only give."

He supposed he should have carried her to the divan or laid her down on the carpet, but he was selfish. He wanted all of her, all for himself. All of her weight in his arms, all of her heat against his body. He did not want to share her with a sofa or a carpet, or even something so slight as a chair.

Wrapping his arm tight about her middle, he bound her to him. With his other hand, he coaxed and explored her sex. Desperate for her secrets.

There were few things that gave him more satisfaction in life than bringing a woman pleasure. In so many ways, it was like solving a puzzle. Each woman had the same anatomy. But the crucial bits came in all shapes and sizes, fit together in different ways, and each responded to a unique set of strokes and caresses. The same techniques might not work from one woman to the next. The process of discovery was humbling and intoxicating.

But when he triumphed—when he found just the right touch to apply in just the right place for just as long as she needed it—ah, the sweet thrill of success. Victory was a heady drug. He loved feeling a woman come undone in his arms. Loved feeling the taut ring of her sex soften and melt for him, then grasp him tighter than a fist. He loved learning each little expression and sound that heralded her orgasm. Some women sighed, some wept, some laughed, some whimpered, some begged, some screamed. Some were wickedly grateful in the aftermath, and others grew endearingly bashful.

He didn't know what Pauline would be like when she reached her peak. But he knew he must find out. Deep inside, he expected transcendence. Something utterly different than anything he'd experienced before.

He gathered a handful of her shift and drew the fabric upward.

"You can say no," he murmured.

"I don't want to."

Thank heaven. He slid his hand beneath the linen, skimming a slow, patient touch up her thigh. When he reached her cleft, his patience left him. He had to be inside her, somehow. He parted her folds and plunged a single finger into her tight, wet heat.

She gasped. Her hands clutched at him. The delicious bite of her fingernails made him wild.

"Are you frightened?" he asked, holding still. "Do you want me to stop?"

"Yes, I'm a bit frightened." She looked up at him and swallowed hard. "And no, I don't want you to stop."

He kissed her again, thrusting his tongue in

rhythm with his touch. Slowly in, then out. When he felt she was ready, he added a second finger. Her intimate muscles stretched and contracted around the combined girth, gripping him tight. His cock throbbed vainly in his trousers, trapped in a painful state of arousal.

She nestled close to him, and her belly pressed against the aching ridge of his erection. It wasn't nearly all that he desired, but the friction provided some relief.

She broke the kiss and rested her head on his shoulder, slack-jawed and breathing hard. Her hips writhed as she worked herself against his hand, grinding against him in the way that pleased her most.

He began to whisper against her ear. He knew she'd passed the point of coherence, so he said any foolish thing that came to mind. How lovely she was in the moonlight, and how proud he was of her courage. How she'd enchanted him that very first night, and he still hadn't found his way back through the magic cabinet. How he adored her neck and her sharp green eyes. How sweetness clung to her, and how he fantasized spending blissful hours slowly lapping it up with his tongue.

"Here," he whispered, skimming his thumb up and down her crease. "I'd taste you here. You'd be so sweet. And then . . ."

He pushed his fingers deep, driving them to the hilt. With his thumb, he worried the swollen nub at the crest of her sex.

"Griff," she pleaded.

"Yes," he said. "That's right."

She gave a few charming little hitches of breath. Like an ascending scale on the pianoforte. And then she came with one perfect sighing, shuddering moan.

A lovely sound, that moan. Her intimate muscles contracted deliciously around his fingers. But all in all, her orgasm was not quite the epic, transcendent experience he'd expected.

What stunned him breathless was his own reaction.

That was entirely new.

The surge of emotion he felt—it wasn't just the usual triumph of bringing a woman pleasure. An unbearable font of tenderness welled in his chest. Mingled with protectiveness, fondness. The impulse to not just pleasure her, but cherish her, guard her. He pressed kiss after kiss to the crown of her head, as if he could expel this painful excess of emotion.

"It wasn't you," he whispered, nuzzling the delicious lobe of her ear. "Whoever he was, he was a fool. Or a boor. Or just too damned young to know what the hell he was doing. But it wasn't you. Understand?"

She clung to his shirtfront for long moments, breathing hard. Finally, she looked up at him. "Will you take me upstairs?"

He'd never wanted anything so much. To simply take her upstairs, let his world explode, and then contend with the rubble later.

"I wouldn't expect anything," she rushed on. "I'm not asking for promises. I just want to know what it's like when it's good. And I might go my whole life without another chance. I'm not a lady with a reputation to guard. There's no one to care."

Damn it, *he* cared.

He *cared*, and he could no longer deny it. He'd brought her into his house, taken her under his protection. Lady or not, he wanted to treat her well.

Her hands slid up his chest, then trailed down his arms. She pressed a light kiss to his neck. "Griff, please."

His cock throbbed in eager agreement.

Her, his stupid heart whispered. *I'll take her.*

But beneath all this, his veins ran cold with a deep, dark current of fear. It was too great a risk for them both. He couldn't take her like this when she'd never be his for the keeping. That way lay danger and months of despair.

"I can't." He stroked her hair. "It isn't you. I want you more than you could possibly know, in ways you couldn't even fathom. But I just can't."

He released her with abruptness—because that was the only way he could do it at all.

Chapter Fourteen

Pauline came late to breakfast. She considered skipping the meal entirely—pleading headache or fatigue—but she didn't want to invite any questions.

She wasn't sure how she'd even look at the duchess this morning. The woman had the perception of a hawk. She would have to mind her every move, word, and glance to avoid giving anything away.

As she neared the breakfast room, she stopped in the corridor and took a moment to compose herself.

She could hear voices from within—both the duchess's and Griff's.

Drat.

He wasn't supposed to be awake this early. How was she going to manage this?

The same way he managed it, she supposed. After their encounter in the dining room the previous morning, she knew Griff would have no difficulty. He would barely acknowledge her presence, no doubt.

In fact, that was probably why he'd come to

breakfast at all—because he worried that she would blurt out over toast that she'd shamelessly thrown herself at him mere hours ago. He wanted to quell any speculation.

Just pretend nothing happened, she told herself. *You were not alone with him in the library. He did not gather you in the most tender, needing of embraces. He most especially did not lift your skirts and give you delicious pleasure while whispering the most tender, arousing words to ever caress your ear.*

The memory was so acute, she bit her knuckle to keep her reactions in check.

When she had her resolve firmly in place, Pauline turned the corner and entered the breakfast room. She kept her eyes downcast.

"Beg pardon for my tardiness, your graces. I slept rather—"

The scrape of chair legs interrupted her. The sound froze the blood in her veins.

Oh no. Surely he hadn't.

She looked up in horror.

He had.

The eighth Duke of Halford had come to his feet when she entered the room. Without thinking, apparently, because he couldn't possibly have meant to do such a thing. Gentlemen rose to their feet when ladies came in. They did not rise for servants.

No man had ever stood for Pauline. Not once in her life. It was the best, most thrilling sensation. But when it came to the cause of discretion, this was complete disaster.

And then he made it worse—he inclined his handsome, dark head in a sort of bow. "Miss Simms."

Up went the duchess's eyebrow. "Well."

That one syllable spoke volumes. Her grace knew everything. At least, she knew *something* had happened. Pauline could only pray the details remained a rough sketch in her imagination.

"Be seated, Miss Simms," Griff said.

She shook her head. "You first, your grace."

"Both of you, remain as you are," the duchess said. She rose from her own chair. "I was just about to leave for the morning room, and now I've saved you the trouble of rising twice."

"Do we have lessons this morning, your grace?"

She gave Pauline a strange look. "No. It's Wednesday. My day to be at home to callers. I expect a great many inquisitive ladies this morning."

"You don't want me to sit with you?"

"Best to keep them wondering, I think. If they want another look at you, there's the fete at Vauxhall Gardens this evening. For now, you may be at your leisure."

Pauline curtsied as the duchess exited the room.

As soon as the older woman had gone, she whispered to Griff, "What are you doing, standing for me? You shouldn't stand for me. You saw the duchess's face just now. How smug she looked. She'll think something has changed between us."

"Everything *has* changed between us."

Everything changed inside her, at that statement. Her internal organs began scouting for new neighborhoods.

He said, "When you've finished your breakfast, get your things. We're going out."

"We? Out? Where?" Pauline was aware she sounded something like a yipping dog. But her mind was full of questions.

"You and I. Will go out of the house." He walked his fingers in demonstration. "On an errand. Did you have some other plans for the morning?"

Pauline had just been contemplating an hour or two of reading, followed by a nice long nap.

"I don't have any plans," she said.

"Very good. Meet me in the entrance hall when you've fetched your wrap."

She still wasn't sure what last night meant to him. Or even what it meant to her. But this morning she couldn't turn down the chance to spend time with him.

She wanted to be with Griff more than she wished to be anywhere else.

In her heart she knew this meant she was on the verge of something emotional and treacherous—and at serious risk of falling in.

Be careful, Pauline. Nothing could come of it.

For today, she decided to ignore the posted warnings and dance on the edge of heartbreak. Surely she could teeter on this brink a few hours longer without falling completely in love with the man.

After all, it was only an errand.

Except that it wasn't only an errand.

Oh, no. It was something far better. And far worse.

He took her to a bookshop. *The* bookshop.

When the coach pulled up before the familiar Bond Street shop front, Pauline's heart performed the strangest acrobatics in her chest. It tried to sink and float at once.

The cruel words echoed in her memory. *I'll chase you off with the broom.*

"Why did you bring me here?" she asked, accepting Griff's hand as he helped her down from the carriage.

"It's a bookshop. If you mean to open a circulating library, don't you need books? They don't sell very many of those at the fruiterer's or linen draper's." He tugged at her hand. "Come, we'll buy up every naughty, scandalous, licentious volume in the place."

He pulled her toward the shop entrance, but Pauline held back.

Griff looked bemused. "If you're too proud to accept a gift, I can deduct it from your thousand pounds."

"It's not that."

"Then what is it?"

She chided herself for her reluctance. He meant well. He meant more than well. He'd brought her here for the express purpose of making her dreams come true.

"Isn't there another bookshop in London? A bigger one, with a larger selection? This one looks rather small."

"Snidling's is the best. My family has patronized this shop for generations. They offer bindings done to order, of the finest quality. That'll be important for your circulating library. You'll want the books made to last."

Her heart ached at all the evidence of how much thought he'd given this. This was the extravagant shopping trip her heart yearned for—not a whirlwind of pink in the dressmaker's shop, or hours spent poring over trays of gold and jewels. And the fact that he understood it meant he knew *her*.

"You were right yesterday," he said, more softly. "About Hubert and the hat. I can't just hand you a thousand pounds, brush the gold dust from my hands and walk away. If this is your dream, I want to be sure you'll make a go of it."

Oh, Griff.

"I can't go in there," she blurted out.

"But of course you can."

"No, I mean I'm . . . I'm not welcome there."

His face went serious. "What makes you say that?"

There was nothing for it but to tell him the truth. As Pauline related the tale, he received it with a stony, impassive expression. It hurt to own up to the humiliation. But if she were going to refuse his help, he deserved to know why.

"So you see, I can't go in. Not this shop."

He didn't answer her. Not in words. When his footman opened the door, Griff ushered her into the bookshop with a firm hand.

The shopkeeper rushed out from behind the counter to greet him with a deep bow. "Your grace. What an honor."

Griff removed his hat and placed it on the counter.

"How may I serve you this morning, your grace?"

"This is my mother's friend, Miss Simms. She is looking to acquire some books for her personal library. I believe you made her acquaintance earlier this week."

Snidling's gaze flicked to Pauline and his tongue darted out in a reptilian manner. "Er . . . I'm afraid I don't recall, your grace. Please forgive me."

"I understand. This is a busy shop."

"Yes, yes. So many people come and go, you see. I can't possibly remember each face."

The snake. Pauline knew he recognized her. His gaze kept darting in her direction, and his face was showing hints of crimson.

It was on the tip of her tongue to confront his lies. She wasn't afraid of him. Not now, with a duke at her side. This time, she would stand up for herself.

But Griff's hand pressed against her back, relaying an unmistakable message: *Allow me.*

"So you do not remember Miss Simms?" he asked the shopkeeper once again.

"I'm afraid not, your grace."

"Let me shake your recollection," the duke said, imbuing the word "shake" with the crisp ring of a threat. His voice was smooth, aristocratic, commanding, and honed to a blade-sharp edge.

Pauline thought it was the most arousing thing she'd ever heard.

"You had a conversation with her," he continued evenly. "About oranges, Leadenhall, the Queen of Sheba, and chasing vermin off with brooms."

The man's stammering became a violent tremor—nearly as violent as the bloodred flush of his cheeks. "Your g-g-grace, I humbly and abjectly apologize. I had no idea the young lady—"

"It is not I who deserves your apology."

"Of course not, your grace." The scaly man turned to Pauline. He barely met her eyes. "Miss Simms, please accept my profoundest apologies. I didn't realize. I am deeply sorry if you interpreted my remarks in any way that offended you."

"Well?" The duke turned to her. "Do you accept his apologies, Miss Simms?"

Pauline glared at the shopkeeper. His was the

worst, most insincere apology possible. To say "I'm sorry you were offended" was not the same as apologizing for the offense. She didn't believe he was sorry in the least, and if she'd been alone and feeling brave, she would have told him so.

But she was here with Griff, and he'd meant this to be a pleasant errand. Part of her fairy tale.

So she said quietly, "I suppose."

"Very well, then." Griff clapped his hands together. "Let's begin an order. Take a list, Snidling."

The shopkeeper's relief was plain. He scurried behind the counter and turned his ledger to a fresh sheet before dipping his quill in ink.

Griff began to dictate, rattling off titles and authors with an arousing tenor of authority. "We'll start with all of Mrs. Radcliffe and Mrs. Wollstonecraft. All the modern poets, as well. Byron and his ilk. *The Monk, Moll Flanders, Tom Jones*, a good translation of *L'École des Filles* . . . *Fanny Hill.* Make it two copies of that last."

Snidling looked up. "You did say these are for the young *lady's* library, your grace?"

"Yes."

"Your grace, might I suggest—"

"No," Griff clipped. "You may not offer suggestions. You will continue to write down the titles that I name."

Her mouth dried. Good heavens. If he'd torn every scrap of clothing from his body and held the shopkeeper at the point of a glimmering sword, every muscle flexed in anger—she could not have found him more attractive than she did right now.

He went on listing titles and dictating names. They were all a muffled stew in her ears.

When the list filled an entire page, front and back, he said, "I suppose that will make a start. Now, for the bindings."

Griff turned to Pauline and waved her over to view samples of leather. As she neared him, her heart began to pound. Last night he'd skimmed his rough, hungry touch over her breasts, filled her with his wicked fingers. But nothing—none of the previous night's exhilaration—could compare to this moment.

She stood next to him, buffeted by the full, soul-rattling force of her adoration. How could he fail to notice? How could the world not have changed around them? She'd been struck by lightning, and he just went on speaking in that same, even tone.

"You must have Morocco bindings, of course. It's the best. Gold leaf embossing for the title and the spine. Do you have a favorite color?"

"Favorite color?" She was lost in his dark, inquisitive stare. "I . . . I like brown."

"Brown?" he scoffed. "That's too commonplace."

"If you say so." Pauline ran a loving touch over the scrap of fawn-colored leather she'd admired the other day. Just as butter soft as it appeared, but wholly impractical. She tried to focus her attention to the samples of Morocco he'd suggested.

"I should think red," she decided. "Red, for all of them." She lifted a scrap of supple crimson kidskin. "Red is the best color for naughty books, don't you think?"

"Indubitably."

"And people will know at a glance they came from my library. It will be a good advertisement."

"Red it is, then. With marbled endpapers and gold leaf. Write that down, Snidling."

The shopkeeper scribbled greedily in the margins. Pauline could tell he was already tallying up the outrageous profits he'd turn on this one order alone.

"May I view the list?" the duke said.

"But of course, your grace." Snidling turned the ledger so the duke might view the page.

Griff ran his finger down the list, nodding with approval.

Then he grasped the page and ripped it from the ledger. "Thank you," he said, folding the paper in two and creasing it smartly. "This will prove helpful when we place the order with your competitor."

The shopkeeper flashed a nervous smile. "Your grace, I don't understand."

"Really? Don't you? Then permit me to make it clear." He approached the man until the difference between their heights was evident. "Perhaps Miss Simms accepts your measly, insulting apologies. I do not."

"B-But, your grace—"

"I would offer you a farewell, but I don't bother with insincerity. I hope you fare very ill indeed."

Pauline wanted to cheer and applaud. Kiss him, in full view of everyone. Or at least stand there and gloat a few moments longer.

But Griff was eager to leave.

He ushered her out the door. "Don't worry. We'll find another shop."

"We don't have to do that right now."

"Yes, we do," he replied. "I sent the coach around the corner to wait. Do you mind walking?"

"Not at all."

He barely paused to gain her agreement before storming down the sidewalk at a terror of a pace. His boots hit the pavement with crisp reports, and his gloves flapped comically in his grip. Pauline had to dash to keep up with him.

"Sorry." When he noted her struggles, he slowed his pace. "I'm angry at the moment."

"Thank you for being angry. And for what you just did. The way you handled him was marvelous."

He stared into the distance and snapped his gloves against his thigh.

"Griff, I'm going to work so hard for you the rest of this week," she promised. "Starting with Vauxhall tonight. I'll be the best, most comprehensive failure you could imagine."

He made a dismissive wave, brushing off her vows.

"No, I mean it. Truly. That was . . ." There was no other way to say it. "It was the best thing anyone ever did for me."

He stopped, then turned to her. "And that, Simms, makes me angriest of all."

The fiery look in his eyes . . . it undid her. She knew that look. It mirrored the fast-blooming vine of devotion and rage that grew inside her whenever Daniela was harmed. She knew it well—the pure, unreasoned fury at a world that would allow such things to happen, coupled with the frustration that she was powerless to prevent it from occurring again.

Griff felt that same frustration right now. On *her* behalf. And he wasn't even bothering to hide it.

If she'd harbored any hope of not falling in love

with the man, it vanished that instant. It was only a matter of time. She would love him before the week was out, and it would be gloriously terrible, wonderfully hopeless.

Her heart was now a coin with two sides—dread and joy—and it seemed to flip back and forth with every racing beat.

"Miss Simms?"

At the sudden address, Pauline startled.

"Why, it is you." Lady Haughfell appeared on the pavement before them. "And your grace. What a pleasant surprise. We've just come from your house."

"Is that so?" Griff replied.

"Yes, we came hoping to make a social call and further our acquaintance with dear Miss Simms. We do so long to hear more about her and her people. Our copy of *Debrett's* was curiously of little help."

Pauline didn't miss the implication in Lady Haughfell's words. *You're not one of us. I know it, and I mean to learn the truth.*

"We were out," Griff said.

"Obviously," the lady replied.

"My apologies for the inconvenience," he said coolly. "Perhaps you will be so good as to call another day."

"Yes, yes. And allow me to express my deepest concern for the duchess's health and my best wishes for her speedy recovery."

"What?" His voice changed instantly.

Lady Haughfell arched a brow. "Were you unaware? The butler informed us. Your mother has taken gravely ill."

Chapter Fifteen

Griff couldn't get home fast enough.

The carriage was too far away, the traffic too congested. Time dallied in a most impertinent way.

Pauline tried to mollify him. "She's fine, I'm sure. Perhaps she merely said she was ill so she wouldn't have to entertain the Awfuls."

He nodded, hoping she was correct. Still, he could not rest easy until he'd confirmed it with his own eyes.

When they reached Halford House, he took the stairs two at a time and stormed down the corridor to the duchess's suite. He flung open the door and saw her lying in the center of her bed, eyes closed and hands clasped atop the bedcovering.

Motionless.

His veins became ice floes. This couldn't happen. Not yet. He knew she was getting older and that inevitably her health would fail. But she was still so strong-willed, so alive. She couldn't do this to him now.

He wasn't ready to be alone.

"Mother?" When she gave no answer, a knot stuck in his throat. *"Mother."*

At last her eyes opened, with an innocent flutter of lashes. Her voice was weak. "Griffin? Is that you, my dear boy?"

Devil take it.

He knew in that moment that this was all a ruse. In all his life, his mother had never once referred to him as her "dear boy." He would have remembered.

The duchess was alive, well, and cunning as ever. He was going to throttle her.

"Come closer." Her pale hand groped the air. "I want to look on your face one last time."

Really, her acting skills were most impressive. She should take to the stage.

She mustered a pathetic cough. "My only regret . . . the fete at Vauxhall tonight."

"Never mind it. We won't go."

"No." The volume of her protest seemed to revive her a bit. "No, you must attend. Everyone's expecting you."

"Then why are you playing ill?"

"I'm not playing." She smoothed the bedcoverings with one hand. "I'm simply too weak for Vauxhall this evening. The drafts, the fog by the river, all those stairs. I feel a chill coming on, just to think of it. The two of you must go without me. I don't want to ruin your evening."

"I find that hard to believe. You were all too eager to ruin our afternoon."

Diabolical woman. Did she truly not understand the panic she'd just put him through? It was a thousand times worse than any matchmaking, or even drugging and kidnapping. He couldn't forgive her that.

"You are not ill," he said. "I command you to rise from that bed and be well."

She fixed him with a droll gaze. "Griffin, you are a duke. You are not St. James curing the lepers."

"Tell me, which saint is the patron of beleaguered sons?" He glared at a mysterious lump beneath the counterpane. "What is it you have under there?"

Her hands covered the lump. "Nothing."

"It's not nothing. I can plainly see you have something under that blanket. What is it?" He reached for the counterpane and bed linens, planning to draw them back.

She tugged them close. "Leave me be."

"I will know what you're hiding."

They tussled back and forth for several seconds. Until something sharp stabbed him in the wrist.

"*Ouch.*"

He pulled back his hand. Incredulous, he rubbed at a small round wound. She was stabbing him with pins now? Good Lord. She'd be a terror with a saber.

"I revise my previous statement," he said. "You *are* ill. Seriously ill. And when this week is over, we're going to discuss living arrangements for your decline. I hear there are lovely sanitariums in Ireland."

Pauline waved him to the side of the room. "It's all right," she whispered. "It's for the best. If I'm to be a social disaster, it will go much easier without her there."

Griff wasn't so sure. He knew exactly what his mother had in mind. She wanted to force the two of them alone. So they'd spend the whole evening together in a hopelessly romantic setting, and then . . .

"It's not a good idea," he said.

Her green eyes pleaded with him. "I'm only in London this one week. Chances are, I'll never return. I was looking forward to seeing Vauxhall. And to earning my keep, at last."

He sighed and leveled a single finger at her nose. "Your comportment had better be dreadful."

She lifted a hand in mock salute. But her fetching smile gave him grave misgivings. Soon, there'd be nothing he could deny her.

On his way out of the bedchamber he addressed the vigilant butler. "Higgs," he said, "see that my mother does not move from that bed. And summon the doctor. Not the gentle-mannered one, either. The one with the leeches."

Once the duke had left the room, Pauline approached the duchess's bed. "Really, your grace. That wasn't kind of you. He was terribly concerned."

He'd been more than concerned. She'd watched his face go pale as ash, and he'd clenched his hands until his knuckles bleached to bone. Didn't they realize how fortunate they were to have each other? She'd never known two people who so clearly loved each other yet spent so much time and effort denying it.

There was phlegm, and then there was sheer obstinacy.

"I should think this sort of ploy is beneath a duchess."

She clucked her tongue. "Very well, I admit it. I'm not truly ill. I'm desperate. Look."

The duchess threw back the counterpane, revealing a misshapen baby blanket large enough to swaddle a calf. Not even just a bovine calf, but possibly an elephant calf. The yarn had been changed twice, partway through. So one-third of it was peach and another third was lavender. Now she was working her way through a ball of pink.

Skeins of white, green, and blue lurked ominously nearby.

Pauline whistled at it. "That *is* dire."

"I know it. And it's growing worse by the hour. This evening is the chance we've been waiting for. You'll see."

"No, your grace. I'm going to be a disaster. I have to be. Elegance, comportment, accomplishment, elocution . . . all of it. I don't possess any of the qualities a duchess needs."

The older woman waved a hand. "Forget all that. There is exactly one quality, and one quality only, that makes a woman a duchess."

"What's that?"

"She marries a duke."

Pauline shook her head. "It's not going to happen."

"I know my son, girl. He's half in love with you already. It started that very first day, and then this morning . . . ?" She hmphed. "One strong push in the right direction and he'll fall hard. Don't try to tell me you're not feeling something for him."

She sighed, not knowing how to argue. He'd declined to take her to his bed. But after the bookstore today, she believed that Griff did care about her. At least a little. And she knew herself to be dangerously close to falling in love with him.

But what did it matter? That didn't mean he'd want to *marry* her. Or that she could ever marry him.

She rose from the bedside. "I'll leave you to your rest."

"One last thing," the duchess said just as Pauline had reached the door. "You're to have the amethysts tonight. I'll tell Fleur."

The amethysts?

Pauline was stunned. "But, your grace, I couldn't possibly wear—"

"You're ready for them. And what's more, he's ready to see you in them." As she left the room, the duchess called after her, "I'm counting on you, girl."

Too many people were counting on her, it seemed. Her loyalties were growing more and more divided. The duke had hired her to save him from matchmaking. The duchess wanted to be rescued from a creeping tangle of yarn. Pauline was coming to care for them both—and she knew they each needed something more.

But somewhere, much too far away, there was poor Daniela, faithfully gathering eggs and counting the days until Saturday. Her sister needed her most of all.

Pauline drew to a halt in the corridor and cast a look at the porcelain shepherdess she'd nearly demolished a few days back.

What am I doing here?

To these people, country life made for decorative figurines. She knew it to be backbreaking, ceaseless work. No matter what delusions the duchess suffered under, she could never belong in this aristocratic world.

All she wanted was a little shop in Spindle Cove and a circulating library of naughty books. Not to *mean* well, but to *do* well—for her and her sister both. She couldn't start dreaming of the wrong fairy tale.

She was a hardworking girl, and she'd been hired for a reason. To be a comprehensive catastrophe.

"Colin. *Colin*, something terrible has happened."

Colin Sandhurst, Lord Payne, looked up from the letter he was writing. His wife stood in the doorway of his study—as always, an enticing vision of dark hair and plump, kissable lips.

But her lovely eyes had gone grim behind her spectacles.

He rose from his desk at once. "Good God, Min. What is it?"

"We must do something," she said.

"Of course we will, darling." He crossed the room to her. "Of course we will. I could crash through the window this instant, if you asked. Or pen a strongly worded letter to *The Times*. But the actions we take will be more effective if you explain to me first what's going on."

He took her by the shoulders and guided her to the divan.

"It's that horrid, debauched friend of yours," she said. "From before we married."

He chuckled. "That description fits a shocking number of people, I'm afraid. You'll have to narrow it down."

"The duke. That grabby, disgusting duke from Winterset Grange."

"Halford?"

"Yes, that's the one. He's got Pauline Simms. Our Pauline, from the Bull and Blossom. And he's holding her hostage here in Town." She shuddered. "God knows what he's done to the poor thing. Probably made her his sordid love puppet."

Colin struggled not to laugh. "Minerva, I'm trying to follow you, but you're making it quite difficult. Perhaps you can start again and tell me what actually happened today."

"I saw them together. I was going to the bookshop to . . ." She blushed a little. "To see if any more copies of my book had been sold. I can't help it."

"And had they?"

"Yes," she said proudly. "Three."

"Excellent, Min. That's brilliant." Colin had only purchased two of them himself.

He knew she'd throttle him for buying them up, but he couldn't help it. The market for geological treatises wasn't especially robust. But she was so damned adorable when she was pleased with herself—and especially creative in bed. His motives were entirely selfish.

"Anyhow, as I was approaching the bookshop, I saw the two of them leaving it. The Disgusting Duke of Halford and Pauline Simms. Clear as day."

Colin sighed. He hated to prod at a sore spot, but this was too much to be believed. "Were you wearing your spectacles?"

She gave him an offended look. "Of course I was."

"Still. I think you must have been mistaken."

"I'm not. I know I'm not, Colin. Don't you believe me?"

"I believe, without a doubt, that *you* believe you saw them." He clasped one of her sweet little hands in his and stroked it soothingly. "But I still think it a great improbability."

"It's true that two more different people never existed," Minerva agreed. "That duke is vile and debauched. And Pauline is so well-meaning."

"Well. Opposites do occasionally attract. And Spindle Cove women 'abducted' by rakes are not always so unwilling as the observer might suspect."

She smiled. "I suppose that's true."

"Before we go haring off on a rescue mission, let's consider a few bits of information. From all evidence, Pauline had no means of traveling to London. Secondly, I know Halford. The man would never be near a bookshop. And last"—he placed a light, affectionate touch to her nose—"you *have* been complaining that your spectacles need new lenses. A mistake seems the most likely explanation."

"Colin—"

"However," he added, "I will do all I can to set your mind at ease. Today, I'll ask around at the clubs. See what gossip there is of Halford."

"That's a good idea. I'll pay a call on Susanna

and Lord Rycliff. If anything were amiss in Spindle Cove, they would have heard."

"Excellent. And if our little fact-finding investigations turn up nothing, we'll perform an experiment. We'll call at Halford House tomorrow."

She nodded. Her eyes misted with tears.

"Darling Min." He stroked her cheek. "Are you truly that concerned?"

"No," she said. "Oh, Colin. I'm just so proud." She squeezed his hand. "You're using the scientific method."

Chapter Sixteen

Griff kept busy for the rest of the day. He had a full slate of appointments that afternoon, all related to the business of his estates.

It still wasn't enough. All his meetings with solicitors and land agents and secretaries . . . They were like cannonballs stuffed in a crate. They were weighty, and they took up space—but they didn't make the crate truly full. Thoughts of Pauline slipped in to fill every void, like a million grains of sand.

Or crystals of sugar, it might be more appropriate to say.

Somehow he made it to late afternoon, when he surrendered to the attentions of his valet. He emerged an hour later—smooth-shaven, fully dressed, and completely unprepared for the vision coming down the staircase.

Good Lord.

One look at her and Griff knew it was over. The evening was a failure before it began. No one would ever believe her to be a common serving girl. Not tonight, not looking like this.

She wore a gown in deep, lush pink, with gauzy layers of skirts billowing out from a fitted, off-the-shoulder bodice. Matching elbow-length gloves. Her hair was curled, looped, and pinned—but all in a way that managed to look effortlessly lovely and elegant. Quite a trick, that. Fleur deserved a rise in wages.

She carried herself well, too. Her neck was a pale, slender column, and her bare shoulders . . . ah, her shoulders looked sculpted from moonlight. Delicate and serene, mysterious and feminine. A rope of pale amethysts dipped sensuously above her décolletage, catching the light with a thousand facets.

He was a duke and a libertine, he reminded himself. He'd seen many a beautiful woman in his life. Finer gowns than this, more lavish jewels than these. Rationally, he knew that Pauline Simms could not eclipse everything and everyone who had come before her. And yet, somehow she did.

There wasn't any one feature he could point to, or any particular gesture she made. It was just . . .

Her. I'll take her.

"Well?" she prompted.

Finally, he looked her in the eyes—those bright green, cat-tipped, intelligent eyes, set in a heart-shaped face. They were anxious tonight, and transparently vulnerable.

Lord above. She had no idea. She had him enraptured to the point of drooling incoherence, and she had absolutely no idea.

She lifted an eyebrow.

She's waiting for your reaction. React. But not too much. Only the appropriate amount. A well-chosen word or two.

What he said was, "Guh."

Oh, hell. Had that unformed syllable actually escaped his throat?

Pauline blinked at him. "What?"

Apparently it had. He cleared his throat with a loud harrumph, then searched for a way to amend his statement. "Good," he pronounced, clearing his throat again. "I said good."

A pretty flush rose on Pauline's cheeks. Still, she bit her lip, looking hesitant. "What kind of good?" she asked. " 'Good' as in 'rather bad,' which aids our purpose? Or 'good' as in 'actually good,' and you're displeased?"

Griff sighed inwardly. What was he to say? *"Good" as in "Good God, you are the most radiant, lovely thing I've seen in all my life, and I'm a speechless, shuddering fool before you." Does that clear matters?*

"Good as in good," he said. "I'm not displeased."

Her mouth pulled to the side. "Then that's . . . good."

This was now officially the most inane conversation in which Griff had ever been a participant— and that included a drunken debate with Del over ostrich racing.

"The color isn't too awful?" She twisted a fold of the skirt. "The draper called it 'dewy petal,' but your mother said the shade was more of a 'frosted berry.' What do you say?"

"I'm a man, Simms. Unless we're discussing nipples, I don't see the value in these distinctions."

Her lips pursed into a chastening pout.

"Whatever shade it is, it looks well on you." *Too well.* He tugged his black evening gloves on and gathered his hat from Higgs. "Let's be going."

The carriage was readied and waiting. He turned to Pauline. She obviously needed help, what with those ungainly skirts. Without hesitation, she took the hand he offered and clutched it tightly, borrowing his strength. The warm clasp of her satin-clad fingers nearly undid him. He was unsteady himself as he made his own way into the coach and sat across from her on the rear-facing seat.

He turned his head to the window. He needed to bring himself under control. They were only just leaving the house, and the whole evening lay ahead.

When they reached the place for the river crossing and alighted from the coach, twilight had descended. The air was heavy with wisps of fog and shadow. An air of romantic mystery lingered, despite all Griff's attempts to discredit it.

"We're going to cross the river in boats?" she asked, eyeing the boat launch with alarm. Her grip tightened on his arm.

He nodded. "It's the only way to Vauxhall. Eventually there's to be a bridge, but it isn't complete."

"I've never been in a boat. Not in my whole life."

"Never? But you live by the sea."

"I know. It's absurd, isn't it? Sometimes the ladies go boating, but I never had a reason to join in."

"Don't be frightened." He reached for her. "Here."

Helping her into the boat was even more precarious than handing her into the carriage had been. Griff went first, wedging his boots fast against the floorboards and steadying his balance.

Pauline accepted his hand and took a cautious step onto a seat near the bow. But just then the waterman launched the boat. She stumbled. Griff had to catch her by both arms as she fell against his chest.

"Oh, bollocks." She struggled to correct herself, and the boat lurched.

His stomach nearly capsized. He had a vision—a brief, waking nightmare of a thought—in which she tumbled straight into the black water and all those heavy, embellished skirts dragged her straight to the depths.

"Don't move," he told her, tightening his grip. "Not yet."

He held her close and tight. For long moments they stood absolutely still—swaying in each other's arms while the boat regained its equilibrium.

"Are you well?" he whispered.

She nodded.

"Your heart is racing," he said.

"So is yours."

He smiled a little. "Fair enough."

When the boat finally steadied, he helped her onto the seat and motioned to the waterman, who ferried them across the Thames in smooth, even strokes.

"See?" he murmured, keeping her close. "There's nothing to fear. Just imagine we're traveling through that crystal cabinet in the poem. On our way to another world. Another England. Another

London with its Tower. Another Thames and other hills."

She relaxed against his shoulder. "A little lovely moony night."

"Exactly so." There she went again, enchanting him.

Griff had never been the fanciful sort, even as a boy. When he was with Pauline, the world *was* different. She forced him to see things through fresh eyes. Suddenly his library was the eighth wonder of the world, and Corinthian columns merited blasphemy. A ferry across the Thames was an epic journey, and a kiss . . . a kiss was everything.

Deep down, beneath the overworked, sharp-tongued serving girl, he saw a woman who craved the poetry in life. She'd never been given anything—not even favorable odds. But there was a liveliness in her spirit that fed on simple possibility—soaked it up like a wick and shone the brighter for it.

And tonight? Griff tilted his head westward and regarded the setting sun. Less than an hour from now her world was going to explode with brilliant possibility.

He wanted nothing more than to be near her when it did.

Pauline found Vauxhall rather overwhelming. And that was before they even entered the place.

When they disembarked on the far side of the river, her stomach took several moments to cease bobbing. They ascended a long flight of stairs, leading up the riverbank to a grand entrance gate. The higher they climbed, the louder the music grew.

Cor, she thought. She didn't say it aloud, not tonight. But it was the constant thought in her mind as they made their way through the gate and into the gardens proper.

Cor, cor, cor, cor, cor.

She didn't know nature could be tamed to this degree. The greens were perfectly flat. The shrubs were pruned in squat shapes. The trees were planted in straight lines.

Stately colonnades ran in various directions, marking covered pathways. At the end of each aisle vast paintings were hung. From this distance she couldn't quite make them out. She glimpsed a white orchestra pavilion in the form of a giant seashell, with carvings and embellishments all over it.

Suddenly, she realized her mouth had been hanging agape for the past few minutes. And the duke had noticed.

He gave her an amused look.

"It's growing dark," she said. "Should we head toward the pavilion?"

"Not yet," he said, catching her arm. He guided her off the main walk, into a darkening grove of trees away from the colonnades.

"What is it?"

"Something is about to happen, and I want you to see it. I want to be with you when you see it."

She popped up on her toes, craning her neck to look in all directions. "What is it we're waiting to see?"

"It's starting," he said, turning her head. "Look."

Pauline looked. She caught sight of a glowing orb. One single ball of light, hanging in the distance.

She blinked, and there were two of them.

And then ten.

And then . . . thousands.

A warm glow spread through the gardens like a wave of light, touching here a red lamp, there a blue or green. Breathless with delight, she tilted her head back. The trees above them were strung with lamps on every branch. The glow traveled from one to the other, and before long the entire grove was illuminated. The effect was similar to standing beneath a stained-glass church window at the sunniest part of the day. Except this was night, and all the colors had a luminous richness. The lamps were like a thousand jewels, hanging from every tree and carved stone archway.

Pauline couldn't even come up with words. She laughed and clapped a hand to her cheek. "How do they do it?" she asked. "How do they light them all at once?"

"There's a system of fuses," he explained. "They only need to light a few, and the spark travels to all the lamps."

"It's magical," she said.

"Yes," he said, softly. "I think it is, rather."

She turned to the duke, giddy with the beauty of it. He wasn't looking around at the thousands of lit globes hanging from the trees.

He was watching her.

A shiver passed over her bare shoulders. She crossed her arms to warm herself.

"Let me," he said, placing his gloved hands on her upper arms, then rubbing up and down.

The supple leather slid over her bare skin, warm and buttery. It was a lovely gesture, but it wasn't doing a dratted thing to cure her of gooseflesh.

His gaze caressed her mouth. "Perhaps coming here was a mistake."

"No," she insisted, hoping her words weren't drowned by the mad thumping of her heart. "No, I promise I can do this."

"Halford!" The voice carried to them through the glen. She turned to spy Lord Delacre waving at them from the colonnade. "Come along, then. We've a booth over this way."

"That's my cue," she said, giving Griff a wink. "Time for me to earn my thousand pounds. Prepare for disaster."

They made their way to the colonnade and found the booth Del had reserved. Pauline slipped away to mingle with the group. Griff watched her laugh and joke, sip champagne and devour slice after slice of wafer-thin ham.

For his part, Griff stood to the side, nipping brandy from his pocket flask and finally coming to grips with a painful truth. He needed to find some new friends.

Martin had his Drury Lane songstress in tow, and Delacre had taken up with that widow again. A few well-dressed prostitutes hovered at the edges of the group, hoping for their glasses to be filled before they wandered away. Without even making an effort, Pauline was the most refined woman in the booth. If she made any ill-informed remarks about the Corn Laws, no one would care.

All the halfway decent fellows who'd once been part of their circle had drifted away in recent years—married, come into their titles, settled down. Griff would have liked to drift away, too—without the marrying part—but it was harder to leave a circle when you were the center of it.

"When are you opening the Grange this year, Hal?" Martin asked, one arm draped about his mistress's powdered shoulders. "Ruby here fancies a holiday in the country. She'll bring friends. Quite friendly friends."

The painted blonde gave him a coy promise of a smile.

In years past, Griff had spent the colder months at Winterset Grange. The house was the first thing he'd purchased after reaching his majority. Even with six family properties, he'd felt the need for a place of his own. Other men had bachelor apartments. He was a duke; he had a bachelor estate. There, for several years after leaving university, he and his Oxford friends had taken the country house party tradition to new heights—or lows—of dissipation.

Always the generous host, Griff famously opened his door to any and all guests—especially the pretty, female variety. Days were for sleeping. Nights were for gambling, drinking, and other vices of the flesh.

The Grange had become such an institution that when Griff failed to open the house last winter, rumors of his insolvency had circulated.

He hadn't been broke, of course. Just broken.

"You *are* opening the Grange this year, aren't you?" Martin asked.

"I hadn't decided," Griff replied. "Perhaps not."

"Oh, come along, Hal. You *must*. Last winter I was forced to go home to Shropshire. A crashing bore, I tell you. The old man's after me to join the Church."

"Second sons and their problems."

Griff wasn't interested in opening his house just so Martin and Delacre and every other over-grown adolescent in England could come laze barefoot on his furniture and organize drunken billiard tournaments that lasted three days and three nights straight. It had been good fun when they were youths, but now . . . He supposed his patience and his generosity had run out.

Or been redirected.

He could see himself opening that house for one reason only—and her name was Pauline.

As soon as the idea flickered through his skull, his mind pounced on it. He knew she had her dream of opening a bookshop in Spindle Cove. But perhaps she dreamed of that simply because she couldn't conceive of more.

He could give her more.

She turned to him then, as though she could feel the force of these new, visceral intentions. Sidling her way through the crowded booth, she made her way to his side.

"Lord Delacre has asked me to dance," she whispered. "I haven't the faintest idea of the steps. If I time my stumble at *just* the right moment, I think I can take us both into the punch bowl. Will you give me a ten-pound bonus?"

He smiled despite himself. "Twenty."

He watched her as she drifted away on Del's arm, headed out to join the colorful whirl of dancers.

Oh, he couldn't marry her. He couldn't marry at all. But he could take care of her, see that she never struggled again. At the age of twenty-three, she'd worked enough for a lifetime. She shouldn't have to toil anymore. She deserved to be spooned delicacies, pampered with the softest linens, waited on by a dozen maids, and bathed in deep copper tubs.

Delacre swung her through the dance. In that blush-pink gown, her light figure was a dream. He hoped she was enjoying herself, at least a little. In a more just world, she would have been given her own coming-out ball, with dozens of admirers queuing for her hand. Then again, he could admire her enough for dozens of men. He couldn't take his eyes from her now.

The dancers turned a corner, and Griff caught a glimpse of her face.

Damn.

He recognized that expression she was wearing. He didn't like it.

Before he'd even decided on a course, his feet were in motion. He had to get to her, immediately.

Something was wrong.

Chapter Seventeen

"How long have you known the duke?" Lord Delacre led her capably through the dance. He was so elegant a dancer, she scarcely had the opportunity to misstep.

"Only this week," Pauline answered truthfully. "And you, my lord?"

"We were at Eton together. Close friends ever since." He fixed her with an unreadable gaze. "We have a pact, you know."

"A pact?"

"Yes. A pact, blood-sworn on our crossed blades. To protect one another in the face of all threats—treachery, betrayal . . ."

"Death?" Pauline finished.

"No, worse. Marriage."

She laughed. She couldn't help it. "How old were you when you swore this pact?"

"Nineteen. But it never lapses, you know. It automatically renews."

"I see." She tried to look thoughtful. "Lord

Delacre, if a duke wishes to avoid matrimony, isn't he capable of protecting himself?"

He shook his head. "You really are new in London, aren't you? A man like Halford needs a trusted friend to watch his back at all times. The *ton* is rife with fortune-hunters. And as fortune-hunting goes, his fortune is the elusive white tiger's pelt. The greatest prize to be had. There are women in this town who'd stoop to poisoned darts and mantraps just to bag him." He arched one brow and swept a playful look around the crowd.

His gaze returned to her. "You never know when they'll strike."

"So you think I'm one of those women," Pauline concluded. "A fortune-hunter like the rest. My lord, let me assure you—I have no designs on the duke. No sharpened arrows or slingshot in my reticule. I possess no qualities that could remotely tempt a man like Halford into marriage."

Where was that punch bowl anyway? She didn't feel like explaining her bargain with Griff to Delacre, but acting it out might serve the same purpose. Surely he wouldn't view her as a marital threat once he was drenched in arrack punch.

"You're aware of Halford's reputation, I hope," Delacre said. "Fling your favors at him all you like, but he won't marry you."

"What makes you think I'd 'fling my favors' at anyone?"

"I beg your pardon, Miss Simms," he said stiffly. "I didn't intend any such implication."

Liar. He'd meant exactly what he'd said. As though he could look at her—without having any knowledge of her humble, common origins—and just know she was *that* sort of girl.

What was worse, he was right, to a point. In her youth, she hadn't guarded her "favors" as closely as she should have. But Griff knew about that, and he never made her feel lesser for it.

Pauline looked about, growing desperate to end this. She wanted to get back to Griff.

Aha. There it was. A vast silver tub of punch, shaped like an open clamshell. As soon as they reached the far end of the dance floor, she'd ask Lord Delacre for some refreshment. They'd approach the bowl . . . he'd lean over to dip with the ladle . . .

And from there, just one good push would do the trick.

"Lord Delacre, your friend is in no danger from me." Mentally, she added, *You, on the other hand . . .*

"I'd like to take you at your word, Miss Simms." Delacre's eyes wandered to a spot beyond her shoulder. "If only Halford himself weren't about to prove you wrong."

"What?"

"That'll be enough." Griff appeared out of nowhere and stopped them in the middle of the dance. "I'll take it from here."

Delacre resisted. "Oh, come along, Halford. Let us get through one dance. We're having a conversation."

Griff gripped his friend's lapel, pulled him away from Pauline and lowered his voice to a growl. "I said, she's mine."

Delacre raised his hands. "Very well. She's yours."

With a little bow—and a wary look in Pauline's direction—Delacre disappeared.

As Griff took her in his arms and resumed the dance, Pauline stared at him, amazed. "Why did you cut in? I was on the cusp of brilliant disaster."

He shrugged. "I decided I didn't care to watch you dive in the punch bowl. Someone worked too hard on that gown you're wearing. And on the punch. Not to mention, there's a breeze this evening. You might catch cold."

Might catch *cold*?

"You do realize," she whispered, "that for our bargain to work, sooner or later you *will* have to let me stumble."

"Well, it won't be tonight. Tonight, I'm here for you. And I will not let you fall." He leaned close and whispered in her ear. "I could see you were upset, Pauline."

Her heart twisted. The fact that he'd been able to tell from all that distance—and wasted no time coming to her side—it warmed her deep inside. She didn't care what anyone said about his past or reputation. This was a good man.

She clutched his shoulder tight.

"It's all right." He firmed his hand against her back. "Just follow my lead."

He danced her to the side of the pavilion—the one opposite his friends' booth. Instead of rejoining the party, he steered her away from the orchestra and onto a dimly lit path. Once they left the crowds behind, he turned her to face him.

"What happened?" he asked, bracing his hands on her shoulders and searching her face. "Was it something Del said? I can easily kill him for you."

Pauline smiled weakly. "Please don't." Even though Delacre had insulted her, she knew he was trying—in his own, warped way—to be a good friend to Griff. She didn't want to be caught in the middle.

"Did someone else insult you? Are you ill?"

"No. Nothing like that."

"You're homesick, then."

"I am homesick." It wasn't a lie. "This place has me awestruck. Everywhere I turn, I think, 'Daniela would love to see this.' And from there . . ."

He drew her close. "Another landslide."

She nodded.

"It will pass. A walk will help."

He offered his arm, and she took it. Together they ambled away from the orchestra and into a darkened grove. Once again she found herself wondering how he understood her feelings so completely. Almost as if they were his own.

"May I ask you something?" she said.

"Only if it's nothing to do with cataclysmic smelting."

She smiled. "It's about my sister. You were perfect with her. Just perfect. Do you have someone like Daniela in your family?"

"No," he answered. "I have no siblings at all. Not anymore."

So he *had* lost someone. She squeezed his arm. "Griff. I'm so sorry. I didn't know."

"It's not like you're thinking. I mean, it is, but it isn't. My mother bore four children, but I'm the only one who lived longer than a week. I have no clear memories of my brothers and sister." He moved a low-hanging branch out of Pauline's way, and she ducked under it. "I found Daniela charming. You're lucky to have her."

"I am. I didn't always know it. But I am."

Pauline wasn't a saint, and neither was Daniela. Like any sisters, they had their episodes of bickering and resentment. And there'd been that shameful day in their girlhood when they traveled to market with Father. Pauline, perhaps eight years old, had run off to make new friends, steal a bit of joy from someone else's life. And when Daniela caught up with their merry group, Pauline had been embarrassed.

"Is that dummy your sister?" a boy had sneered.

"Lud, no," she'd replied. "Never saw her before in my life. Make her go away."

Even now she could still see her sister's horror-stricken face. The guilt had crushed her like a millstone. She'd known, in that moment, she'd denied the only person who loved her most in the world. And for what? To impress a few children at market? She had dashed after Daniela, begging forgiveness. They'd clasped each other tight and cried and cried. It was a painful memory, but one she didn't dare forget.

She would never let anyone make her feel ashamed. And she would never betray her sister again.

"I am lucky to have her," she repeated. "And no one else understands that. No one."

"Perhaps they have siblings to spare. We aren't all so fortunate."

With that, he fell quiet.

Pauline stared at him, tracing his handsome features in the lamp-lit darkness. He was a complex man, with a rich family legacy and responsibilities she couldn't begin to fathom. Who was she—a serving girl, from Sussex—to tell him anything?

But she had to try. There was no one else who could.

She turned to him, placing a hand on his sleeve. "Griff . . ."

"Don't." At the new tone in her voice, his eyes narrowed. He backed away, leaning against a nearby tree. "Don't, Simms. Don't start this."

"Don't start what? I merely said your name."

"But in that *tone*. I know that tone. You're embarking on some vain attempt to fix me, mend the brokenness of my life . . . Whatever fool womanly notion you're entertaining, abandon it now. You'll only embarrass yourself."

Good heavens. The man was so transparent, it was like she could look at his waistcoat and see straight through to the tree trunk he leaned against.

If he thought a few boorish words could shake her off, after the way he'd clutched her to him last night . . . the sweet words he'd whispered . . .

"You are being ridiculous," she said calmly. "So ridiculous, I can't even be angry with you, so don't think you're pushing me away. Griff, I know you're hurting somehow. I know it. I could feel it, even that first day, and—"

He turned his gaze. "I'm not having this discussion."

"Fine. Deny it. I don't care. I don't know if that's male pride or aristocratic phlegm. But whatever quality it is, it's not one I possess. You can pretend you're not hurting. I can't pretend not to care."

She steeled her courage to continue. "I'm not asking to be in your confidence. I can understand why you wouldn't share your problems with a girl like me, but . . . perhaps you shouldn't dismiss the idea of marriage entirely. I hate to think of you alone."

"Who says I'm alone?" he scoffed. "I don't lack for companionship if I want it."

"Yes, yes. You're a great rake and libertine—or so I hear. But I haven't seen any evidence of it. From my observation, you're just an impulsively generous, occasionally decent man who roams the house alone at night and tinkers with old clocks."

His arm shot out and he pulled her tightly to his chest. "Don't mistake me for a decent man."

In one swift move he had their positions reversed. His broad chest pressed her against the tree. She struggled just a little, and the gauzy fabric of her dress snagged and caught on the bark.

She would not let him see her trembling.

"You declined to ravage me last night," she said. "Surely you don't expect me to fear it now."

"Not at all." He leaned forward, until they were nose-to-nose. "I expect you'll enjoy it."

He took her mouth in a deep, demanding kiss. His tongue moved against hers, again and again, and he angled his head to slide deeper still. Exploring her, possessing her. Relentless.

And it didn't stop there. His hand slid to her bodice, claiming her breast.

Oh, sweet heaven.

He cupped the batting-enhanced mound capably, his fingers lifting and stroking. His thumb skimmed back and forth, searching for her nipple.

The padding thwarted him. He gave up with a curse and tugged at her off-the-shoulder sleeve, working her neckline downward.

She sucked in her breath. He couldn't mean to do this *here*.

Or perhaps he could.

With a firm, unapologetic motion, he gathered what there was to gather and lifted, hiking her breast above the border of her corset and exposing it to the cool night air. It was dark, but she felt thrust into a spotlight, vulnerable and quivering.

He kissed her again, exploring her mouth with possessive sweeps of his tongue. As their tongues sparred, he rolled her nipple with his thumb. His masterful caresses destroyed all will, all reason. Somehow, between the delicious sparks and shivers of bliss, one simple, straightforward goal began to coalesce.

This time she wanted to touch him, too.

She slid her gloved hands inside his coat, surveying the ridged, stony muscles of his torso and chest. Even through his waistcoat the power in his body was palpable.

She yanked his shirt free of his waistband and thrust her hands beneath. He growled in encouragement as she ran her flattened palms over the hard cobblestones of his abdominal muscles and traced the light furrow of hair bisecting them. Then she swept her touch upward, grazing over his nipple and centering on the fierce thump of his heart.

Boom.

Something exploded. She felt the concussion of it in her chest, and thought it might have been her heart bursting. Then flashes of sparks from the heavens lit the space between them.

She laughed at herself as the realization dawned. Of course. "Fireworks."

With one last brush of his lips against hers, he lifted his head. She held her breath, expecting him to speak. But he didn't say a word. He just stared down at her, the same way he had that first day in Spindle Cove—as though she were the most wonderful, terrible, puzzling, perfect thing he'd ever beheld.

No, no. This was all too much.

She held his heartbeat in her hand. He treasured her small, insignificant breast with his. And overhead, great bloody fireworks exploded with trails of silver and gold.

The power in the moment was soul-rattling. Without the shield of a kiss, she couldn't hide her own feelings. There was nowhere she could look but straight into his dark eyes.

Her own pulse was an incoherent flutter, but there was no hesitance in the rhythm beneath her palm. No stutter, no doubt. Just a strong, insistent beat of wanting.

Pauline, she could almost imagine it to say. *Pauline, Pauline, Pauline.*

That couldn't be right. It had to be saying something else.

Probably, *You fool, you fool, you fool.*

Somewhere nearby, love was an ominous, gaping hole in the earth, widening every moment. Unless she were very careful, she'd be sure to fall straight in.

"Griff," she whispered. "You need someone. Everyone needs someone."

With an impatient motion, he hiked her bodice, covering her breast. Then he stepped away.

"You don't understand this." His words were dark and fierce. "Don't tell me I need someone. My whole life has been an endless string of someones. Another 'someone' is exactly what I don't need. I most especially do not want to stand in a room of pitiful, lackluster young women and hear, 'It's your duty to marry, Halford. Just choose *someone*.'"

She reeled away from him, stung. "Oh. I see."

He cursed. "That's not what I—"

"No, you're right." She edged away in small, hurried steps. "Choosing a lackluster girl from a crowded room. What a nightmare. No good could ever come of a scene like *that*."

"Pauline, wait."

She turned and ran, leaving him in the darkened grove and emerging into an open square where a crowd had gathered to watch the fireworks. She stopped in her tracks, working for breath. All around her, people were laughing and cheering and gasping with joy.

An unseen man bumped into her, hard. The old Pauline would've elbowed him back, but she didn't have the heart for it right now. Instead, she turned to face him, laying her hand to her throat in apology.

Oh, God. Oh no.

He was gone. It was gone.

Griff made his way through the grove, searching for her.

At last he caught sight of her gown on the far

side of the crowded green. That throbbing blur of pink, illuminated by gold pulses from above. He felt as though he were watching his own heart, separated from his body.

Then a man emerged from the shadows—and his heart stumbled.

"Pauline!" he shouted.

She didn't hear him—or didn't turn, if she had. Instead, she paused for a moment. Then she rucked up her skirts and tore away, darting into the night.

She was chasing someone. He heard her call, "Stop! Stop, you bloody thief!"

Thief?

Griff ran after her, but he still had the crowd to navigate, and she had a formidable lead. He was amazed at how fast she could run in all those skirts. She was giving the villain—whoever he was—quite a chase through colonnades and across lamplit groves.

And as she ran, profanity unfurled behind her like a brightly colored banner. Whatever gains she'd made in elocution this week all disappeared.

"Bastard!" she shouted, jostling past a bemused gentleman Griff recognized as an Austrian ambassador. "Stop, you black-'earted devil!"

Well, if she'd wanted a disastrous public spectacle—she had it. No punch bowl necessary.

"I'll 'ave your bollocks, you filthy whoreson!"

Griff made an apologetic *No, no, not you* grimace in the direction of the royal booth, not daring to slow down long enough to explain. He would have laughed if he weren't so breathless—and so worried for Pauline.

They reached the borders of Vauxhall and plunged out into the surrounding neighborhood—a jumble of factories and shipping merchants' homes and tenements. None of the streets were lit. God only knew what dangers lurked in the alleyways.

Still, she charged on.

What was she thinking? Whatever the brigand had taken, it wasn't worth risking her life.

She was losing ground on the thief, but Griff was gaining on her.

"Pauline!" he shouted, digging deep for breath. "Let him go!"

"I can't!"

She turned a corner in pursuit and Griff lost sight of her for a few bleak, endless seconds. He kicked up his pace, just praying that she'd still be whole and unharmed—so he could catch her and shake her silly.

Just as he neared the same corner, a short, piercing scream rent the air.

Holy God. Please.

He rounded the corner, and there she was— crumpled to the ground in the middle of the lane.

"Pauline. Pauline, are you hurt?"

"Don't stop for me," she cried. "Run after him."

"He's gone." Griff didn't even bother to look. "He's gone. And even if I could catch him, there's no way in hell I'd abandon you here."

People were already filing out from the nearby dwellings, having a good look at the fine lady and gent in the street. Griff made his posture strong and turned a wary glance in all directions, letting any ruffians know that they'd better not take their chances.

"What's happened?" he murmured, crouching down before Pauline. "Did he hurt you? Strike you with something?" He began searching for splashes of blood. A horrid thought struck him. "He didn't have a pistol or a blade?"

"No," she sobbed.

He breathed again. Thank God.

"Nothing of the sort. It's just these dratted shoes. I caught my heel between the paving stones and my ankle turned."

She lifted her skirt, and he could see her stockinged ankle, caught at an angle that made him wince.

He freed her foot first, then the shoe. With gentle fingers, he explored her swelling ankle. She choked back a sob of distress.

"Is it so very painful? Perhaps it's broken."

She shook her head. "It's not broken. And the pain isn't so bad. It's just . . ."

"What?" he said darkly. "What did the villain do to you?"

"Oh, God. You'll despise me."

"Never."

She slumped against him, as if all the fight and fire had gone out of her. "Griff, he took the necklace. Your mother's amethysts. They were worth thousands. And now they're gone."

Chapter Eighteen

That was it, then. Pauline gave up. She surrendered to his care, not knowing what else there was to do. She'd always considered herself a resilient person, but tonight she was beat.

London one, Pauline nothing.

Less than nothing. Even considering the thousand pounds in wages Griff had promised her, she was now several thousand in his debt. The duchess would never forgive her. How would she ever pay them back?

The duke was still crouched at her side.

"Put your arms about my neck," he directed.

She obeyed, halfheartedly lacing her wrists about his shoulders.

"Hold on tightly," he admonished, muttering a curse. "You're a farmer's daughter and serving girl. I know you can do better than that."

She willed her muscles to flex. He was right, she had a sturdy frame—which meant she wasn't precisely a feather's weight. She owed it to him to do her part.

He lifted her with a low grunt of exertion, shifting his arms until her weight settled against his solid chest.

"The shoe," she said feebly.

"Damn the shoe."

She supposed he was right. What difference did a shoe make, when she'd just lost a necklace worth thousands of pounds?

He carried her to the end of the street, down a different way than they'd come in pursuit. She thought about pointing out the discrepancy, but decided he knew where he was going. His face, when she now and then glimpsed it in the weak light thrown from a window, was a mask of stern determination.

"I'm so sorry," she said.

He gave a terse, dismissive shake of his head. "Don't."

He didn't speak to her further on the way home. Not in the boat that ferried them back across the Thames. Not in the carriage back to Mayfair.

When they arrived at Halford House, she heard him giving quiet yet firm orders to the house staff. She found herself whisked into the Rose Salon and propped up on the largest available divan.

"I'm calling for a doctor," Griff said.

"Really, I don't need it," she protested.

He left the room. And that was the end of that argument.

So Pauline sat in the Rose Salon while the doctor poked and prodded and looked over her.

The swelling seemed to be improving already. No lasting harm done. Not to her ankle, anyway. Other parts of her might never recover.

As the doctor was on his way out, Griff appeared in the doorway to confer with him. He'd removed his coat, rolling his shirtsleeves to the wrist.

Pauline rose from the chair and hobbled to meet him in the center of the carpet. "Well," she said. "I finally proved a catastrophe. I must have appeared to be a foul-mouthed harpy, swooping across those manicured greens."

He didn't seem to see the humor in her statement. "Come. I'll help you upstairs."

She waved off his help. "It's not a bad sprain. The doctor said it will quickly mend."

He insisted on placing an arm about her waist, guiding her toward the stairs. She didn't know how to refuse. The juxtaposition of his glowering expression and his solicitous attentions made everything seem worse.

She took the first stair with her good foot. "You're angry with me."

"I am angry," he said. "I cannot deny it. But I am struggling not to direct my anger at you."

She hobbled up another stair.

"I'm so sorry. I'll pay it back somehow. Beginning with the thousand pounds, of course. As for the rest of it . . ." She stopped and looked up at him. "I don't know how. But I swear to you, I will make this right."

He looked down at her with an expression of absolute bemusement. "What on earth can you mean?"

"The necklace. I'll pay for it somehow." She clutched the banister and took another step.

He didn't move with her.

"This is absurd," he muttered.

Ducking, he wrapped one arm under her thighs and lifted her straight off her feet—into his arms. He carried her up the rest of her steps, and at the top of the staircase, he didn't continue up another flight to her bedchamber.

He turned toward his private suite.

Balancing her weight in one arm, he opened the latch, carried her through the entry, and kicked the door shut behind him. After toting her through a sitting room, he dropped her onto a bed.

His bed.

It was an enormous bed—a four-poster of solid mahogany, with velvet hangings on all sides.

She tried to struggle up on her elbows, but her heavy gown worked against her. Before she could make any progress, he had her caged. He knelt over her, straddling her thighs.

Then he framed her face in his strong hands, forbidding her to look anywhere but at him. His eyes were wild and fierce. Her heartbeat slammed against his.

"I am angry, Pauline. I have immense rage for that brigand who dared to touch you. I am furious that you've been hurt. And I'm angry with you, yes. For chasing after him, putting yourself at such risk. Do you know what kind of people lurk in those paths and alleyways?"

"I didn't know what else to do. He took your mother's—"

"Necklace. What of it? She has dozens."

"But this is a valuable one. I know she prizes it. That's why she wanted me to wear it tonight, so . . ."

So you could see me, and look at me as a true lady. So you'd fall in love with me and want me to be your bride. What a laugh.

"You believe I'd value a strand of jewels above your life? I know we've had our differences, Simms, but that's low. You truly think so little of me?"

"I . . . No. I think a great deal of you."

"I happen to think a great deal of you, too."

Kind words, but he spoke them so viciously.

"Tomorrow," he said, "I can buy my mother another necklace. A better one. A half dozen of them if she likes. Jewels can be replaced."

"So can serving girls."

"Don't. Don't play that game." His brow pressed to hers. "When I heard you cry out . . . it was like a saber to the gut. I wanted to die."

I wanted to die.

The words pushed a wave of doubt through her. He couldn't mean that. Just exaggeration, surely.

"I could have found you broken or bleeding, or—" His voice broke. "Or worse. Don't tell me I care about polished rocks on a chain. I want to believe you know me better than that."

"I do."

"And yet you believe I'd be so upset about a necklace that I'd send you away?"

She gestured uselessly. "You'd just said you didn't want me at all."

"I said no such thing. You ran off before I could finish." He ran a hand down her body. "I said I didn't need 'someone.' Because you're not just someone to me. You're remarkable and stubborn and lovely and too damn brave for your own good." His hand fisted in the fabric of her gown.

"You're you. I want you. From the moment you stumbled through that tavern door, I wanted you."

She pressed a hand to her mouth, stifling her emotion.

"Don't." He pulled her hand from her mouth. "Don't hide. Don't ever run from me again."

He kissed her hungrily, desperately, and she opened herself to his sensual invasion, welcoming his tongue with her own and aching to hold him tight.

With labored breaths of effort, he pulled away. His eyes burned into hers. "If I asked you to stay with me . . ."

"I couldn't." Stunned, she went still in his arms. "You know I couldn't. I must go home to Daniela. I promised her, and you gave us your word."

"If I offered you a home. A house in the country, with everything you and your sister could ever need."

"I couldn't be a kept mistress. Not even yours. I'd lose respect for myself, and for you."

His gaze clouded. "I can't marry you."

"I know." Sadness pressed down on her heart. "There's no way this can last beyond week's end."

He cupped her face with one hand and stroked his thumb over her cheek. "Well, know this. I am damned well going to make love to you tonight."

Excitement jolted through her.

Yes.

"Yes, Griff. Please."

He gathered her skirts, tugging them upward. His fingers curved around her thigh, stroking up and down. "Are you sure you're well enough? You're not too bruised or hurting under all this silk?"

His concern for her well-being touched her heart. "I promise. I'm fine."

"I'll judge for myself." He turned her on her belly and began to tug at her hooks and laces. "Off with these things. I've been wild to see you naked again."

Again? "When did you see me naked before?"

"That first night in the library."

"But . . . I was wearing my shift the whole time."

"I know." He pulled the gown down over her hips, then set about untying her petticoats. "But your shift was gloriously thin. When you stepped in front of the lamp, the light shone right through it. I could see everything."

"Everything?"

"Everything."

Pauline didn't know how to take that. She merely went limp as he unlaced her corset and flung it aside. Then, pulling her to a half-sitting position, he lifted the chemise up and over her head. She flopped back on the bed linens, completely nude except for her stockings.

He sat up and began to remove his own clothing. Waistcoat, cravat, shirt. She watched him as he stripped off layer after layer of elegance, down to the man beneath it all.

"Cor," she breathed.

He was perfect. Broad in the shoulders, lean at the waist. Muscled everywhere. A sprinkling of dark hair on his chest.

He turned away, sitting on the edge of the bed to remove his boots and unbutton his breeches, giving her ample time to admire the sculpted planes of his bared back.

"There," he said, tossing the last bit of clothing aside.

He stretched out beside her, and she suddenly felt abashed. He was so perfect, everywhere. The ideal form of a man. And she wasn't the ideal form of woman. Not at all.

For the first time, she felt truly unequal to him.

His gaze swept her body first, but his caress soon followed suit. He cupped her breast in his hand. She began to hope, foolishly, that he might say he liked what he saw. She didn't need to hear "Beautiful" or "Lovely" or "Perfect." Something like his terse "Good" earlier that evening would do.

When his thumb found her hardened nipple, he did something much better. He gave a low growl of satisfaction, deep in his throat. The sound was so primal and unambiguous. So utterly male. It called to everything feminine in her, and the response that welled from deep inside was a faint, sighing moan of relief.

"Just as arousing as I remember," he muttered. "More. You wouldn't believe how hard you made me that first night. Every night since."

A self-conscious laugh escaped her. "I'm built like a fourteen-year-old boy."

"Bollocks. I've been a fourteen-year-old boy. I tell you, my breasts were nowhere near this enticing." He traced her areola, then the curve beneath her breast.

She writhed, undone by the intense sensations. "So you're one of those men who actually likes his women small-breasted?"

Her well-endowed friends had always consoled her with the promise that such men existed, but she'd yet to meet with one in the flesh. She'd grown to think of them as mythical beasts, in the same class as pixies and dragons.

"I never understood that way of thinking." As he spoke, he kissed her breasts and swept bold touches over her belly and down her thighs. "It's like those old men who come to the club for dinner every night and always take the same meal, sitting at the same table. What good is life if a man can't appreciate variety?" He drew one nipple into his mouth, circling the taut peak with his tongue.

A sigh of pleasure eased from her throat. Beyond that, she didn't know how to respond. She supposed a duke would have ample access to "variety," if he wished it. After she returned to Spindle Cove, perhaps he'd find a buxom, fair-haired beauty for contrast.

As if he could sense her unease, his demeanor changed. "You're an intensely attractive woman. You do know that, don't you?" To her silence, he replied, "You'd believe me if you could see yourself."

"I *have* seen myself. That's the snag, you see."

He shook his head. "No, no. Not in a mirror. I know how mirrors work. They're all in league with the cosmetics trade. They tell a woman lies. Drawing her gaze from one imagined flaw to another, until all she sees is a constellation of imperfections. If you could get outside yourself, borrow my eyes for just an instant . . . There's only beauty." He pressed his hand to his heart. "I swear it on the seven Dukes of Halford before me."

Several moments passed before she could speak.

"Well. I've seen their portraits. I'll concede that I'm prettier than they were."

He chuckled. "Thank God for that."

He wedged his hips between her thighs, spreading her wide. The hard curve of his erection pulsed hot and urgent against her core.

"Let it be now," he said, burying his face in her neck. "Next time, I'll go slowly. Kiss you everywhere, touch you for hours. But I can't be patient any longer. I need . . . God, I need you. I need you."

"Yes." She kissed him, tilting her hips in invitation. She needed him, too. So desperately.

He positioned himself at her entrance and thrust.

When their bodies joined, she cried out—but not in pain. Despite the hurried foreplay, she was ready for him. She'd been ready for days, and waiting on this sensation for years. The size and heat of him were formidable, but she welcomed both feelings. The fullness. The searing pleasure.

At last, she was with Griff. Beneath him, around him, holding him, kissing him, stroking his hair and shoulders.

At last, this was how a man made love—not a fumbling youth, but a proper man. One who understood not only what he wanted, but what she wanted as well. He loved her in a smooth, powerful rhythm, delving a little deeper with every stroke. Just when she thought there couldn't be more of him to take, he proved her wrong.

At last, his pelvis met hers. He was fully buried inside her. She was stretched to her limits. The tension burned like the sweetest fire.

He lowered his body to hers, and her breasts flattened beneath his chest. Their heartbeats sparred, punching back and forth like pugilists. He began a slow, steady roll of his hips. His firmness slid in and out of her in cautious increments, teasing whorls of pleasure from her center and spreading bliss throughout her body.

He stared into her eyes, looking strangely bewildered. "This is . . . This is good, Simms. I'm no stranger to pleasure, but this is . . . *good*."

"You did say it's been a long time for you."

He nodded. "Months and months. And you?"

"Oh, ages. Years."

He paused mid-stroke. "I suppose that must be it."

He bent to kiss her, moaning against her lips as he eased forward. She clutched at his shoulders and back, trying to urge him faster. Deeper. Wilder. She felt sure he wasn't the sort of man to make sweet, careful love.

"Griff," she pleaded.

He paused. "I don't want to hurt you. I'm trying to be gentle."

She pushed against him just enough that she could meet his gaze. "Just be you. I want you."

Something feral sparked in his eyes. He rose up on his arms and dug his knees into the mattress, thrusting hard.

"Yes," she gasped, thrilled by his strength. "Again. More."

He gave her again. He gave her more. He gave her stroke after stroke of pounding bliss, and she was utterly laid waste.

This was raw, primal sensuality, but the emotions were what made her ache. He could be teasing and nonchalant with words. But each pummeling thrust was a confession of just how much he desired her, how desperately he wanted this—with every muscle in his body, every pulse of his blood.

Oh, and the intensity in his dark, captivating eyes . . . it turned her inside out. She was exposed, vulnerable in the face of such bald determination. He would hold nothing back in pursuit of this pleasure. He would give her everything he had.

She lifted her arms overhead and braced her hands against the headboard, pushing back at him with everything *she* had.

"That's right," he grunted, never breaking pace. "Move with me."

Her body arced off the bed as she strained to meet his thrusts. Their joining verged on painful, but she was beyond any such cares. She couldn't take him deep enough, couldn't stretch tautly enough around the smooth, hard curve of his cock.

The contrasts were exquisite. The two of them rutting like beasts amid all the embroidered pillows and clouds of discarded petticoats. The helplessness of her splayed posture beneath him only added to the surge of sensual power she felt. When she wrapped her stockinged leg over his hips, sliding the silk across his bare thigh, he gave a fierce, primitive growl.

He was so animal and so elegant . . . and so powerfully arousing, she couldn't possibly last.

With every stroke, his body rubbed hers in just the right place. Her head rolled back and her eyes squeezed shut. She felt the pleasure building, drawing tight all through her body. Release was so close.

He groaned deep in his chest, and the sound sent worry shooting through her. Perhaps release was close for him, too.

They hadn't discussed what would happen at the end. The anxiety was enough to drag her back from the edge.

"Let go," he said.

She opened her eyes. He was looking down at her, his face a mask of resolve. His rhythm never faltered for an instant.

"I have you. Just let go."

And that was when she realized . . . he wouldn't stop until she reached her peak. He just wouldn't. He would stroke on. And on. And on for hours, if she needed it. Plowing his hardness into her over and over again, just as many times as it took to reduce her to quaking, shuddering bliss.

This man would not be denied.

"I have you." His whispered words were hoarse. "I have you now."

He covered her hands with his, pinning them to the bed. And she let go. Her arms went limp and her hips thrashed beneath his. Little sobs began to escape her as each thrust drove home.

Through it all, she stared into his eyes, unable to look away. Those dark eyes were her anchor.

"Come. For the love of God. Come, Pauline."

Hearing her name from his lips . . . it undid her. Because it let her know this was for her. All this heroic, erotic effort was for her.

Her crisis broke, rocking her with waves of keenest pleasure. The climax went on and on—battering her, body and soul, with fierce, unparalleled joy.

He slid back on his haunches and took her by the waist, lifting her body with those powerful arms.

"Griff . . ." she whispered, hoping she wouldn't need to say more.

"I know." He grimaced with pleasure. With a growl and a desperate jerk of his hips, he withdrew and spent himself somewhere in all those folds of sheets and petticoats.

Afterward, he collapsed beside her on the bed, perspiring and working for breath. They lay that way for several minutes, staring wordlessly up at the bed's canopy and struggling for air.

What now? she wondered. Perhaps now that his desire was slaked, he would feel regret. Perhaps whatever emotions he'd imagined he had for her were obliterated by the force of his climax.

The longer they lay there, side by side but not embracing, the more anxious she became.

She'd known this couldn't last beyond the week. But was it already over?

Finally, with a soft groan, he put an arm about her. "Come here." He rolled her close and pressed a tender kiss to the crown of her head.

She couldn't help it. She wept with relief.

He pulled her tight, tucking her head to his chest and guarding her with his body. He didn't try to stop her weeping, didn't chide her for nonsensical tears. He just allowed her to have her feelings, and he held her all the while. As though he understood that all other men had failed her in this one simple way, and he was determined to make it right.

After some time, she laid her head on his chest.

"I'd only been with one other man before you. Errol Bright, the shopkeeper's oldest son. He said he loved me. He said a lot of things, and made a great many promises he never saw through." Her face pinched in embarrassment. "I'm just telling you this because I don't want you to think I'm expecting more. I don't want promises from you, Griff. But I hope you understand that I don't do this often, or with just any man. Even if it's only this once, it means something to me."

Her head rose and fell as he took a slow, deep breath. His hand found hers and clasped it. "Pauline? Please believe I say this in all sincerity. I am honored."

Her breath rushed out in a relieved sigh. She didn't know what she'd been hoping to hear—but what he'd said was even better. There was a ring of newness in those words: *I am honored.* Somehow, she doubted he'd spoken them to a woman before. Not in bed, at least.

She turned in his embrace, skimming a possessive touch over his chest. He groaned in encouragement. She loved that she could be free to touch him now, explore him everywhere.

Her fingers found the red, not-quite-healed slash on his biceps, and she traced it. "Are you in pain?"

"No, not . . . not there."

His words had the deep resonance of a confession. She treasured those two syllables of raw honesty.

"Is it this?" she asked, touching the small bruise on his cheek from where she'd punched him yesterday.

"No."

"Somewhere else, then." She dropped her hand to his bare chest, covering his thudding heart. "Somewhere deep inside. You're hurting."

He nodded. "Like the devil."

Her curiosity was intense, but she resisted the urge to press him for explanations or details. He'd trusted her with this much. Perhaps he would trust her with more, in time.

"Can I kiss it better?" She gave him a playful smile.

"I don't think so." He thoughtfully brushed a lock of hair from her face. The glint in his eyes went from wounded to wicked. "But I could be persuaded to lie very still while you exhaust yourself in the attempt."

Chapter Nineteen

In another hour's time they'd exhausted each other.

Griff stroked her hair, forcing himself to relax and surrender to the simple pleasure of being kissed. Her lips touched his chest, his shoulders, his neck, his belly. She was as thorough as she was sweet, covering every inch of him with tender brushes of her lips. She didn't manage to heal all his deepest, darkest wounds with her attentions—but she made his mind go blank, which was almost as good.

And when her tongue traced a path from his navel downward, he reached a breaking point.

"I need you again." He took her by the waist and lifted her above him, trapping his hard, aching cock at the apex of her cleft. "Take it in your hand. Guide me in."

If she felt any trepidation at his bold request, she didn't show it.

A rosy flush bloomed over her chest as she

reached between them. She held him in place as he moved her slowly down, lowering her heat to envelop his full length.

She fit him like a well-made glove, hugging him tight as he guided her up and down, teaching her how to ride him.

Clever girl that she was, she caught the spirit and rhythm of it soon enough. Her palms braced flat against his chest, pinning him to the bed. Her thighs flexed as she dragged herself up and down. Those pert, delicious breasts bounced and swayed. If he'd ever beheld a more erotic view, he couldn't recall it.

"Simms."

She moaned, lost in pleasure.

"Simms," he said again.

Her eyes opened, drowsy and heavy-lidded as she looked down at him.

"How long has it been since you last made love?"

She bit her lip. "Twenty minutes?"

"Right. Same for me. Give or take thirty seconds."

Laughing, she braced her hands on his chest. "Why do you ask?"

"Because the first time was shockingly good." He guided her up and down again. "But this . . . this is extraordinary. Even better. I'm trying to understand. It can't merely be the long drought, can it?"

"Do you always talk this much while making love?"

He shook his head. "No. That's different, too. Everything is different with you."

Tighter, sleeker, hotter, wetter, sweeter. Not

dreamlike or perfect, just more real. And so damn good, he feared hurting them both in that mad, frantic race to the end.

He struggled to a sitting position. It wasn't enough to watch. He wanted to feel her breasts' softness and heat caressing his bare chest. Cushioning the mad beat of his heart.

He wanted to kiss her as he made love to her.

He brought her close, guiding her legs over his hips and locking her ankles at the small of his back.

With one arm wrapped tight about her waist, he guided her in a brisk rhythm. He worked the other hand between them and pressed his thumb to her pearl, working the nub in small, tight circles until she seized and shuddered in his arms.

And he didn't stop. There would be no laziness with her, no half measures. This woman was going to get his best. He kept up the same attentions, kissing her neck and murmuring words of praise against her ear until she reached another, more devastating peak.

"Oh," she whimpered in the aftermath, clinging to his neck. "Oh, Griff. Oh, God."

Her words made him *feel* like a god. Or at least a demigod. A pagan, rutting, immortal being of pleasure.

He would have tried to bring her to a third crisis, but the clasping heat of her sex had pulled him too close to the edge. He lifted her off his cock, and she reached between them to encircle his erection with her small, delicate hand.

"Like this," he said, demonstrating.

She followed his lead. "This?"

"Ah. Yes."

Her grip was gentle, but strong. Her thumb rubbed perfectly along the sensitive underside of his shaft, and with each tug, his crown grazed the silky slope of her belly. He threw his head back in surrender, clutching at the twisted sheets. Within moments she had him gasping, growling—and spilling over her fingers in hot, forceful jets.

She smiled, looking very pleased with herself.

He was pleased with her, too. So damned pleased, there seemed no room for any other emotion in his heart. In his life.

And it couldn't last. It couldn't last.

God, he didn't know how he'd ever let her go.

So he kissed her instead, wrapping his arms about her torso to haul her close. Using their closeness to conceal his weakness.

After lazy, lovely minutes of deep, languid kissing, she sighed against his lips. "I should leave."

"No." He gripped her tight. "No, no, no. Not yet."

"I can't risk falling asleep. You know I must go to my room. We can't be found here together. The servants . . ."

He shook his head. "The servants are servants. Who cares what they think?"

She pulled back and blinked at him.

He winced. "I beg you. Pretend I didn't say that. Or at least pretend you didn't hear it."

"Never mind." Moving off his lap, she reached for her discarded chemise. After untangling the shift, she slipped it over her head and pushed her arms through the cap sleeves. "I don't want to quarrel."

"Well, that's a new development." He tugged at his ear.

"I just don't want to waste what we have."

"What is it we have?"

She held his gaze. "A few days," she said quietly. "And a few more nights together. That's assuming we're not discovered tonight."

He would have liked to argue the point, but in the end he couldn't. "I'll see you back to your bedchamber."

"No, stay. Rest." She pushed him back against the bed with a hand to his shoulder and a firm kiss to his brow. "I won't get lost in the corridors this time."

She gathered her discarded gown and stockings into a bundle, then made her way toward the side door—the one that opened onto his dressing room.

"Are these rooms all connected?" she asked. "If I slip from one to the next, I won't have to travel so much of the corridor. I'll be much less likely to be seen."

He nodded, suddenly drowsy. She'd sapped him of everything. "Yes, they're connected."

She plucked a candlestick from the night table, then headed through the dressing room.

He lay back, listening. He heard her opening the door that led from the dressing room to his personal sitting room. From there, she could slip out into the corridor or cross into—

Oh, Christ.

"Wait." He launched from the bed, stumbling into his trousers in pursuit. As he dashed through the dressing room, he snagged a fresh shirt from a hook. "Wait, Pauline. Don't—"

Too late.

"I didn't mean to," she said, standing in the center of the room.

The room.

"I'm sorry. I truly didn't mean to invade your ..." She swallowed hard. " . . . your privacy."

He rubbed his neck with one hand. No getting around it now. He'd have to face this at last. He was seized by the terrible lightness of inevitability. The sense of just having jumped off a cliff.

"Did you paint all these?" she asked, holding the candlestick aloft. "They're, uh . . . they're lovely."

"No, I didn't paint them."

"Oh. Good. I mean, not that there's something wrong with a grown man painting a room with rainbows and ponies. They are quite nice rainbows and ponies."

"Do you truly think so?" He crossed his arms and leaned against the wall.

"Oh. Yes. How could I not? They're . . . why, on this wall they're frolicking, aren't they? Just look at them, frolicking and—" She swallowed hard. "—prancing."

Good Lord. She was utterly flummoxed, trying to find some way not to give offense. For no particular reason, she was valiantly striving to spare his feelings. Making a hash of it, but the thought was sweet.

"I so admire the way this one's mane is rippling in the breeze. Quite majestic." Her head tilted to the side. "In the meadow, are those buttercups?"

He couldn't hold back any longer. He laughed. It felt good to laugh in this room. It was a place he'd planned to fill with smiles and laughter, but God had taken all his careful plans and torn them to shreds.

"The ponies are ridiculous," he admitted. "The artist who painted them specialized in portraits of Arabian racehorses. His patron owed me a gambling debt, so I engaged his services for this room. He got rather carried away."

"And what do you do in here?" she asked.

"Not much of anything. It was never finished, as you see." He waved toward the blank southern wall. "The decor wasn't intended to please me. It was meant to appeal to feminine tastes."

Her expression battened. "Oh. I see. So you planned to move a woman into your house. Into your suite. A woman who likes rainbows and ponies."

He rather liked the obvious envy in her tone, and he might have teased it out a bit longer—had the truth been any different.

"Not a woman, Pauline. A little girl." A knot formed in his throat, and he cleared it with an impatient cough. "My little girl."

Pauline watched him closely for any signs of teasing. She found none.

"You have a daughter?" she asked.

"No. Yes."

"Which is it?"

"I . . . *had* a daughter. She died in infancy."

Her breath left her. She'd known something was weighing on him, but she'd never imagined this. He'd lost a child? The other day at the Foundling Hospital—of course the atmosphere had rattled him. It wasn't any wonder he'd wanted to leave. And then to have that baby thrust in his arms . . .

The poor man. How the landslide must have flattened him. She'd been so insensitive without even realizing.

"Oh, Griff. I'm sorry. So, so sorry."

He shrugged. "Such things happen."

"Perhaps. But that doesn't make them any less sad."

She wanted to go to him. But when she took a step in his direction, he began to pace the room, evasive.

"Anyway, that's why the room was never completed." He walked about the perimeter of the chamber, stopping at the window. "Never got around to installing the nursery grate. There wasn't time."

"Your mother has no idea?"

He shook his head. "She was in the country at the time. I've kept this chamber locked ever since . . . Well, ever since it became unnecessary."

"You should tell her the truth. She's noticed there's something going on in here. She thinks you're sacrificing kittens, or living out perverse fantasies."

He chuckled. "No wonder you looked so shocked at the paintings. I can't imagine what you must have thought."

"I don't really care to admit to it." She swept another glance around the room. "So your little girl's mother was . . ."

"My mistress," he confirmed. "Former mistress."

Former mistress. Try as she might, Pauline

couldn't bring herself to express condolences on that part of things. "Did you love her?"

"No, no. It was purely physical." He pushed a hand through his hair. "She was an opera singer, and we . . . It's disgraceful, I know. But it's far too easy for men of my station to get away with such arrangements. It's just the done thing."

"You don't have to make excuses, Griff," she said. "Not to me."

"If I had any excuses, I would owe them to you first and foremost. But I don't. We weren't close. I saw her less and less, and I was on the verge of breaking it off entirely. Then she told me she'd conceived."

"Were you happy to hear it?"

"I was furious. I've always been so careful, and she'd assured me she was careful, too." He paced the room again. "But I accepted my responsibility. I set her up in a cottage a short ride into the country, where she could wait out her confinement. I arranged for a maid and a midwife, set aside funds to support the child. Because that's what men of my station do, when they impregnate their mistresses."

"It's the done thing," she supplied.

He nodded. "I visited her in the new cottage, to see that she was settled and to make my final assurances of support. And just as I was about to leave, she grabbed my hand . . ." He regarded the blank wall, as though the distant memory were painted there. "That alone was a shock. We never held hands. But anyhow, she grabbed my hand and plastered it flat to her belly." He held his open hand outstretched in demonstration. "And the child—*my* child—gave me a wallop of a kick."

He slowly brought his hand to his chest. "So strong. This little life—a life I'd helped create—declaring itself in such fierce, unspoken terms. I swear, that kick split my heart wide-open. Had me reeling for days."

She smiled a little to herself.

"After that, I couldn't stay away. I went back, again and again. Visited her more often than I ever had in Town, just to lay my hands on her swelling stomach. Did you know babies can get the hiccups, even in the womb?"

She shook her head no.

"I didn't, either. But they can. I was enchanted by each little jump. I can't even explain it. For the first time in my life I was . . ."

Falling in love, she finished in her mind. Because he wouldn't say it aloud, but the truth was plain. He'd fallen headlong, irretrievably in love with his own child, and in love with the idea of fatherhood. The loopy joy of it was written all over his face—and frolicking all over the walls of this room.

"Her family was in Austria. With the war finally over, she wanted to go home—but she didn't think they'd accept her with an illegitimate child. She asked me to find a family here to foster the babe. I told her no."

"No?"

"I decided I would raise my own child. In my house, with my name."

Pauline gazed at him in quiet admiration. For a duke to raise a bastard child in his own home, with his own family name . . . that would be extraordinary.

It was most decidedly *not* the done thing.

"That's when I cleared this chamber and brought in the artist." He stopped in the center of the room and looked to the ceiling. "I know nurseries are usually up in the dormer rooms, but I didn't like that idea. I wanted her close."

He stared at the room's lone blank wall for several moments. "I never had the chance to bring her here. She caught a fever that first week. It's been months now. I should repaint, but I haven't found the will to do it."

"And no one knows of your loss? Not your friends, either?"

He shook his head.

Her heart ached for him. Naturally he'd been withdrawn these past months. He'd been grieving. And what was worse, grieving all alone. The duchess thought him reluctant to have children, and the truth was just the opposite. He'd been ready to welcome his daughter with an open heart—and then all his hopes were crushed.

She wanted to take him to bed and just hold him, for days and days.

"So you see," he said, "I truly don't need a fresh-faced young thing to teach me the meaning of love, make me want to be a better man. I already found that girl. She was about so big"—he held his hands just a foot apart—"with very little hair and no teeth. She taught me exactly what would give me true happiness in this life. And that I can never have it."

"But that's not true. In time you'll—"

"No. I can't. You don't understand. My father was an only child. My mother bore three other children after me. None of them survived a week. I was young, but I remember the whole house in mourning. That's why I delayed even attempting a family until the issue was forced—precisely because I'm the last of the line. All those generations of difficult childbearing didn't bode well for my chances. But then that fierce little kick . . . It gave me hope that things could be different."

She went to his side and touched his arm.

He steeled his jaw. "I can't go through that again. The Halford line ends with me."

"You sound very resolved."

"I am." He looked around at the room. "I trust you won't tell anyone about this."

She knew he wasn't concerned about her telling just "anyone." He didn't want his mother to know.

"You have my word, I won't tell her. But I think you should."

"No," he said firmly. "She can't know this. Ever. I'm serious, Pauline. That's the whole reason I—"

"The whole reason you brought me here. I know. I see it now."

She understood, at last. It wasn't simply that he was a rakish libertine, reluctant to marry. He'd decided he couldn't marry, and he didn't know how to break the news. The duchess wanted grandchildren so desperately. He couldn't bring himself to tell her she *had* one grandchild she'd already lost, and now there'd never be another.

He knew it would break his mother's heart.

So he'd kept his grief a secret, determined to manfully shoulder all the heartbreak himself.

"Griff, you needn't go through this alone. If you

won't tell the duchess, I'm here for a few more days. At least talk to me."

"Isn't that what I just did? Talk to you?"

Not really.

Throughout their conversation, his tone had been so calm. Almost eerily matter-of-fact. She knew it was a façade. He hadn't been able to fully grieve. It wasn't possible to do so in a cold, secret room. He needed to talk, to rage, to cry, to remember.

He needed a friend.

"You've been locking all your grief away. Months and months of it now. You can try to keep it secret, pretend it's not there. But until you open your heart, give it a good airing out—no sunlight can come in."

She reached for his hand. "Won't you tell me more about her? Did she favor you or her mother's side? Did she smile and coo? What was her name?"

He remained silent.

"You must have loved her very much."

He cleared his throat and pulled away. "You'd better go. The servants will be coming around soon to lay fires."

So that was that. As close as they'd come today, as much as they'd shared . . . it still wasn't enough.

She nodded, then moved to quit the room. "If that's what you want."

Chapter Twenty

"Good heavens. This is the worst yet."

In the morning room the following day, her grace was most displeased.

"Let me see." Pauline leaned forward on her yellow-striped chair.

The older woman held up her knitting needles. From one of them dangled a grayish, shapeless lump with no conceivable function. It resembled nothing so much as a dead rat.

"It is rather hideous," Pauline had to admit.

"Wrong. It is *hideous*." The duchess clucked her tongue. "*Hideous*. Back to your diction exercises, girl. We've made great strides, but those *H*'s must be clear by tomorrow night. We can't have you curtsying before 'Is Royal 'Eyeness, now can we?"

"I shouldn't be going anywhere near the Prince Regent at all."

Just the thought made her stomach twist. There was to be a ball at Carlton House, the Prince Regent's own residence, tomorrow. The duchess had seized on the invitation as Pauline's last and best chance to make a splash in London society.

"Even if I *can* say proper *H*'s, I don't belong in a palace. Your grace, I wish you'd abandon the idea."

"I'm not abandoning anything. It's our only remaining chance, after last night."

When Pauline had appeared at breakfast that morning and Griff had not, the duchess concluded that her Vauxhall hopes had been for naught. Though her assumptions about the intervening hours might be faulty, she had the end result correct.

"Don't say I didn't warn you," Pauline said. "I've told you and told you, he won't marry me."

"Perhaps not willingly." The duchess resumed her seat and began furiously working her needles again. "But he will be forced to propose tomorrow. That was the bargain. If I make you the toast of London, he promised to marry you."

Pauline shook her head. "You must accept reality, your grace. It's just not possible."

"It *is*. I know it looks unlikely. But this is the point where we rally and make a triumphant finish. Diction this morning. I have a dancing master coming by the house later. We'll practice your curtsy and greetings, too. I've bought you a set of lovely chimes to replace your water goblets. And of course, we've ordered the finest gown available. I'm not surrendering." She held up her hideous knitting. "I can't."

With a resigned sigh, Pauline cracked open the Bible. "*Holy*," she read aloud. "*He. Hath. Hosanna.*"

Out of the corner of her eye she glimpsed a familiar figure entering the room.

"Oh, *hell*."

Griff.

So many impulses flooded her. She wanted to fly to him, hug him, shake him, kiss him, tackle him to the carpet. She didn't know how she'd even look at him without giving everything away.

But she needn't have worried. The duchess was too mortified to notice Pauline's reaction.

The woman jumped to her feet. That ghastly gray rat still dangled from her knitting needles, and she had nowhere to hide it.

The duke frowned at his mother, then dropped his gaze to the knitting. "What on earth is *that*?"

A very good question—and one Pauline hoped the duchess would now be forced to finally, honestly, answer.

"This?" the duchess asked.

"Yes. That."

"I will tell you exactly what this is." She lifted her chin, then turned to Pauline. "It's exceedingly poor handiwork. Very bad indeed, Miss Simms. I expected better of you." She cast the entire mess of yarn into the coal grate.

Pauline rolled her eyes at the Bible. "*Hypocrite,*" she pronounced softly, with perfect diction.

Ignoring her, the duchess smoothed her hands down the front of her gown. "Well, what is it?" she asked her son.

"I need to tell you something."

Hope jumped in Pauline's chest. Perhaps he'd changed his mind, seen the benefit to revealing his painful secrets and unburdening his heart.

She looked up from the Bible and sent him an encouraging look. *Please. You'll feel so much lighter.*

But he didn't even turn her way.

"I've sent your amethysts to the jeweler for repair," he told his mother smoothly. "The clasp broke while Miss Simms was wearing them last night."

Pauline released her breath, frustrated. There went her hopes of honesty.

The duchess's eyes narrowed to suspicious slits. "It broke?"

"Yes." He tweaked a button on his cuff. The ducal calm was in top form this morning. "You'll have them back in a few days."

Surely the duchess would, Pauline thought. Just as soon as the jeweler had time to recreate the entire piece, in meticulous detail, so the duchess could never know the difference. What an absurd amount of effort. Why didn't he just tell her the jewels had been stolen? Pauline would feel much better.

"You're certain it can be repaired?" the duchess asked. "Perhaps I should have a look at it myself."

"No need. Just a simple matter of mending the clasp."

"Hah," Pauline interjected.

When the duke and duchess swung on her with questioning gazes, she pointed one finger at the Bible page and added:

"—llelujah."

Why didn't anyone in this family simply talk to each other? For the entire season, they'd been residing in the same house, dining at the same table . . . and all the while holding these deep secrets. The duchess was desperate for creatures to comfort. Meanwhile, her own son needed a great deal of comforting. Pauline was caught in the middle—everyone's confidante, but sworn to secrecy on all sides. This was miserable.

They were privileged in so many ways—wealthy, well-placed, well-regarded among their peers. But mostly they were just so damned lucky, the two of them, to have each other. Only their aristocratic reserve was in the way.

"*Hogwash*," she muttered.

Griff snapped his fingers at her. "Verse."

"Hm?"

"Chapter and verse." He craned his neck, looking over her shoulder. "I should like to know where, precisely, in St. Paul's letter to the Ephesians, he uses the word 'hogwash.'"

She twisted in her chair, shielding the Bible from his view. "It's penciled in the margin." He wasn't the only one who could prevaricate.

"Someone scribbled in the family Bible?" The duchess arched a brow at Griff.

"What?" he said. "It wasn't me. You know I never read the thing."

"Hmph." The duchess rang the bell, and when the housemaid appeared, instructed her to bring every servant into the room.

Once they were all lined in a perfect row, from Higgs the butler down to Margaret the scullery maid, her grace addressed them.

"Someone has vandalized the Holy Scriptures. Let the offender come forward."

No one came forward, of course. So Pauline did.

"I made it up," she said, rising from her chair.

"And there's more you should know, your grace. The duke's keeping something from you."

The room went utterly silent.

And the look Griff sent her—oh, it chilled her to the marrow. It was a hard glare brimming with anger, betrayal. *Don't you dare*, that look said.

She knew in that moment, if she broke her word to him and revealed the truth of his daughter, he would never forgive her. It wouldn't matter that he cared for her, or what pleasure they'd shared last night. He would excise her from his life completely, even if it felt like slicing off his own arm.

She swallowed hard.

"The amethysts," she whispered. "The duke is good to shield me, but he's not telling the whole truth, your grace. The clasp didn't break on its own. A thief tore it from my neck."

The assembled servants gasped.

"Oh, Miss Simms," the housekeeper said. "You weren't hurt?"

"No," she assured all of them, grateful for their concern. "No, I'm fine. But my reputation took a few blows. I might have chased after the thief, shouting blasphemy all through the pavilions of Vauxhall. And the necklace is gone." She turned to the duchess. "I'm so sorry. But I feel much better, having told the truth. As they say, confession is good for the soul. While we're all assembled here, perhaps there are other secrets weighing heavy on our minds. Matters that would benefit from fresh air and sunlight."

She looked from Griff to the duchess and back. *For the love of God. Just talk to each other.*

"You're right," someone said. "Miss Simms is right. I've done wrong and I must confess."

In the corner, Cook was wringing her apron. Tears rolled down her floury cheeks. "Last month, her grace ordered turbot for dinner. Well, I searched and searched the market, and there weren't any turbot to be had." She buried her face in her apron. "I served you cod. *Cod.* I sauced it heavily so no one could tell. But I've felt terrible about it ever since."

Pauline went to the crying woman's side and offered a sympathetic pat. "There there. I'm certain her grace will be forgiving."

"I let a cinder fall on the drawing room carpet," one of the housemaids blurted. "It burnt a hole."

"But don't you feel better now for having the truth out in the open?" Pauline asked.

The housemaid sniffed and raised her head. "I do, Miss Simms. I truly do. It's like a weight's been lifted."

"I'm so glad. No one should live under the burden of secrets."

Young Margaret spoke up, eager to have her part. "I saw Lawrence in the pantry, fumbling with a housemaid!"

The duchess straightened her spine. *"Lawrence."*

The footman in question paled.

The duchess addressed the housemaids sternly. "Which one of you was it? Step forward now."

Three of them did, in unison. When they looked around the room and realized they weren't alone, they each turned on Lawrence with vicious glares.

Lawrence twisted under their anger. "I . . . I . . ." He thrust his chin forward. "Higgs wears a corset!"

If he meant to divert attention from himself, he succeeded. All around the room, eyebrows soared.

Poor Higgs. His cheeks went beet red. "It's not a *ladies'* corset. A butler must cut a respectable figure."

For a long, uncomfortable moment, no one had anything to say.

And then . . .

"I'm not French."

This came from Fleur.

"What?" the duchess exclaimed. "Impossible."

"I'm not. I'm n-not." The lady's maid gave her confession in halting, poorly enunciated English. Her accent was even more common than Pauline's, and she had a painful stammer. "I knew I'd never f-f-find a lady's maid post, speaking as I do. So I let on that I was French and full of airs, so's I wouldn't have to talk. My real name's Fl-Fl-Flora. I'm so sorry. I'll pack me things."

She fled the room in tears.

The duchess went after her. "Fleur—or, Flora . . . Whoever, you are, wait!"

In their absence, a stunned silence filled the morning room.

Griff clapped his hands together. "Well. Thank you, Miss Simms. This has been a most illuminating morning."

Pauline put a hand to her temple. Oh, Lord.

The doorbell rang. No one moved.

"Here's a thought," said Griff. "Why don't I answer that?"

Higgs shook himself and lurched into motion. "Your grace, allow me."

Griff held up a hand. "No, no. I confess, I have long harbored a deep, secret yearning to answer my own door."

As he left the room, Pauline dashed after him. "I'm sorry. I had no idea all that would happen. But don't you see? This house is full of secrets, and it's making everyone unhappy. No one more than you. You need to disclose your sorrows, open your heart."

"The only thing I'm opening right now is the front door." He strode to the entrance and yanked on the door latch. When he saw the visitors standing outside, he muttered, "Brilliant. Just what this morning needs."

Pauline froze in disbelief. On the doorstep stood not one, but two familiar people. The woman she'd known in Spindle Cove as Miss Minerva Highwood. And Miss Minerva's husband—Colin Sandhurst, Lord Payne.

"I knew it," Minerva said, pushing past the duke to catch Pauline in a desperate hug. "Never fear, Pauline. We've come to save you."

Having opened the door, Griff took on the duty of closing it. As he did so, he felt heartily sorry that these two visitors were on the wrong side.

"It's been too long, Halford." Payne offered a hand and a genial smile.

Not long enough. For his part, he could have lasted a week or two more.

Lady Payne looked up at him, eyes burning with violence behind those wire-rimmed spectacles. "You revolting trilobite."

Charming. And here he had been wondering what Payne saw in the girl.

"If only I hadn't left my reticule at home," she said bitterly.

He hadn't the faintest idea what that signified, but he supposed this wasn't a conversation to conduct in the entrance hall.

Griff showed them to his study—it was one room he felt certain would not be occupied by a sobbing housemaid. Ringing for tea seemed a chancy prospect. He poured Payne a brandy and made the offer of a cordial to the ladies. Another episode in today's adventures in self-sufficiency.

"Pauline, what's happened?" Payne's excitable wife asked. "What's he done to you?"

"My lady, he's only employed me. I'm in this house working as a companion to his mother, the duchess."

"Oh, really." Lady Payne's voice was rich with skepticism. "And where is the duchess now?"

"She is upstairs," Griff said. "Dealing with a small crisis of the house staff."

"So," she huffed. "Servants in this house are often unhappy." She slid her gaze between Pauline and Griff. "And I'm to believe nothing untoward has happened between you?"

"You're to believe it's none of your concern," Griff answered. "Why are you so suspicious of me?"

"I'm not suspicious. My dislike of you is formed on abundant evidence. I've been to that ghastly pleasure palace you keep." She turned to Pauline. "Do you know he has a den of iniquity in the country?"

Pauline shook her head. "No, my lady. It wouldn't be my business to know that."

Griff frowned. Why had she become so docile and compliant all of a sudden? This was hardly the same Pauline he knew. Certainly not the same Pauline who'd pressed him back against his bed last night and dragged her tongue over every inch of his chest.

"It's called Winterset Grange. I was there last year," his bespectacled inquisitioner continued, speaking to Pauline. "Colin and I stopped the night there on our journey to Scotland. Oh, it was disgusting." She shuddered.

"Not so disgusting that you declined my hospitality," Griff said, leaning against the desk and crossing his arms. "And if you'll forgive me for saying it, Lady Payne, I'm not sure you have the moral high ground in this particular tale."

"What can you mean?"

"By your own admission, you'd run away from your family with a scandalous rake. And, I might add, lied to my face about your identity. I seem to remember Payne introducing you as Melissande, some sort of long-lost Alpine princess and cold-blooded assassin who spoke not a word of English. I mean, really. An Alpine princess-assassin. You will call *me* depraved?"

She sat tall, indignant. "You made inappropriate overtures to me. And you suggested Colin wager my favors in a game of cards. What can you say to that?"

He spread his hands. "Alpine. Princess. Assassin."

She fumed at him.

Griff said, "I admit that the scene you wandered into was one of flagrant vice. I'm just pointing out that you were hardly the saint in the lion's den. Isn't it conceivable that we've all changed in the past year?"

"People don't change *that* much," she said. "Not in essentials."

"Well, that's where you're wrong," he replied angrily. "In essentials."

He stalked toward the window. This conversation was making him angry, and a little bit afraid. It had been a full year since he'd engaged in anything like Lady Payne described. His heart and his life *had* fundamentally changed. And no one saw it. Not Payne, whom he'd once thought a close friend. Not even his own mother. Society still linked him with opulent debauchery, and those assumptions would color the way they perceived anyone close to him—including Pauline.

So this was the price he paid for a misspent youth. Last autumn he'd wanted nothing more than to give his daughter a respectable life. Perhaps it was best she hadn't lived to feel the brunt of his failure. She would have been ashamed to be his.

He tossed back a large swallow of brandy, feeling it burn all the way down.

Payne approached him and spoke in confidential tones. "Listen, Halford. My wife can be protective, but we're truly not here to grill you on your life choices. We're just concerned for Pauline. I spent many dark nights in that village tavern. It's not much of a stretch to say her friendly smile and quickness with a pint saved my life a time or two. She's a sweet girl, and she means well."

He bit back a curse. "You don't know her at all. You never took the time to learn anything about her."

"I know her family situation. I know she hasn't anyone to look out for her."

"She does now," Griff said. The words came from his gut.

Payne's eyebrows lifted meaningfully. "Oh, does she?"

"Yes."

"And you're certain that's what she wants, too?"

"She's an intelligent, free-thinking adult. Ask her." With a gruff sigh, Griff moved away from his conference with Payne. "Miss Simms, if you are concerned about my personal history, or unhappy with the terms of our arrangement—if you want to leave this house for any reason at all—I will write you a bank draft this moment, and you can go with Lord and Lady Payne."

Her gaze alternated back and forth between him and their visitors. As though she were giving it close, thoughtful consideration.

Good God. Perhaps she *did* want to leave him.

"Well?" he asked again, somewhat hoarsely this time. "Do you want to go?"

Chapter Twenty-one

Pauline halfheartedly wished she had the strength to say yes. It would be the easiest way. She and Griff would have to part eventually, and the parting would only grow more difficult.

But she couldn't go this morning. Because she loved him. She *loved* him, and she couldn't let him go just yet.

"No, your grace," she said. "I want to stay."

"Well, then." He turned to Minerva. "I assume you're satisfied."

Lady Payne didn't even speak to him, instead approaching Pauline. She pushed a small square of paper into her hand. "Here is our calling card. I've written our direction on the back, and Lady Rycliff's as well. If you need anything—anything at all—you can always come to us. Day or night, do you understand?"

Pauline nodded. "You are very good, the both of you. I'm grateful for your concern."

Even if she didn't need it, it felt good to know they cared.

Griff showed them out. When he returned, he was glowering. "What was that?" he asked.

"I don't know. They seemed to have the wrong idea."

"Well, you didn't leap to correct them. You barely spoke at all, except for all that 'your grace'-ing and 'my lord and lady'-ing."

He was angry with her? "What else should I say? He *is* a lord. She *is* a lady. And you *are* a duke."

"But on intellect and character, you are the equal of anyone in the room. Why would you defer so easily to them, when you've never been anything but impertinent with me?"

"It's different with you. Everything's different with you. But you can't blame this all on me. You were rather standoffish yourself. It's not as though you jumped to tell them we're having a deeply passionate *affaire*."

He waved at the door. "Because I knew how they'd receive it."

"Precisely. The same way everyone would receive that news. As an impossibility, at best. At worst, something shameful and sordid."

Pauline understood why he was upset. She felt the same way. The people who'd just visited them were the closest thing they had to mutual friends, and if even *they* wouldn't credit a relationship between Griff and her, it was truly hopeless. No one would accept them together. No one.

She sighed. It shouldn't come as a surprise. It didn't matter what the poems said. There was no other England, no other London with its Tower. There was only this world they lived in, and it was unyielding on matters of class.

"There are thirty-three ranks of precedence between a serving girl and a duchess," she said quietly. "Did you know that? The chart takes up three pages in *Mrs. Worthington's Wisdom*. I have it all in my head. Duchesses are at the very top—after the queen and princesses, of course. The order goes duchesses, marchionesses, countesses . . ."

As she recited the ranks, she ticked them off on her fingers. " . . . then wives of the eldest sons of marquesses, then wives of the younger sons of dukes. Then come the daughters. Daughters of dukes, daughters of marquesses. Next viscountesses, then wives of eldest sons of earls. Then daughters of earls . . ."

"Pauline."

" . . . that's ten ranks already, and I'm not even to baronesses yet. Let alone all the orders of knighthood and the military ranks. And below those, you have—"

He approached her and tipped her face, forcing her to look him in the eye. "Pauline."

"I'm not even on the chart." She blinked hard. "A girl like me, Griff . . . I'm so far below you. When we're alone together, we might be able to forget it. But no one else will."

"*Forget* it? You think I forget who you are when we're together?"

She fidgeted. He must forget, a little. From their very first meeting, he'd afforded her more respect and attention than any nobleman would ever intentionally give a servant. "What matters is, we have to remember ourselves eventually. If we don't, society will force the point."

He stared at her for a long moment. "Perhaps you're right. We should remember ourselves."

"I'm glad you agree."

He crossed the room, closed the study door, and turned the key in the lock. The tumbler gave an ominous click.

"Clear the desk, Simms."

"What? I don't see—"

"Don't argue," he clipped. "You're a serving girl, and you wanted me to recall it. I'm the duke in the room, and I've bid you to clear the desk. It's what you do, isn't it? Clear tables?"

Is that what he was initiating, then? Playing roles? The libertine duke and the naughty serving girl?

Well . . . After about two seconds' pause, Pauline decided she could get inspired for that.

She reached for the inkwell and cautiously moved it to a nearby lamp table, where it wouldn't spill. Then with one hand, she made a broad sweep across the desktop, sending blotter, papers, sealing wax, and more crashing to the floor. "There."

"Such impertinence."

"It's what you like."

He tugged at his cravat, loosening it as he crossed the room. "You need to learn your place."

"Is this my place, your grace?" She pushed herself up to sit on the desktop, legs dangling.

"For now." He sat in the desk chair before her, boots sprawled on either side of her dangling legs, and fixed her with a dark, commanding gaze.

The moment stretched into a thin, brittle thing. Pauline sat very still, just waiting for it to snap.

"Lift your skirts," he said.

Whoosh.

His words were a starting pistol, and her pulse took the cue to race.

After kicking off one slipper, she toed the other one loose. Both dropped to the floor. She placed her stockinged foot on his thigh and slowly drew the lacy hem of her frock higher, revealing her leg all the way to the knee. "Like this?"

"Higher."

She dragged her lacy hem upward, inching it along her thigh. Her garter peeked through the edge of her petticoat—a saucy wink of lavender ribbon.

"More."

She slid her foot to his groin, cupping the growing bulge in his trousers. With slow motions, she teased him harder, rubbing her silky instep up and down the long, firm ridge. Soon, the sounds of labored breathing filled the air. Both his and hers. The smooth friction against the sensitive arch of her foot was a surprising source of pleasure.

And the way he looked at her . . . Unashamed of his rampant arousal, penetrating her with his dark, intense gaze. He had her panting and wet for him, without so much as a kiss.

"Higher," he demanded, encircling her ankle with his strong grip. "All the way to your waist. Show me everything."

The dark command in his voice thrilled her. She wriggled on the desk, working her skirts higher. Until cool air rushed over her exposed, aroused cleft.

"Yes," he said, sitting forward in his chair. "That's it."

He caressed her calf, running his hand up and down the silky curve. His thumb pressed against the hollow of her knee, and her thighs fell apart. As if he'd found some hidden lever.

He grabbed her by the hips, jerking her to the edge of the desk. His fingers traced the dewy folds of her sex, slipping over her aroused flesh. Such sweet, sweet torture.

"Take me," she pleaded.

He clucked his tongue. "I shall do as I please. And it pleases me to taste you."

As he lowered his head, she squirmed away, breaking the little scene they played.

"Griff, wait. No one's . . ." She licked her lips, nervous. "No one's ever done that for me."

He raised his head. His smile was slow to spread and overtly wicked. "If you hoped to dissuade me, that was the wrong thing to say."

He framed her hips in his hands and pulled her forward again, pressing his mouth to her core.

And as promised, he kissed her. *There*.

So shocking. So indescribably arousing.

She jolted in his arms, but his grip on her body was like iron. He was not going to let her escape this erotic embrace. So she reclined, limp, on the mahogany surface, surrendering to the inescapable bliss. She spread her arms wide, covering the full span of the desk. All the papers and correspondence were gone. At this moment she was his work. And he was attending to her thoroughly. Single-mindedly.

Masterfully.

His tongue explored her most feminine, intimate places with confidence and zeal. She relaxed her thighs, spreading herself for his kiss, trusting that he knew what he was doing.

And he did. Oh, he was good at this. A true champion. She had no basis for comparison, but she'd wager the entirety of her thousand pounds on the fact. If there were an order of knighthood awarded for proficiency in pleasuring women, he would have achieved the top rank.

He licked up and down her slit, savoring her as if she were most delicious course in a royal banquet. When he lavished attention on that tight, swollen bundle of nerves at the crest of her sex, she couldn't help but moan. Then he parted her folds with his thumbs, using his tongue to delve inside her sheath. He moved his tongue in and out, in shallow thrusts that mimicked intercourse.

"Griff." She writhed on the desk.

He didn't pause to reply, but answered her by sliding one hand to her breast, squeezing and kneading her through the fabric.

She clutched at his head, shoving impatiently through layers of petticoats to weave her fingers into the lush, dark waves of his hair and grip tight. She held him fast to her, grinding against his hot, wet, talented mouth.

"Yes," she panted. "Please, don't stop."

He wouldn't stop. He showed no signs of flagging in the least. His every lick and thrust pushed her higher. She began to whimper, wordlessly begging him for release. He moved his head back and forth, nuzzling her pearl.

"Oh. *Oh.*"

She arched straight off the desktop, rocketing through an intense, soaring climax. He pressed the heel of his hand to her mouth, giving her that something she needed to bite and moan and cry out against.

Eventually the tremors of bliss subsided, and he let his hand slip to cup her breast again. For several moments she stared mutely up at the ceiling while he fondled her breasts and dropped lazy kisses along her thighs.

There were no words she could utter. None.

"Did you enjoy that?"

"Yes," she managed. There were no words, save that one. "Yes, yes, yes."

"Do you believe that I worship every inch of this lithe, delectable body? Do you understand that I would take a saber to the kidneys before letting you come to harm?"

She nodded, breathless.

"Good." His expression darkened. "Because now I'm going to teach you a lesson."

He lifted her to her feet, spun her about, and then moved her toward the desk until she bent at the waist. Her breath rushed out as her breasts met the unyielding surface of the desktop.

Behind her, Griff pushed up her skirts with brisk motions, gathering all the heavy fabric of gown and petticoats and shoving it above her hips.

His hand cupped her backside, and his knee nudged her thighs apart.

"This is what happens to serving girls who forget themselves with a duke. They get a firm reminder."

At the playful sternness in his voice, Pauline felt the slope of her inner thighs erupt into gooseflesh. Her nipples hardened against the cool, polished wood.

"Impertinent minx."

His palm spanked lightly against her bottom, and she let out a breath that was part startled laugh and part sensual excitement. There was no pain, only a stinging pleasure.

"Saucy temptress."

Another delicious smack.

She knew he wouldn't hurt her—this was a fantasy for him. If she could play at being a seductress, he was welcome to play his role, too. She liked that he would be playful. It meant he felt safe with her.

He leaned over her, pinning her to the desk with his body weight. His breath was hot against her neck. "You are a very naughty girl."

As he whispered to her in a rough, needy voice, his hand worked between her legs, rubbing her aroused, sensitized sex.

"You like this," he said. "You like to imagine that you drive me out of my mind with wanting. Until my cock does all the thinking, and I forget myself completely."

"I . . ." Her voice failed her as his fingertip brushed over her pearl.

"Answer me," he demanded. He slipped a finger inside her.

"Yes."

"Yes, what?" He thrust his finger deep.

She moaned. "Yes, your grace."

"Know this," he said. "I do not forget my place. And you will not forget it, either."

Oh, how she hoped his rightful place was deep, deep inside her. She wanted him so badly, she would have said anything he pleased. Called him by any name he liked.

He slid his finger almost entirely out of her slickness before pushing back in. "Who am I?"

"A duke," she managed.

"And what do you want of me?" He withdrew his fingers, leaving her empty and aching for more.

"I . . ." She writhed on the desk. "I want you to tup me."

At her use of such crude language, she felt his cock jump against her thigh. Despite all his chastisement, she knew her words excited him. This language was who she was, after all. Common. Low-born.

"Manners." He gave her bottom another teasing smack. "Remember whom you are addressing."

"Please, your grace." By now she was desperate for him. She made her voice as sultry and enticing as she could. "Tup your humble servant, I beg of you."

"That's better."

He lifted her hips and slid into her in one smooth, thick stroke. Her moan of satisfaction echoed his.

She was wet and ready from his earlier efforts. He didn't need to proceed slowly, so he wasted no time setting a brisk pace. Driving deep, and deeper still.

Pauline gripped the edges of the desktop to keep from being tupped straight off the desk. The heat and fullness of him thrilled her. He was reaching unexplored places inside her, showing her new, dark facets of herself. The pleasure consumed her.

"Harder," she gasped. "Harder, if it please your grace."

He growled. "Oh, it pleases me."

He lifted her by the waist until her toes left the carpet, holding her off the ground as he pumped his hips harder, faster. She bit the soft flesh of her forearm to keep from crying out. He had her weightless, utterly at his mercy as he rode her at whatever angle and pace he desired. He was using her for his pleasure, and using her well.

Then he lowered her feet to the floor and bent forward, looming over her on the desk. His hands covered hers where she clutched the edges of the desktop. She felt a drop of his perspiration splash against her exposed shoulder.

"Who am I?" His voice was so close—and so guttural. Her intimate places pulsed in response.

"A duke."

"Which duke?"

"The eighth Duke of Halford . . . your grace."

Her whole body throbbed for release. His cock was so long and solid inside her. Why had he stopped? She rolled her hips, trying to entice him back into a rhythm.

He held firm, motionless. "The courtesy titles. Recite them, too."

Oh, God. "I don't recall."

"I recall. I never forget who I am. Not even when I'm this deep inside you and so desperate to come I could explode." His hips flexed. "Do you understand?"

He began to move again. This time his pace was slow but relentless. He drove into her with such force, a dry sob wrenched from her throat with his every thrust.

"Griff," she pleaded.

This "lesson" of his was both arousing and devastating. When they were together, alone, she did want him to forget the thirty-three rungs between them on the ladder of English society. But he couldn't. And she couldn't. The truth would never go away.

"I'm the Duke of Halford," he said, plunging deep.

She shut her eyes, trying not to cry. It was all too much—the emotion, the pleasure. The hopelessness.

"I'm the Marquess of Westmore."

Thrust.

"I'm also the Earl of Ridingham. Viscount Newthorpe. Lord Hartford-on-Trent."

Thrust. Thrust. Thrust.

"And I am your slave, Pauline."

Oh, mercy.

She sobbed in earnest that time. She couldn't help it.

He stopped, the full length of him buried deep inside her. Filling her, lifting her, shaping her to his desire. When they parted, she would ache with emptiness for him, always.

His voice was edged with need. "Do you hear me? Do you believe it now? There could be a thousand ranks between us, and I would not give one damn. Every blue-blooded vein in this body pounds with desire for you."

He slid an arm beneath her torso, lifting her as he drew himself tall. Her back fell against his chest. He held her up with that strong, powerful arm, and his other hand burrowed under bunched petticoats until his fingertips grazed her pearl. A shiver of ecstasy had her trembling on her toes.

"Look up at me," he rasped. "Kiss me."

She did as he bade, and gladly, turning her head and stretching to press her lips to his. His tongue plundered her mouth, and his cock filled her sex, and his fingertips worked her just where she needed it. He had her wrapped in strength and adoration.

She didn't want to come. She didn't want this to ever end. This was the purest bliss she'd ever known.

But he was wicked and skillful and so cursed efficient. Within moments her whole body was racked by waves of pleasure.

His thrusts quickened, lost their elegance. Once again that coiled power in his thighs had her toes lifting off the ground. He broke the kiss and buried his face in her hair. Profane, inarticulate mutterings rained on her ear, making her pulse drum even harder.

"I don't forget who you are," he whispered. "And it's you I want. So . . . damned . . . much."

He withdrew, finishing with a few last thrusts between her thighs. His primal growl gave her a thrill of satisfaction.

And then he held her so tightly it grew difficult to breathe. But she didn't mind.

"Well," he said finally, hoarsely. "I hope that's settled."

"Quite."

He slumped into the armchair and pulled her into his lap. They sprawled there, tangled and sweaty, filling the silence with ragged breaths. He lazily stroked her hair with one hand.

She pressed her face to his shirtfront. "Griff, that was . . ."

"I know," he said. "I know. It was. I don't mind saying I'm rather proud of it."

"You should be."

His chest rose and fell with a deep, satisfied sigh. "I feel like jaunting over to Piccadilly to wait for someone in passing to ask me, 'How do you do?' Simply so I could reply, 'Just had the best sexual encounter of my life, thanks for asking.'"

She laughed, imagining that exchange. "Best of your life?" she couldn't help but ask. "Truly?"

"Until later tonight, at least." He nuzzled her neck. "Pauline. Every time with you is the best of my life."

And how many more times would they have left? Too few, too few.

Ding . . . ding . . . ding . . .

As if it were some fateful portent of their time growing short, a nearby timepiece chimed the hour. Pauline looked over at the side table. She recognized it as the clock he'd been tinkering with all week.

"You were able to repair it," she said.

He shushed her, and his breath warmed her earlobe. "Watch."

From a little window in the front, a tiny couple emerged. A soldier and a lady. In halting, mechanical motions, they bowed to one another, twirled in a little waltz, then parted and retreated back into the clock.

"Oh, that's charming."

"I always loved watching it when I was a boy."

A hint of melancholy deepened his voice. No doubt he'd hoped his own offspring would one day love watching it, too. Now he believed he would never have someone to share it with.

At least she could share it with him now. She slid an arm around his back, hugging him tight. Listening to the last chimes of the clock and the fierce thump of his heart.

"I was thinking I'd donate it to the Foundling Hospital," he said. "I thought perhaps the children in the infirmary would enjoy it."

"I'm sure they would."

"Well, then. I'll have my mother take it when she visits next."

She twisted in his lap and peered up at him. "I have a better idea."

Chapter Twenty-two

The plan might have been Pauline's idea, but Griff quickly took control of it. This wouldn't be any namby-pamby Ladies' Auxiliary tour of the establishment. If he was going to visit a foundling home, he was going to do it his way. The dissolute ducal way.

With authority, extravagance, and unabashedly wicked intent.

His arrival was unannounced—all the best, most dramatic appearances were. He led a parade of servants through the gate, each of them laden with treasures: sweets, oranges, playthings, competently knitted caps—and at Pauline's suggestion, storybooks.

By the time they marched this bounty straight into the central courtyard, the entire place was in upheaval, with brown-clad children pouring out from every classroom and dormitory.

The matrons were not pleased. Their already dour expressions reached new excesses of sternness—many a new wrinkle would be carved that day. But the matrons had no recourse, unless they wished to refuse the thousands he gave them per annum.

It was good to be a duke.

Once all the children were assembled, Griff called out, "Where's Hubert Terrapin?"

The lad shuffled forward. He was easy to spot—the smallest in his queue.

"Hubert, I'm appointing you quartermaster," he said.

"What's that mean, your grace?"

"You're to supervise distribution of all this. It's quite a job. Can you manage it?"

The youth pulled himself tall. "Yes, your grace."

"Good. The rest of you, fall in line. Youngest first."

The file moved painfully slowly. As good-natured, oft-slighted children are, Hubert was painfully fair in his apportionments, solemnly counting out sweetmeats and sections of orange.

"He's so conscientious," Griff whispered to Pauline. "We'll be here until tomorrow."

"It's dear, isn't it? But I'm not surprised. Squabbling over too little is just human nature. But it says a great deal about a person, what they do with abundance." She put a boiled sweet in his hand. "Something to chew on."

He smiled to himself as she drifted away. Apparently, she'd found time this week for duchess lessons in subtlety, or lack of it. But she was wrong if she thought these few hours of spontaneous generosity were some sort of saintly exercise on his part. Whether he bestowed it on charity or lost it at the card table, parting with money had never been a trial for him.

Parting with her, on the other hand . . . God, he couldn't even think about it yet. The hours remaining before her inevitable departure were growing too few. He needed a task to occupy himself or he'd go mad.

"Hubert," he said, "pass me one of those oranges. Let me give you a hand."

Sometime later he congratulated the lad on a job well done, left the courtyard littered in orange rinds, and went in search of Pauline. At last, he found her in the infirmary.

Such a cozy scene. His repaired clock occupied the center of the fireplace mantel. On the hearth rug, Pauline had three little ones piled in her lap like kittens, as an older girl read aloud to them all from a book of fairy stories.

The irony ripped open his chest and went straight for his heart. This picture before him—Pauline, children, sweetness, the fairy-tale ending—it was everything he could want in life. And everything he could never have.

He hadn't wanted to fall in love with her. Lord knew, he'd tried his best to avoid it. But now it was too late. And he couldn't even employ the younger man's trick—talking himself out of the emotion, pretending he felt something less. Perhaps his heart did lie at the bottom of a black, fathomless well, where he'd succeeded in ignoring it for years. But he'd dug deep while waiting for his daughter. Now the pump had been primed.

He knew what it was to love. And this was it.

God help him.

He remained silent in the doorway, unwilling to interrupt. Not knowing what he'd say, if he dared. He'd probably blurt out a stream of desperate raving. *Don't leave me, I love you, I can't go on without you.* He'd send the children screaming. They'd have nightmares for weeks.

So he just stood there, silently reeling on the edge of life-long desolation.

Until a thin, high-pitched sound pushed him over the edge.

Pauline snuggled the little ones close. Beth had reached the most delightfully gory part of the story—the bit with the dragon who plucked out black hearts with a single claw. But just as the heroine of the story prepared to face the ultimate test, they were interrupted by the high, keening cry of an infant.

"Oh, it's that new one," Beth said. "Always wailing. He'll be sent to the country soon, I hope."

"Poor thing," Pauline said. "I didn't know we were so close to the nursery."

Beth turned a page. "It's straight across the corridor."

She looked up, toward the corridor in question. *Oh, no.*

Griff stood in the doorway, mildly rumpled and devilishly handsome as ever. But his face . . . Oh, his face had gone the color of paper. One look at him and she knew. He was in torment.

"I have to go, darlings. Beth will finish the story."

They fretted and mewled and tugged at her skirts. "Will you come back, Miss Simms?"

"Can't, I'm afraid. I'm going home tomorrow night. I have a sister who's missing me. And I'm missing her." She gave Griff a cautious smile. "Perhaps his grace will visit another day."

"I . . ." From the other room, the babe wailed again. He winced.

"I know," she said to him and hurried to gather her bonnet and wrap. "We'll leave at once."

They made hasty strides for the front gate. Pauline struggled to keep pace. She knew Griff was racing his emotions, determined to outrun the epic landslide those cries had set off.

He couldn't outrun it forever. The grief would catch up with him eventually, but she didn't want to see him plowed under here. Not with so many people about.

She hurried toward the front entrance.

But then, without a word, he turned and passed through a side door instead. Pauline changed course and chased after him as they made their way to the street. His face had that same blank, unfocused look he'd worn the other day—the day when he'd walked off into the London streets and wandered them all night.

"Griff, wait," she called. "You can't leave me behind."

"The carriage is in front. The coachman will take you home."

"But what about you?"

He gestured aimlessly at the bustling, anonymous streets. "I need a walk. Some time. It will pass if I can just . . ." His voice failed.

Her heart ached for him. Perhaps he had successfully outrun these emotions for months now. But this was one race he was losing.

"Just leave me."

"No," she said as they reached the curb. "Not this time. I'm not leaving you alone."

With a brisk wave, Pauline hailed a hackney cab. "What's the name of that church?" she asked the driver. "The one all the way on the other side of London?"

The black-clad driver peered down his sharp nose at her. "St. Paul's, you mean?"

"Right. We're going there." She climbed into the cab, knowing Griff would have to follow. He wouldn't let her drive off alone.

"I don't want to go to a bloody church." He slung himself down across from her, folding his long legs into the cramped, dark cab.

"Neither do I, really. I just needed some destination that was far away. I know you need time, but you need to be with some—"

She bit the word off. He didn't need *someone*. He needed her.

"I'm not leaving you alone right now," she said. "That's all."

He tugged a silver flask from his breast pocket and began to unscrew the top. His fingers were too clumsy to manage it. With a disgusted curse, he hurled the flask into the corner of the cab.

Pauline bent to retrieve it, calmly unscrewed the cap and held the flask out to him. "Here."

"You need to leave me." His hands were clenched into fists on either knee. "I'm not in control of myself. I . . . I might lash out."

As if he could ever hurt her. "I'll duck," she promised.

"I might weep."

"I'm already weeping." She dabbed her eyes with the back of her wrist.

"I . . ." He bent over, bracing his elbows on his knees. "Jesus. I think I'll be sick."

"Here." She held out her bonnet. "Use this."

He stared at it.

"Really. It's so ugly. You could only improve it."

His eyes met hers, wounded and dark. "I can't make you leave me?"

"No."

"Damn it, Simms." As he looked away, he pressed a fist to his mouth, as though to suppress a flood of emotion.

But she could sense there were cracks in the dam.

She moved forward on the seat until their knees met in the center of the coach. "You're safe," she whispered. "In this space, with me—you're safe. Whatever happens in this cab will remain here. I will go home tomorrow night. No one need ever know."

With a curse and the swiftness of desperation, he reached for her, grasping her by the hips and lowering his head to her lap. His hands fisted roughly in the fabric of her gown.

At last, with his face buried in her skirts, he released a sound. A growling, razor-edged howl of anger and anguish. It built from his gut and erupted through his body. She could feel the force of it sending tremors all through his joints—and hers. His fingers tugged at her, drawing her closer, holding her more tightly.

Every hair on her body seemed to lift on end. The sheer violence of his emotion terrified her. Her instinct was to shrink from it, but she beat down the fear.

She laid one hand flat on his shuddering back and touched the other to his hair.

Though her heart yearned to soothe him with crooning words, she resisted the urge. There was no good in telling him she understood, or that everything would be all right. It wasn't true. She couldn't possibly understand his loss—the sheer agony racking his body was beyond her comprehension—and everything would *not* be all right. He'd lost someone who could never be replaced, and he'd been holding in the sorrow much too long.

"God." His voice was muffled by her skirts. "God damn it. God damn it."

She wrapped her arms about his quaking shoulders, pressing a kiss to the top of his head and embracing him as tightly she could.

They stayed like that as the coach rattled on through streets and neighborhoods she'd never seen before and would never visit again.

Pauline had never dreamed how much a father could love his child—her own upbringing hadn't given her a clue. But Griff showed her today. If one took every battered hope in a grieving father's heart and laid them all down end to end—they could stretch across London.

Mile after mile after mile.

Sometime later, emptied of all that pent-up emotion, he lay sprawled with her on her seat.

"Tell me about her," she whispered. "Tell me everything."

"She was exactly this big." He touched the tip of his longest finger, then the crook of his elbow. "Her hair was like little wisps of spun copper."

"She must have taken after you."

"My hair is dark."

"But your beard is ginger when it grows in." She grazed his cheek with her fingertip. "I noticed it that first day. Did she have your fine brown eyes as well?"

"I don't know. They were that cloudy blue-gray, but the midwife said they'd darken." He rubbed his face with one hand. "She rarely opened her eyes while I held her. I don't think she ever saw me at all."

"She knew you were there." Pauline laid a hand to his chest. "She could feel these strong arms holding her. She would have known your voice. And your cologne. You have the most wonderfully comforting scent. I don't think I'd have ever left Spindle Cove with you if you hadn't smelled so marvelous. She probably kept her eyes closed because she felt so safe."

He let out a deep breath. "I was so happy when she was born a girl."

"Truly? I thought men want sons."

Her own father had wanted sons. When he received daughters instead, he'd never recovered from the disappointment. He even refused to give them names other than those he'd chosen for boys. It was only by the grace of the old vicar's pen that she and Daniela weren't named Paul and Daniel.

"I wanted a girl," he said. "An illegitimate son would have had a harder time of it. He could never have been my heir, and I would have worried he'd feel lesser, no matter what attempts I made to be a good father. But a daughter . . . a daughter, I would have been free to spoil and cherish. I had so many plans. You can't imagine."

She bit her lip, grief-stricken for him. "Oh, I can imagine."

"It wasn't just the nursery room. I had birthdays, holidays, outings all planned out. Nursemaids already hired."

"Had you chosen her finishing school yet?"

A wry smile tipped his mouth. "I'd started investigating possibilities."

"I'm sure you had." It eased her heart to see him smiling. Even a little.

He closed his eyes. "She lived less than a week. It's been the better part of a year. How can it be that I still mourn her this much?"

"I can't pretend to understand how love works." Pauline sifted her fingers through his hair, smoothing a touch over his brow. "How many days have I known you? Not many more. And I doubt I'll ever go a day without thinking of you, even if I should live to see ninety. I . . ." She couldn't help it. "I love you so."

His eyes flew open.

"I'm sorry," she said. "It's a poor time to say it."

"When would be a better time?" He rose to a sitting position next to her.

"I don't know." She knotted her hands in her lap. "Probably never. But I'm not good at hiding these things, and you deserve to hear it. I fell desperately in love with you this week."

He pushed a hand through his hair. "I don't understand. We had an agreement, Simms. How did this happen?"

"I don't know. Vauxhall, the bookshop, those first kisses in your library . . . When I try to understand how it began, I go back and back. I don't know how it started, I just—" She made herself look at him. "I just feel rather sure it's not going to end. Ever."

"Pauline." He cupped her face.

"Still, I can't be sorry for it. I won't be. I know we have to part, and my heart will break. But even if it's aching, at least I'll always know it's there." She gave him a weak smile. "And the naughty books will make so much more sense."

His mouth thinned to a solemn line. He inhaled slowly. Then he raised his fist and banged on the coach top to signal the driver. "That's it. We're going home."

"Because you're unhappy?"

"No." He gave her a look that said, *Isn't it obvious?* "Because lovemaking in a moving carriage isn't all it's purported to be."

"Oh."

He hauled her into his lap and swept her into a passionate kiss.

"Pauline." His voice was a dark murmur against her lips. "My heart, my dearest love. We are done with this cab. To do every wicked, delicious thing I mean to do to you, I need a bed. And hours."

Chapter Twenty-three

There was no denying it. Despite a week's worth of duchess training, Pauline remained a farm girl at heart. Once again she woke before first light.

Griff lay tangled with her, snoring softly. His dark head lay heavy on her breast. She wished she could let him sleep all morning. After his efforts in this bed last night, he'd certainly earned his rest.

But all too soon it was dawn. She could hear servants stirring on the lower level of the house.

"Griff," she whispered. She teased her fingers through the dark, tousled waves of his hair. "Griff, I have to go. It's nearly morning."

He clutched her tight about the middle. "It can't be morning. I won't let it be morning."

She smiled. "I don't think even the Duke of Halford can make time stand still."

"He can try."

He pulled her down and yanked the bedsheet over them both, making a sort of tent for two.

The early morning light shone through the linen, painting their naked bodies with a warm, honey-gold glow.

Pauline ceased worrying about what would happen later that day, and for the rest of her life. She was here now. In his arms. His touch could make her forget everything.

Except the muffled crash and scrape of a grate being cleaned downstairs. That was hard to ignore.

"Is the door locked?" she asked.

He made a nod of confirmation as he tongued her nipple. "It's locked."

"Are you sure?"

"I'm sure." His hand delved between her thighs.

She put a hand to his chest, holding him back. "Please go check. I'll feel safer."

He stared at her for a moment. "Well, then." He rose up on his haunches. "I won't have you feeling anything less than safe in my bed."

With a quick kiss to her brow, he rose from the mattress and made his way toward the door. Pauline rolled onto her side, watching him.

As he covered the distance in easy strides, she admired the long, lean muscles of his calves and the sculpted tone of his shoulders and back. And his arse . . . Lord above. The world had not seen such a perfectly formed arse since the sixth day of Creation. His buttocks were taut, rounded domes of pure muscle. As he walked, tantalizing hollows appeared on each cheek, alternating with every step.

Right, left, right . . .

He reached the door and rattled the latch. "Locked," he confirmed aloud.

Then he turned around—praise be—and began the walk back.

If he was arousing to view from behind, he was devastating in the approach.

"Wait," she said. "Stop there."

He halted. "Is something wrong?"

"It's just . . . I've lied to you about something."

His dark eyebrows gathered like storm clouds. "What?"

"I wasn't truly that concerned about the door latch," she confessed. "I just wanted to watch you walk across the room."

He laughed, startled. His abdominal muscles tensed in a delicious manner.

She reclined on her elbow and sighed languidly. "You're so beautiful. If 'beautiful' is the right word to use for a man."

"I wouldn't know. I don't often compliment naked men." He tugged at his ear in a self-conscious gesture. "I'm starting to feel like a display in the British Museum."

"You belong in a museum." She shook her head, amazed. "How do you stay so fit? You're a nobleman, but that body puts farmhands to shame."

He scrubbed a palm over his washboard of a belly. "I just stay active. It's important to me. One winter at Oxford, I caught a pneumonia. Lay sick in bed for months and nearly died. It was a difficult time."

Pauline could imagine it would have been. Not only for him, but for his parents. Griff was their only child remaining of four, and if something had happened to him . . .

He confirmed her suspicions. "I was already a disappointment to them. But it seemed the least I could do was stay alive, you know? As soon as I was able, I worked hard to recover my strength." He stretched and flexed one arm. "Not only strength, but balance, reflexes. And I've tried to stay fit ever since. Lately, it's mostly the fencing."

She smiled. "All that thrusting has served you well."

"Fencing's not only about the thrusting." He drew closer. "It's about quickness of mind and body. Flexibility. Concentration. Strategy."

The dark quality in his voice was making her intimate places swell and ache. Her gaze dropped to his eager, arcing cock. Seeing how badly he wanted her . . . it made her desire him even more.

Just to tease him, she moved back to the middle of the bed. "Let me gaze a bit longer, please. It might be my last chance."

"It won't be your last chance."

The mattress dipped as he joined her. He rolled atop her and settled between her thighs. Thanks to his brief sojourn out of bed, his body was cool. Cool and solid as marble.

"This will be the last time," she whispered.

He slid into her with one long, powerful stroke. "It can't be the last time."

She wrapped her legs over his. He worked in and out of her, bracing himself on his hands and staring down at her, deep into her eyes. The intensity was piercing. She felt so exposed, so raw and vulnerable. Her hands began to tremble where she touched his arms. She hoped he wouldn't notice.

He stopped, holding still within her. A slight frown wrinkled his brow.

"What's wrong?" she asked.

"Nothing," he said. "I wouldn't change a single thing. You're perfect."

Her heart wrenched in her chest. At last, that word again. And it didn't come when she was dressed in a silk gown and draped with jewels, but just here. Here, when she lay naked beneath him in the full light of morning. Nothing hidden, nothing concealed. Nothing between their bodies but musk and heat.

It was worth the whole week's wait, to hear it now.

She slid her hands to his back and arched her hips, drawing him deeper. "Take me hard. Hold nothing back. I want to be sore. I want to feel you for days."

She didn't have to ask twice. He did as she asked, lifting her legs and guiding them around his hips so he could ride her hard and well. Her breasts danced to his rhythm. His thighs smacked against hers with every deep, penetrating stroke.

She raked her fingernails down his back, scoring his flesh—so that he'd feel her for days, too. She rode the wave of his deep, forceful thrusts.

He pressed his brow to hers. "I don't want to withdraw. I want to be deep inside you when I come."

She was stunned. "Griff, no. The risk is too great."

"I want the risk." He kissed her lips. "I never thought I'd say that again, but I want it. I want you, always."

He was talking madness. Lust had addled his brain. She had to leave; he must stay. They were both completely unprepared to deal with those consequences. But some crazed, unthinking part of her wanted the same. The decision would be made. No undoing it. He couldn't shut her out of his life. And how wonderful it would feel, to someday place a cooing, healthy infant in his arms. Her heart melted at the idea.

She could make him so, so happy.

He paused above her, tensing every muscle. And when he began to thrust again, she sensed a now-familiar shift in his rhythm. His peak was near.

"Don't stop me." He pumped hard and fast. "I can't let you go."

"Griff . . ."

"Take me," he breathed, driving deep. "Take everything. Just love me."

"Yes." Her own climax broke, sending her into a place beyond thought or reason. "*Yes.*"

The door crashed open.

Pauline shrieked. They jolted apart, and she burrowed under the bed linens, still shuddering with the last tremors of orgasm.

Oh my God. Oh my God, oh my God.

Griff cursed and flipped onto his back, drawing her into a protective embrace. The hard, frustrated ridge of his cock throbbed against her hip. "What the devil?"

Lord Delacre stood framed in the entryway. He lifted a hand to shield his view. "It's worse than I thought. My eyes."

"I thought the door was locked," Pauline whispered, clutching the bedsheets to her chest.

"It *was* locked," Griff said through gritted teeth.

"I broke it in," Delacre said. "This is urgent, Halford. Do you know this girl you've been squiring all around the *ton* is a bloody barmaid?"

Oh, Lord. Pauline's face blazed with humiliation. Griff's arm slipped from its protective perch around her shoulders. She felt his erection flagging, too. He slowly sat up in bed, rubbing his face with both hands.

"How did you know?" she asked.

"Everyone knows," Delacre answered. "Eugenia Haughfell ferreted out the truth, and now it's all over Town."

She should have known. Those cursed Awfuls.

"No doubt this week has been quite the lark for you, Miss Simms. But it's at an end." He walked a few paces into the room, plucked Griff's discarded breeches from the floor and flung them at him. "You've had some narrow scrapes, Halford, and I've seen some brazen fortune-hunting schemes in my time. But this beats all. Seduced by a barmaid in the ancestral bed."

Calm and silent, Griff collected the breeches. He turned aside—away from Pauline—and slid his legs into them one at a time. His back was to her as he stood and yanked the breeches to his waist.

Farewell, she thought wistfully. *Farewell, finest arse in Creation.*

This was it, then. She'd known they were down to their last few hours of bliss, but this was a mortifying ending.

She wanted to disappear under the mattress.

Delacre went on, "At least no one can expect you to marry the girl. The gossip will deem her just another of your debauched larks. Toss her a bit of money and send her off. But I hope you've been careful not to get a brat on her. She probably hid it from you, but there's imbecility in the bloodline."

Griff paused in the act of fastening a button on his breeches falls. He looked up at Delacre for a brief moment.

"Del," he said, in a low, easy voice, "it will take me about ten seconds to button these. That's how much time you have to run."

Lord Delacre shook his head. "I'm not going anywhere until I'm certain this—"

"Run." Griff finished the last closure. He swung his arms at his sides, shaking his fingers loose. The expression on his face was thunderous. "I mean it, Del. You had better flee. Because I fully intend to kill you."

Griff could tell by the look on Del's face that his oldest "friend" didn't believe him.

"Come along, Halford." He held up his hands. "You can't be serious."

Griff pulled back his right fist and crashed a full-force punch into Del's gut. "Convinced?"

Del doubled over, eyes wide with shock. "Jesus."

"That's right, say your prayers. You're going to need them." He threw another punch, this time catching Del on the jaw.

Realizing he was at a disadvantage, Del scrambled down the corridor. "Stop and think about this, Griff!" he called. "We had a pact, remember? I'm trying to be a friend. Rescuing you from entrapment. Saving you from greater scandal."

"You had better save yourself."

They raced toward the salon, where they'd begun so many days together.

They wouldn't be using blunt practice swords today.

Griff yanked a short sword from its wall mount and swung it, limbering his arm. "I've something to tell you, Delacre. All these years we've been perfectly matched fencing opponents?" He raised his blade. "I've been holding back."

As soon as Del had armed himself, Griff went on the attack, swinging in savage blows, driving his opponent backward until he had him against the wall.

Griff let the blade press ever so slightly against Del's cheek, until a thin line of blood appeared. "Oh, too bad. That might leave a scar."

"Women are mad for scars. I'm still miles better looking than you." Del smirked. "Perhaps barmaids aren't particular."

"You vermin. She is not a barmaid, and she will never be one again."

"Do you mean you *knew*?" Del lifted one boot and kicked Griff in the chest, sending him reeling back a step.

Griff recovered quickly, but the brief separation gave Del enough time to raise his weapon and defend himself.

"Wait, wait, wait," Delacre said, panting. "Are you . . . God, you can't believe yourself to be in love with that girl."

Griff shook his head, but not in denial. Love was too small a word for what he felt. Just now, when she'd been beneath him . . . He'd never thought he would feel that way again. Ready to brave any sorrow just to keep her at his side. Perhaps the impulse wasn't logical or reasoned, but it was real and true. It was choosing hope rather than despair. Seizing the one sparkling possibility in a roomful of someones.

It was her. All her.

He'd been dead inside. She'd brought him back to life.

"I'd die for her," he said. "And I'd kill for her. The rest doesn't concern you right now."

"Devil take me. You *do* love her." Del ducked, parrying Griff's enraged strike. "Oh, this is even worse. Just what are you expecting to come of it? You plan to make her your mistress?"

"Guess again."

"Well, I know you don't mean to marry her." Delacre laughed. "That would be rich. I can see the scandal sheets now: 'the Barmaid Duchess.'"

They locked swords. Griff flexed his arm, pushing the crossed blades forward until one edge lodged against Del's throat.

"I think the papers will carry a different story tomorrow. One about the late Lord Delacre."

He mustered all the strength in his arm and prepared to flex.

"Griff! Griff, no!"

Chapter Twenty-four

Pauline skittered to a halt in the doorway, having hastily dressed in yesterday's discarded frock. "Don't do this," she called. "He's your oldest friend. You don't want to hurt him."

"Oh, I want to hurt him," Griff said evenly. "I want, very much, to hurt him."

Fair enough. She couldn't deny that after hearing his cruel words, watching Lord Delacre squirm conveyed a particular sort of pleasure. But it had to stop there.

"Griff, please." In cautious steps, she approached the men. "His life isn't worth one-tenth of yours. Your mother is in the house somewhere. You don't want her to see this. And if nothing else moves you, think of the servants. There would be a horrific mess."

"Do you hear that, Del? That's the lowly barmaid pleading for your life. The woman you insulted, begging me to spare your loathsome skin. I think you ought to thank her." Through gritted teeth, he added, "Now."

Delacre nervously cleared his throat. "Thank you."

"'Thank you, Miss Simms,'" Griff demanded. "And make me believe it."

"Thank you, Miss Simms. I owe you my loathsome skin."

Griff inhaled through his nose. Then slowly exhaled. After a long moment, he shoved away, and both swords clattered to the floor.

Delacre slumped to the ground with relief.

Pauline felt like doing the same.

"When next you see her," Griff said, giving Delacre a light kick in the ribs, "you will greet her with respect and address her by her rightful name. As her grace, the Duchess of Halford."

Now Pauline's knees truly buckled. "What?"

"What?" Delacre echoed. "Halford, we had a pact."

"For God's sake. Leave off about the stupid pact. We were nineteen. At that age, we thought midnight grouse hunts were a grand idea, too."

Griff crossed to Pauline and took her hands in his. "I can't let you leave today."

She shook her head with vigor. "No, no. Griff, I can't stay. My sister. I promised her."

"I'll take care of her," he promised. "I'll take care of you both. Always. From this moment on you will never need to work again. Never need to be anxious or fearful. I will take care of everything."

Oh, Lord.

"But you must stay with me and see this through. If you retreat today, the gossips will claim their victory." His thumb caressed her hand. "We can have a future together, but we must seize it now. We can be married today."

"*Today?* Are you mad?"

"Not at all. There are only a few men in England who could procure a special license on such short notice. I'm one of them. We'll marry today, and tonight you'll appear in public as the Duchess of Halford. No one will dare to cut you, just on the basis of a rumor in the scandal sheets. You're beautiful and gracious and clever, and you have that whole silly etiquette book memorized. We'll show them all tonight. You can do this."

She wanted to believe him. She did. But how could she, when she could see very well the reaction of his own supposed best friend?

"She will never be one of us," Delacre said. "Not even if you marry her. You know it, too, Halford. Be honest with yourself, and with her. The gossip will be savage. You will lose almost all of your social connections." He struggled to his feet. "It gives me no pleasure to say this. But I'm trying to be your friend."

"You are not my friend," Griff grated out. "Get the hell out. And pray I don't send my second with a challenge tonight."

"I *am* your second," Delacre said as he left the room. "You don't have anyone else."

See? she wanted to exclaim. It was happening already. Perhaps Delacre wasn't much of a loss, but there would be others. She didn't want to see Griff estranged from *all* his friends.

As for her, there was no question. She must go home, tonight. If she didn't come back as promised, Daniela would feel betrayed and abandoned. Pauline couldn't live with herself then. She'd sworn to never make her sister feel that way again.

She had to end this now. In no uncertain terms.

The duchess entered then, dressed in a quiet gray silk enlivened by a collar of sapphires and diamonds. "What on earth is going on?" she demanded, her keen gaze sweeping the room. "Griffin, explain this commotion."

"Delacre's a jackass. And I'm in love with Pauline."

"Well," the duchess said after a moment's pause. "I already knew both of those things. Neither quite explains the state of my salon."

Griff's eyes never left Pauline's. "I'm going to marry her."

"No, your grace," Pauline countered. "He's not."

The duchess arched a brow. "Does that mean I cast the deciding vote?"

"No," Griff and Pauline said in unison.

She seemed unconvinced. "We'll see."

Pauline drew him aside and whispered, "Griff, this just can't happen."

"Why can't it?"

"How many times must I point out the obvious? You are a duke. I am a serving girl."

"You won't be a serving girl tonight. You will be a duchess. A beautiful, poised woman who can hold her head high anywhere. And I will be the proudest man alive to stand at your side."

"But what pride will I have, when I'm pretending to be someone I'm not?"

"I'm not asking you to pretend."

"Yes, you are." Her voice faltered. "You told me I wasn't a 'someone' to you. You called me perfect, said you wouldn't change a thing."

"Yes, but—"

"But what? You don't mean to stand before all of London's Quality and tell them you're in love with *me*. A serving girl with a coarse, yeoman farmer for a father and a simple-minded sister. Do you?"

He didn't answer. Which was answer enough.

"No. You want to dress me up in a fine gown, throw your name over me like a cloak, and pretend this barmaid everyone's gossiping about just doesn't exist. As if you're ashamed of me." She pressed a hand to her chest. "I can't hide the truth of who I am."

"I am asking you to *live* the truth of who you are. The full truth." His tone was impatient now. He took her by the shoulders and gave her a mild shake. "There is so much more to you than a common serving girl, Pauline. Inside you, there's a remarkable woman who soaked up poetry and squirreled away etiquette lessons, turned cruelty into dreams and plans—because she knew she was meant for better things. I saw that woman the first day we met. I don't know why you won't let the world see her, too."

"You would chastise *me* for hiding secrets? For not living the truth? You, with that locked room upstairs?"

The color drained from his face. He darted a gaze at his mother, then lowered his voice. "This has nothing to do with—"

"Of course it does." She retreated a step. "You're asking me to trust you'll love me openly. That you'll never be embarrassed or resentful of my origins, my family. How can I believe those promises when you won't tell your own mother about her?"

The duchess stepped forward. "Griffin, who is she talking about?"

"No one."

Pauline gasped in shock. "You would *deny* her? She's not even a 'someone,' but a 'no one'?"

He drilled her with a fierce look. "You gave me your word. You promised. Stop this now, Pauline. Or I can never trust you again."

She felt a twinge of guilt. She *had* given her word, and she knew she was pushing him toward a dangerous edge. But someone had to. After today she'd never have another chance.

"You never told a soul she existed, Griff. Then she died, and your heart splintered into a thousand pieces, and still you didn't say a word. How am I to believe that you'll protect me and my sister? How am I to trust that Daniela won't be hidden away in some locked, shameful room?"

"How dare you suggest that I'm ashamed of her."

"Prove you aren't, then! For God's sake. Love shouldn't be a secret. You gave her a name, and you can't even use it."

His eyes flashed.

"Did you love her?"

"You know I did. I do."

She raised her voice. "Then say her name."

"*Mary.*" His angry shout echoed through the room.

Pauline went very still, absorbing the quiet swell of his fury. She knew he would never forgive her for this. But at least, at long last, he might be able to heal.

"Her name was Mary," he said. "Mary Annabel York. Born the fourteenth day of last October, died the following week. She lived all of six days, and I loved her more than my own life." He turned away from her, leveling a small table with a single, savage kick. "God damn it."

"Oh." The duchess pressed a hand to her mouth.

Pauline rushed to her side, afraid the older woman might swoon. She helped her to the nearest chair. "I'm sorry. I'm so very sorry."

She said it over and over again. Words of regret, apology, condolence. But she knew they couldn't be enough.

"I'm sorry. But I've come to care so deeply for you both, and I can see plainly how you love each other. How you're hurting each other, too. Please. You can hate me forever, but talk to each other."

Griff stared out the window, emotionless. "I'll call for the coach to be readied. You can leave within the hour."

"I didn't want it to end this way. I hoped we could part as—"

"As friends?" He tapped one finger against the window glass. "If you don't believe that I'd change anything, give up everything, move heaven and earth to keep someone I love, even if it's only been a week . . . ? Then you don't know me at all." He fixed her with eyes gone cold. "It seems I was wrong about you, too."

Reeling backward, she fled the parlor. Then she turned and ran down the corridor, headed for the entrance hall.

"Pauline," the duchess called after her. "Wait."

She only ran faster. What more could be said? Nothing would change.

When she reached the front door, she wrenched it open and darted through.

Outside, a crowd greeted her with a roar.

Good heavens. The square was jammed with carriages and people, all of them thronged about the steps of Halford House, craning their necks for a look.

A look at *her*, apparently. Lord Delacre hadn't been exaggerating. The word was all over London, and now all of London had converged on the duke's front step.

"There she is! That's her!"

"Miss Simms!" a man shouted. "Is it true you're a barmaid?"

"Five pounds for an interview for the *Prattler*!"

Pauline cowered in the doorway. She couldn't go back inside and face Griff again. But this crowd churned with enough curiosity and excitement to pulverize her. Even if she managed to escape these people, where would she go? She had no money. No possessions, save the clothes on her back.

She wasn't even wearing shoes.

"Pauline!" A familiar voice filtered through the din. "Pauline! It's me, Susanna."

Her heart leaped. Shading her brow with both hands, she scanned the crowd until she saw a friendly wave from a gloved hand, and a halo of red hair.

A friend.

As Pauline pushed toward her, people grabbed at her disheveled clothing and jostled for a glimpse of her face. She felt buffeted about like a cork.

At last she and Susanna made their way to each other. "Oh, Lady Rycliff. I can't . . . I don't know how to—" Overwhelmed, she clapped a hand to her mouth.

Susanna folded her in a protective hug. "It's all right, dear. It's all right. You're coming home with me."

Chapter Twenty-five

Ensconced at Rycliff House, safely away from the crowds, Lady Rycliff—who now insisted Pauline call her Susanna—poured another cup of tea. "What a week you've had, dear."

Pauline watched the fragrant liquid filling her porcelain cup. Lady Rycliff serving *her* tea. The world had turned upside down.

"It has been eventful." And the story had taken the better part of two hours to relate, from the first tossing of clayed sugar to the cold, bitter end.

Of course, she hadn't told *everything*. She left out the amorous details. And Griff deserved his privacy where Mary Annabel was concerned. She'd never tell another soul about that.

"I knew Halford was a villain." Lady Payne—who insisted Pauline call her Minerva—plucked a biscuit from the tray and took a vengeful bite.

"You're mistaken," Pauline said. "He's a good man. The best kind of man."

And she'd hurt him. Whenever Pauline closed

her eyes, she saw his angry, betrayed expression. The image was stamped into her memory, embossed in guilt. Perhaps she shouldn't have pushed, but she'd been so concerned for him . . .

And so afraid.

Griff was right. She'd been so very afraid for herself.

"Did he truly propose marriage?" Lady Rycliff asked.

Pauline nodded.

"And you refused?"

She nodded again. "You must think me a fool."

"You are not a fool." Susanna reached to squeeze her hand.

No. Pauline supposed she wasn't. In truth, she was a coward. She'd panicked and pushed him away.

His suggestions had been such madness. The two of them, marry? Her, become a true duchess? An elegant lady, admired by the London elite?

It just couldn't be. The crowd outside Halford House knew the truth. She could still feel them tugging at her clothing, shouting in her ears.

Griff could claim not to care about gossip—but that was easy for a duke to say. He'd never been the object of mockery and scorn. He didn't know how it felt to be at the bottom of the pecking order, and if Pauline tried to live in his world, that was exactly where she'd be. Always. Even if she could withstand a lifetime of snide remarks and subtle cruelty, she couldn't expose Daniela to that treatment.

"You were right to refuse him," Minerva said. "But we can't let it end this way."

We?

Why should either of these ladies care how her week ended? Pauline felt lucky enough that they'd offered her a place to gather herself and help finding transportation back to Spindle Cove.

"This ball tonight," Minerva said, adjusting her spectacles. "You must go."

"Why would I do that? I doubt the duke will attend."

"Even if he doesn't attend. Go for yourself. Just to let those gossips see you, undefeated and proud. Simply to prove you can."

To prove you can.

But could she, really?

Pauline shook her head. In Spindle Cove she'd half listened as Minerva Highwood lectured the other ladies on the most impossible topics—vast underwater caves and giant prehistoric lizards. This latest suggestion seemed no different.

"I can't attend the ball tonight," she said. "I wouldn't even know where to go, or how to get there. I haven't anything to wear."

"Leave all that to us," Minerva said, tapping Susanna on the arm. "We'll handle the arrangements. You need only supply the courage. Spindle Cove ladies band together."

"I'm not a lady, my lady."

"We would stand by you even if you were a serving girl," Susanna said. "But I believe you've always been something more."

Pauline warmed a little. She *did* have more inside of her, and maybe Griff wasn't the only one to notice. To be sure, she wasn't up to the standards of Lady Haughfell and her set, and she certainly was no duchess. But neither were Susanna or Minerva, or any of the other ladies who sought refuge in Spindle Cove.

She belonged there. Her heart expanded with a sense of certainty. She knew her right place in the world. She was going to have her cozy, welcoming, wonderful-smelling library, and it would be a home for any girl who needed it.

And she would have her sister—the one person who loved her wholly, without shame or reservation. That was something even the fourth-largest fortune in England couldn't buy.

"I want to go home," she said. "As soon as it can be managed."

"Go to the ball first," Minerva urged.

Pauline shook her head. "I must be back in Spindle Cove tomorrow. I promised my sister."

"You can do both. The mail coach is the fastest way home, and it doesn't leave London until after midnight. Isn't that right, Susanna?"

"I suppose," Lady Rycliff replied. "Pauline, if you wanted to attend the ball for an hour or two, we could still have you to the mail coach in time."

Pauline hesitated.

"My lady?" A housemaid entered the room, looking apologetic. "I beg your pardon, but there's someone here for Miss Simms."

Pauline's heart fluttered. "If it's the duke, I . . ."

The maid looked confused. "I didn't see any duke, ma'am. It's a lady caller. She's brought a good many parcels, too."

A young woman entered the sitting room, laden with a tower of boxes. Pauline couldn't even see her face for all the packages.

"Miss Simms, it's m-me."

She rose to her feet. "Flora? What are you doing here?" She helped unload the parcels from the maid's arms.

Once unburdened, Flora dropped her gaze. "They've s-sacked me."

"*Sacked* you? Oh, no."

"It's what I deserved. Her grace let me go without a reference, and I haven't any way to find a new p-post. I thought, perhaps if I readied you for the ball tonight—so's everyone was dazzled by your beauty, and it made it to the papers—maybe someone would hire me anyhow." She grabbed Pauline's arm. "Please, Miss Simms. It's you who'd be d-doing me a favor."

"Flora, I'd like to help. But I don't know. Perhaps you could dress Lady Rycliff or Lady Payne."

Flora shook her head. "It has to be you. I want to see you do this, Miss Simms. You worked so hard all week. We all d-did. And then there's this. It was made for you. It won't fit anyone else."

From the largest box, she withdrew a breathtaking flash of silver.

Oh goodness.

The gown seemed to be at least three-fourths skirt. The bodice was small and tight, boned for stiffness and fitted with the shortest puffs of sleeves. The skirts were a cloud. A great shimmering, airy, fluffy cloud of tulle overlaying satin. Little sparkling things were affixed to the tulle by the thousands. It truly was a thing of wonder.

"Oh, Pauline," Susanna said. "If any man can look at you in that and not simply fall to his knees before you . . ." Her voice trailed off.

"He'll eat his own hat." Minerva clapped with glee. "Do it. Do it for every young woman who ever felt scorned or overlooked. This is your chance, Pauline."

Pauline ran a touch over the beautiful silver fabric, spangled with seed pearls and tiny crystals. She didn't *need* to prove her worth to anyone. She didn't *need* a lavish wardrobe or the wealth that accompanied the title of duchess.

But she needed to wear this gown, just this once. It was made for her. Literally.

"Very well," she said. "Let's do it."

"One question," said Susanna. "Do we tell the men about this?"

"No," said Minerva stoutly. "Colin will steal all the credit. This is going to be *our* grand success. We'll show everyone what Spindle Cove ladies can do."

Pauline wasn't so certain about that "success" part. She still doubted that she could ever blend in at such an event.

But after tonight, she could go home with her pride. No one could say she wasn't brave enough to try.

"Corinthian." As the carriage rolled up before the Prince Regent's grand residence, the word just rolled from her tongue.

"What is it, Pauline?"

"Those columns on the portico. They're Corinthian."

Amazing. This week in London had taught her the strangest things. What an odd assortment of lessons she would bring home with her.

She still hadn't learned how to hide her anxiety, however. It helped that Susanna and Minerva were clearly nervous, too.

"We're not much good with balls, either," Minerva confided. "Perhaps we should have warned you beforehand."

"It's all right," said Susanna. "We'll all go in as a group."

As they made their way into the entrance hall, Susanna—the tallest of them—craned her neck to look over the crowd.

"Oh, drat," she said. "They're checking names against a list."

That wasn't good news. Pauline knew she'd been on the list earlier that week. But today's gossip had no doubt removed her from it. Or perhaps moved her to another list—one written in red and headed with the words, *Not to be admitted under any circumstance.*

"You could give another name," Minerva suggested. "You could be me. I don't mind. Everyone will just assume I've removed my spectacles for once and undergone a thrilling transformation."

"No." Pauline smiled. "It's kind of you, but I can't. I must be here as myself or not at all."

When the crowd shifted, she quietly remained in place and let her friends drift away. If this evening proceeded as disastrously as she suspected it might, she didn't want Lady Rycliff and Lady Payne to be tainted by association. They'd brought her this far, but she must face the rest on her own.

Surely there was another way into the ballroom. There must be a smaller passageway for the staff. She was a servant; she could find it.

After a few moments' surreptitious investigation, she turned down a narrow corridor. She passed near a clashing, steamy din that must have been the palace kitchen. When she spied a footman returning with a tray of empty glasses, she knew she needed to proceed in the direction he'd come.

Pauline traversed a passageway with stairs. At the top, she listened for the sounds of chatter and music. Turning toward the noise, she rounded a corner . . .

And reeled to a halt when she nearly collided with a finely dressed man.

"I'm sorry," she started to apologize. "I—"

When she swept a look from his boots to his face, she gasped.

Oh, bollocks.

Fitted tailcoat. White gloves. An angry red line running down his left cheek.

"Lord Delacre."

Griff had been right—that wound would probably leave a scar. Not a disfiguring one. Just a thin, indelible reminder.

Good.

"I knew I saw you here," he said.

"Please excuse me."

When she tried to move past him, he grabbed her arm. "I won't let you do this. I've known Halford all his life, and I know what's best for him even when he doesn't."

Her heart jumped. Did that mean Griff was here?

She pulled against Delacre's grasp. "Let me go."

Delacre didn't frighten her—but he was a

man, much larger and more powerful than she. Moreover, this was his native environment. His friends at this event numbered in the hundreds. She could count hers on one hand and still have a good many fingers left over.

She was outsized, outranked, outclassed. And unless she figured out a way around him, she would remain outside that ballroom forever.

"Is it money you want?" He released her arm and slid a bank note from his breast pocket. She could just make out the writing on it.

Five pounds.

He waved it at her. "Take it, then. And use the servants' exit. This isn't the place for you."

That's not for you, girl.

Her cheeks burned. With those words, he wasn't Delacre anymore. He was every book that had ever been ripped from her hand. Every door that had ever been slammed on her.

She wanted to fight back, throw something. Spit in his face.

But this situation called for a different sort of phlegm.

She pulled her spine straight, lifted her chin and fixed him with a cool, direct look. "Go to *hell*."

While he stood sputtering, she dashed past him and rejoined the crowd near the ballroom entry. Before she could lose her nerve, she cut ahead of the queue of waiting guests. Impolite, perhaps. But the gossips already knew her to be a serving girl—it wasn't as though they could think much worse of her.

She gave her name to the majordomo, and he announced, "Miss Simms of Sussex."

The ballroom went utterly silent, except for the thunder of her heart. Her hands trembled at her sides.

Breathe, she told herself.

And then: *Go.*

She let that transparent cord at her navel pull her forward, guiding her as she descended the small flight of stairs. As she walked, her gown caught the light of hundreds of candles and lamps, sending arrows of light in every direction.

Once she reached the bottom of the staircase, she sought refuge behind a cluster of potted palms and scanned the crowd for familiar faces. Where were Minerva and Susanna? She knew she'd resolved to go this alone, but she didn't feel so brave anymore.

And then—

Griff.

He strode toward her, wearing an immaculate black tailcoat and carrying a wicked gleam in his eye. So assured, so handsome.

Oh, the flutterings. She had flutterings all through her. They were so strong, they just about carried her away.

"I didn't think you'd attend," she breathed. "I was hoping, of course. I just wanted to see you again. To tell you I'm sorry, and that you were right. I was afraid. I'm *still* afraid, to be honest. I don't think I can do this at all. But if you—"

He didn't let her finish. "You shouldn't be here."

She was seized by a pulse of pure terror. It didn't matter to her if the rest of the gathering scorned her. But if even Griff would cast her out . . .

He didn't cast her out.

He took her by the hand.

"You shouldn't be here," he said, more gently this time. "The most beautiful woman in the room does not belong in the corner with the potted palms. Come out from there. Or else Flora did all this for nothing."

She pulled up short and stared at him. "*You.* It was you. You sent Flora. And the gown. You didn't sack her at all."

A little smile played about his lips. "You wouldn't have come if I'd *asked.*"

Of all the tricks. She couldn't believe it. "I thought you were furious with me."

"I *was* furious with you. For about . . . ten minutes. Perhaps a full quarter hour. Then I came to my senses." He tugged her forward. "Come. We have a bargain to complete. There's someone to whom you should be properly introduced."

Not the Prince Regent, she prayed.

Worse.

He steered her straight toward the Haughfells. All three of them—mother and daughters—were united by the grim sets of their mouths and their refusal to even look at Pauline.

What was Griff playing at now?

"Lady Haughfell." He bowed. "What a happy coincidence. I know you've been longing to further your acquaintance with Miss Simms. And here she is."

Sheer horror flickered across the matron's powdered face. "I do not think—"

"But this is ideal. What better time or place? In fact"—he took a dance card and its small attached pencil from the older Miss Haughfell's hand—"let

me write down the key details. Just so there can
be no question in the scandal sheets tomorrow.
Miss Simms hails from Spindle Cove, a charming village in Sussex. Her father is a farmer, with
thirty acres and some livestock."

As Pauline looked on in amazement, he narrated
the entire tale for them. His mother's kidnapping
ploy, their arrival in Spindle Cove. Pauline's appearance in the Bull and Blossom—sugar-dusted
and muddied. His visit to her family's cottage and
their eventual bargain. He spared no detail, but
told the story plainly and with good humor. Occasionally, he noted an important fact on the dance
card:

Bull and Blossom.

Thirty acres.

One thousand pounds.

"You see," he said, "I brought Miss Simms to
London to thwart my mother's matchmaking
schemes. She was supposed to be a laughable failure. A hilarious joke."

One of the Misses Haughfells began to giggle.
Her mother smacked her wrist with a folded fan.

"No, no," Griff said. "Do laugh, please. It's most
amusing. A barmaid, receiving duchess lessons.
Can you imagine? The best part was the diction
training. My mother was forever drilling Miss
Simms on her H's."

"Is that so?" Lady Haughfell arched a brow. "I
don't suppose she made much progress."

"Oh, but she did. Show them, Miss Simms."

Pauline smiled. "*H*ideous. *H*am-faced. *H*ag." She
looked to Griff. "There. How was that?"

"Brilliant." He beamed at her.

"Write it down?"

"Of course." As he scribbled the epithets on Miss Haughfell's dance card, he went on talking. "But you haven't heard the funniest bit, Lady Haughfell. See, I thought I was playing a trick on my mother—and all London—but it turns out, the joke was on me."

The matron stiffened. "Because you have lost what remained of your family's honor and society's good opinion?"

"No. Because I fell desperately in love with this barmaid and now cannot imagine happiness without her." He looked up and shrugged. "Whoops."

All three Haughfells stared at him in mute, slack-jawed horror. Pauline wished she could have a miniature of their expressions to keep in a drawer forever and pull out on dull, rainy days.

Griff sharpened the pencil stub with his thumbnail. "Let's make sure to have that down. It's important." He spoke the words slowly as he inscribed them. "Desperately . . . in . . . love."

"Don't forget the 'whoops,'" Pauline said, looking over his shoulder. "That was the best part."

"Yes." He looked up, and his dark gaze caught hers. "So it was."

They stared into each other's eyes, utterly absorbed in affection and silent laughter.

The moment was perfect. *He* was perfect. Teasing, wonderful man.

"Is that a waltz they're playing?" Griff suddenly asked. He stared at the marked-up card in his hand before handing it back. "Pity your card is full, Miss Haughfell. I suppose I'll dance with Miss Simms instead."

He led her to the center of the ballroom and slid one arm about her torso, fitting his hand between her shoulder blades. Together, they joined the waltz.

Almost immediately, other couples began to disappear. One by one, at first. Then two or three at the same time. And the more alone they grew, the less self-conscious she became. Soon it felt positively magical. Here they were, dancing under the full weight of society's disapproval. And it felt as though the orchestra and canopied ballroom and general resplendence of the setting had all been arranged just for the two of them.

"I suppose I've fulfilled my end of the agreement," she said. "I'm not going to be the toast of London tonight, nor any night."

"No. You won't."

With that, she thought surely Griff would put a stop to the dance, but he didn't. He just twirled her into turn after turn.

"I think we've done enough," she whispered. "I'm a confirmed disaster."

"Oh, yes. A comprehensive catastrophe. A beautiful, perfect failure." He pulled back to regard her. "And I could not be more proud."

His words settled as warmly as a hug. They both knew she could never have sustained any pretense at gentle breeding. Families like the Haughfells would not have been fooled. Instead, he'd embraced Pauline for her true self—publicly and completely, in a manner that ensured they'd never accept her at all.

But by letting her fail, he'd made her a success. At long last, she was a triumph. The serving girl who'd conquered not society, but its most recalcitrant duke. A huntress, draped in the elusive white tiger's pelt.

Just for tonight.

He swept her with an adoring look. "Radiant. Just as you were that first day."

She laughed. "I am sure I look nothing like I did that first day."

"You do. You sparkled."

"That was the sugar."

"I'm not convinced. I think it was just you." His voice softened to a caress. "It was always you."

A lump stuck in her throat. She swallowed hard.

Out of the corner of her eye, Pauline spied a few of the Prince Regent's hussars conferring in the corner, hands on their sabers. If they didn't leave the dance floor soon, armed guards might chase them from it. *That* would be a night to remember.

"We're down to minutes, I think."

"So let's make them count," Griff said. "Here I am, a duke. Waltzing with a serving girl. Holding her improperly close, for everyone to see." He shivered for effect. "What's that I feel? Could it be the social fabric unraveling?"

Her mouth twisted as she tried not to smile. "It's probably just the gout. I've heard dukes are gouty."

"Well, I've heard serving girls taste like ripe berries." He touched his lips to hers.

She gasped. "Griff."

"There. Now I've kissed you, in front of everyone. Shocking. And look, I'm going to do it again."

He stopped dancing and used those strong arms to pull her close, and claimed her mouth in a passionate kiss.

When they parted, he wore a sly, roguish smile. "What would Mrs. Worthington say?"

She didn't know about Mrs. Worthington, but somewhere a clock began to chime the hour. Pauline's heartbeat stuttered.

The mail coach.

"I have to leave," she said. "I must go, or I'll never make it home in time." She tugged out of his embrace. "I'm sorry. I promised my sister. You promised her, too."

She dashed away from him, streaking out of the ballroom, back through the crowded antechambers, to the portico and down the stairs—just as fast as her slippers would carry her.

"Wait." He called to her from the top of the stairs.

"Don't," she called over her shoulder. "Don't make it harder, Griff."

"Pauline, you can't leave yet. Not like this."

She tried to hurry but his footfalls outpaced hers easily. These stupid heeled slippers. When she tripped again, she kicked one off and threw it over her shoulder.

He dodged the flying slipper and caught her by the arm. "Wait."

"Just let me go."

"I'm not trying to stop you," he said.

All the fight went out of her. She blinked at him. "You're not?"

"No. I'm not." His expression turned serious. "You need to go. Go home to your sister and open that circulating library. It's your dream, and you've earned it. As for me . . . I have some work to do, too. I think it's time I lived up to the vaunted Halford legacy."

"Truly?"

He nodded, solemn. "To start, I'm going to be a man of my word. I promised to have you home by Saturday, and so I will."

This was it, Pauline realized. He was truly letting her go. She would return to Spindle Cove and be a shopkeeper, and he would become a respectable duke. They would be further apart than ever.

Oh, God. They might never meet again.

"I have my carriage and fastest team waiting to see you home. But first there's something I owe you." He rummaged in his pocket.

The thought of him paying her made her stomach turn. The words spilled from her lips. "I can't. I can't take your money."

"But we agreed."

"I know. But that was before, and now . . ." She shuddered, thinking of Delacre and his five-pound note. "It would make me feel cheap. I just can't."

"Well. You must take this much, at least." He pulled a coin from his pocket and placed it in her hand. He folded her fingers over it, still breathing hard. "For Daniela. I don't have a penny."

Oh, Griff.

"I expect great things of you, Pauline." He touched her cheek. "Do me a favor and expect the same of me? Lord knows, no one else will."

As he retreated back into his glittering, aristocratic world, she opened her fingers and stared at the golden sovereign on her palm.

Dukes and their problems.

Chapter Twenty-six

Griff watched his mother closely as she turned in place, taking in the walls painted with incongruous rainbows and frolicking Arabian colts.

"I did want to tell you." He took a seat on a wooden stool draped with a Holland cloth. "I just didn't know how. She was gone so quickly, and then afterward . . ."

His voice trailed off, and the duchess raised a hand in a firm, silent gesture, letting him know further words were unnecessary. She was no stranger to quiet suffering, holding her aristocratic grace through all manner of trials. He knew this news would hurt her deeply—it was why he hadn't wanted to tell her. But she *was* the duchess. If he knew his mother, she would cling to her composure. Bear up under the weight and never crack.

Perhaps he didn't know his mother at all.

She turned to him with tears in her eyes. "Oh, Griffin. I've been so worried for you. I knew you were hurting, and I knew the cause must be something horrible. You've *looked* horrible."

Griff rubbed his face with both hands.

"No, I mean it. Just perfectly wretched."

He made a gesture of helplessness. "My apologies."

She sighed. "I was so hoping it wouldn't come to this. Stay right there."

She left, and returned within a minute, approaching him where he sat in the center of the room.

From beneath her arm, his mother unfurled the ugliest, most malformed knitted muffler he'd ever seen. She wrapped it once, twice, thrice about his neck.

It was the tightest, warmest hug he'd ever received.

He stared up at her, bewildered. "Where did this come from?"

"The knitting? Or the affection it represents? I'd rather not talk about the knitting. As for the love . . . it's always been here. Even when we haven't discussed it."

He rose to his feet and kissed her on the cheek. "I know."

For so many years now they'd been all the family each other had. He suspected they'd avoided admitting how much they meant to each other, for the simple fear of acknowledging how close they were to being alone.

She touched one of her cool, papery hands to his face. "My darling boy. I'm so sorry."

"How did you bear it?" he asked. "How did you bear this three times?"

"Not as bravely as you have. And never alone." She looked around at the painted walls. "The loss was keen. In my heart, I have a room something like this for each of them. But even in the darkest hours, your father and I took comfort in each other. And in you."

"In me? God. I never felt good enough to be one son. Let alone take the place of four."

"I hate that you felt that way. Looking back, we should have been more nurturing. But we were so afraid of coddling you, when we knew the strong man you'd need to become. Left to my own devices, I could have hugged you to my bosom and held you there until your sixteenth birthday."

"Well." His mouth pulled to the side. "I suppose I'm glad you resisted that urge."

She patted his cheek. "Griffin, I've always looked at you and seen a generous, good-hearted man. I've merely grown impatient waiting for you to see the same."

"I wanted to be better for her." He lifted his eyes to the ceiling. "I didn't hide all this because I was ashamed of Mary Annabel. I was only ashamed of myself, my dissolute life. I'd resolved to make myself a better man. I didn't want anyone to look at my daughter and see one of my mistakes."

Mistakes he kept right on making, it seemed.

"She was right," he said. "Pauline was right about our chances, but she had the blame laid wrong. If society won't accept her, it's not her fault. It's mine. A stodgy, boring sort of nobleman might fall in love with a commoner, and society would give her the benefit of the doubt. An even chance to prove herself, at least. But with my sordid history, people will always assume she's just a debauched duke's latest, greatest scandal. She deserves better than that. I want better *for* her."

"It's not too late," his mother said. "Let her come here. Not just for a week, but months. You can take our place in Lords, and we'll introduce her to society slowly next year. You'll see, people will eventually—"

"No. No, that's just it. She doesn't want this life, and I don't blame her. I don't even want it, but I know it's my duty now." He sighed. "There may never be a ninth Duke of Halford, but I want the eighth to be remembered well. For my daughter's sake."

"And what about Pauline?"

Pauline, Pauline, Pauline. She'd been gone from his life a matter of hours, and he already missed her so acutely. He would spend his life digging out from landslides.

"I just want all her dreams to come true."

Had the cottage always been this small?

Pauline stood in the lane, just staring. Uncertain how to approach her own home. Major the guard goose came honking toward her, alerting those within the house.

"Pauline?" Her mother's face appeared in the window. "Pauline, is that you?"

She dashed a tear from her eye. "Yes, Mum. It's me. I'm home."

Later, up in the sleeping loft, Pauline and Daniela hugged and cried. Then they brushed and plaited one another's hair and laid out their Sunday dresses for the next morning.

As always, Griff's sovereign went straight in the collection box.

During the church service, Pauline could feel all the curiosity of Spindle Cove focused on her. She knew she'd have to answer a great many questions, but she just wasn't ready yet.

And even though she managed to delay her first trip to the All Things shop for another several days, she still wasn't prepared to answer them.

Sally Bright pounced on her the moment she walked through the door. Aside from being her oldest and dearest friend, Sally was the most inquisitive, gossipy person in Spindle Cove. Pauline knew the curiosity must be gnawing at her friend with a hundred teeth.

"You"—she lifted and waved a stack of newspapers—"have so much explaining to do! Did you really attend a ball? Make a duke fall madly in love with you?"

"Sally, I don't wish to speak of it yet. I just can't. It's all too . . ." Her voice broke.

Sally didn't press for more. She hurried out from behind the counter and wrapped Pauline in a tight hug. "There there. We'll have years to talk it over, won't we?"

Pauline nodded. "Sadly, I think we will."

She'd been harboring the absurd hope that Griff would come chasing after her, perhaps show up at the farm cottage some morning, unshaven and smelling of cologne. But as the days passed, her hope seemed more and more like a fanciful dream. That wasn't the fairy tale he'd promised her.

"I have some news that will cheer you," Sally said.

"Oh? What's that?"

"It's nasty old Mrs. Whittlecombe. She's moving to Dorset to live with her nephew."

"Truly? That is good news, I suppose. For everyone but the nephew. I thought she'd never leave that tumbledown old place."

Sally shrugged. "Well, she did. And cleared out of the neighborhood quickly, too. Now I'm stuck with a half-dozen bottles of her noxious 'health tonic.' I don't suppose anyone else is going to want it." Her eyebrows lifted. "And there's something else. Something for you."

"What's that?"

"Come see."

Sally pulled her over to the storeroom. On the floor in the center sat an immense wooden crate, labeled with Pauline's name.

"A man delivered it special yesterday," she said. "It didn't come through the regular post. But he told me it wasn't to go to your cottage, ever. I must wait until Miss Simms came to the shop, and I couldn't speak a word of it to anyone. It was all just painfully mysterious." She gave Pauline's arm an impatient shake. "Can't we open it now? It's heavy as anything. I'm dying to know what's inside. *Dying.*"

Pauline nodded. "Of course."

Sally gave a little cheer of excitement. With the help of a slender crowbar, she pried the top from the crate and sifted through a top layer of straw.

"Oh," she said flatly. "Well, that's disappointing. I hope you didn't have your hopes too high. It's only books." She lifted a red-bound volume off the top and peered into the crate. "Yes. Books, all the way down."

"Let me see," Pauline said, snatching the book from Sally's hand.

She ran a palm over the fresh red Morocco binding, brushing aside a blade of straw so she could read the cover: *Memoirs of a Woman of Pleasure: The Life and Adventures of Fanny Hill.*

"Who's this Mrs. Radcliffe person?" Sally lifted

a handful of books from the crate. "She wrote a great many books."

"Be careful with them, please." Pauline went to her side and began to sort through the volumes. Radcliffe, Johnson, Wollstonecraft, Fielding, Defoe. All the books on the list that Griff had dictated that day in Snidling's bookshop.

He'd remembered. And he'd known not to send them to her home, for fear her father would pitch them all into the fire. She lifted the book to her nose and inhaled that aroma deeply—her second favorite smell—before setting it aside to look at the rest.

Halfway through the crate, she found a small volume not bound in red Morocco, but instead covered in the softest, most impractical fawn-hued leather. *Collected Poems of William Blake*.

Tears welled in her eyes as she opened the cover. Inside, right on the exquisite marble endpaper, there was affixed a bookplate with a stamp.

FROM THE LIBRARY OF MISS PAULINE SIMMS

"Oh, Griff."

This crate wasn't merely stuffed with books. It was full of meaning. Messages too complicated to explain and too risky to send in a letter.

He knew her, this crate of books said. He knew her to the deepest, most hidden places of her soul. He respected her as a person, with thoughts and dreams and desires.

He loved her. He truly did.

And most poignant of all, this crate of books held one clear, undeniable message:

Goodbye.

Chapter Twenty-seven

A few months later

If there was anything better than the smell of books, it was the smell of books mingled with the scents of strong tea and spice biscuits—and all of it on a rainy afternoon.

A celebration was in order. The Two Sisters circulating library was exactly one month old today.

All the Spindle Cove ladies had come to their party. The small shop was crowded with young women poring over scandalous books and dunking their biscuits into cups of milky tea.

Pauline loved this shop, as she'd never thought she could love something that was supposed to be work. And she did work hard—every day, from dawn to dusk—but the labor was a fatiguing kind of joy. Spindle Cove was bustling with a new crop of ladies on holiday, all of them eager for new reading material.

Some days, a young woman might come

through the door looking rather lost. And then she'd find an old friend sitting on the shelf, bound in red Morocco. Or perhaps a new, exciting acquaintance. She'd leave with a book in her hand and a smile on her face. Those days made all the hard work worthwhile.

And she never worked alone. She had her sister.

She and Daniela had traded one sleeping loft for another. They lived above the shop now, the two of them. Except for visits to Mama on Sundays, they kept their own hours, made their own meals, cleaned as little or as much as they liked. They were wildly extravagant with candles, burning them late into the night and reading verses to each other.

This place truly was home.

"Who's that walking across the square?" a lady said, peering out the window. "Do we know him?"

A second young lady laughed. "I think we might."

"Oh goodness," said Charlotte Highwood. "Not him again."

It couldn't be. He wouldn't have come. But in the end, curiosity won out. Pauline made her way to the window and peered out through the rain.

Oh, Lord. Oh, Lord. It *was* him. Even with the rain, she'd know those strong features and broad shoulders anywhere. The Duke of Halford was walking straight toward her shop.

Griff.

Her pulse began to pound. Why was he here now, after months had passed with no word? Just when she'd gathered the pieces of her heart and built it a new, safer home.

"Don't worry, Miss Simms," Charlotte said. "I'll devil him before he can trouble you."

Pauline stepped toward the rear of the shop, trying to steel herself.

He opened the door, ducking his head to enter. "Is this the—"

"Halt." Charlotte blocked the doorway with a broomstick. "Are you looking for someone?"

"No." His deep voice rang out. "I am most certainly not looking for 'someone.' I'm looking for Pauline Simms and no other."

Her heart skipped a beat.

Charlotte held firm. "The cost of entry is a verse. No exceptions."

Griff looked past her, scanning the crowded shop until his eyes locked with Pauline's. Heavens above. He was even more handsome than she remembered.

"Miss Simms," he said. "May I—"

"No exceptions," Charlotte repeated. "A verse."

"I don't know any verses."

"Write one."

"Very well, very well." He pushed a hand through his dark, damp hair. "There once was a libertine duke. He . . . He . . . preferred trout and cod to fluke. He let his love go, but he wants her to know—"

Pauline turned away, unable to look at him anymore.

He shouted after her. "I haven't ceased thinking of you since that night, Pauline. Not for a moment."

"That's a terrible verse," said Charlotte, holding the broomstick turnpike in place. "Doesn't even rhyme."

"I don't know what else rhymes with duke."

The ladies muttered among themselves, debating possibilities.

"I have it." Charlotte's voice rang out over all. "Puke! 'He let his love go, but he wants her to know . . . that thoughts of her face make him puke.'"

"That won't do," Griff said. "That's not right at all."

"At least it rhymes," Charlotte grumbled.

"Rebuke," Pauline declared, exasperated. "He deserves a stern rebuke."

"Excellent," Griff said. "I'll take that one. May I pass now?"

Daniela threw a biscuit. It bounced off the duke's forehead. "Go, Duke. Leave my sister be."

"Daniela has the right of it," Pauline said. "You should go. I can't imagine what you want after all these months."

"I wanted to see you, see how you've done." He looked around the shop. "This is brilliant, Pauline. I knew you'd make a go of it."

That was all? He'd made the journey all the way down from London just to have a look at his investment, so to speak?

"Well, now you've seen me," she said. "So you can go."

The other ladies in the room agreed, adding their voices to the call for Griff to leave.

"Listen, if you'll all just give me a moment alone with Miss Simms, I—"

"Just go," she shouted, her nerves in tatters. The scent of his cologne was wafting its nefarious way to her, and soon she'd be reduced to a puddle on her newly painted floor. "You might be a duke, but you can't make a habit of this. Popping into my place of work unannounced and turning my life on its ear. I won't have it. I just can't. So unless you've come here to fall on your knees, grovel for forgiveness, and beg me to marry you, you can leave this moment and never return."

He didn't leave. He merely stood there, staring at her.

Then he went down on his knees.

"Oh, no." Pauline pressed both hands to her face. "Griff, no."

"You can't refuse before I even ask." He ruffled his hair with one hand. "Why is this all happening backward? I knew you'd be surprised to see me, and no doubt angry that it's taken me so long. But I thought you'd at least let me have a few words. I had a whole speech prepared, you know. A good one, too. But now that you've ruined the surprise . . ."

He reached into his pocket and removed a small velvet pouch.

Pauline peeked at it between her trembling fingers. By now she was crying messily. She swiped impatiently at the tears with both wrists, straining to make out the ring he shook free onto his palm. An emerald, set in a thick gold band and ringed with tiny diamonds.

Well, at least she knew he'd chosen it himself.

It was beautiful.

She turned away, burying her face in her apron. Griffin Eliot York, the eighth Duke of Halford, was here, on his knees. For her. Ring in hand, with the whole village watching.

It was too much. Too much impossibility to accept. To much joy to comprehend.

"I love you, Pauline Simms. I've loved you since the day we met. In fact, I suspect some part of my heart loved you long before then. There was no woman for me before you, and if you refuse me, there'll be no one after. I know I'm no prize, but—"

She interrupted him with a burst of indelicate laughter. "No prize?" Turning, she dabbed at her eyes. "Griff, you're a duke."

"Yes, I'd noticed that. So?"

"So . . . we settled this. A duke can't marry a serving girl. Or even a shopkeeper."

"You were right. Our lives *were* too different. For the two of us to make a go of it, something had to change. I couldn't change the world. And I didn't want to change one thing about *you*. It seemed clear, however, that I was overdue for some improvement."

"Improvement?"

"You're familiar with the Halford legacy. I come from a long line of scholars, explorers, generals. They amassed quite the string of accomplishments and a vast amount of wealth. And I finally realized there's one thing I had the heart to do that none of the rest of them could."

"What's that?"

"I could give it all away."

The shop went very quiet.

"All of it?" Pauline echoed.

"Oh, no," Charlotte moaned. "Now he's worse than an arrogant, debauched duke. He's a *poor* duke."

"I'm no pauper," he said. "You needn't look so

stricken. A duke can't surrender his title. There are entailed properties, trusts. It's boring solicitor business, that part. The short version is, I'll always be a wealthy man. I might sink from fourth richest in England to somewhere about fourteenth. But even so, there was a great deal of money I was free to part with. And it went easily, once I applied myself to the task."

Pauline eyed him, wary. "I don't understand. What are you telling me?"

"I found my natural talent. I was born to give money away. But no more of this 'squander a few thousand here or there' nonsense. This is a full, systematic divesture of the family's dispensable fortune. The eighth Duke of Halford will be remembered as the single largest charitable benefactor in England's history. This will be my legacy."

She stared at him, shocked. But he did look happy. Entirely at peace with himself and his place in the world. Not precisely humble. She didn't suppose that rakish arrogance would ever wear off, nor did she wish it to. But he looked like a man with purpose and direction.

And the best part was, she knew he hadn't given any of it up for her. He'd done it for himself.

"I confess, I did make one last selfish purchase." A sly grin tipped his mouth. "A crumbling farmhouse, of all things. At the arse-end of Sussex."

"*You* purchased the Whittlecombe farmhouse? That was you?"

"It was the only land for sale in the parish." With a muttered curse, he shifted his weight. "Will you say yes soon? This floor is damned hard. And you're much too far away."

She moved closer. "I don't remember hearing a question."

"I don't know what to ask, truthfully. 'Will you be my wife' or 'be my duchess' or just 'be mine' . . . they all sound dangerous. I don't want to put names or titles to it, or you'll find some way to argue. I don't even care if you wear the bloody ring." He tossed the velvet pouch to the floor.

"I'll wear the ring," Charlotte offered.

Pauline sent her a look. *Don't touch it.*

Griff held out his empty hand. "Pauline, I'm here asking you—begging you, if it comes to that—to take my hand. Just take my hand, and promise before God you will never let it go. I will vow the same. Can we arrange for that to happen, someday soon? In a church?" After a moment, he added in a quiet voice, "Please?"

She put her hand in his. His fingers curled around hers in a grasp that was as poignant as a hug, as iron-forged as a promise. And she knew, in her heart, that the church vows would only be formalities.

This was the moment. And from here, the world only grew warmer.

He raised her hand to his lips and kissed it. "Tell me this means yes."

"Yes," she said. "Yes, to all the questions. To every question. And I'd be honored to wear your ring."

Excepting Charlotte, who muttered "Drat," everyone gave a hearty cheer.

Hours later, after all the biscuits were eaten and the teapot down to dregs, after Daniela had gone up to sleep upstairs, the two of them stood on opposite sides of the shop counter, holding hands and trading fond looks back and forth.

"I've just noticed something," Pauline said. "I always feel most in love with you when we're surrounded by books."

"Well, then. I must speak with the architect designing our new house. I'll instruct him to install floor-to-ceiling bookcases on every wall of our bedchamber."

She smiled. "It's enough that you're here. I confess, I'd lost hope. I read in the paper that you went home to Cumberland."

"I did. My mother went with me. I settled matters with my land steward so I wouldn't have to return for some time. And we placed a stone for Mary Annabel in the family churchyard."

"Oh, Griff. I'm glad you were able to do that together."

"So am I." He cleared his throat and looked around at the shop. "How did you manage all this without the funds?"

"I started with the books you sent, of course. The ladies helped me gather more. And for the shop rental, I took out a loan from Errol Bright."

Jealousy flashed in his eyes. "Errol Bright made you a loan?"

She nodded. "A friendly loan. That's all. I'm halfway to paying him back already."

"I'll bet you are." He kissed her hand and stroked it fondly. "I will demand some compromise, you know. Spindle Cove is home now, but I have other properties that need attention. Responsibilities in London, as well. I'm now a governor of several charities. And I suspect the next year or so will teach us who our true friends are. If we're invited to a ball or party, I should like to attend and show off my beautiful wife."

"I'd like that, too."

His brow furrowed as he studied the notch between her second and third fingers. "I can't promise you children. You know that. I'd love nothing more than a family with you, but . . . there are no guarantees."

"I know."

"All I can offer you with certitude is a devoted husband and devious mother-in-law. Can it be enough?"

She smiled. "More than enough."

"Well, and we can't forget Daniela. She'll be with us, too. I know change is difficult for her, but I've given it a great deal of thought. We'll arrange for her to have a bedchamber in every one of our residences, each arranged and decorated exactly the same. So she'll always feel at home. And we can hire her a companion, if you like. An excellent one. You know I only employ the best."

Her throat itched so fiercely, it was all she could do to squeeze out, "Thank you."

"There's no need of thanks. You know I was raised an only child. It will be my joy to have a sister. If you'll share her."

There was nothing—*nothing*—he could have said that would have meant more. He was the best of men. She should never have doubted him, not even for a moment. She never would again.

He said, "Daniela and my mother will get on like thieves, I suspect."

The image made Pauline smile through her tears. "Goodness. The shopping trips alone."

"Never mind the shopping. Imagine the knitting."

They laughed together.

She touched a hand to her brow. "It's too much. You're being too perfect. Quickly, say something horrid so I know this isn't a dream."

"Very well. I have a creeping skin condition, and I hoot like a barn owl when I reach orgasm."

She laughed. "But I know very well those things aren't true."

"They weren't true a few months ago. I think you'd better strip me naked and make sure nothing's changed."

"Hm. I might know of a quiet hayloft."

He leaned across the counter and kissed her. Warmly, leisurely. It was possibly the best kiss he'd ever given her.

It was an everyday kiss.

"I love you," he said.

"It's truly going to be all right," she said. "Isn't it?"

His lips quirked, and he squeezed her hand in his. "Sometimes it will be all right. But for the most part, it's going to be wonderful."

And it was.

Epilogue

Five years later

"**D**o you have a name picked out for her?" Victor Bramwell, Lord Rycliff, reclined in his chair at the Bull and Blossom and stacked his arms over his chest.

"Her?" Colin echoed. "How do you know the babe will be a 'her'?"

"It's certain to be a girl," Bram said. "Susanna calls it the Spindle Cove Effect. There's my Victoria. Thorne has little Bryony. Susanna even had a letter from Violet Winterbottom—twins. We've all had firstborn girls." He cocked his head, indicating Griff. "Save for Halford, of course."

Griff didn't correct him by mentioning Mary Annabel—this wasn't the time—but took a thoughtful sip to her memory.

"I wouldn't place any bets," Colin said. "Nothing about this has gone according to custom or reason. Minerva wasn't supposed to give birth for a month yet. We wouldn't have imposed on Halford for a visit otherwise."

"Just as well you're here, and not in London," Griff said. "In Spindle Cove, she has her friends around her. And there's certainly space enough at the house."

They'd razed the crumbling old Whittlecombe farmhouse years ago, replacing it with a home that was grand enough for a duke and his duchess, but not too overwhelming for Daniela or too ostentatious for the neighborhood. He and Pauline thought of it as the honeymoon cottage to their larger homes in Cumberland and Town. It was the one residence that was all theirs—not populated by generations of history.

And most of the year, it was home.

But while it boasted twenty rooms and the finest in modern construction, the house wasn't soundproof—nor big enough to contain three anxious noblemen while a woman suffered through childbirth upstairs.

Susanna, exhausted by assisting the midwife *and* replying to constant requests for updates, had shooed the men down to the village for a drink. She promised to send word as soon as there was anything to report.

Cowardly as the retreat might have been, all three of them took it gratefully. Griff bought round after round of ale in the cozy, familiar tavern, and the hours stretched. If this dragged on until nightfall, he suspected they'd need to move on to something stronger. Brandy or whiskey, perhaps.

"You'll have a girl," Bram said again. "So have a name ready."

"Minerva insisted I leave the naming to her." Colin drained his tankard. "She said I'll undoubtedly call the child everything *but* her proper name anyhow." He blew out his breath and drummed his fingers on the tabletop. "How many hours will this take? As long as Min and I waited to start a family, I find my patience is exhausted. This is torture."

"Think how your wife is feeling, my lord." Becky Willett served them a fresh round. Fosbury hadn't lost his weakness for smart-mouthed serving girls.

"He *is* thinking of his wife," Griff said softly. "That's why it's torture."

If anyone thought Colin's moaning was excessive, they should have seen Griff the first time Pauline began her labor pains. He'd been a right bastard. Barking for doctors, shouting orders at the maids, prowling up and down the corridors. He'd needed to put up a strong front, lest anyone see the sheer terror eating him from the inside. If anything had happened to her . . .

"Trust me," Bram told Colin. "When it's over—once you see she's well, and the midwife places your red, shriveled *female* offspring in your arms—all this worry will be forgotten."

Griff hoped that would be the case for his old friend. It certainly hadn't worked that way for him. He hadn't slept for a fortnight after his son's birth. He'd hovered over the cradle, walked the halls with him swaddled in his arms.

Finally, Pauline had found him in the library one early morning.

He'd nodded off in a chair, little Jonathan tucked

into the crook of his elbow. When he awoke, it was to the vision of his lovely wife, her hair unbound and haloed by new sunlight. So beautiful, she could have been an angel.

She didn't say a word—just took their child from his arms, kissed the cheek Griff hadn't shaved in days, and smiled.

In that moment a sense of peace had descended on him. For the first time since they'd learned Pauline was with child, he stopped worrying about everything that could go wrong and began looking forward to everything that would go right.

Almost four years now, and he hadn't looked back.

He was sure his peers would look at his life here and find it highly confusing. The duchess kept a circulating library and remained best of friends with the dry goods shopkeeper. Their children frequently wore lumpy, ill-knitted jackets, and they played with children of farmers and fishermen. To balance his charitable work for the local school and St. Ursula's parish, Griff hosted a weekly card game that was legendary.

It was an unconventional life for a duke, perhaps. But an unquestionably happy one.

"Well, if it isn't young Lord Westmore." Fosbury's voice boomed from the kitchen. "And her grace and little Lady Rose with him."

"No sweets, please, Mr. Fosbury." Pauline's voice. "Their grandmother spoils them enough. No, Rose. You mustn't touch."

Griff smiled to himself. So many years since she'd worked in this tavern, and his wife—his *duchess*—still entered the establishment through the rear door.

And even with frazzled hair and two small children in tow, she still took his breath away. Every time.

Colin shot to his feet. "How is she?"

"Which 'she'?" Pauline led Jonathan by one hand and had little Rose propped on the opposite hip. "Do you mean your wife or your daughter?"

Bram thumped the table, triumphant. "Told you it would be a girl."

"They're both well," Pauline hurried to add. "In excellent health and enjoying some hard-earned rest."

"I . . . That's . . ." Colin paled and dropped to the chair again as his knees gave out. "Oh, God."

Pauline came to Griff's side and nodded at Colin's dazed state. "Is that from the drink or the shock of fatherhood?"

"Both, I suspect. Give him a moment, he'll recover."

She released Jonathan's hand and shifted Rose from one arm to the other. "Will you watch them while I pop over to see Sally? I'm expecting a new parcel of books for the library."

"Of course. But I expect a reward for my trouble."

She kissed his cheek and whispered a husky, "Later."

"I'll hold you to that." He caught Rose and lifted her into his arms, tweaking the snub of her tiny nose. "Look at you, darling. You're all spangled with sugar."

Author's Note

The poem Pauline quotes is "The Crystal Cabinet" by William Blake.

The Foundling Hospital was a real institution in London. Though today we use the word "hospital" for institutions that care for the sick, at the time the word simply referred to a safe place. It was a home for the abandoned children of unwed mothers. Visiting the Foundling Hospital was a popular charitable outing for gentlemen and ladies of the day; however, those visits were typically confined to observing the children in the dining room and perhaps passing them sweets.

Some readers might be wondering about the modern medical explanations behind parts of this story. Why did all of Griff's siblings die in infancy? Was it some sort of hereditary disease? If so, wouldn't he and Pauline risk a string of similar tragedies in their future?

Even though the historical setting prevents me

from inserting the medical rationale into the story, I do write with it in mind.

With Griff's parents, the problem was Rh incompatibility. This complication occurs in women who have Rh-negative blood but conceive children with an Rh-positive partner. The firstborn child (in this case, Griff) might be born in full health. But with subsequent pregnancies, the mother's body has been "sensitized" and will treat the Rh-positive fetus as a threat. These pregnancies can result in miscarriage, stillbirth, or infants who are born too weak and jaundiced to survive.

Fortunately, modern medicine understands this problem. Doctors routinely test for Rh factor, and incompatibility is preventable. As for this story—readers can feel assured that since Pauline is Rh-positive (as are the vast majority of women), there is no reason why she and Griff can't raise as many happy, healthy children as they like.

Next month, don't miss these exciting new love stories only from Avon Books

A Kiss of Blood by Pamela Palmer
Quinn Lennox vowed never to return to Vamp City, and when rugged vampire Arturo Mazza comes for her, Quinn can't forget the betrayal she suffered at his hands. But with her brother's fate hanging in the balance, Quinn will have to risk another journey to the twilight city . . . and another chance at love with a ruthless vamp.

It Happened One Midnight by Julie Anne Long
There's nothing like a gypsy prophecy to make a man rethink his priorities. For Jonathan Redmond, that priority is now avoiding the one thing he can't seem to escape: matrimony. But on one fateful midnight, he's drawn into the world of the intoxicating Thomasina de Ballesteros and suddenly he's rethinking everything—including the possibility that succumbing to prophecy might just mean surrendering to love.

Anything But Sweet by Candis Terry
Ex-Marine Reno Wilder is determined to protect the town of Sweet, Texas, from any and *all* intruders. Especially intruders like Charlotte Brooks and her TV makeover show. Reno may be gorgeous and a one-man *unwelcoming* committee to boot, but Charli isn't taking no for an answer. When push comes to shove, she's gonna show this gruff cowboy just how fun a little change can be . . .